Beneath the Hood

EMILY MCINTIRE

Beneath the Hood
(Sugarlake Series, Book Three)
By: Emily McIntire

Edited by: Ellie McLove, My Brother's Editor
Proofread by: Rosa Sharon, My Brother's Editor
Cover Design: Emily Wittig Designs

Ebook ISBN: 978-1-7349994-6-4
Paperback ISBN: 978-1-7349994-7-1
Hardback ISBN: 978-1-7349994-8-8

BENEATH THE HOOD PLAYLIST

1. This City - *Sam Fischer*
2. Lonely - *Justin Bieber (with benny blanco)*
3. Smells Like Teen Spirit - *Nirvana*
4. Someone To You - *BANNERS*
5. Try - *Colbie Caillat*
6. Iris - *The Goo Goo Dolls*
7. The Way I Say Goodbye - *Emily Weisband*
8. Without Me - *Halsey*
9. True Colors - *Justin Timberlake + Anna Kendrick*
10. Best Part - *H.E.R (ft. Daniel Caeser)*

For anyone who has ever hidden behind a happy face.

It's okay to not be okay.

To be beautiful means to be yourself. You don't need to be accepted by others. You need to accept yourself.

— THICH NHAT HANH

AUTHOR'S NOTE

Beneath the Hood features mature and graphic content.
Reader Discretion is advised.

Full list of Trigger Warnings can be found on EmilyMcIntire.com

Beneath the Hood is the third interconnected standalone in the Sugarlake series. There are plot points and side stories that start in book one and run through the series. While not necessary, it is recommended to read in order for a full reading experience.

Read Book One: Beneath the Stars (Free in Kindle Unlimited)

Join Emily's Facebook Group THE MCINCULT to chat while you read!

1

BLAKELY

"You're not eating much."

A knot in my stomach tightens, the way it always does when people question my habits. So I don't want to shove three-thousand calories of grease down my gullet, and end up spending hours in the gym to work it off. *Sue me.*

I smile thinly, the force of my lips pressing against each other causing an ache in my jaw. "I literally ate everything I ordered."

Jared, my best friend Kayla's flavor of the week, scoffs as he glances at my plate. "It was baked chicken and plain cherry tomatoes. You *can't* be full from that."

I shrug, ignoring the way my shoulder muscles pull tight. "And? Your point?"

His brow arches. "Well, aren't you still hungry?"

My insides twist, his questioning making my legs bounce under the table and my lungs compress. People never understand the dedication, but I have an image to maintain. I don't have the luxury of being able to demolish a plate of cheesy fries and guzzle pints of overpriced IPAs. Besides, my body is my temple. I refuse to desecrate it with trash.

My eyes start at the tip of Jared's perfectly coiffed blond hair, trailing down his pink polo with an alligator on the breast—the fabric soaked in his pretension. Kayla's been excited to introduce me to her newest "love," and this is the first time we're meeting face-to-face. So far, I'm less than impressed.

Kayla smacks his arm. "Leave her alone. She looks fucking fabulous. I *wish* I had her willpower."

Her brown eyes swing my way and she winks. My stomach unravels and I grin back at her. *She gets it.*

Jared's hands raise. "My bad, Blakely, I'm just saying. I didn't realize you were on a diet."

"It's not a diet, it's a lifestyle choice," I hiss. My fists clench in my lap.

Looking past him, I notice the audience of paparazzi forming outside of the restaurant. I paste a smile on my face, not wanting them to snap blurry photos of me sneering across the table.

Lazy bastards.

They don't even try to hide in the shadows anymore, knowing I'll play my part every time. They're blatantly looking through the windows, waiting like vultures to catch an unpolished moment. They'll have to keep waiting. I've been training for perfection my entire life. Having a dad who's the *it* producer in Hollywood comes with a set of expectations. A certain standard you can't fall beneath, lest you be picked apart by millions of people who will never understand what it's like to be you. I bring it upon myself at this point, embracing the life I was born into—commandeering the vapid, shallow waters, and steering the sails to make the waves break for me and not the other way around.

Tossing my hair behind my shoulders, I peek down at my shirt, picking off the few stray dark brunette strands. I'm wearing the new Leaxandre blouse and it's the perfect chance to get some candid shots—it's why we leaked to the paps that I was here in the first place, after all.

Jared's hand slinks around Kayla's chair, playing with the ends of her chocolate hair. I squint my eyes, watching them interact. Kayla's addicted to relationships. I can't remember a time where she didn't have man candy on her arm, claiming they were her soul mate.

She calls it love, I call it codependency, but to each their own, I suppose. I've never even had a boyfriend, so who am I to judge?

The problem is, she's also super attracted to preppy douchebags. Ones who buy the Ferraris but don't know how to make them purr. And if they can't handle a machine, how the hell does she expect them to handle her?

Cars remind me of Jackson, my dad's newest star employee, and *my* kitty purrs just from the thought of him. He's way too old for me, and a thousand percent off-limits, but he's hella hot so I can't find it in me to care. Besides, there's something oddly satisfying about slipping under his skin and causing him to shed his calm exterior. I find myself doing things just to get a reaction, and when I do, his irritation sizzles between us and settles into my veins like a current. It makes me feel powerful to incite such a strong reaction in a man who otherwise never cracks.

Besides, it's nice having someone who doesn't bend to my will and lay down at my feet following me around like a lapdog once they find out who I am.

I pull out my phone and type off a text.

Me: Miss me yet, Jackson?

Closing the window, I don't bother to wait for a response.

He rarely texts back, but it doesn't deter me. He doesn't live in Cali full time, which makes zero sense to me since his work is here, but I guess the ties to his hometown are stronger than the pull of the California sun.

Swiping through my apps, I pull up my calorie tracker, mentally calculating my lunch before entering in the numbers. The app has a search with most common items listed, but I've been at this long enough to know the numbers by heart. I don't really deviate from what I know. Always keeping the same restaurants in rotation so I don't have the added anxiety of figuring out what I can and can't eat.

I sigh, gripping my phone tighter. "You guys ready to go? I need to run home before the club tonight."

Jared's brows draw in. "What club?"

"I can't remember the name." I slip on my sunglasses, nodding to the table behind me where my bodyguard, Lennox, sits. I don't go anywhere without him, even before I made a name for myself in the influencer world, my father had Lennox at my side, not willing to take the risk of someone coming after me to get to him.

We live a blessed life of luxury. The kind people can only dream of, and greed breeds corruption from even the most unsuspecting people.

"How do you not remember what club you're going to?" Jared pipes in again.

I shrug. "Sierra knows, but I gave her the afternoon off."

"She's the best." Kayla sighs.

"She really is." I nod in agreement.

Sierra is my manager, and the only reason I'm not a freaking mess all the time. She keeps me—and my schedule—in check. Honestly, she's one of the closest people in my circle, and I trust her more than anyone else in my life.

"Should we go out the back?" Jared asks, glancing toward the paps.

I force a chuckle, my throat tightening around the noise. Clearly, Jared has no clue what this world is like. He comes from money, of course, Kayla wouldn't be seen with him if not, but he's never been in the limelight.

Obviously, Kayla didn't let him know how things work around here.

Releasing my bottom lip from where it's stuck between my teeth, I smile. "Nope, we go out the front. Give them what they're after. I need some good shots of this outfit anyway."

"You *want* them to take pics of you?"

Want is a strong word. I *want* the two-hundred thousand I'm being paid for wearing this outfit. I don't *want* the rest of it. It's just an unfortunate side effect. But I won't tell him that—even to my closest friends I play the part.

Fake it 'til you make it… and then keep faking it forever, even after you do.

The legs of my chair scrape against the tile as I stand,

but right before I grab my purse my phone vibrates in my hand.

I look down and smile.

Jackson: Not even a little bit.

2

JACKSON

My house feels foreign. I can't really place what's causing the feeling, but whatever it is, it's burning a crater in the center of my stomach.

It's the first time I've been back in California with the intention of staying, but I'm no stranger to starting over in new places. Growing up a military brat teaches you to not get attached. To make friends quickly. To bend but not break. Change is the only constant in life, so I can't for the life of me figure out why *this* change feels so damn different. Maybe it's knowing that this time I had a choice. That it was one-hundred-percent my decision to finally move from Sugarlake to California. And while deep down I know it's the right one, it still feels like I'm leaving something fundamental behind. Something beyond a mom I'll go back to visit and memories I wish wouldn't linger.

Right now I'm sitting in my living room, a warm beer in front of me, fireplace crackling and ESPN droning while I relentlessly pour over those memories. The more hours that tick by without distraction, the more my heart screams inside my chest, begging to go back to the people who own it. Unfortunately, those are the same people who have a tendency to break it.

One person in particular.

Alina May Carson, also known as Lee. The sweetheart of Sugarlake, and my best friend for the past decade. I've been her sucker since we were kids—when she plopped down in my Mustang Fastback, grabbed my dad's dog tags and told me "real was beautiful." The chain dangled by my heart, but her fingers tangled into my soul, and I wish like hell she'd loosen her grip. Realize that I *need* her to let go. It isn't fair for her to hold on so tight when she doesn't let me hold her back.

She has Chase for that now, anyway. And really, she's always been his, no matter how much I've wished she'd pick me. *Choose* me.

I was just a stand-in. Her faithful sidekick. A pathetic sponge, absorbing her emotions and holding them when she couldn't.

That's all I ever am. An "in the moment" kind of guy. A distraction. A temporary fixture.

A second choice.

With everyone else, it's a position I've mastered, grasping onto the title and wearing it like a crown. The resident charmer, the king of one-night stands. My legacy in Sugarlake is giving a good fuck—the best—one that provides them with whatever high they're chasing and eases the loneliness of being friend-zoned by the one woman who I've never seen as just a friend.

Sometimes it's nice to feel wanted, to be the center of someone else's everything, even temporarily.

But "temporary" erodes quickly, and if you don't do something to fix the source, eventually, your whole damn soul will crumble. So, leaving permanently was a difficult yet necessary step. I've been Lee's Jax for so long, I don't remember how to be my own.

My phone vibrates across my coffee table and I groan, leaning forward to snap it up. I forgot to call my mom and tell her I made it back okay, so I assume it's her checking in.

I'm wrong.

Blakely: Miss me yet, Jackson?

My teeth clench, irritation making my chest pull tight and my heartbeat rev. *Blakely.* Everything about the girl bothers me and I'm not sure why. I swear to God it's her personal mission in life to get under my skin. She's always just *there*, her sparkly iPhone at the ready, and her long as hell legs in my face. Legs that make my dick twitch and guilt spiral through my system because I definitely should not be attracted to a nineteen-year-old girl whose biggest asset is her follower count and her most genuine feature her inability to take no for an answer. So, I lash out and she bites back and I end the day feeling like a gigantic asshole, even when that's the last thing I want to be.

My parents raised me right, taught me that respect is both something that's earned and something to take pride in giving. And if there's anything I strive to be, it's someone my parents can be proud of.

My free hand reaches up, the pads of my fingers rolling

along the metal chain of my necklace, the thought of my dad snapping my purpose back into focus.

He's the reason I'm in California in the first place, after all. After he finished his military service, we spent his last days in a small two-bedroom house right on the coast of Monterey—every free second spent beneath the hood of some rusted-out car, turning a hunk of junk into a masterpiece.

I have a lot of good memories with my dad, but California is home to some of my favorites. If I close my eyes, I can still feel the rays of sun as they'd sprinkle in through the open garage, casting an orangey hue on oil-stained cement while he taught me how to jet the carburetor and see the potential of beauty in even the ugliest of shells. And at night, once the sun had slipped beneath the horizon and taken the last of our light, I'd sit on the concrete steps that led to the back door, and watch in awe while he scrubbed Gojo soap on his hands, the water running black while he waxed poetic about our cars being on the big screen.

He was so sure in his conviction, I never doubted him for a second. But cancer ravaged his blood, taking him from this life before he was ready—before any of us were ready—to say goodbye.

So now his passion lives on through me.

And if working with the biggest producer in Hollywood, James Donahue, and letting his bratty kid annoy the hell out of me is what it takes to get my cars in the movies, then that's what I'll do.

But did I miss her?

Not even a little bit.

3

BLAKELY

My hand brushes across the wall absentmindedly, steadying myself from stumbling, exhaustion wringing my bones. It's been a long night and I can't wait to pass out. My finger snags on the corner of a picture frame, making my steps falter, my fingertip throbbing from where it jammed against the metal. Cursing, I glare at the portrait responsible for my pain.

It's of my mother. They *all* are photos of my mother, encased in ornate frames and hung throughout our house like a shrine. A way for my father to gaze at her beauty without having to admit out loud he's never moved on after her death. *After I killed her.*

She was the great love of his life—at least that's the way the story goes—and sometimes I can't help but think the reason he's a workaholic is so he doesn't have to stare at me too long, afraid he'll start blaming me for taking her away.

I have her eyes. Only five percent of people in the entire world have them, and sometimes, I stare at her unblinking face in the photos and search for familiarity. For *forgiveness*. The canary yellow swirls into deep brown, dipping into the center of her irises—a kaleidoscope of colors frozen in a portrait, making me ache to see the amber hues warm. They don't, of course. Snapshots can't capture a soul, only a memory.

I'm sure my dad would tell me anything I wanted to know, but every time I bring it up, grief tugs on his happiness, trying to make it rip off his skin and disappear into the ethers. Once it's gone, who knows how long it will be until it comes back—until *he* comes back. So, I don't like to ask.

Something sharp slices down my insides at the thought, dulling the pain in my finger, and making me break from my stare down with a woman I've never known. Continuing the trek to my bedroom, I try to shake away the tumultuous thoughts so I can get at least a few hours of sleep, but it's no use. In these late-night hours—the only ones where I'm truly by myself—the thoughts always creep up and find me in the darkness. Thoughts that whisper like the most vicious kind of bully, tormenting me with cutting words and truths I keep shrouded in the shadows.

After changing out of my dress and slipping into a robe I step into my en suite. *Mozart's Moonlight Sonata—Third Movement* plays softly from the built-in speakers, just like it does every night. I methodically strip off my makeup, pumping the face cleanser onto my Clarisonic brush three times, ensuring the droplets form directly in the middle before moving it along my skin. Thirty seconds for each side, then again for my forehead and chin. No longer, no less.

It's the routines that keep me focused. Keep me sane.

After applying the last of my creams and elixirs, I drop the robe and walk to the full-length mirror for my nightly inventory.

Drawing in a deep breath, I step on the scale, closing my eyes tightly and counting to twenty-five, envisioning the result I'd like to see. Slowly, I slide my lids open, the knot in my stomach tightening as the light filters back in. My eyes blur for the slightest second before the bright red numbers come into focus.

One-hundred and twelve point six. *Shit.*

That's point three over what it was yesterday. My mind races, mentally calculating everything I ate and drank today, a tidal wave of regret surging through my system, rising up my esophagus and making my insides pull.

It's the vodka sodas, I just know it.

Normally, when I make appearances, I don't drink. Being underage is usually reason enough, but for some reason, when I was offered a drink tonight, I convinced myself that just one would be fine. But then one turned into two. That's one-hundred and ninety-two calories, assuming the bartender didn't overpour—which they probably did—so who knows how much it actually was. My heart rate accelerates, my throat closing around the uncertainty.

My body feels heavy, and as I step off the scale and stare in the mirror, I can almost *see* where the extra calories are already making a home. My face sours, the tang of disgust settling thick on my tongue.

Scoffing, I turn away, my lack of self-control smacking

against my insides and making the haziness of exhaustion disappear, an antsy energy whipping through my muscles and pushing me toward my closet.

I can't believe I put that poison in my body.

Weak, Blakely. Fucking pathetic.

Throwing on a sports bra and leggings, I glance at the clock on my nightstand, grimacing when I realize I'm supposed to be awake in four hours and headed to Donahue Motors. To the job my father has forced me into so that I can "start to take life seriously."

For just a moment, I consider giving myself some leeway, and slipping between my sheets, but the overwhelming need to watch the calories burn away on the elliptical wins, choking me with impatience.

As I rush down the hall and toward the staircase, I keep my head down, not wanting to see identical eyes on a stranger's face staring back at me.

Judging me, just like everybody else.

"You look tired." Jackson's voice rumbles across the entrance of Donahue Motors, his wavy, dirty-blond hair swishing against his jaw.

My stomach flips, and I push my sunglasses to my head as I stop in front of him. "That's usually code for you look like shit, so thank you, once again, for your never-ending kindness."

His thick arms cross against his broad chest, the tendons in his forearms flexing at the movement. My gut clenches.

Damn, he's pretty.

His brow quirks, and he leans forward. "Fine. You look like shit. Better?"

The words—even though I pushed for them—cause anxiety to creep through the cracks of my makeup. My fingers strain against the urge to pull out a mirror and make sure I don't actually look like a train wreck. It's early, and nobody here gives a damn one way or the other, but you never know when someone will be lurking—when a photo will be taken and end up circulating online. It only takes a second, and I can't afford a shitty picture. It doesn't fit the brand.

The longer I internally panic, the more Jackson's eyes narrow, his grassy, green gaze sharp and penetrating, like he's trying to strip away my paint and see the bodywork underneath.

A thrill zips through me, loving the weight of his stare. My chest relaxes from where it was gripping my lungs tight.

I swallow, meeting his gaze and daring him to dig deeper. To press further.

"Jax, honey, your order came in this morning." Karen, the office assistant, walks in from the back hall, causing Jackson to break our connection. Charm glides over his body like an aura, polishing away his grit—a blinding white smile spreading across his face as he spins to face her.

His elbows rest on top of the reception counter. "Karen, what would I do without you?"

I watch, fascinated, as the hue on Karen's cheeks bloom a deep shade of rose and she legit giggles like a schoolgirl. *Gross, Karen. You're like sixty. Get it together.*

"Oh, hush. You'd do just fine."

Jackson's smile grows, his hand leaping to his heart. "I beg to differ. You're the cherry to my pie, sweet thing."

She playfully pushes against his arm. "And you're an insufferable flirt, has anyone ever told you that?"

"I just call it like I see it." He winks.

I snort, my hand slapping over my mouth at the noise. Jackson's back stiffens and he looks toward me. "Something funny, Blake?"

I bite my lip and shake my head. *Blake.* Why he gives me a nickname when he won't give me the time of day is beyond me.

He runs his big hand through his hair, and my eyes track the motion. Normally, I'm not a fan of longer hair on guys, but for some reason with Jackson, I can't imagine him any other way.

And I have imagined him. Frequently. Not that I'd ever admit it out loud. He's not my type, and definitely not the kind of person who I could have on my arm in public. He may have the movie star looks, but he doesn't have the pedigree. At the root of everything, he's blue-collar. My father's employee and someone who would never understand the lifestyle.

He's too old for me anyway.

He taps his knuckles on the countertop. "See ya later, Karen. Don't work too hard or I'll be forced to come back up here and take you out for an extra-long lunch."

She smiles, her blush deepening as she waves him off.

He turns, sparing me a single glance, and disappearing through the glass doors leading to the garage.

Smiling softly at Karen, I walk closer. "I'm at your service today, Karen. Put me to work."

The grin she held for Jackson slips from her face, transforming into a grimace as she regards me. "Like usual, Miss Donahue, not much for you to do other than manning the front desk and answering calls. I can handle the rest."

Irritation surges through my insides even as I keep a smile pasted on my face. "It's just Blakely, Karen."

Karen hums and grabs a stack of papers as she walks

away. I plop in the reception desk chair, spinning around and sighing as I resign myself to my fate. I have to play nice, for my father's sake, but being here makes me itch. Every minute that ticks away on the clock is another wasted second that I could be dedicating to my career. The one nobody takes seriously except me. They don't understand the dedication, and I don't think they ever will.

There was a moment when I thought my father saw the truth. When he sat me down, saying he wanted me to take up a position with Donahue Inc., my chest warmed, thinking that he saw how hard I worked at being an influencer. At the business I conduct behind the scenes. But, of course, he didn't. He sees the pictures in the papers and falls for the act, just like everyone else.

So instead of giving me a real chance to prove my worth, he stowed me away at Donahue Motors, a branch of his conglomerate responsible for making prop cars used in the movies he produces.

Out of sight, out of mind.

I could have told him no, I suppose. But I know he's doing it out of love, even if it's misguided, and I don't want to disappoint him. He's the only family I've got.

Besides, he's not a *bad* father, just an absent one.

A squeak from the hallway brings me out of my thoughts. Karen comes back around the corner, huffing and puffing, pushing a dolly with large boxes.

I jump out of my chair, rushing to her side. "Let me do that, Karen. Where are they going?"

"Oh no, Miss Donahue, don't worry about me. I've got years left in these bones yet," she protests.

I don't listen, moving her to the side, my hands replacing hers on the handle.

She doesn't put up a fight. "They're going out to the garage. It's the order Jax has been waiting on."

"On it." I smile, winking at her. I'm overcompensating, trying for the thousandth time to gain her approval, but it doesn't work. She gives me nothing more than a small lift in the corner of her mouth and goes behind the front desk, already on to her next task.

Pushing through the glass doors that lead into the expansive garage, I roll the boxes over to the shelving of inventory and glance around, looking for broad shoulders and sun-kissed hair.

I find him hunched under the hood of a forest green convertible. I'm not sure what kind of car it is, only that it looks old and expensive.

"You know," I say, my stomach tightening as his back straightens from my voice. "I sincerely hope you come with better lines than what you used on poor Karen when you're trying to snag some vag."

He sighs, straightening up and looking at me with a blank face. Turning, he sets his tool down and walks around the car, leaning against the driver's side door.

"Should you be leaning against that?" I gesture toward the convertible.

"Should you be using words like 'snag some vag?'" he bites back.

A pang of excitement slams into my stomach. Jackson's feisty today.

"Well, I don't know what lingo you old folk are into these days, but vag is short for *vagina*." I smile big and wide.

His jaw twitches. "I'm familiar."

Smirking, I eye him up and down, wiggling my eyebrows. "Oh, I have no doubt." Walking over and peering inside the front of the car, I wrap my fingers around a rod that's holding up the hood. "What ya working on?"

I feel the heat of his body as he comes to stand next to me. His hand wraps around mine, the weight of his touch as he peels my fingers off the metal making my breath stick in my throat.

"Be careful, please. You could hurt yourself," he murmurs next to my ear.

Blowing out a shaky exhale, my stomach clenches. "Careful, Jackson. It almost sounds like you care." Spinning around, my eyes rest on his Adam's apple, the intensity of his attention wrapping around me like a blanket.

I peer up at him through my lashes, marveling at the sharp angles of his jaw, inhaling the scent of rubber and oil, mixed with a delicious spice I can't place. It's heady, and it makes me lightheaded.

He takes a step back, snapping a hairband against his wrist. "Look, Blakely, I don't have time for this. This car is supposed to be on your dad's set tomorrow, so if you're not in here to help, then get the fuck out."

I raise my chin, my defenses rising at his brush-off. "My dad sent me here to help. I doubt he'd like to hear you're anything less than nice to me."

"He sent you here to be watched, because you're still a kid who can't take anything seriously for one goddamn second," he snaps. "So, go ahead. Run and tell your daddy I've been mean. He'll give me a bonus on my next check for not falling at your feet like your vapid friends and empty followers."

My gut twists, his accusations ringing in my ears. "My *father* doesn't take the time to learn what it is that I actually do, and instead decides to believe what he sees." I take in a breath, batting away the hurt that tries to leach from my bones. "But at the end of the day he's still my father, and if he feels like I'm being treated unfairly, he won't stand for it."

"And Jackson." I step back into him, close enough where I can see the faint outline of a necklace underneath his shirt. "I'm still looking for a *daddy*. Know anyone up for the challenge?"

Jackson's nostrils flare, his fists clenching at his sides, and like a hit of nicotine, my head buzzes with satisfaction. He's right, after all. He doesn't treat me the way everyone else does, and in a world of perfect photos and staged happiness, there's something intensely gratifying about the realness of his irritation. The rawness of his anger.

I like knowing I'm the one who draws out the passion that hides beneath his laid-back charm.

The truth is, I'm addicted to Jackson's hatred.

4

JACKSON

"You should come to the club tonight," Blakely says.

I cringe, my stomach jumping at her question. "No."

"Oh, come on, Jackson. I wanna see those corny lines work in person." She laughs, walking over to my industrial toolbox and jumping up to sit on its surface.

"Pass."

Her long, tanned legs swing back and forth, the heels of her shoes hitting the metal drawers, creating a tapping rhythm that echoes through the garage.

"You're a bore," she complains, sticking her shiny bottom lip out.

"That's what happens in old age." I shrug, biting on my cheek to keep from smiling.

A spark hits her eyes and my chest pinches. I shouldn't make jokes, it will only encourage her, which is the opposite of what I want. In fact, I've been doing everything in my power to dissuade her.

My brain knows she's off-limits, but my dick disagrees, and since she doesn't seem to even know the meaning of the word boundaries, I need to be careful with our interactions. "How would your father feel about you asking me to go?"

A wicked grin splits her face, but then her eyes move past me and her smile falters.

"How would I feel about what?" a deep booming voice interrupts.

I look behind me and see the father in question, James Donahue, walking across the garage.

Blakely beams at him, shrugging. "I'm trying to make friends with Jackson, and he isn't being very nice about it."

His thick, black eyebrow arches, his hands resting in the pockets of his three-piece suit. "Is that so?"

"Yep," she continues. "Asked him to go with me to the club appearance I have."

Mr. Donahue's lips twist, his forehead creasing as he looks between us.

Blakely sighs. "Don't worry, he said no."

"You should consider saying no too," he says, his stare pointed.

She scoffs. "It's work, Dad."

He looks around, his arms spread wide. "*This* is work, Blakely. Something tangible. Something you can build on. What you do is slave away for an algorithm just to feed your ego."

Unease pours through my veins at her flinch. *Damn, that was harsh.*

James Donahue is a dick. He expects excellence at every level, and if something gets between him and what he wants, he'll slice you quicker than a paper cut. I hate kissing ass, but I'm willing to do almost anything to make sure my dad's dream comes to fruition, and the Donahue name has a stranglehold on the industry.

"How are things going around here?" Mr. Donahue walks around, stopping to peruse the Austin-Healey 3000 that's due on set tomorrow.

"Great." I nod. "Right on track."

He smiles, stopping next to where Blakely sits on my toolbox, and for the first time, I notice the resemblance between them.

"She's not distracting you, is she?" He turns to Blakely. "What are you even doing out here, Blakely? Karen says she's been looking for you. Your purpose here isn't to distract the other employees."

Blakely's shoulders slump, her shiny lips parting as she tucks a strand of hair behind her ear.

"She was helping," I rush out.

I don't know why I say it, especially when it's a lie. She *was* distracting me. But there's something about the way her sparkle dimmed that tugs at my chest, making me want to buff away the look in her eyes just to see them shine. "I asked her to help me unload the new order," I continue. "Wanted to make sure I could stay on track with the Healey."

Mr. Donahue looks over to Blakely. "Good. You should still make sure to let Karen know where you are, so she doesn't waste time looking."

Blakely nods. "You're right, I'm sorry. I'm gonna go see

if she needs anything." She hops down, brushing off her jeans and gazing up at her father. "Will you be home for dinner?"

He shakes his head and the remainder of her confidence deflates, longing screaming from her eyes. She blinks and it's gone, a smile pasted on in its place. She goes up on her tiptoes to kiss her father's cheek, then brushes by him, her dark brown hair swishing as she rushes to head back inside.

Mr. Donahue watches her walk away, his eyes turning down in the corners. "Thank you for putting her to work," he says, finally breaking his stare down with the door.

I clear my throat, my fingers running along the chain around my neck. "It's no problem."

He smirks, leveling me with a knowing look. "Karen says she doesn't do much."

A flicker of irritation licks at my bones. *Why would she say that?*

Sure, Blakely doesn't really want to be here, that's obvious, but I haven't seen Karen go out of her way to try, choosing to delegate her to reception to answer the phones instead. There's only so much you can do when you're stuck at a front desk for a business that doesn't have customers.

"She seems to do fine with what she's tasked with," I say carefully. I'm not sure why I'm defending her. It would work in my favor to convince him she doesn't belong. Maybe then he'll move her to a different branch. Stop her from pushing herself on me when all I want is to keep her away.

"Mmm," Mr. Donahue hums. "Well, you'll keep an eye on her then."

An uncomfortable feeling slinks through my insides, churning my gut. I nod slowly. "I'll do what I can when she's here, sir. No problem."

He rubs his jaw as he assesses me. "That club she's going to tonight… I want you to go with her."

My heart drops, taking my stomach with it. "*What?*"

He glances at the watch on his wrist. "She insists on playing out this role of 'celebrity.'" He finger-quotes as he speaks the word *celebrity*. "One who doesn't do anything, choosing to live off our last name and my legacy, instead of working for her reputation. This world is filled with people who will use her and toss her to the side when they're done. People that will influence her to make bad choices. I'd much rather have someone with her that I can trust."

I chuckle from the feeling of pure disbelief that's flowing through me. "With all due respect, that's not my job."

His eyes flare. "I'm asking you to *make* it your job."

Shit.

I don't want to fuck this up—my chance of achieving what I've been working toward for years. And as much as I'd like to think that James Donahue is a man of honor and integrity, I also think he's a man who doesn't like to be told no by the people on his payroll.

Nausea swirls in my stomach, my mind racing to figure out a way to stay on his good side while also avoiding the torture of babysitting a nineteen-year-old socialite.

I come up blank.

So even though I should say no, I *want* to say no… I say yes instead.

How bad can it be?

5

BLAKELY

Sweat drips down my brow, and I soak in the feeling as it coats my skin. Glancing at my Apple watch, I check how many calories I've burned. *Seven-hundred and three.* Once I get to one thousand, I'll stop. Realistically, I'd love to hit at least fifteen hundred, but time won't allow it. I ramp up the intensity on the treadmill.

Tonight, I'm making an appearance at Club Ransom, and while I'm so exhausted I may need to glue my eyelids open, I bask in the chaos of a constantly busy schedule. It keeps me from standing still—and every still moment is a wasted second.

"You need to be in makeup at seven. We'll arrive to

Ransom at eight-thirty. Twenty minutes on the press line, ten minutes for pictures, then you'll be taken inside to host. They want an hour minimum of you up front… Blakely, are you with me?" Sierra snaps her fingers in my face.

I nod along, her voice drowning out the tap of my feet as they slap against the treadmill. "Who's the DJ tonight?" I huff out.

"DJ Andelo."

My brows draw in. "Am I supposed to know him?"

Sierra shrugs. "I don't think you've met." She spins, pulling two hangers from the rack of clothes set up behind her. "Now, do you want to go with the Amber Allen or the Retzy top?"

I *want* to wear my sweats, but that definitely wouldn't draw the right attention. I can see the headlines now.

"Let's go with the Retzy." I've been putting off wearing it because I know once I do, I won't see it again, and it's one of my favorite pieces.

I've never been photographed in the same outfit twice.

The doorbell rings—most likely my glam team—and Sierra rushes out of the gym to let them in.

I glance over at Lennox, who's currently lounging in the corner at a small table, his buzzed head buried in a worn paperback of *Dracula.* My father hired him on when I was a kid, and even though I've spent more time with him than anyone else, we might as well be strangers. All I know about him is he's thirty-three, and he's extremely skilled in fighting. When he's not at my side, he's lost in a book, and sometimes I feel envy crawl through my chest, wishing I could take his place and lose myself between the pages of someone else's story.

But there's no time for that.

My phone vibrates from where it's resting in the treadmill's cup holder. I snatch it up quickly, wondering who would be texting me that isn't already in the house.

Jackson: Still want some company tonight?

My heart skips. I slow the treadmill for a two-minute cooldown as I text him back.

Me: ...are you fucking with me?

Jackson: Nope. Are you taking back your invitation?

I chew on my lip as I contemplate how to respond. When I asked him to come with, I didn't expect him to say yes. The truth is, going to these clubs isn't a party, it's an obligation.

Me: It's not really going to be fun. I'll be working.

Jackson: Working? At the club?

Me: Yeah... I didn't think you'd take my offer seriously. I don't think you'll have a good time. :(

The treadmill beeps as it comes to a stop, and I stand there for a few long seconds, waiting for him to text back. I'm caught off guard by him texting me, and even more so by him wanting to hang out. Something takes flight inside me at the thought, soaring through my chest and whipping around my stomach.

Jackson: Look, your dad wants me there. Make it easier on both of us and just let me tag along to keep an eye on you, princess.

I inhale sharply, hurt shocking the breath from my lungs. *Of course, there's an ulterior motive.* Silly me, thinking he'd had a change of heart. For just a second, I consider telling him to go fuck himself. But as much shit as I give Jackson, I don't want him on my father's bad side.

Sighing, I text him back the address, telling him to meet me at the house and ride with us. I walk over to where Lennox sits and stare down at him, sweat beading on my cooling forehead, my hands on my hips. "I have a friend showing up here soon, his name is Jackson. Tall guy, shaggy blond hair. If I'm busy will you make sure he's let in?"

Lennox grunts a response, his icy blue eyes glancing my way before sliding behind me, his fingers tightening around the edges of his book. I spin around to see what stole his attention.

Kayla comes prancing into the gym and a smile overtakes my face. I've known Kayla since the first day of prep school. Her father is a sought-out director who works with mine frequently, so we bonded quickly, both of us knowing what it's like to grow up in the belly of the beast that is the Hollywood elite.

"Hey, girl. I didn't know if you were gonna make it tonight." I wave.

She grins. "Duh. Why wouldn't I?"

"Thought you'd be busy with *Jared*." My nose scrunches as I say his name.

Kayla's smile dims. "Nope, I cut him loose."

"Why?" I'm not really surprised. As quick as Kayla falls in love, she falls out faster. Even a perfect man would eventually fall off her pedestal.

She shrugs, running her hand through her pin-straight locks. "He kept asking about *you*. Wouldn't shut up about it, really. I've got literally zero interest in toting around somebody who's only using me to get to you."

My stomach tightens, her words jabbing me, even though I'm sure she didn't mean them that way. "Really? He was kind of a dick to me."

She shrugs again. "Probably because you weren't giving him the attention he wanted." She sighs, sticking her bottom lip out. "It sucks though. I really thought he was gonna be the one."

I squint my eyes. "You always think that."

"Yeah, well… one of these times, I'll be right."

Laughing, I toss my towel in the hamper near the door. "Your optimism is inspiring."

"Good." She smiles, plopping down across from Lennox. "Hi, Lenny."

I stifle my smirk as I watch his jaw tense, his eyes boring holes into the pages of his book. Kayla is forever flirting with Lennox, and he's forever ignoring she exists. Not that it deters her.

"Okay, you two play nice, I'm gonna go grab a shower."

It isn't until I'm rinsing the shampoo from my hair, the warm water cascading over my sore muscles, that the stillness creeps in. It allows me a free moment to drown in my thoughts, recognizing that in a houseful of people—all here for me—I've never felt so alone.

THERE ARE butterflies doing flips in my stomach, and I have no idea why.

Okay, that's a lie.

I have a *little* bit of an idea why, and he's currently sitting across the club, the ends of his blond hair brushing against his sharp jaw. It's down tonight and has a slight wave, like he dipped in the California sea and let the salty water mold the strands.

My nerves meld into a different type of flutter when Kayla throws her head back, her white teeth gleaming as she laughs at something he says.

Why did I think it was okay to leave them alone together?

Jackson never showed up to the house, and Sierra wouldn't let us wait, so I texted him to meet Lennox outside the club. But it didn't cross my mind that my love-starved best friend would be his entertainment while I was working.

It doesn't matter, I guess. I should be happy that he doesn't seem bored to death. Clubs don't really seem like his type of scene. To be honest, they're not really mine either.

Kayla's hand shoots out, caressing his arm. My fingernails press into my palms. Deep down I know I have nothing to worry about. As soon as she realizes he's my father's employee, someone who works on cars for a living, she'll lose interest. But it doesn't stop my stomach from tightening with irritation, because while I'm stuck on stage, a headache pounding between my ears, and a DJ who loves to play grab-ass—Kayla gets to enjoy the attention of Jackson Rhoades. It doesn't seem fair. Even worse, he seems to be enjoying her company.

I skim along the lines of Kayla's barely-there curves, her perfectly toned legs front and center. Green gusts of jealousy burn through my chest as I watch her guzzle big gulps of her blue drink. I wonder what it feels like to enjoy something so freely—to savor the taste as it rests on your tongue. To not have regret attacking your psyche with every sugary sip.

My eyes bounce to Jackson, his perfect smile pulling up one side of his pouty mouth, and his black T-shirt snug around his biceps. I've always thought maybe he was putting on a show with his flirtations—with his laid-back attitude. But in this setting, watching from afar, I realize it's his natural gait. The charm exudes from his pores like it's overflowing from the tap, and I know the second I walk over, it will disappear.

Am I that unpalatable? Is Kayla that much better?

Maybe he can see the difference in us, can tell that while she's effortless, I'm a constant struggle.

A never-ending work in progress.

A fraud.

I feel the brush of a palm along my lower hip, and I turn, staring into the gray eyes of DJ Andelo.

Gripping his wrist, I smile. "Watch your hands."

He smirks, his neon pink headphones pressed between his shoulder and his ear, while he leans forward and shouts into the mic. "Everyone having a good time tonight? Give it up! We've got the *stunning* Blakely Donahue in the house!"

Cheers erupt, a sea of hands and hair flying as they jump to the beat.

Anxiety eats away at my insides, and I try to find my center.

Deep breath in. One. Two. Three. Deep breath out.

Slowly, the rubber band around my chest loosens, allowing the Blakely Donahue they all expect to come to the forefront. Knowing that as long as I play my part, they won't look too deep. Won't see through to my core and realize I'm an imposter.

I've tricked the world into thinking I'm somebody, when really, I'm nothing more than what they pay me to be.

A walking, talking billboard.

But I'm damn good at it.

Closing my eyes, I throw my hands above my head, and move my hips to the beat, hoping they'll get some candid shots to circulate online. My goal is to come across lost in the music, having the time of my life, even though I'm anything but.

Controlling the narrative is everything.

Suddenly, a frisson of energy snaps at my skin, sending a rush of tingles up my spine. I don't even have to look to know it's him. There's a magnetism whenever his eyes are on me, an attention that splices me deep and tries to draw out everything I keep locked inside.

I open my eyes, our gazes locking like pieces of a puzzle.

He's not smiling. Just looking.

Watching.

A grin grows on my face as I hold his stare, my hips moving faster to the beat.

He shifts uncomfortably, and my eyes trail down his body, warmth shooting through my stomach and pooling between my thighs at the sudden urge to know what it would feel like to move my hips in his lap instead of on a stage.

Smirking, he leans back, spreading his legs out in front of him. Kayla's mouth is moving, and he nods to whatever she's saying, but his eyes stay on me, burning me from the inside out.

Just the way I like it.

6

JACKSON

She's nineteen.

Maybe if I say it enough times it will sink into my brain and my cock will calm the hell down from where it's pressing painfully against my zipper. I shift on the club couch, trying to relieve the pressure. Unfortunately, adjusting moves me closer to Blakely's friend who seems to have issues with personal boundaries.

But she's a distraction from the girl I shouldn't be looking at, so at least for the moment, I lean in closer and indulge her.

"What did you say your name was?" I flash her a smile and watch the blush rise on her high cheekbones.

"Kayla." She grins and keeps talking, but my attention is stolen away by the thump of the bass and the lithe body that's moving to its beat. Heat flares in my veins as Blakely opens her eyes and stares directly at me. My stomach flips, but I don't drop her gaze. She's always brazen, but in this setting she's impossible to look away from. She's in her element. Gorgeous in the spotlight.

I've just convinced myself to look away, and find someone I can actually take home, when I see that fucking idiot DJ grab Blakely and pull her roughly into his side.

Anger spikes in my gut at the way he's manhandling her, but I shake the feeling before it has a chance to fester. *This is ridiculous.* I don't even like Blakely, there's no reason I should care about who's touching her.

"Are they together?" I blurt.

"What?" Kayla cups a hand over her ear, scooting in closer until her thigh presses against mine. She glances at me from under her lashes. "Sorry, hard to hear over the music."

I smirk. This girl is cute, but not very skilled in the art of seduction. I wonder how confident she'd feel if she knew that drink she's slurping has turned her mouth blue.

"I asked if they were together." I nod my head toward the stage. "Blakely and that guy. The DJ."

She laughs. "Oh, no. Blakely doesn't date. A *virgin*," she whispers dramatically, taking another sip. "I don't think they've ever met."

My brows lift in shock. Blakely's always so confident in her advances, I assumed she had more experience. I glance back toward the stage. "Should he be touching her like that then?"

She cocks her head to the side. "Like what?"

"Like he doesn't give a fuck if she wants it or not." My

jaw clenches, and I try to temper the bite in my voice. I don't like to cause scenes, content to learn people's traits by observing rather than making knee-jerk decisions. But in this moment, I want to jump on stage, and rip that skinny prick's hands from Blakely's body. Force him to apologize for touching what doesn't belong to him.

Kayla chuckles again. "Oh, don't worry about her." She brushes the hair off her shoulder, setting her drink on the table in front of us. "She's used to it."

Mr. Donahue's words from earlier today whisper in my head—how he doesn't trust the people in her life—and for the first time tonight, I'm thankful I'm here, because I'm beginning to think he was right. She does need someone to look out for her. To make sure she's taken care of.

"Hmm," I mutter. My eyes are drawn back to her hips as they swing like a pendulum, lulling me into this fucked up hypnotic state—taunting me with what she's offering. What she's *always* offering.

She's nineteen.

BLAKELY'S BEEN a master of the VIP room ever since she walked in. She smiles when appropriate and takes photos with fans who've paid God knows what to get the privilege. All run-of-the-mill stuff, I'm sure.

But it's all so fake.

She is fake.

Anyone who cares to look can see it's forced. But as I watch from the back corner as Blakely flits from place to place, I realize that in a club filled with hundreds desperate to stand in her shine, none of them really *see*. And maybe that's the problem.

You learn a lot about a person from paying attention to what they don't say. And Blakely Donahue doesn't say a lot.

I wonder if anyone has ever listened to her silence.

The blaring music starts up again, the bass vibrating so loud it rattles my bones, and I sigh, tired of the charade. Ready to go home. I head to the outside bar, both to get a break from the music, and to get away from a bunch of kids who aren't even old enough to be here. Pulling out my phone, I check for any missed calls or texts, my chest pinching when I see a blank screen.

I don't know why I'm surprised. My friends in Sugarlake still have each other, like they did before I moved there when I was sixteen. I've always been the transplant. The added feature. One that makes your life easier but doesn't sever your ability to function once it's gone.

Knowing that doesn't make it hurt any less.

"You look like you've got good stories." The raspy voice of the bartender pulls me from my thoughts.

She leans over, and my eyes drop to her cleavage, appreciating how they bounce as she wipes the bar top down. It would be rude not to watch since she's putting on such a show.

"Do I?" I smirk, meeting her almond eyes.

I hold her gaze, waiting for that spark to flare, the same way it did earlier with Blakely. I *need* it to flare. To prove its lack of sex making my body react, and not something else.

Unfortunately, disappointment is the only thing that flickers.

Still, she'll be a good distraction. I can't give her stories, but I *can* give her thirty minutes in the stock room closet.

"Babe, who's this?" Arms slink around my waist, my

heart jumping at the voice, my skin sizzling from the touch. *Goddamnit.*

Blakely peers around the side of me, her fingers lightly scratching against my abs, making them tense against her palms. I stare down at her, my brow quirking.

She looks at the bartender. "I'd love a water."

The bartender clears her throat, eyes dimming as she straightens and nods. "Sure thing."

I grab Blakely's hands, intent on pushing them away, but instead my fingers tighten around hers, moving them from around my waist and dragging her until she's standing in front of me. My hands slide up her arms, goose bumps sprouting underneath my fingertips. My cock is fucking aching, and what the hell am I even doing? Clenching my jaw, I take a step back, dropping my hands.

"Cute, *babe,*" I say.

She laughs. "I was doing her a favor. Saving her from those atrocious pickup lines."

My lips twitch, amusement dripping through my chest. "See, that's your first mistake."

"What is?" Her head tilts to the side.

"Thinking I need lines."

My eyes follow her tongue as it peeks out, swiping along her bottom lip. She shrugs. "So maybe I was saving you. Honestly, it was pathetic. She looked like a sacrificial lamb, waiting for the big bad wolf to eat her up."

I lean in until my lips are next to her ear. "Maybe I was hungry."

She sucks in a breath, her supple cleavage brushing against my chest. My heart slams against my ribs as I think of how her tits would feel wrapped around my dick. *Fuck.* I need to get this back in control. I straighten, reaching up to grab the chain around my neck.

Her eyes flare, no doubt noticing my struggle.

"I can think of several ways to *feed* you, if that's what you need," she says.

My cock throbs, images of her moving her hips the way she did on stage assaulting my mind, but this time she's sitting on my face while I feast on her pussy and drown in her juices.

I clear my throat. "Stop that."

She smirks, leaning in and rising up on her tiptoes until I can taste the mint on her breath.

"Or what?" she whispers.

My nostrils flare, hands tingling with the need to palm her ass until it hurts—make her realize she can't handle a man like me.

A flash goes off, and it jolts me out of my daze. I step back, turning my head to the side, noticing a group of girls with their phones out, all of them directed toward us. I sweep my eyes slowly over the patio, watching as some avert their gazes while others blatantly stare.

Blakely and I have everyone's attention.

My eyes find hers again. The flash must have knocked some sense into her too, because in an instant she transforms, that thousand-watt, picture-perfect grin spreading across her face. It's quite the dichotomy, watching her face light up and frame the darkness in her eyes.

I sigh, running a hand through my hair. "Blake, listen, I—"

"Don't." She shakes her head slightly. "We should go. Sierra will kill me if she sees me out here with you."

My lips press together, her words reminding me of the bruises on my heart. "I get it. Bad look to be seen with the babysitter."

It's a low blow and I know it. But fuck her for saying

that to me. Like I'm not good enough. Like I'm just a stand-in. Cracking my neck, I wave my arm. "After you, princess."

She hesitates, sucking that pouty bottom lip between her teeth, and I stare at a spot behind her head, not trusting myself to look into her eyes. Finally, she squares her shoulders, turning to walk inside.

I follow close behind, my gaze locking on to the way her ass bounces with the sway of her hips. My gut clenches, my cock thickening, and I grasp the chain around my neck, the tiny metal balls biting against my skin.

She's nineteen.

7

BLAKELY

There's a picture of Jackson and me on TMZ. Usually, a photo in the tabloids is the goal, after all, there's no such thing as bad promo, but the fact someone snapped a photo of *this* moment—where it felt like Jackson was dipping into the depths of my soul—makes nausea curdle in my stomach.

Blakely Donahue's Mystery Man.

That's what they're calling him. Like he's a puzzle for them to solve. Like he's *mine*. The reality is he's neither of those things, but people aren't interested in facts. That's not what sells.

Truth has no place in the spotlight.

They'll want him, that's for sure. You can't look the way Jackson does and not have agents and slobbering fangirls banging down your door.

Anxiety tightens my insides, my foot tapping against the leg of the glass table. I've been sitting here for the past hour, hiding away in the enclave off the kitchen, trying to force myself into believing I don't care about this headline.

But for the first time since I met him, I wish Jackson was just a little bit uglier. A little less perfect. A little less likable. Because if they get their hands on him, they'll either change him into something unrecognizable or they'll destroy any sense of reputation and honor he has. Either way, he gets eaten alive. There's no way to come out whole once you're in the jaws of Hollywood.

It was stupid as hell, letting myself get lost in the moment. A rookie mistake, one I'll never let happen again. But it caught me off guard last night. I didn't expect the air to become our foreplay, swirling in the space between us, and sinking into my skin, teasing me with its tension. I didn't know playing with Jackson's fire would make it lick at my insides, desperate to have him strip me of my products and love me bare.

I don't have much experience with men, and even less with sex, but I've never felt anything like what I felt last night. And now it's staring me in the face from the front page of TMZ.

"I think it's great." Sierra's voice filters through my thoughts as she plops down across from me.

Turning my head, I look at her, my brows rising. "What is?"

She nods toward my computer and my eyes follow. It's not a great photo. It's grainy, like someone snapped it on their shitty phone, and sold it to the highest bidder. But there's no denying the way our bodies are pressed so close you can't see the space between us. No way to mask the look in his eyes or the smile on my face.

"He's hot. They're practically salivating trying to figure out who he is."

I cringe, guilt weaving its way into my chest. I can't imagine he's the type of person who craves notoriety. And that's what being seen with me will give him. A bad name and a bad reputation, whether he wants it or not.

"Use it to your advantage," she continues. "Invite him to more things." She pauses briefly, tapping her stiletto nails on the tabletop. "But not *too* many things. We want them curious, not confident. We still need plausible deniability."

"Mmhm." I'm only half paying attention to what she says, choosing to scan the article instead, my stomach churning more with every word I read.

"What's wrong?" Sierra asks.

"Hmm?" I glance up at her. Clearing my throat, I push my laptop to the side. "Nothing. I'm just tired."

"You're being weird. You don't..." She tilts her head to the side. "You don't *like* this guy, right?"

My stomach flutters at her question and I scoff, scrunching my nose. "Please, Sierra. He's like thirty."

"And your dad's employee," she says pointedly. "Maybe we should leak his profession. Blakely's mystery *mechanic* has a nice ring to it, yeah?"

"He's not a mechanic," I snap.

She shrugs. "He's close enough." Her eyes narrow as she leans back, running a hand through her blonde hair. "Shit. You like him, don't you?"

I roll my eyes. "Get real, Sierra."

"I'm always real, B. You're the one who has to put on a show, not me. Let's not forget that."

Her words hit their mark, bruising the tender spots in my soul and dripping into my conscience.

She sighs. "It's probably for the best if we don't use him then."

My eyes widen. "You literally *just* said we should."

"Well, that was before I knew you were getting attached." She leans in, resting her palms on the table. My eyes flash to where her hands press into the glass, and I bite the inside of my cheek so hard I taste blood. Having her talk about Jackson makes my lungs squeeze tight.

Closing my eyes, I try to stay calm and focus on the conversation.

Deep breath in. One. Two. Three. Deep breath out.

My heart rate starts to level, and I reassure myself that Sierra is wrong. I'm not attached, I just like the way he makes me feel. He doesn't expect me to be anything, he just lets me simply *be*.

"I'm not getting attached. I just… he doesn't treat me like everyone else." I shake my head, huffing out a laugh. "He doesn't even *like* me. How pathetic is that? The realest person in my life, and he can't stand the sight of me."

Sierra tsks. "He seems to like the sight of you just fine if that picture's any indication."

My eyes glide back to the computer screen, my stomach jolting from the memory of what it felt like to be spinning in Jackson's orbit, even for a moment.

"Look, B. I'm gonna keep it real. He's good for the gossip but he's not good for the brand. Not long-term. Cartier doesn't want to dangle off the wrist of someone whose man can't afford to put it there."

My brows draw in. "Cartier isn't even one of my sponsors."

"And they never will be if you fall for this guy."

"Ughhhh," I groan, throwing my head back. "Will you shut the hell up? Nobody is *falling* for anyone. God, he was only there because my father told him to be."

Sierra shrugs. "I'm just saying... let's keep it that way. He's hot, and he's a great tool to keep your name in the headlines, but that's all he is, you know? *A tool.* Product placement."

Her words scrape against my ears, making me cringe at the harsh reality of my life. You either play the game or you don't, that's what she's really saying.

Dance, monkey, dance.

In my world, consent is an illusion, an act put on for the masses. It's all fake. And Jackson is just so damn real.

But I'm not.

And that's why I know I'm going to agree even before my head starts to nod. Even though there's a sour taste on the back of my tongue, and a weight pulling down my chest. Because I'll do anything to rise to the top.

To be seen.

8

JACKSON

I woke up this morning after tossing and turning all night, worried like hell about how Lee was handling things back home. Wondering if she misses me, even just a little. If she's surrounded with a good support system, or if she's breaking apart from holding the weight of her alcoholic father and her estranged brother on her back.

Leaving was the right choice, though. I've lived the past decade watching her give someone else the beats of her heart, leaving me alone with its echo. Staying would have only been hurting myself, and even though I've loved Lee through my pain, I'm not a masochist.

It's hard enough coming to terms with the fact it's her

first love, and my ex-best friend, Chase, who's drying up all her tears. I don't need to stay around to see it. I *can't.* But not speaking to her like I'm used to leaves an ache behind that not even the strongest liquor has been able to numb.

But last night, something finally did.

Blakely.

She's always been simply my boss's brat daughter, with a silver spoon up her ass, and a knack for never leaving me the hell alone. A minor inconvenience because of the way she gets under my skin, but one I would have done anything to distance myself from.

Now, things feel different. I'm confused. Twisted up in ways I didn't know had any slack left to tangle, and I'm not sure what to do with the realization that the one thing screaming disaster is also the one thing that dulls the pain.

Last night, for the first time in years, my mind wasn't stuck on Lee. My heart wasn't wading through the muddy waters of unconditional love and unreturned feelings.

It wasn't until later—after I got home and jerked off to the thought of my cock down Blakely's throat—that I realized it had been hours since Lee was even a passing thought. But the guilt quickly washed away any relief that was there, heartbreak pumping through my body and whooshing in my ears until the only sound left was the hollow ring of longing.

Maybe that's why when I see Blakely's driver pull her S-Class Maybach up to the curb, I drop what I'm doing and go inside to meet her. Because she's the perfect distraction, a reprieve from the constant feeling of being second best. Besides, I can't really watch over her the way her dad wants if she doesn't think we're friends.

By the time I make it through the doors from the garage, Blakely's already seated behind the front desk, her face barely visible over the high top that doubles as a counter.

I peer down at her. "Hey, princess."

"Jackson." She stares at me, chewing on her bottom lip.

"What?" I ask, my brows rising.

"Nothing, you're just—" She waves her hand around. "Chipper."

I point to myself. "I'm *always* chipper."

She snorts. "Not with me."

A stab of guilt pricks me in the chest. I've never taken joy in being seen as an asshole, but I don't know how else to handle her without letting her get too close.

Humming, I flip through the Donahue Motors pamphlets sitting in the display case to my right. "So, what's on the agenda for tonight?"

She scrunches her nose. "Why? You gonna play babysitter again?"

I smirk. "Let's not pretend you don't like it."

She cocks her head. "You're not mad at me?"

"Should I be?" Dropping the pamphlets, I lock my gaze with hers, the yellow center of her eyes spearing me right in the fucking chest.

"Noooo." She draws out the syllables, like even she doesn't believe the word as it leaves her lips. "You haven't…" She hesitates, running her hand through her shiny hair. "You're not online much, huh. No Facebook or anything?"

I shake my head. "Nope."

"How come?"

"My friends—" The thought of Lee and Chase makes me pause, and I clear my throat to cover the break in my voice. "I learned a long time ago that nothing good comes from people being in your business. Some things should stay private."

She sucks on her teeth, nodding slowly.

My stomach clenches, something settling over my body —a warning. "Why?"

Cringing, she toys with the cord of the phone's headset, twirling it between her fingers. "There may or may not be a photo of us from last night."

"A photo…" I repeat her words, thinking about what that means. I don't really *want* my picture anywhere, but I'm not an idiot. I knew it was a possibility when we went out—especially once I realized she was more well-known than I gave her credit for.

I sigh, resting my chin in my hand, letting the silence stretch uncomfortably before I finally smile. "Was it a good one?"

Her eyes widen, a grin creeping over her face. My stomach jumps.

"Duh." She flips her hair behind her shoulder, her eyes peeking at me from under her lashes. "I thought you'd be more… upset?"

"Upset because…?"

Picking up her phone, she stands, leaning over the desk and showing me the headline on TMZ.

I take in the photo of us, my breath stuttering as my heart kicks against my ribs.

"This is why. I wasn't sure how you'd take being plastered all over… how you'd like being seen with me. The *princess* you love to hate."

My lips curl up, but my eyes stay glued on the picture, the memory of that moment diving straight into my chest and squeezing. I was *so* close to feeling her under my hands.

To sucking the brat off her tongue and bending her body until it broke me of my grief.

Sliding my gaze away from the screen, I lean in close, her mouth a slight twitch away from touching mine. "I don't hate you, Blake."

She sucks in a gasp, drawing my eyes to the way her cleavage rises with her breath. "You don't?" she whispers.

I shake my head slowly, careful not to let my lips graze hers with the motion.

"What do you feel, then?"

"I—"

Laughter from the hallway cuts me off and I jump back, the sound dousing me in icy water. I run my hands through my hair, glancing down the hallway, seeing Karen meander toward the reception area.

Fuck.

I back up, pointing toward the photo still pulled up on her phone. "I'm not mad, but it doesn't mean I like it."

She scoffs. "Like I do? Please…"

"Then we should be more careful."

"Fine." She crosses her arms.

"*Fine.*" Amusement at her attitude warms my chest, and I copy her stance, stifling my smile.

Her eyes narrow. "I'm having a photo shoot at my house tonight. Do your babysitting duties extend to in-home activities?"

"They probably should." I nod.

The truth is, I have no idea if Mr. Donahue's request extends past her public appearances, but at this point, it doesn't matter.

When I'm at home, I have time to think. Time to *feel.*

I'll take Blakely over the hurt any day.

9

BLAKELY

It isn't healthy to read comments online, especially ones under articles that are filled with speculation. But for the first time in what feels like forever, I do. I justify the decision by convincing myself that I'm checking to see how it comes across. After all, I haven't heard anything from my dad, so I assume he either hasn't seen the photo, or it's not actually as bad as it feels.

But I should know better than to look.

Who is that? He looks like a Greek god.

Not to be dramatic, but if this man doesn't wife me up and father my children, I will die.

How's a frigid bitch get a guy like that?

OMGGGG He's fine af.

Her pussy must be gold. Have y'all seen her w/out photoshop? H-I-D-E-O-U-S. In it for the $$.

It's the last one that makes me pause, the barbs slicing through my thick skin, and festering in my psyche. Setting my phone down, I head into the formal living room—the one that's just been transformed into a set for the photo shoot—trying to ignore the way it suddenly feels like a thousand bugs are crawling under my skin.

Immediately, my eyes take in the scene. Sierra is standing to the side, hands on her hips, her messy blonde hair thrown up in a bun. A beige knitted sweater slouches off one shoulder and drapes on top of black leggings. She looks cozy, and envy hits my chest, jealous of how she's able to throw on comfortable clothes and not worry about being seen in something off-brand.

The sun hasn't set yet, but it's close, pinks and purples grazing against the horizon, spreading their glow through the wall of windows and casting everything in a stunning hue of twilight.

It's a calming aura, and if I were anyone else, maybe I'd enjoy the moment, and be thankful that my life is as blessed as it is. But instead of relaxing, my fists clench tight, fingernails pressing into my palm, threatening to cut through my skin with the pressure.

There's a scent in the air. Baked dough and tomato sauce. Gooey cheese and peppers. My nostrils flare, letting the stench flow down to my empty stomach, hoping it will be enough to curb the craving.

My foot starts tapping against the tigerwood floor as three guys in black huddle in a circle, not a care in the world, the large slices oozing grease from their hands.

Sierra walks toward me. "Blakely, be ready for glam in

fifteen." I close my eyes and continue breathing deep, a tendril of anxiety wrapping around my insides.

One. Two. Three.

"You okay?" she asks.

"Fine," I snap. "I'm just… I'm hungry."

Her eyes widen and she gestures toward the pizza.

Scoffing, I cross my arms, irritation swimming through my chest and pulling it tight. "That's *pizza,* Sierra. I need food I can eat and not want to die from later on."

Sierra huffs out a laugh, rolling her eyes. "God, you're so dramatic. Have a piece of pizza, you're gonna spend all night in the gym anyway, and we both know it. We don't have time for one of your prepped meals *or* one of your tantrums."

My jaw clenches tight. *Tantrums.* Like I can control it. Shame courses through me, my mind waging war against my stomach.

I can have half a slice. Or just a few bites. One time won't kill me.

Walking to the table, the smell of baked crust and oregano slam against my senses and my mouth waters, urging my hand to snatch up a piece before my brain can talk me out of it.

I take a bite.

Oh, my fucking god.

My eyes close, the flavors exploding on my taste buds in a way that baked tilapia and lettuce with no dressing just can't replicate. I lose myself in the moment—in the absolute freedom of enjoying every precious bite, and by the time I come back to myself the entire piece is demolished.

"Damn, girl. I've never seen someone eat pie that way."

My head snaps to one of the men in the corner,

stomach churning in disgust at both my lack of restraint and my stupidity. *Anybody* could have recorded me shoveling pizza in my mouth like a fat ass.

I give a tight smile to the man, not trusting myself to keep from snapping back, and not wanting to give him anything to sell to the tabloids if I do.

Slipping my phone from my pocket, I pull up my calorie tracking app.

One slice of cheese pizza is…

I choke on my inhale. *Three hundred and four calories.* A burning heat slams through my body, my forehead becoming damp from the sudden shift.

Lennox's voice draws my attention away, and I turn toward the hallway where he walks in with Jackson beside him. They're chatting, a smile on both of their faces, and for just a moment, I forget about my failures, too busy wondering how the hell Jackson got through Lennox's cold exterior in a matter of moments.

Jackson's gaze scans the room, locking on me and widening slightly.

Why is he looking at me like that?

My eyes bounce between him and the empty plate of my mistake, and I can actually *feel* my heart ramming against my chest. My mind races, making me woozy with the need to burn off the calories before they're able to stick to my cells and turn into fat.

There's no time. The shoot will last hours and by then it will be too late.

Stupid, Blakely. Pathetic.

Months of hard work and discipline thrown down the drain because of one weak moment. And even if I get to the gym, the damage will be done. Visions of my measuring tape reading higher numbers flash through my mind, thoughts twisting into a spiral.

My lungs wring tight. I close my eyes and try to focus.

Deep breath in. One. Two. Three.

It's only four hundred calories. The three from the pizza and an extra hundred to make up for my lack of control. I can be on and off the spin bike in thirty minutes.

Deep breath out. One. Two. Three.

My legs bounce erratically as I scan the room, briefly locking eyes with Jackson before continuing on to find who I need.

"Sierra." I try to make my voice nonchalant, but it comes out pinched. "How long do I have?"

Sierra drops the pillow she's rearranging as she turns to look at me. "Not enough time for you to do whatever you're thinking. Just wait until later."

My heart stutters, and a sharp pain spreads across my chest.

Panic tightens around every piece of me and squeezes until I'm sure I'll burst at the seams.

Nausea curdles my stomach, the urge to heave so strong I press the back of my hand against my mouth.

My breaths come shorter, my eyes darting from the table pushed against the wall to the garish studio lights that are looming over the makeshift set before settling back on Jackson. Someone drags an end table to the side, and the sound of it scratching against the hardwood grates against my ears and rakes down my insides.

Jackson cringes from the noise but his eyes stay locked on me. My vision narrows.

I'm spiraling and I know it, but it's an out-of-body experience and I can do nothing but watch. A helpless bystander. A spectator to my own destruction. If I were in my right mind, maybe I would feel shame for being so vulnerable in this moment—in front of the one person who will see what's happening and won't be content with pretending it never did.

I try to take deep breaths. Try to steady my nerves, but once the panic has started, there's no reasoning with the madness.

Deep breath in. One. Two. Three. Deep breath out.

It doesn't help. My hands reach up and pull at my roots. "Stop!" My voice is loud, echoing off the high ceilings and reverberating across the empty space.

The men moving the furniture freeze in place. My glam team, busy putting out their tools, spin to face me. Jackson continues watching. And Sierra, ever the businesswoman, ignores me completely. "Keep going, guys. She's just having a moment."

My nostrils flare. I wouldn't even be *having* this moment if it weren't for her. If she would have just let me make my food, we could have avoided this entire situation. But instead, I gave in. Let her dictate what goes in my body and desecrated myself with garbage.

The thought reaches up and strangles me.

Deep breath in. One. Two. Three.

"No, I'm not having a moment. I need…" The race of my heart pounding against my chest makes my words stutter. "I-I need everyone to stop what they're doing and get the hell out. I can't do it. I can't do it right now."

Sierra sighs, walking over to me. My gaze jerks across the room to Jackson, standing effortlessly calm and collected, hands in his pockets, his eyes *still* never leaving me.

"Blakely," Sierra says. "We can't stop. This is on your schedule, has been for weeks. If we push it back, then you'll be behind. Again." Her words are slow. Soothing. Like she's trying to bait and lure an animal into its cage.

My head shakes, unable to focus on anything other than the fact that it's now been over ten minutes since I finished stuffing straight-up trash down my throat, and every second wasted is another ounce of fat. One that, no doubt, every single person on the internet will notice.

"I don't care," I hiss through clenched teeth. "Get them out. *Now.*"

"Look." Sierra clicks her tongue. "I know you're a control freak, okay? I get it. You're mad that I took over and had you eat what the common folk do." She gestures toward the empty boxes.

My insides flare, chest burning with her words. "I'm not a control freak, I just..." Closing my eyes to try and shake the dizziness, I continue to inhale.

One. Two. Three.

"Blakely, look. Take deep breaths and just... go sit in the makeup chair." She waves her hand. "Let them make you pretty."

My chest pulls tighter.

Suddenly, the air shifts, heat dancing through the chill that's pricking on my skin.

Sierra's eyes flick behind me. "Hi, Jackson."

He ignores her, walking around and standing in front of me. Embarrassment drowns my system, blood rushing to my cheeks and making them hot. I don't want him to see me like this. Never wanted him to know about this part of me.

Bile teases the back of my throat, chunks of the pizza I just ate threatening to come back up and remind me of what I just gave up *months* of restraint for. The acid burns my esophagus, and I swear to God I can feel the extra weight already dragging me down with every minute I stand here.

Jackson's palms reach up and cup my face, angling my head to meet his eyes, the mossy green searing through me. I suck in a breath at the way my mind zones in on his gaze, and I'm suddenly desperate for more of his calm.

"Don't leave," I gasp.

His thumbs brush my jaw, and I focus on the feel of his calloused fingers as they scratch against my face. "I'm not leaving. Are you okay?"

There's a burn behind my eyes, and Jackson goes blurry as I stare back at him, something warm blossoming in my chest and rising to my throat. I shake my head no, my hair brushing against his forearms with the movement.

His jaw tics. "What do you need?"

My heart cracks open at the question, the pressure against my lungs easing, just a bit.

"I need… I need them to leave." My tongue jets out to wet my dry, chapped lips. "And you to stay. Please." My heart palpitates, stuttering against my ribs. My hands jump to cover his.

"Everybody out." His voice is strong. Commanding. I sink deeper into his hold.

His eyes never leave mine, his fingers tightening against my skin, and I focus on the brown specks that dot the forest green of his gaze.

One. Two. Three. Deep breath out.

Sierra scoffs. "This is ridiculous. They need to finish setting up."

I don't respond. I can't do anything other than focus on Jackson's eyes. If I break away, I'll lose the rest of my sanity.

"No." His voice is sharp.

"What do you *mean,* no?" Sierra bites out.

"Have them leave, *now.* Or I'll make them leave."

"Listen," Sierra continues. "She does this sometimes, has these… moments, and we always get through it. We don't need you coming in here and concerning yourself with the way things work."

His eyes finally leave me and my stomach heaves, twisting until it breaks into a thousand pieces and prods against my edges. My nails dig into the back of his hands. His fingers tighten against my jaw.

"The only thing I'm concerned with is Blakely," Jackson snaps. "And you. Getting. The. Fuck. Out."

His eyes come back to mine and the knot in my gut loosens.

Deep breath in. One. Two. Three.

He's my anchor. The only thing keeping me from being lost in tumultuous seas. And even though it makes me weak, I let him keep me steady until I'm able to stand on my own.

10

JACKSON

I've been holding Blakely in my hands for the past ten minutes. Her skin is soft underneath my palms, her trembling jaw vibrates through my fingertips until I feel her unease like it's a tangible thing, sinking into my bones and locking me into place.

I don't know what it is she's going through, but I know panic attacks when I see them. Most of my childhood was spent helping my father navigate through his when he'd wake up in a cold sweat, having post-traumatic stress attacks from his time overseas.

My dad always needed a focus object. Something to keep him anchored, so he wouldn't get lost in the darkest parts of his mind. So his memories wouldn't overtake his reality.

And maybe it's the way Blakely latched onto me the second I arrived. Or maybe it's seeing the same haunted look in her eyes that kept me awake so many nights with him. But there's *something* that has me holding steady and keeping her in my grasp. Something that sucks me in like quicksand, telling me to stay.

So, I don't move from my spot.

Not when that bitch of a manager screeches in my ear, and not when every other person who didn't give a fuck that Blakely was breaking down, leaves. I hear them moving, hear their whispered complaints and groans of disapproval… but still, I stay.

Letting her focus on me so she doesn't focus on the chaos.

It's not until every last person is gone, our syncopated breathing matching the heavy beats of our hearts, that I let her go.

She tenses the second my fingers leave her face.

My hands fly back to her jaw, bringing those wild eyes to stare into mine. "Tell me what you need."

Her head shakes back and forth, the movements small, short, and frantic. Like she's trying to control the tremors that so obviously ooze from her nerves.

Those pouty lips part, but instead of speaking out loud she mouths silent words, and when I look closer I realize they're numbers. *One, two, three.*

She's been doing that since I walked in, and it hits me that this is her coping mechanism, which means this is something that happens often enough where she has methods to try and maintain control. My heart sinks at the thought.

"You can get through this," I say. *Just like I used to with my dad.*

Her eyes squeeze shut, nostrils flaring as she breathes in deep.

"Good. Concentrate on your breathing. Stay in the present."

I'm not sure that what I'm saying applies to the current situation, but I'm going off what I know, hoping the sentiment behind the words is enough to help keep her centered.

Her fists clench at her sides, knuckles turning white from the force.

"I need… I need to go change," she finally stutters out.

I step forward. "Okay. Do you want me to come with you?"

She nods sharply, her face scrunched. "Yes, I…" She opens her eyes and exhales a shaky breath, taking a step back, leaving my palms to grasp the air. Her fingers stop digging into her hands long enough to run through the strands of her hair. "Yes."

"Okay."

She nods again, her shoulders relaxing the slightest amount, and the pounding in my chest eases along with them. But then a clock from somewhere down the hall chimes nine times, and like a light switch, her eyes squeeze tight once again.

My stomach jumps, her anxiety reaching out and tightening the knot in my gut.

I won't lie, I'm nervous. Scared that the small tricks I remember—the things my dad's therapist taught me—won't be enough. That I won't be able to help her through whatever the hell this is.

But I have to try. I won't be able to walk away from this

situation. Whether she breaks apart or gains control, I'll be here to mend the frays. *Someone* needs to be.

"I need to get out of this room." Her voice is stronger than it was before, but I can practically taste the tension off her words. Still, she doesn't move. Instead, her chest heaves, rising and falling faster with every second, and I can see the war being waged in her brain, wanting to go, yet being frozen from hysteria.

So, I do the only thing I know, without a fucking clue whether it will help.

I tell her what I used to tell my father.

And even though my nerves shift higher with every clench of her fist, I keep my voice steady. Strong. Controlled. "It's not the place that's bothering you, Blakely. It's the thoughts."

The words fly out of my mouth, whizzing by her ears, and for a moment I'm convinced they've missed her completely. But eventually, she nods. And then she starts to mouth the words. Over and over, her fists once again white-knuckling against her sides.

Relief pours through my veins that she heard me, that it seems to be making at least a little bit of difference. My fingers reach up, twisting the chain on my necklace, giving her space and praying like hell she knows herself enough to know what she needs.

But I see her.

My eyes are my weapon as I slice her surface, searching for what she hides down deep, desperate to meet the real Blakely. To learn who she is by watching how she acts in the fragile moments.

Guilt weaves through my chest, realizing I've spent all my time so worried about keeping her at a distance that I've never cared enough to actually look. I thought I had her pegged from the second I met her, convinced I didn't like what I saw.

Nausea rolls in my gut. That's not me. That's not who I strive to be as a person. I'll stay and help her through her panic, and I'll keep coming back to make sure she's *seen*. Not because I'm craving to spend time with her, and not because I feel responsibility, but because I know what it's like to be lost in your head—to feel so alone while you're spinning at its mercy. I know what it's like to spiral so fast and so deep you fear you'll never see straight again. I *know* the pain of hiding your grief, and doing it so well, so convincingly, that no one realizes they should be looking to see if it's there.

That was my reality with every one of my dad's deployments. My mom hiding her tears, thinking I couldn't hear through our thin walls at night, and me, hiding my terror at the thought of him never coming home.

That was me suffering with every round of his chemo. Through the good days and the bad. The times he was thankful for life, and the times he begged for death.

That was me drowning from the emptiness he left behind. From not being there in his final moments. For allowing God to take him away when I still desperately needed him here.

So, I'll stay in my spot.

And I'll keep coming back, so she isn't alone. The lighthouse to her darkness, guiding her through the shallow waters.

11

BLAKELY

Jackson stays through everything. He walks behind me as I rush up the winding staircase to my room, and is still here, staring at photos of my mother, when I come out in my sports bra and shorts.

He's here while I head straight to our basement gym, making himself comfortable at a small round table in the corner while I spin my ass off for who knows how long. And when I'm finally feeling semi-normal—once the control has started to settle back in, clicking into place one calorie at a time—he's *still* here.

I look at my Apple watch. One thousand and seventy-four calories.

Once I hit two thousand, I'll stop.

The knot of anxiety in my chest loosens as I slow down to a normal speed on my bike, and for the first time since the pizza hit my taste buds, I can breathe. My muscles are past the point of burning, the lactic acid having morphed into a dull throb that sends satisfaction racing through my veins. I can feel the grease as it drips from my pores, and if I close my eyes, I can actually visualize all of the impurities purging from my system. A renewal of health through my hard work and dedication, despite my moment of weakness.

Finally, I ease to a cooldown and grab my water bottle.

"Feel better?" Jax asks.

My stomach jumps at his voice and I look over to where he's sitting leaned back in his chair, watching me.

Why did he stay?

"Yes," I respond slowly before taking a sip of my water.

He nods, his hand coming up to rub the scruff on his chin. "Good."

Slowing to a stop, I take him in, shame working its way through my system and blooming under my skin when I reflect on the past few hours. On how absolutely pathetic I must have looked. "You didn't have to stay, you know."

His hand rubs at his chest, a tinkling of metal jostling underneath his white tee. "I wasn't going to leave you alone."

My heart stutters when he says it, and I can't for the life of me figure out what his angle is here. Why he's acting like he wasn't witness to something that most people would *kill* to know—to hold against me.

Why is he acting like I'm not broken?

"Why did you?" I ask.

"Why did I what?"

"Stay."

"I just told you. I wasn't going to leave you."

I huff. "Yeah but… *why*?"

He shrugs, his eyes darkening as they stare into mine, but he's silent for long enough that I think he won't answer. That I've hit a nerve without meaning to, and he's about to close back up—become the Jackson he's always been around me. The one who creates distance and won't ever let me in.

Sighing, he runs a hand over his head, rustling a few strands of wavy hair from his bun. "Sometimes... you just need to know you aren't alone."

It's immediate—the way my chest rips open from the strength of his words, but besides the sharp, sudden inhale of breath, I do my best to mask the feeling.

I'm not sure anyone has ever said that to me before, and even if they have, I'm sure they've never meant it.

My eyes trail up his form, from his black boots to his dark jeans, over that plain white tee he wears so well, all the way to that chiseled jaw and ethereal gaze. He's so effortless. So calm. And in my most vulnerable of moments, the ones I'm desperate to hide from the world, he's the strongest, surest thing I've ever seen.

It makes me feel off-kilter. I've never experienced that type of security before.

He clears his throat, shifting in his seat. "Does that happen a lot?"

"Does what happen a lot?" I know what he's asking, I'm not an idiot. I'm just hoping if I pretend, then maybe he will too. Just like everyone else.

Jumping off my bike to grab a towel, I stop for a moment, closing my eyes and basking in the post-workout high. Lightheaded and almost dizzy, a warm buzzing fills my body. I let the feeling of accomplishment cling to my skin like a second sheen of sweat, the satisfaction a warmth that swims through every cell.

"Come on, Blake, you know what."

The fuzzy feeling disappears and my teeth grind, irritation slicing through my contentment. *Why can't he just let this go?*

"Why do you call me that?" I snap, spinning around.

His brow rises. "Call you what?"

"*Blake*. No one calls me that. It's not my name."

He lifts a shoulder, a smirk pulling at one side of his mouth, hinting at what I know is a perfect smile. "Why do you call me Jackson? Everyone else calls me Jax."

"I'm not everybody else," I retort.

"Neither am I." He pauses. "Besides, I didn't realize I was doing it."

My eyes narrow. "I don't believe you."

His smirk widens. "Guess we'll never know."

Huffing, I cross my arms over my chest, biting my cheek to keep from grinning. "You're ridiculous."

"Just trying to stay on your level." He winks.

His eyes drop quickly to my breasts before coming back to my face. Heat surges from between my legs, and pools low in my stomach, causing my heart to ram against my chest.

The feeling is so new, so *different* from what I'm used to feeling when it comes to men, and it unnerves me. "W-well, don't call me that," I stutter. "It makes me..."

He stands up from his chair and stalks toward me. My hands tighten around the terry cloth towel, the fabric rough against my suddenly clammy palms.

Why is he coming so close? I'm disgusting right now.

My icy thoughts freeze the warmth before it can grow

into something more. I can't believe I didn't think about it until this moment.

I have no makeup on.

He's going to see the chickenpox scar on my forehead. The one right between my eyes that gets covered with makeup and shopped out by my team.

He's going to see my stomach. The one I stupidly didn't cover, too lost in my panic of burning off calories to worry about the extra flab that's been on display. Jiggling with every motion.

Embarrassment slams into me, and I back up a step from the impact. My head starts shaking, trying to warn him. To tell him without words that he shouldn't come closer. I don't *want* him close.

But he doesn't stop, not until he's right in front of me.

I suck in a breath, squeezing my eyes shut so I don't have to watch the realization pass over his eyes when he notices my flaws in the garish gym lights. Nausea churns in my stomach, my lungs squeezing tight, until suddenly…

It stops.

Jackson's hand is on my neck, his thumb rubbing the underside of my jaw. And his touch, it calms the storm swirling inside. Slowly, I open my eyes, and my heart skips from a different type of nerve.

Because Jackson is *looking* at me. And he's not running the other way. Not telling me to change or to make sure I clean up. Not listing off all the ways we're going to adjust the "unedited" version of me the world gets to see.

Jackson just *is*.

And I don't really know what to do with that.

"It makes you feel *what,* princess?" he rasps.

My stomach tightens at the rumble in his voice, and I

turn my head to the side to break the tension. Chills spread down my neck from the loss of his touch.

"Like we're friends," I say, tossing my towel in the bin, and putting my hands on my hips. "And you've made it perfectly clear that we're not."

His jaw tics. "We can't be friends."

My forehead scrunches. "How come?"

"You're nineteen."

"And?"

"I'm twenty-eight." He points to himself.

"And?" I repeat, throwing my arms to the sides.

He doesn't respond and a giggle bursts out of me, my hand smothering my mouth to try and keep it down.

"What?" He grins.

"You're just… astonishingly good at math." I pause. "And bad at coming up with excuses."

He laughs. "You're kind of a little shit, you know that?"

A tingling sensation unfurls inside me, expanding through my chest and trickling into my stomach—spreading through my limbs until I feel lighter than I have in years.

I smile. "Yeah, well… just trying to stay on your level, *friend.*"

His head cocks slightly as our banter dies down, and the silence surrounds us, pulling the air until it's stretched so thin it steals your breath.

A ringing interrupts the moment, and he's quick to grab his phone from his pocket. I can't help but lean over and sneak a peek to see who stole his attention away.

Sweetheart.

The term of endearment splices into my newfound happiness, and even though I have no basis for it, no clue of who "sweetheart" is or what story lies behind the sudden sadness in his eyes, a thick spread of jealousy coats over my insides.

I paste on a smile—the kind that hurts my cheeks and fools the world. "Do you need to get that?"

His gaze stays locked on his phone, but he silences the call, shaking his head. After a few seconds, he meets my eyes, but the lightness from earlier is gone, a heavy dose of reality settling in its place.

"Nope. I'm all yours."

12

JACKSON

Blakely and I settle in to watch a movie, but when she passes out on her couch halfway through, I take the opportunity to slip through the front door and head home, my phone burning a hole in my pocket since the moment it rang.

Sweetheart.

Alina.

It took everything in me not to pick up when she called. *What if she's hurt? What if she's breaking and all alone?*

Memories of the times I've held her together play on a loop, a physical ache spreading through my chest.

I've happily been Lee's shield, protecting her from the

impact every time her world crumbled, but if I continue to jump and say how high whenever she comes running, I'll never move on.

And I *have* to move on.

It just sucks I'm losing my best friend in the process, at least temporarily. Maybe one day I'll be able to hear her voice—look her in the face and not feel my heart fracture from the longing that slices through it. Won't feel the disappointment wrapping around my chest and sinking into my gut, knowing the guilt in her eyes is because she doesn't love me back.

It isn't her fault, after all. You can't choose who your soul aches for. It's *my* stupidity that's to blame. For seeing all the signs and not listening to them. For believing I'd be okay with second best if it meant she was mine for even a moment. For falling while she was busy waiting for someone else.

So, I silenced my phone and gave my attention to Blakely. The girl who *does* need me.

Blakely didn't ever answer my question about her panic attacks, but I didn't keep pushing. I can tell by the stiffness in her shoulders and the bite in her words it's a subject she doesn't like to talk about, and while I'd love to help, I'm not her therapist, so I let the subject go.

I don't need her to open up to me, I just need her to know she's not alone.

But I'm intrigued by her now, which is both a problem and a blessing.

A problem because she's done nothing but throw herself at me at every turn, and my body has done nothing but try and convince me to give in.

A blessing because she can be my focus, a distraction

from the thoughts of Sugarlake and everything that comes with it.

She's a solution. A way for me to help someone who needs it, keep my boss happy, and keep my mind occupied until I can heal my heart enough where it doesn't sting with every beat.

But Blakely isn't here right now. And when I get to the silence of the kitchen, I can't stop from grabbing my phone and pressing play on my messages.

"Hey, Teeth." Lee's voice fills the empty space in the room.

I roll my eyes at the nickname as I fill a glass with water, my stomach tightening from the vision it brings up. From the smell of banana bread as it warmed my hands and a blue-eyed, honey-blonde-haired beauty smiling wide on my front porch.

"Are those your real teeth?"

Something sparks in my chest, lighting up my insides like fireworks as I watch her eyes grow big and round, like she didn't mean to say the words but couldn't control her mouth.

"You think I have fake teeth?" I grin.

She shrugs. "I mean… maybe?"

Shaking my head out of the memory, I chug the tepid water, resting my hands on the counter, my head hanging as I listen to the rest of her message.

"I was just callin' to check in. See how things are goin' out there in sunny Cali." She sighs. "I know you said we had to say goodbye. You know, to appreciate the hellos and all. But," her voice breaks. "I was hopin' this could be one of those hellos? I promise I'll appreciate the crap out of it. I mean, dang, Teeth, I don't know if we've ever gone more than a week without talkin'... it feels like a lifetime."

The knot lodged in my throat grows, tears sprouting along my lower lids as I swallow down the burn.

"... and there's so much that's changed around here already. Feels wrong you're not a part of it."

Like usual, my stomach twists, every single pathetic beat of my heart whispering the *what-ifs* through my veins.

What if she needs me?

I could go home on some weekends still… check in on my mom—check in on *her*.

"Anyway, Daddy's in rehab. The whole dang town knows about his drinkin' problem now. I reckon most already did."

My eyebrows draw in. *She thinks everyone knew?* I was by her side for years, and I had no idea. I'm not sure if that's a reflection on how talented Lee is at hiding things or how good I've gotten at choosing to be blind.

"It's been hard, but Chase has been a godsend."

My teeth grit at his name, and the hole that blazes in the center of my ribs flares. *Chase fucking Adams.* My closest friend. My biggest lapse in judgment. The one Lee welcomed back with open arms when he popped up eight years after leaving. After destroying everything he had.

Fuck her for forgiving him so easily. And fuck her for not realizing he hurt me too. That this hurts me too.

Anger swirls in my gut and I press end before hearing the rest of her message. *Chase.* It always comes back to Chase.

I'm missing her, and he never has to.

Not anymore.

THE HEALY HAS BEEN GONE for two days, and I've moved on to a cherry red Ferrari 458, one of my personal favorites. Shame the inside isn't as pretty as the out, but since they're planning to blow this car up, there's no need for the fancy interior. Just the illusion of perfection.

As I work on detailing the badge, a sadness teases at my conscience. This was always my dad's dream, but in these moments I wonder whether he'd want any part of it if he knew what it was really like.

Dad lived for the satisfaction of polishing potential. Unearthing something beautiful. Unique. Something to take pride in. There's no pride in empty cars with pretty faces.

My knees crack as I stand from the front of the Ferrari, and a flash of chocolate brown hair catches my eye through the glass doors. My stomach flips and I'm heading inside before I can stop myself.

Walking to the reception desk, I peer over the counter, a smirk splitting my face as I see Blakely. She's talking on the phone, her hair thrown up in two gigantic buns, and she's sitting on a large blue ball.

She gazes up at me and smiles—a *genuine* smile—the first one I've ever seen her give. My lungs squeeze tight, forcing me to suck in a breath at its beauty. It's slightly crooked, pulling up just a smidge higher on the left, scrunching the corners of her eyes.

My smirk transforms until I'm grinning wide back at her.

It's nice to see her this way. So… light. Fun.

My eyebrow quirks as I watch her, amusement dancing its way through my chest at her antics. She looks ridiculous with those Star Wars buns and a giant exercise ball for a chair.

Her eyes stay locked on me even when she speaks into the phone. "Thank you so much, sir. I'll be sure to let Karen know it needs to be adjusted and have her call you back with the final numbers."

Hanging up, she resumes her vigorous bouncing. "What?" she pants.

Nodding toward the ball, I shrug. "What are you doing?"

She glances down before bringing her gaze back. "Exercising. What's it look like?"

I rub my jaw. "Didn't you work out enough last night?"

Her eyes darken. "It's a new day, Jackson. Calories don't burn themselves."

"Actually, they do."

"Semantics." She waves her hand in the air. "Did you have a purpose for coming in here or are you just hanging around to annoy me?"

I bark out a laugh. The audacity of this girl to think that *I'm* the one annoying *her*. "That's cute, princess." I lean on the reception counter. "So, what are we doing tonight?"

Her head cocks as she stops moving. "What makes you think we're doing anything?"

My hand covers my heart. "You don't want to hang out with me anymore? You've been begging for *weeks,* Blake."

She clicks her tongue. "Guess you didn't live up to my expectations."

I scoff. "I am extremely offended by that statement."

"Facts don't care about your feelings." She smiles.

My eyes narrow. "Did you just quote Ben Shapiro to me?"

She laughs. "He's a quotable guy."

My forehead scrunches. "Is he? Give me another one then."

"Bring a bucket *and* a mop."

I grin. "I'm pretty sure that's Cardi B."

She lifts a shoulder. "Some might say his best quotes are from her."

Shaking my head, I bite back a chuckle. "Sometimes it's so hard to forget how young you are."

"Well, maybe you could use a little youth and vitality in your life." She winks.

She resumes her exercise and my eyes drop, grazing along the top of her cleavage, her breasts jostling from the movement. My stomach clenches, frissons of heat spiraling from my skin, daring me to reach out and touch her. Begging me to just *give in*. It would feel so damn good to feel her bounce on my lap instead of on that ball.

I lean in, my voice raspy from the image. "Just so you know, I wasn't trying."

Her body falters from the steady up and down motion. "Trying at what?"

"To meet your expectations."

She sucks in a breath. "Maybe you should."

I smirk. "Be careful what you ask for."

She stops moving entirely, her breasts grazing the edge of her desk. "I know *exactly* what I'm asking for."

My cock jerks as I stare her down, debating on whether this is a road I want to go down. If I can keep my dick in check long enough to actually try and be her friend.

Sighing, I tap my knuckles on the counter. "Be ready tomorrow at noon."

"For what?"

I lower my voice. "If I told you, then you'd get those pesky *expectations*. Better to keep it a surprise."

Her fingernails click methodically against the top of the desk. "Is this a date?"

My heart stutters. *A date?* "No. Definitely not a date."

She tilts her head. "Well, how am I supposed to know what to wear?"

I shrug. "Wear your pajamas for all I care."

"I sleep naked." She grins.

My gut jolts, and I shift to relieve the pressure of my dick pressing against my zipper. "I don't care what you wear, Blakely. Just be ready at noon."

Walking away, my heart slams against my ribs.

I don't think of Lee for the rest of the day.

13

BLAKELY

It's eleven fifty-eight on Saturday morning and Jackson isn't here.

Is he standing me up?

Not that this is a date anyway. He made that perfectly clear. But that doesn't stop the tension in my stomach, or the anticipation that thrums through my insides when I think about where he might be taking me.

"What do you mean you won't be home?" Sierra hisses over the phone.

Putting her on speaker, I set my cell down beside me. "I mean, I have plans, Sierra. You know, an actual *life* for once."

"Plans with who?"

"With the man that *you* told me to do things with!"

She breathes out slowly. "Okay. Okay. That works. Text me when you end up wherever you're going, so they know where to be."

Groaning, I pinch my nose, trying to stop the headache from pulsing between my eyes.

She's talking about the paparazzi, of course. It's normal to leak our location so we can control the narrative. Ensure the headlines that spread across the internet both have my name in them and are the right kind of headline. And since it's the norm, I really can't be annoyed with her. She's just doing her job, and up until recently, I've been more than happy to go along with it. In fact, it's usually me at the helm, steering us into the murky waters of internet celebrity.

But I just wanted this *one* thing.

One day where I could sneak away and pretend to be normal. Silly me, thinking *normal* is something I could ever be.

And really, Sierra is right. Today is the perfect setup to get some candid shots of me with Jackson. Make sure that my *mystery man* is still at the forefront of everyone's minds. There's nothing people love more than trying to solve a mystery.

"Yeah, sure. I'll let you know." I run a hand through my hair.

"Okay, great. And don't forget we're redoing the shoot we never finished from the other night. Make sure you're back by five so we can get it done."

"You got it." Guilt slams its way through me with every word she says. *God.* What's wrong with me? Have I really let myself become so distracted I've lost sight of what's important? Of all the goals I've been working toward?

"I'll be there. And I'm sorry, okay? I have no clue what's been up with me the past few days."

She exhales heavily. "It's fine."

There's a knock on my bedroom door and Lennox peeks in. "Your ride's here."

Nodding, I give him a thumbs up. "I gotta go, Sierra. I'll text you the details."

Hanging up, I run to grab my black Docs, double-checking my appearance in the mirror. I wasn't sure what to wear, so cozy and casual is what I went with. Now that I know we're staging paps on the scene, I wish I would have put more thought into my attire. Maybe had my glam team put together a look.

Hindsight is twenty-twenty, I guess.

Grabbing my ChapStick and shoving it in my back pocket along with my credit card, I skip down the stairs, smiling big at Lennox who's holding open the front door.

I stop at the entrance, my hair swishing against my back as I turn toward him. "Don't linger too close today, okay?"

His jaw clenches but he nods, pushing me out the door. Stumbling slightly, I shield my eyes from the glare of the sun and peer around the circle drive for Jackson. I find him leaning against the passenger side of a royal blue beauty, the Mustang emblem glinting in the light.

The loose gravel from the driveway crunches under my shoes as I approach and he looks up. "Blake."

"Hiya." I grin. "Nice whip."

His lips twitch. "*Whip?* Who'd you hear that from, your grandpa?"

My eyes widen. "Yeah, just trying to be 'on your level.'"

He grins, tapping the end of my nose and opening my door. "Your chariot awaits, princess."

It's the first time he's called me princess without it sounding like an insult, and the way it rolls off his tongue sends a shot of adrenaline straight to the center of my gut, waking up the butterflies that were lying dormant.

I slide in and breathe out a sigh as I melt into the buttery leather of the tan seats.

The sun dances off the strands of his blond hair as he walks around to the driver's side door, sliding behind the wheel. Reaching up, he grabs Ray-Bans off his visor and winks at me before throwing them on and turning up the radio.

My heart skips.

God, he's hot.

A few minutes into the drive, and I'm still staring at him like an idiot, wondering how I've managed to go such a long time without ever truly admiring his beauty.

He glances my way and turns down the music. "Okay. What is it?"

I shrug, warmth scorching my cheeks at being caught ogling. "Nothing. I just… you don't look twenty-eight, you know?"

He side-eyes me. "You don't look nineteen."

I fidget in my seat, the heat flaming stronger on my face and racing through me until it settles between my legs. Throwing my feet on the dash, I stretch my arms, trying to lighten the mood and ignore the reaction my body is having. "So, where are we going?"

His eyes flash to my feet and I grin, a tingle lighting up my insides. "You okay?"

He smirks. "I'm perfect. Thanks for asking."

"You sure? Seems like you might have something you'd

like to say." I move slightly, pressing the soles of my shoes onto the cherrywood front of the glove compartment, trying to get a reaction.

Everything about this car is pristine. There's no way this doesn't bother him.

"If I had something to say, I'd say it."

We drive over a hill and pull into a parking lot, bright blue letters on what looks like an arena spelling out *AnaMaria RaceTrack*.

My stomach drops, anxiety tightening my throat.

He parks and turns to me, smiling. "You ready?"

My nose scrunches as I glance hesitantly at the building. "I'm not sure."

"You'll be fine, I promise." He laughs as he jumps out of the car, and suddenly I feel bad for playing such a childish game on the way over. For not respecting his car when I know it's probably a prized possession. Especially when he's going out of his way to be so *nice*.

I've been dying for this side of Jackson, and I don't want to ruin the day before it even starts.

He jogs over to my side, opening the door and reaching out his hand. My heart sputters in my chest at the gesture. The only people who have ever opened my door were always paid to do it.

The second my hand grazes his, my stomach flips, warmth sending tingles up my arm. I swallow, trying to ignore the way he's affecting me.

"Sorry about defiling your car," I mutter.

His hand squeezes my fingers and he leans in, his lips teasing the shell of my ear. "If anything, Blake, you improved it."

My heart bangs against my chest, arousal splitting me in half with how quickly it surges through my body. My chest physically arches into his and I bite the inside of my cheek to keep from gasping.

Clearing my throat, I step away. *Not a date, Blakely.*

"What are we doing here?" I ask.

A blinding smile lights up his face. "We're gonna drive."

14

JACKSON

It was a risk bringing her here, and honestly, if it weren't for the fact the racetrack is closed today, or that my only friend in California is one of the directors of operations, we wouldn't have come.

But I called in a favor, and my friend Timmy set everything up. I'm not even sure she'll be into it, but I wanted to offer her something different—an experience that isn't just for the sake of how good it will look on the internet. Wanted to give her something sincere, because there's this sinking feeling in my gut that she doesn't have much authenticity in her life.

And everybody deserves something real.

"Wait, wait, wait! What do you mean we're driving?" she screeches, scrambling after me as I walk into the building. "I don't even drive myself on normal days, you expect me to drive a *race car*?"

I bite back the laugh bubbling in my chest. "Why?" I spin toward her, walking backward. "You don't think you can handle it?"

My voice echoes off the concrete floor, reverberating through the empty hall we're in.

"I don't… I mean, I can't…" she gasps out. The smile slides off my face as I take in the sudden stiffness of her shoulders. My eyes trail her posture, my stomach dropping when I notice how her fists clench and unclench at her sides.

I move toward her, gripping her hands first and then running my palms up her arms until they're cupping the back of her neck.

Her eyes are closed and she's mouthing numbers.

Shit.

"Look at me."

Her eyes snap open, and my heart wavers when I see the panic swirling in their depths.

"You're not driving," I tell her. "Okay?"

She nods, her chest heaving with her short, stuttered breaths, and my fingers tighten around her neck, anchoring her in place, wishing there was more I could do. She reaches her hands up, gripping the front of my shirt in her fists.

"I'm sorry." My thumbs slide across her skin, and when goose bumps sprout under my hands, my stomach flips. "I didn't mean to keep it from you, I just wanted it to be a surprise."

She blinks, breathing out in slow, measured increments. "It's okay," she whispers.

"It's not." I shake my head. "Do you trust me?"

I'm not sure why the question makes my chest pull, or why it suddenly feels like I'm dangling myself at the edge of a cliff, teetering back and forth as I wait for her answer.

"Yes," she grasps my shirt tighter.

The satisfaction of her response sends a flood of tingles through me, and for some reason her trust gives me the confidence to continue trying to bring her back. To keep her from spiraling.

"Listen to me," I continue.

She leans in, making my words stall from the warmth of her breath on my lips. I swallow down the urge to close the gap—see if the temptation wanes once I've tasted her sweetness. The strength it takes to remain focused makes my jaw clench tight. "I promise I won't let anything happen to you."

"Okay," she murmurs.

"Do you need a minute?"

She nods again, her fingers tightening around the fabric of my shirt, pulling me further into her. I move her to the wall, wrapping my arms around her waist as I slide us to the floor.

And that's where we stay.

We sit in the empty hallway, her body trembling beneath my arms, her hands grasping at my chest, and I let her do what she needs to bring herself back.

To calm her thoughts.

After a few minutes, her fists relax, and she smooths the wrinkles in my shirt as she gazes up at me. "I'm sorry."

My hand cups her face. "Don't be sorry. Don't ever be

sorry for being real with me. *I'm* sorry that I brought you here." I tuck a loose strand of hair behind her ear. "We don't have to do this, I just thought it would be fun."

She shakes her head. "No, I want to. I just—sometimes they happen for no reason… if I let my thoughts run away from me. I normally have it under control, but I'm also usually…"

"In a routine?" I guess.

She nods. "Yeah, exactly."

"I get it."

"Do you?" Her brows rise, disbelief painting her features.

I stare at her, debating on how much I want to tell. I'm no stranger to being open with people, but my father is something I've always held close to my chest. I don't talk about him, not to anyone.

Besides, no one's ever really cared to know. Even my friends back home were too busy with their lives to spend much time asking about mine.

"My dad was a Marine. He spent a lot of time overseas, and at first, he would come home with these amazing stories." I pause, smiling. "I missed him so bad my stomach hurt, but I remember feeling *giddy* at the thought of all the stories he'd have when he got back. Adventures he went on, the cultures, the people he met…" My throat tightens. "All the ways he would remind me that he was my hero."

"He sounds like an incredible man," Blakely says.

"He was." I nod. "But after his third deployment, the stories never came."

My hand reaches up, fingers tangling around the metal chain that rests around my neck. "He only brought home nightmares that time. Ones he tried to hide but couldn't.

He'd lash out at me. At my mom, and she…" I blow out a breath. "It broke her heart every time she had to say goodbye, but I think it killed her soul when he came back and she wasn't what he needed. When she didn't know how to help."

I gaze down at Blakely, tears glossing over the amber color of her eyes. One falls down her cheek and my thumb reaches over to wipe it away.

"Mom convinced him to go to therapy, but it was *me* who ended up bringing him back whenever he'd get lost. When the panic would overwhelm him, and he'd be stuck, his brain like quicksand, pulling him into the memories of where he'd been."

"That's so sad." Blakely lays her head on my chest. "What's he do now that you're not home? Is he… is he better?"

My hand comes up and smooths over her hair, the motion calming the wave of sadness that's crashing through my insides, threatening to pull me under. "He passed away on my sixteenth birthday." My eyes close, the words exploding through my throat and singeing the back of my nose.

I brace myself for the empty apology—the one that always follows when someone finds out about his death. But it never comes, and I've never been so grateful for someone's silence.

The torn muscle in my chest rattles against my ribs, reminding me that some pieces of a heart don't ever heal. They just exist, broken and bleeding, reminding you to appreciate what you have when you have it. Because you never know when it will disappear.

We don't make it to the racetrack. I never show her how to drive.

But sitting here, in the middle of an empty hallway, as I spill a story I've never told a soul about the greatest man I've ever known, the frayed stitching that holds my broken heart together starts to mend.

And it's the realest thing I've ever done.

15

BLAKELY

It isn't until we're back in Jackson's car that I pull out my phone and realize I never texted Sierra. Honestly, I didn't think of her once, and even though there's dozens of missed calls and texts, I'm glad for my lack of communication.

It would have felt wrong to take advantage of Jackson after how raw I still feel from his realness. From his unwavering support in the face of my vulnerabilities.

I freaked out. *Again*. It's been a long time since I've had two panic attacks so close together. Years of figuring out routines—of making sure every second is planned—have allowed me at least a modicum of control. It's not because I enjoy being busy. It's because when I'm still, the thoughts creep in, weaving into my nerves, creating a spiral of panic that never lets me go once it's taken root.

But there's something about Jackson that inspires me to slow down. For the first time, I *want* to enjoy the quiet moments. If only my brain would let me. Still, even though today started as a disaster, I'm happy I'm here.

Who knew my vulnerability would inspire the same in him?

I've never been a secret keeper. No one has ever shared the most intimate parts of their soul. I like the way it feels to hold something so valuable in the palm of my hand.

And I *love* the way it feels when Jackson holds me in his.

I don't think about the age difference. Or the fact he's technically only with me because my father asked him to be. That I annoy him on my best day and make him hate me on my worst.

All I think about is how unbelievably safe it feels. How right. How there isn't anything on this earth that would make me want to walk away. And maybe that's why I didn't text Sierra. Because I was enjoying letting someone see *me* and reveling in the feel of them liking what they saw.

Jackson glances at me, one hand on the steering wheel and the other on the gearshift. "You okay?"

"Yeah." Leaning my head against the window, the chill of the glass sends a shock of cold shooting down my spine. "Sierra's just pissed."

Jackson hums. "Why?"

I bite the inside of my cheek so I don't blurt out the truth. That he's supposed to be a prop, and the only thing that matters to her—and usually to me—is how to spin a situation in my favor.

"She's always pissed these days." I sigh.

"What's her job again?"

I look over at him. "She's my manager. She literally runs every part of my day. I don't know what I'd do without her."

He grunts.

I laugh. "What?"

Huffing out a breath, he shakes his head. "I mean… you pay her, right? So, is it really her place to treat you the way she does?"

Defensiveness swirls in my stomach, the need to stand up for Sierra surging through my veins, urging me to lash out. She's been the closest thing I've had to a mom, and I'm not sure what to do with the fact that Jackson is telling me she's taking advantage.

What does that say about me if the only person in my life who gives a damn is only *giving* a damn because I pay them to?

"You don't know what you're talking about," I snap. "Things are different for someone like me."

His head cocks. "Because you choose for them to be or because they just are?"

My eyes widen, irritation brewing in my gut. "You don't have any idea—"

He cuts me off with a laugh. "Calm down, princess, it's just a question."

"A shitty one," I mutter, crossing my arms.

He grins. "So does the wicked witch need you back in your castle, or do I get a few more hours of your time?"

I bite my lip to stop my grin, thankful he's changing the subject. "What'd you have in mind?"

"Let's go back to my place, we can cook some food."

A knot of tension tangles in my stomach at the thought, but I smile and nod. I've already been enough of a hassle today, no need to make it worse. Still, my brain jumps into overdrive, outlining all the ways I can avoid putting whatever he makes into my body. Or how many hours I'll need at the gym to work it off.

"That sounds good." I hesitate. "I'm on a pretty strict diet though."

His forehead creases. "For what?"

Shrugging, I tense my fingers in my lap. "Because I don't like eating trash?"

He smirks, rolling his eyes. "You're right, delicious food is absolute garbage."

I force a giggle to cover up the exasperation that's sneaking its way into the moment. *Of course he doesn't understand.* "I didn't say that. I just… in my line of work, you have to stay in shape. Besides, it's better for me mentally when I'm not desecrating my body with junk. Food is fuel, not enjoyment."

A frown drags down his face. "That's pretty sad, Blake."

"Being healthy is sad?" I lift my hands in a shrug.

"Healthy…" His brow quirks. "Is that what you are?"

Usually, a question like that would send hot rage spewing through me like lava, but instead I'm holding back something else. *The truth.* For a split second, I try to find the words to tell him, but I'm not sure where to look. I don't even know what they *are.* So, I push the feeling back down, letting it find another deep, dark spot to hide, somewhere I can ignore that it exists.

He doesn't really want to know about things like that anyway.

We turn into a neighborhood, surprise flickering through me as he pulls into the drive of a cozy, single-story house with white shutters and a dark wood door.

"This is where you live?" I blurt.

He turns off the ignition and leans into his car door, a slow smile spreading across his face. "Not grand enough for you, princess?"

I shake my head. "No… no I like it."

Walking in the front door, I take in my surroundings, the subtle notes of tan and white furniture offsetting the emptiness of the space. There's a complete lack of personality, like it's a temporary place for him to sleep, not somewhere he could make a home. Fear skirts around inside of me at the reminder that even though he lives here, his home is somewhere else.

With other people.

I didn't expect the thought to bother me so much, but I guess I didn't really expect Jackson, either. Now, there's nothing I want more than for him to stick around so I can soak in his presence.

With him, even when I'm still, the seconds don't feel wasted.

"Okay, princess. I'll give you the tour later. First, you can look for something that's good enough to be your *fuel*." He walks into the kitchen, gesturing to the fridge.

I smile, skipping after him, relief untangling the knot that's been in my stomach since he mentioned food. Walking to the stainless-steel fridge, I open the door and bend down, searching through the shelves. His fridge is surprisingly well-stocked with a variety of choices and it doesn't take me long to find something I can handle.

Grabbing some chicken breasts, romaine lettuce, cherry tomatoes, and an avocado, I stand back up and spin, a grin stretched across my face. But my smile slips when I see that Jackson is frozen in place, leaning against the kitchen counter, his eyes burning through my clothes, singeing my skin as they slowly trail up my body. The green in his gaze is dark. It makes heat flood between my legs, my heart kicking against my chest.

I swallow, taking slow steps toward him, feeling the warmth of his stare as I set the food next to a wood cutting board.

"Any of this will work, so you can choose," I mumble.

"Can I?" His voice is low and it sends pinpricks of pleasure trickling down my spine. My fingers grip the edge of the counter and I breathe in deep.

One. Two. Three.

"Yeah." I spin toward him. "Anything in front of you, you can have."

His Adam's apple bobs and it makes my clit throb, a deep ache settling in my womb.

"Anything?" he rasps, taking a step closer.

I nod, my stomach flipping and free-falling with anticipation, my heart pounding against my ribs.

His cell vibrates on the counter next to me and I look down, the word *Sweetheart* dancing across the screen. Reality drops into my gut like a rock.

God, I'm such an idiot.

He glances to his phone, the muscle along the bottom of his jaw tightening as he reaches out to silence it. By the time his eyes come back to mine, the moment is lost. He sighs, running a hand through his hair and walking to the cutting board, starting to prep the chicken.

"Don't wanna get that?" I nod toward his phone.

He shakes his head. "It'd be rude to answer while I'm with you."

"I don't mind."

I *do* mind, but the need to know who "sweetheart" is

and why he doesn't want to speak to her when I'm around is strangling me and I think I mind that more.

"Who's sweetheart?" The question rolls off my tongue without my permission, my throat tightening.

His nostrils flare. "A friend from back home."

"Must be a good one," I quip.

"The best." He nods.

My fists clench at my sides, but it doesn't stop me from asking questions I have no business knowing the answers to. "Is she *just* a friend?"

"She's..." He groans, looking up at the ceiling. "Yeah... she's only ever been a friend." His voice hitches and I peek at him from my peripheral. My chest squeezes tight when I see the grief etching itself on his face, and even though jealousy sears my insides, the look in his eyes has me biting my tongue, because I realize that it doesn't matter who she is. Or that she always manages to steal his attention even when she's thousands of miles away.

All that matters is his pain. And all I want to do in this moment is dive inside of his chest and grasp his heart in my hands, so she can't hurt it anymore.

So I can keep it safe.

16

JACKSON

"I've never seen it."

My jaw drops open. "I'm sorry, *what*?"

Blakely shrugs, popping the last piece of avocado in her mouth then sucking the leftover mess off her fingers. My cock twitches, confusion and desire twirling together and weaving around the edges of my heart, making me wonder how in the *hell* I'm suddenly finding everything this girl does enticing.

Shifting in my chair, I put my napkin on the table. "I think I'm misunderstanding you, princess, because I could swear you just told me you've never seen Die Hard, and that is completely unacceptable."

She smiles while she chews, her amber eyes lighting up as she watches me from across the table. "Only if someone's looking for your acceptance."

"And why wouldn't you be looking for my acceptance, Blake?" I tease. "Still not living up to expectations?"

"You said it, not me." She lifts a shoulder, stifling her grin.

Puffing out my cheeks with a deep exhale, I push my plate away, watching as she picks up her phone, her fingers moving furiously over the keyboard. The smile that lit up her face slowly drains away, a heaviness drawing her features down, making me want to lift away the load.

Smacking my hands on my legs, I stand, walking until I tower over her small frame. Her face lifts from her screen, brows coming together. "What are you—"

She screams as I dive toward her, my arms reaching around her waist, yanking her up and throwing her over my shoulder.

"Jackson!" she shrieks, laughing as her small fists pummel against my back.

A ball of excitement expands in my sternum, my grip tightening around her legs as I carry her through the open archway and into the living room. I throw her on the couch, her body bouncing on top of the oversized throw pillows.

"You. Stay." I point at her as I walk to my small collection of DVDs.

Her giggle turns into a full belly laugh and once I grab the movie I twist to look at her, narrowing my eyes. "What?"

She blows out shaky breaths, her hands holding her stomach as she tries to speak. "Just... just... remembering how... *old* you are." Her laughter finally wanes and she leans back against the pillows, sighing, a satisfied grin on her face. "Who has *DVD*s anymore? It's probably on Netflix."

"I don't even have Netflix."

Her eyes widen as she shakes her head, but there's a soft smile playing on her face as she watches me, her eyes sparkling. "You're so different than anyone in my life."

I start the movie and head over to the couch, sitting down next to her and picking up her legs to settle on top of my lap. "Well thank God you have me in it." I wink.

She grins, her toes digging into my thigh. "You're not wrong there."

A warm feeling rushes through my veins, fusing my broken pieces back together as we sit on my couch watching my favorite movie and just *being.*

No expectations. Nothing left unsaid in the space between us.

It's nice—the most content I've been in ages—and maybe that's why when she falls asleep thirty minutes later, her legs curled around mine, I make sure to stay quiet so she doesn't wake up. So she stays.

My phone vibrates on the end table, my mom's number flashing on the screen, and I move to the kitchen before I answer. Far enough away to not wake Blakely, but close enough where she's still in my line of sight, because for some reason the thought of leaving her alone makes my chest ache.

"Hey, Mom. How's life?" I ask in a low voice.

She chuckles down the line. "My life is the same as always, honey. How are *you* doing? How's California? Still loving your job?"

Homesickness churns in my gut. I miss being close to her, being able to see her at the end of every day, so I can make sure she's okay. Not that she's ever needed someone to lean on. Samantha Rhoades is the definition of independent. Stubborn in her ways and strong in her beliefs, which is why she won't let me take care of her even though now I can afford it.

She says she likes to stay busy, but I think she just doesn't know how to be alone with her thoughts.

"I talked about Dad today," I spout.

"Oh?" Her voice quivers.

She doesn't like to bring him up. But she goes to therapy and she buries herself in her work and that's all that I can really ask of her at the end of the day. She deals with her traumas the best way she knows how, the same as the rest of us. But still, it hurts when I try to speak about him and feel as though I can't. When I worry that she's going to shut down and the conversation will be ruined.

"Yeah... It felt good to have someone who wanted to hear about him, you know?" I pause, running my hand through my tangled hair. "I'm not used to that."

She hums but doesn't respond.

My heart sinks, disappointment pressing on my chest. "Anyway, it doesn't matter. When are you coming out to Cali?" My eyes flick to the living room, an eager type of energy zapping at my nerves and spreading through me when I think about my mom meeting Blakely.

And then shock punches me in the gut, my breath whooshing out of me at how natural it felt to think that. How clear the image was of the two of them together.

Why would she meet her?

She laughs. "Oh, Jax, honey, you know how I feel about planes. I'll just see you when you come back home to visit."

"Well, Mom," I huff, irritation burning between my ribs. "I don't know when that's gonna happen."

My fingers wrap around my necklace, the metal balls of

the chain indenting into my skin and grounding me. Honestly, the entire reason for moving here was for the space it would grant me. So I could gain some perspective.

And even though it's only been a few weeks, I already sense the shift of my thoughts and I'd be lying if I said a huge reason for that isn't Blakely. How these… *feelings* have suddenly sprouted inside of me, I have no idea. I've been convinced my heart was too bruised to feel. All I know is that when I'm around Blakely—when it's just the two of us—she's so much more than what I was expecting.

And that makes me want to stick around.

17

BLAKELY

My arms reach above my head and I relish in the delicious pull of my muscles being stretched. I feel surprisingly well rested and as I rub the sleep from my eyes the room comes into focus and I realize exactly where I am.

It's not where I'm supposed to be.

Springing up from Jackson's couch, I grab my phone, my stomach sinking when I see it's eight p.m.

Shit.

Scrolling past the twenty missed calls and dozens of text messages from Sierra, my mind races, guilt over falling asleep and missing the shoot *again* raging through me.

Nausea curdles my stomach when I think about how

often I've dropped the ball in the past week. But behind the rolling of my gut there's an urge to just turn off my phone and stay where I am, because I know I'll be expected to give up this newfound freedom. I won't be able to sink into the calm that Jackson provides, experiencing things with a safety net, knowing someone will be there to help me when I break.

But it's been nice, being able to relax and just... pretend to be normal. Even for a little bit.

Looking around, I search for Jackson, but the room is quiet. With a deep breath, I call Sierra. She picks up on the second ring.

"Where the *hell* have you been?"

My stomach cramps at her tone and I know this conversation is about to be a shot of reality, burning me on the way down.

Sighing, I run my hand through my hair. "Look, Cee, I'm sorry. I didn't realize what time it was and I..."

"You w*hat*?"

Folding in on myself, my forehead rests on my knees as I close my eyes. "I fell asleep."

The line is silent for long, stretched moments, my chest pulling tighter with each one.

Sierra heaves a deep breath over the line. "Look, I'm not your mother, okay? I didn't sign up to be a babysitter when I took this job, yet that's what I'm here doing."

Irritation snaps at my spine, making me stiffen from her words. "No one asked you to babysit, Sierra. I know I've been off my game the past few days, but god." I huff, throwing my body back into the couch. "I haven't had a day off in years. My entire life has been focused on work, and now with my dad's sudden need for me to be involved in his company, it's like... I don't have any time to breathe."

"B, if you want a day off you need to tell me so we can arrange it. The fact is you have responsibilities that *you* signed up for. No one is forcing you into this."

Jackson's words from earlier whisper in the back of my head, feeding my growing ire at being lectured. "Exactly," I snap. "You work for *me*. Sometimes, I think you forget that."

She scoffs. "Look. If you don't want to do this anymore... if your goals have somehow shifted in the past few weeks and you're tired of being *'Blakely Donahue'*, then let me know. You say the word and we'll stop. I'll go work for someone else and you can slink into the shadows of your father, letting people forget that you ever wanted to make a name for yourself."

My stomach jumps into my throat, my heart seizing. Every word she says cuts my sternum like barbed wire, wrapping itself around me, the sharp edges pressing until I bleed. "No, I want this. *Of course,* I still want it."

"Then act like it, Blakely."

"It was just a few days, Cee. You sound like the world is ending," I mutter, my attention being drawn away by movement from the kitchen.

"And you should know better than anybody that a few days out of the spotlight is a few days too many."

My veins heat with realization, the shame flooding through me. She's right. I've been throwing away years of hard work, and for what? A few normal moments?

Weak, Blakely.

"Yeah... I know."

"Do you?" she continues. "Let's recap, just so you understand the gravity of the situation. You have wasted *thousands* of dollars over the past week. You've had people come in, ready to work, and you weren't here for the follow-through, wasting everyone's time. You've had branded posts which were scheduled to be up that haven't even been shot. Your tantrums and your straight-up irresponsibility have made you unreliable and that's not something that goes unnoticed. People talk and there's only so much PR we can do to save you once the rumors start."

Her words press heavy on my chest, sinking into my muscles and irritating the nerves, making them dance under my skin, ready to burst through at any second.

How could I have been so stupid?

What the hell have I been thinking?

I've let myself get lost in fantasies of a girl I don't even want to be. A girl who may have existed once upon a time but is now nothing more than a memory. A girl I've worked tirelessly for years to bury.

My free hand curls into a fist, my lungs being crushed by the weight of my self-loathing.

Idiot.

Pitiful.

Worthless.

One. Two. Three. Deep breath in.

"Listen, B. Tomorrow we're focusing on this new platform that wants you to help create buzz. They have a contract for you to look over, see if it's something you're interested in."

I reach to the side of the couch, grabbing my shoes so I can get ready to leave, trying to pay attention to Sierra's voice to keep me centered.

"It is *imperative* that you're on time for this, okay? I'll be at your place by eight. Please, please be ready to go. Work on whatever shit you need to tonight and get your head back in the game."

I nod even though she can't see, afraid to try and speak

around the knot in my throat. Sharp pains prick my chest with every inhale.

One. Two. Three.

"*Hello?* Are you listening?

"Ye—yeah." I clear my throat. "I'll be there, Cee."

My voice is small, the weight of our conversation settling on my shoulders, reminding me of everything I've somehow lost sight of.

The harsh truth is that I've been letting myself down, slackening the grip I had on my life, thinking that letting go was relief, when really it was my downfall. My stomach heaves, nausea stealing what's left of my breath when I think of all the ways I've let things slip from my control.

How absolutely pathetic I've been.

So what if I've had a few *moments.* A few precious instances where I was able to break the routine—able to be spontaneous and not feel like the world was crashing down on top of me. So what if I found someone who looks at me without the plastered-on smile, without the illusion of perfection, and still wants me to stick around.

All of that is temporary. None of it will fix my problems. Eventually, they'll float back to the surface and I'll be left wallowing in the constant reminder of everything I've lost, all of the time I wasted just to end up living in my flaws.

Somehow, in the past few days, Jackson went from being a tool—a step on the ladder to my success—into a man who dug his way under my skin, settling in the center of my universe and making me feel things that he'll never feel back.

Things we couldn't act on even if he did.

Jackson Rhoades is bad news for me and I've just been reminded of all the reasons why.

18

JACKSON

Slicing the last of the cheese, I set it on a plate with an assortment of crackers, trying not to eavesdrop on Blakely murmuring from the living room. I wasn't sure what to do once she woke up, I only knew that I didn't want her to leave. So, I'm working with what I've got.

It's not until I've opened the bottle of wine and poured us both a glass that I remember she's technically not even supposed to have alcohol. Hesitating, something pinches in my chest when I'm once again reminded of our age difference. Not being legally allowed to drink is such a distant memory for me, I can barely remember what it felt like. She still has two more years until she's twenty-one.

Jesus, what the hell am I doing?

Honestly, I'm not sure that being friends with someone this young is appropriate, which is one of the many reasons I've tried to keep her at arm's length for as long as I have. But today, something shifted and I'm finding it increasingly more difficult to give a damn.

Shaking off my reservations, I finish pouring the wine, reminding myself that age is just a number and if there's someone I connect with—even if it's a nineteen-year-old—I shouldn't take that for granted.

Plus, it's been nice getting to know the real Blakely. The one I wasn't sure existed until today.

Blowing out a deep breath, I pick up the glasses of merlot and walk into the living room, my heart stuttering along with my feet when I see her pocket her phone and stand, her gaze already trained on the front door.

"Hey." I swallow, feeling awkward as hell, standing here like I expected her to stay when it's obvious she's ready to leave.

She glances at me, her eyes flicking to the wine, then back to the door. "Hey, sorry I fell asleep. Sierra's about to kill me if I don't get home."

"What's she gonna do, ground you?" I raise a brow.

Blakely laughs, but irritation at *Sierra* takes over every bone in my body. There's just something about her that seems off. Something that makes me want to stand by Blakely's side and make sure she's not being taken advantage of. And I sure as hell don't like the way she brushed off Blakely's panic attack like it was an inconvenience.

"I thought you could maybe stick around a bit. Have some wine." I lift the glasses, smiling. "I made a cheese board."

Blakely glances at me again, her lips twitching. "A *cheese* board?" Her eyes fall back to the merlot in my hands but she shakes her head, glancing away. "I really should get back."

Sighing, I ignore the disappointment that's sinking like a rock in my gut and walk next to her, placing the glasses down on the coffee table. "Okay, let me put everything away and I'll take you."

I spin to head to the kitchen, but her hand reaches out, gripping my forearm. Electricity zigzags along my skin from her touch.

"No, really, that's okay. You've done more than enough, Jackson. Lennox can take me home, I'm sure he's just sitting outside." She grimaces.

Of course. How could I forget that our worlds are stratospheres apart? She always has security to drive her around. To protect her. She doesn't need me. The Blakely I experienced today is one that rarely comes to the surface, too busy being smothered behind the cameras and the socialite persona.

Not willing to part with the girl that I've had all day, I blow out a breath and try again. "I don't mind, princess."

"But I do," she whispers.

My stomach churns, wondering what happened from the time she woke up to now—what was said that stole away the girl who's been my catharsis and brought back the Blakely everyone else gets to see.

Turning my body until I'm facing her, my finger dips under her chin, pulling her eyes up to mine. "Can I have Blake back?" I ask.

Her brows furrow. "What?"

"*This*" —my free hand gestures toward her body— "isn't the girl I've been with all day. This is the Blakely the rest of the world gets. I don't have any interest in her."

She flinches, trying to pull away, but my hands reach out and cup her jaw, gripping tight enough to make her stay. "I want the real you, Blake. Let me have her."

I realize after the words leave my lips how they sounded, but instead of taking them back—the way I know that I should, I let them linger in the space between us, my stomach clenching and releasing while I wait for her to react.

Her eyes gloss over, her teeth clamping down on that pouty bottom lip, forcing my gaze to follow the movement. There's a heaviness spinning around us, winding the strings of our energies tight, and if *something* doesn't happen, I think I might break in two.

I'm tired of breaking.

So I decide not to.

Her eyes flare a millisecond before my lips meet hers, our mouths colliding like lightning clashing in the waves of stormy waters.

Damn, she tastes good.

Groaning, my hands move from her jaw, sliding down her arms and cradling her waist, dragging her body into mine until every inch is pressed together. She gasps, allowing me to dip my tongue between her lips. My cock lengthens, throbbing from the taste of her in my mouth and the feel of her perfect body in my hands.

Her palms slide up my chest, leaving sparks in their wake, her fingers tangling into the strands of my hair. She lifts her leg, wrapping it around me, my hips falling effortlessly between her thighs. My hands fumble down to her ass and grab firmly, capturing her moan with my tongue, the headiness of her breath making my dick pulse against the fabric of my boxers.

Suddenly she breaks away, stumbling back and covering her mouth with her hand, eyes wide and frantic.

Shit.

I step into her, grasping her hands, wordlessly pleading for her to stay with me in this moment. Leaning down, I lightly peck her lips, enjoying the hint of berry from her ChapStick.

"Stay," I whisper the words against her mouth.

She blows out a steady breath, her hands trembling as she links our fingers. "Okay."

A torrent of relief rushes through me, knowing that she feels it too.

Whatever *it* is.

I couldn't put a name to it if I tried. All I know is that it's strong, crashing through me like a hurricane, obliterating everything I thought I knew.

Everything I thought I had felt before.

Her fingers squeeze mine as she drops her head to my chest, rolling her forehead back and forth. "Jackson," she rasps. "What are we gonna do?"

My heart falters, afraid she's going to tell me we have to stop. That it's not worth it.

That *I'm* not worth it.

"Let's worry about that later." I push her hair behind her ear.

"I need us to..." She pauses, chewing through the skin of her lip. Withdrawing my hand from hers, my thumb reaches up and tugs, the pad of my finger smoothing over the rough edges where she's bitten through.

She smiles, her eyes softening as she kisses the tip of my thumb, her hands wrapping around my wrist. "I need to go slow if we do this."

Her cheeks bloom the most beautiful shade of pink.

"We don't have to do anything you don't want to do, Blake. I just want to spend time with you." Not able to help myself, I lean down again, pressing my mouth to hers, a thousand fireflies lighting up my chest.

I have no clue what I'm doing. There's no reasoning to my actions. No thought of what tomorrow will bring, or how we'll handle what's inevitably going to come if we decide to be together. Her father. The public.

My heart skips at the thought, my stomach jumping into my throat as I realize that's what I want.

I want to be with her.

I want to try.

Now, I just have to hope she wants that, too.

19

BLAKELY

My lips are still tingling with the memory of Jackson's kiss. Closing the front door, I lean against it, the wood cool against my overheated skin. My fingertips trace along the tops of my chapped mouth, stomach flipping as I replay the feel of his tongue tangling with mine.

What in the world just happened?

My heart flutters as I think about how everything just shifted and how surprisingly, even though it was completely unexpected, I'm okay with it. Now that I've had a taste of him, I don't know if I can let him go. A grin spreads across my face, butterflies bursting from my stomach as I squeal, spinning off the door and skipping to the stairs.

"We don't have to do anything you don't want to do."

He's so much more than I ever expected. Not that I have a lot of experience to pull from. My life has been far too busy—too career focused—to have time for a boyfriend. So even though my body was screaming at me to climb him like a tree—let him devour me whole, my nerves wouldn't let me, terrified of being a disappointment.

Even thinking the word sends my brain into overdrive, making the anxiety that lies dormant perk up and come alive inside me.

I never thought he'd want me. Never realized that maybe all the joking and the forward advances were harder to resist than he showed. Now that I know there's a chance, I can't help but wonder how we're supposed to navigate everything. Our lives are polar opposites, both of us having a million different reasons for why we shouldn't be together. Why we shouldn't explore these feelings that have come out of nowhere and slapped me upside the head.

My dad would kill him.

Sierra would kill me.

But he also makes me happy. Safe. Grounded. And I don't have much of that in my life, so I'll do everything in my power to keep him—even if it has to be in secret.

The uncertainty of our situation bears down on me, the adrenaline from earlier wearing off, allowing the reality of the unknown to fill me up, overflowing with 'what-ifs.'

My stomach turns, the wine from earlier teasing the back of my throat, reminding me I indulged when I shouldn't have.

Why did I do that? And why didn't I add it in my tracker?

Pausing on the stairs, I pull up my calorie tracker, inputting the glass of merlot and trying to remember if Jackson said what type of cheese we were eating. Racking my brain for minutes and coming up blank, I Google "cheese", my fingers pressing against the screen firmly while I scroll, searching for something familiar. But there are so many options and my memory is muddled from the wine. Unease chomps away at my gut, splitting a pit open inside of me, burning with the need to figure it out so I can know my final nutrition stats for the day.

One. Two. Three. Deep breath out.

I jog up the stairs, passing by the eternal beauty of my mother's face and changing into my workout gear.

It's okay. It's just a few pieces of cheese. I say the words like a mantra, trying to keep the focus on my breath, instead of the loathing that's scratching under the surface of my skin.

With every set of weights, I repeat the phrase—*It's just a few pieces of cheese*—pleading with my body to find satisfaction in the sweat, hoping the hours I'll spend here tonight will be enough to stop the clawing of the unknown numbers that are tearing up my mind.

I shouldn't have had the cheese.

Stupid, Blakely.

"They're willing to pay you two hundred and fifty thousand for the first month," my lawyer, Andrew, says through the speakerphone. I scrunch my nose, leaning over to look at the contract while Sierra sits next to me crunching on a piece of celery with peanut butter.

"And I'm expected to post every day?" I look to Sierra.

She nods. "Every day with cross posts on your other social media. It's a video platform, so they'll be ten to sixty second videos."

"What kind of videos? Do we even have time to make them?"

Sierra shrugs. "I think if we block out a day to film content for the week, we can make it happen." She pauses, setting down her half-eaten celery stick. "I *do* think you'll be leaving less time for your other commitments which could affect your bottom line. Two hundred and fifty K looks pretty on paper, but it isn't really enough to make up the difference."

"Hmm..." I lean back, crossing my arms as I think about what she's saying. She's not wrong. If we're blocking out an entire day, that's twenty-four hours we lose. I could do multiple branded shoots in that time. "Andrew, does it say anything about exclusivity?"

"There's a non-compete agreement in place for six months after the contract ends."

I laugh. "Well, that's not gonna happen. How long does the contract last?"

"This one is for three months with the option for renegotiation or extension at the end of the terms."

Raising my arms above my head as I sigh, my muscles stretch, a satisfying pain radiating down the tissue and making me bite back a groan. After last night's marathon workout, I'm so sore it hurts to breathe. It makes satisfaction drip through me with every motion.

That combined with doing my favorite part of this job—negotiating contracts and running a meeting where I call all the shots—has me feeling more like myself than I have in weeks. A skewed puzzle piece slotting back in place.

"How many appearances do we have lined up this next month?" I ask, grabbing a piece of celery for myself, my eyes taking inventory of what's left on the plate.

Three pieces left. That's six total with a tbsp of peanut butter, which is ninety-four calories and three point five grams of protein.

Gratification sinks into my bones as I mentally calculate, relieved to be at home where I can eat things I know the stats of by heart. Where I won't have to waste my energy worrying over what will be offered or how I'll explain away not eating like everyone else.

Having to constantly explain my lifestyle gives me a headache.

Sierra pulls up my calendar. "You have six club appearances and an opening at a new restaurant downtown this afternoon."

I groan, rolling my eyes. "Do I have to do that?"

Sierra smirks. "Yes."

Making a gagging motion, I flip the page of the contract, debating whether or not I want to accept the terms or renegotiate. Rubbing the bridge of my nose, I list out the pros and cons in my mind, crossing them off mentally and allowing the contentment of coming to a decision flow through me.

I push the papers away, leaning over my phone. "Andrew, tell them for that price, I'll post three times a week for one month. Or they can do a three-month contract for five hundred with daily posting. Either way, I'll only sign a noncompete for the duration of the contract. If I'm no longer with them, I want the freedom to go somewhere else."

Chewing my lip, I run over everything I just said. "Oh, and make sure I'm able to terminate the contract easily if needed."

"Got it. I'll write it up and send it over."

A grin breaks across my face, pleasure trickling through

my insides at the feeling of success. Of running my business and knowing I'm doing it well.

I end the call, noticing a text message blinking on my phone.

Jackson: Free tonight, princess?

Nerves erupt in my stomach, sending blood rushing to my cheeks. I school my features as quickly as possible, glancing at Sierra and hoping she didn't notice the way my face lit up.

She watches me with a brow raised as she munches on her food.

Clearing my throat, I place my phone in my pocket, picking up my uneaten celery stick and pointing it in the air as I angle it toward her. "Cheers." I smile wide, my stomach tightening at her inquisitive stare.

The last thing I want is to have to explain things, especially when I'm not even sure what's going on myself.

"What?" I ask, taking a huge bite to try and stem the nerves.

"Nothing." She shakes her head. "It's nice to see you back on your game." She smacks her hands on her legs and hops from the island barstool. "Kayla's meeting us in two hours at the restaurant. You have glam in twenty minutes. Wear the joggers from the Jacob Lancaster campaign, please, so we can get some good street shots."

The contentment from earlier starts to wither away, the strings of my manager tugging from where they're wrapped around my limbs.

I nod and wait for Sierra to leave the room before I slip my phone out of my pocket, glancing at the hallway door to make sure she's out of sight. My heart pounds against my ribs as I click on Jackson's name and reread his earlier message.

Sadness drops in my chest, realizing my schedule won't allow me to sneak away. That I'll have to wait until tomorrow at Donahue Motors to see him again.

Me: My schedule is pretty booked today. See you tomorrow?

My teeth drop into my lower lip, working back and forth as I watch the text bubble pop up on the screen.

Jackson: If you're lucky. ;)

Smiling, a warmth seeps from my heart, pulsing through my chest, sending sparks of anticipation zapping through me.

I don't know what tomorrow will bring. Not sure what he'll say or how I'll react.

But for the first time, in as long as I can remember, I think I'm excited for the unknown.

20

JACKSON

I didn't sleep well. Tossed and turned all night, my stomach in my throat from thoughts of seeing Blakely this morning, wondering if she's been thinking of me the way I've been thinking of her.

I showed up to work earlier than usual, needing to get lost in a transmission to keep my mind off all the uncertainties floating through my head. It doesn't work as well as I'd hoped, my eyes straying to the street every few seconds, waiting to see her Maybach pull up to the curb. The second it rounds the corner, my heart accelerates, beating so fast I feel it in my ears. Her long, toned legs slide from the back seat, desire simmering low in my gut as she walks inside.

The wrench slips from my oil-stained hands and I scramble to grab it, clearing my throat and focusing back on the Stingray's transmission, wondering how the hell it's possible to miss someone who you've only just realized you wanted to see.

Last night, I planned to take her to the beach. Pack a picnic and spend some time together to explore whatever this is.

Dip our toes in the water. *Take things slow*, the way she asked for us to.

Not that I wouldn't dive in if I thought that's what she wanted. Once I make a decision, I'm invested, and over the past twenty-four hours I've had a lot of time to think, my brain going back and forth over pursuing something with her.

Whether we should keep it a secret. *Probably.* Whether it would even be worth it. *Definitely.*

I'm not an idiot, I know going public wouldn't look good. A nine-year age difference with a girl not even in her twenties is sure to push us in the limelight for all the wrong reasons. People love to jump into other peoples' business and this has drama and judgment written all over it.

She's always been stunning, her beauty paired with her advances forcing me to will away the filthy thoughts she'd plant in my mind. But this feeling is deeper than the surface and it came out of nowhere. Hit me in a way I didn't know was possible, leaving me dizzy with lust.

Part of me wonders if it's real, or if it's the vulnerability we've shared that's giving me a false sense of familiarity. A bond that isn't really there.

It's possible, I guess, to have manufactured feelings based on an encounter. But what is life if not the sum of all our experiences?

Regardless, there's this sudden *need* to know her pooling in the center of my chest, threatening to rise up and drown me alive. I woke up Sunday morning with visions of her in my head, the memory of her voice in my ears and the whisper of her taste on my tongue, my body buzzing with happiness.

And that's a welcome change of pace.

It's another hour before I find an excuse to go inside and see her. Stripping off my rubber gloves and washing the oil from my arms, I head through the glass doors, my heart sinking when I realize she's not at the front desk.

Walking to the corner, I make myself a cup of the watered-down, complimentary coffee we keep for the few clients that come through. The caffeine in the break room is better, but I can't bring myself to leave this area, wanting to take in Blakely's reaction when she first sees me, so I can get a feel for what's going through her head.

The flat-screen TV drones above me about some Senator from Oregon and I lean against the counter as I watch, desperate to find a reason to stay inside until Blakely reappears.

"Senator Wells officially announced his second bid for the presidency. This comes after years of speculation as to whether he would run again after the devastating loss of his son, Alexander."

A picture floats on the middle of the screen. A young, polished man donning a black tuxedo smiles wide into the camera, his arm wrapped around a stunning blonde in a floor-length gown. His frame towers over her, but for some reason, it's not his size that captures my attention—it's the look on his face that strikes a chord. The plastered-on grin so similar to the one Blakely wears when she's trying to fool the world.

"Alexander Wells went missing ten years ago, on the eve of his

engagement to the oil heiress, Olivia Sanderson. He has never been found."

"Fan of politics?"

My stomach jumps as I spin, noticing Blakely in front of the reception desk, her arms crossed over her chest.

I shrug, grinning. "I'm always a fan of knowing what's going on in the world."

She nods, her eyes perusing the length of my body. "Yep. I see that for you."

My brows rise as I set down my coffee and walk toward her. "Do you?"

She waves her hand in my direction. "You have that whole 'worldly' vibe going on."

I smirk. "Do I?"

The prettiest shade of pink dusts across her cheeks as I stop in front of her, my fingers reaching out and trailing down her arm, the urge to touch her too strong to resist.

"Ye-yeah," she stutters, the grin slipping from her face. Tension sneaks its way through the air, pulling tighter with every touch of my hand.

"And what do I look like now?" I rasp.

She swallows, and the motion makes my stomach clench, my cock lengthening as I wonder what her throat would feel like massaging my shaft.

Take it slow.

"Like you want to eat me whole," she says.

Pushing a strand of hair behind her shoulder, my lips brush against the shell of her ear. "Accurate."

She drops her head, glancing at me from under her lashes. "Can I tell you a secret?"

My teeth grind as I stop myself from wrapping my palm around her waist and dragging her into me. "You can tell me anything, princess."

She rises up on her toes, leaning close. "No one's ever done that to me before," she whispers.

Her breath sends shockwaves down my spine, her confession sending arousal rushing through me like river rapids—the idea of being the first man to taste her making my knees weak and my mouth water.

The phone rings, making us jump apart, and she shakes her head, giving me a small smile before she saunters to her desk and answers.

I follow, reaching over the high counter, grabbing a notepad and pen from the desktop. Her eyes follow my every move as I write, curiosity shining through her gaze.

Holding up the paper, I wait.

Will you go out with me tonight?

The most beautiful smile blooms on her face, scrunching her nose and puffing her cheeks. It's so damn *real,* and my heart slams against my chest cavity, wanting to find a hundred different ways to make sure it stays.

She twirls the phone cord around her finger and nods, her free hand coming up to stifle her grin.

I cover my heart with my palm as I walk backward before spinning around to leave. I'm sky high, floating in the clouds of my crush, and maybe that's why I don't notice Karen watching us from the hallway until I'm almost at the doors.

My stomach shoots to my throat as our eyes meet, her brows furrowed and her mouth partially open. I paste on a smile and wink, tipping an imaginary hat, hoping that she hasn't been there long. That she hasn't seen just how gone I am for the boss's daughter.

But as I walk back into the garage, there's a sinking feeling in my gut that knows she saw it all.

21

BLAKELY

I'm nervous.

My stomach is tied up in knots for a thousand different reasons, one of them staring me in the face as I try to explain to Kayla why I can't go out tonight.

Anxiety pulses through me when I see it's six-thirty, which means there's only an hour and a half until Jackson picks me up. I need to start getting ready, but when Kayla called on my way home from Donahue Motors, I let it slip that I was getting in an evening workout and she sped over, wanting to "try and emulate my dedication."

"Girl, come on, you're practically a stranger these days," she groans, upping the speed on her elliptical.

I laugh. "I saw you yesterday for lunch."

"Yeah, but that was a paid gig. It doesn't count." Her nose scrunches.

My brow rises, confusion settling in the pit of my gut. "Why doesn't it count?"

She huffs, her breaths coming in short pants as her legs swing back and forth on the machine. "It does, I guess, it's just a little annoying is all. Everything is about *you* when we're out for something like that. The cameras, the attention..."

She trails off and I roll my eyes, ignoring the way my chest pinches from her statement. I should be used to it by now. This isn't anything new coming from her. She's full of passive-aggressive comments that make me feel like shit for being good at what I do.

I love Kayla, but sometimes I have to dim my own success to make sure she shines, and it puts me in an awkward position. On one hand, she's my best friend and I want her to have the world. On the other hand, it's not my fault she doesn't put in the work—that she thinks her family name is enough to get by. She wants the fame, wants the recognition of being known *just* for being known, without realizing there is no such thing. There's only the perception.

She believes the lie instead of being the one who tells it, and you can't master the game if you're a pawn on the board. Instead, she chooses to ride on my coattails, letting my celebrity prop her up to bask in the spotlight. The one that hides *my* blood, sweat, and tears in its shadow.

And because she's my only friend, I let her.

Sighing, I up the incline on the treadmill, relishing in the burn that eats through my leg muscles like acid. "Look, I can't tonight. I'm just... tired. Working at Dad's company really steals any free time and this is my only night to *chill*."

"Maybe you should tell your dad you're not willing to be his bitch anymore," she snaps.

Sadness weaves its way through the holes in my heart at the thought of not being at Donahue Motors anymore.

At not seeing Jackson.

She's not wrong though, allowing my dad to feel like he has control over my life puts a damper on my productivity, making it a thousand times harder to grow in my career.

The one he doesn't believe exists.

I could easily move out, I'm a self-made millionaire from branded posts alone, but the thought of being on my own sends a shot of fear rippling down my spine.

My dad and I are ships passing in the night, but at least if I'm home, he'll acknowledge that I'm there. That I'm his.

At least if I'm home, he won't forget I exist altogether.

"Hello? Earth to Blakely."

Jerking out of my daze, I realize that Kayla is off her elliptical, standing in front of my treadmill and snapping her fingers in my face.

How long was I lost in my head?

Glancing at the calorie counter on my watch, I slow my speed. "Sorry, I didn't mean to zone out."

She laughs, shaking her head, her eyes wide with disbelief. "I wish I could zone out like that, maybe then I wouldn't despise every second I spend on that dreadful thing." She glares at the elliptical. "Is that your secret?" She looks back to me, putting a hand on her hip.

"What secret?"

"You know... how you work out so much. I don't remember the last day you took off." She pauses, her eyes scanning me from top to bottom. "Even bodybuilders take a rest day."

"Oh." I bite my lip, my stomach rolling as I slow to a

stop and hop off the treadmill. "I don't know." I shrug. "I just like being healthy, it's important to me."

Kayla's usually the one person who defends my habits whenever we're around people who like to nitpick—who like to pretend they know what's best for my body, instead of minding their business. But right now, I feel her judgment seeping into my pores and it makes my soul curdle, wondering what nasty things she must be thinking.

I grab my bottle and guzzle, the cool water chilling my throat and chest, distracting me from my thoughts. There's a post-workout high that buzzes through my body, my limbs like Jell-O and my head floating, I focus on those feelings instead of where my brain wants to go.

What Kayla thinks doesn't matter.

If I say it enough times, maybe I'll start to believe it.

"You sure you won't hit the club with me tonight? Final answer?" She sticks out her bottom lip and walks to the corner table, plopping down in the chair, her brunette hair flopping in its bun.

I shake my head, twisting the cap of my bottle closed. "I'm sure."

"Okay," she sighs, leaning against the wall and looking around. "Where's Lennox? Maybe he'll go since you're 'taking the night off.'"

A smile creeps on my face. "I don't know, probably relaxing until I need him."

"I bet I could help him relax." She winks, her brows wiggling dramatically.

Laughing, I toss my sweaty towel in the dirty bin. "You've gotta give it up. He'll never give in."

She grins. "Giving up isn't in my DNA."

"If you say so," I giggle.

Her phone chirps and she's momentarily distracted,

reading something on her screen. Popping up from the table, she grabs her purse and spins toward me. "Well, you're in luck. My plans have changed."

My brows jump. "Oh?"

"Yeah. Gonna go hang out with *Jacob.*"

"Who's that?"

She waves her hand. "He's not important yet. I'll let you know when he is." She blows me an air kiss. "See ya later, babe."

I blow out a breath of relief as she saunters out the door, my mind racing with visions of what it would be like if Lennox *did* go out with her tonight, leaving me truly by myself for the first time in my life.

Solitude is yet another thing that's only an illusion in my world.

It's never bothered me before. When you're used to living a certain way, you become accustomed to it, never questioning the things you may be missing.

But for the first time, there's a reason for me to hate the shadows that linger at my back. A reason for me to wish I wasn't rich. Wasn't well known.

And that reason is Jackson Rhoades.

22

JACKSON

I don't know why I answer when she calls.

But like an addict desperate for a fix, when *Sweetheart* flashes on the screen, I relapse. I tell myself it's because I don't want her to keep calling. The last thing I need is for her to interrupt my time with Blakely. *Again.*

Maybe I'm just weak. Maybe I wanted to see if she'd affect me the same, even when I've been getting so lost in someone else.

Turns out, she does.

Her voice sinks into my brain and filters down to my heart, squeezing around the bruises she caused.

"Things aren't *great*, you know? But every day they're

gettin' better," Lee says. "I just... it's not the same without you."

"Hmm," I hum my response, my dad's dog tags cool against my skin as I slip them beneath my shirt.

Knowing that she's doing well, that she's strong enough to stand on her own, should be relieving. Fear of her shattering without me there to keep her glued together is what made me almost stay.

I shake my head, stomach tossing when I think of how I almost threw my dad's dream away just to make sure she was taken care of, when it's extremely obvious I'm not needed.

Still, I'm thrilled to hear her dad is doing well in rehab. I'm happy her brother, Eli, is sticking around, and that they're healing. I'm shocked to hear she caught him fucking a woman who was not his fiancée and can't help the laugh that bursts out of me when she says it was her best friend, Becca, instead.

I knew Becca looked guilty when I asked her where she disappeared to.

And for just a moment, I let myself believe that the reason it doesn't feel like razor blades splitting open my chest when she updates me on her life is because I've moved on.

But then she says his name. *Chase.* And listening to her talk about the rock that he's been through everything plunges the knife deep, slicing the stitched together pieces and reminding me they bleed.

Every love-infused word she says is a bitter pill coating my tongue until I can't swallow around the taste.

Fuck Chase.

Still, I don't speak up. I don't tell her how it hurts every time she speaks about them together. I don't tell her how it feels like there's a gash gaping open between my ribs when I think about how none of his growth and healing had anything to do with me. That it's yet another glaring reminder of how I'm good enough to be a friend, but not important enough to be a priority.

And I don't tell her about Blakely. Not about how things have changed, at least. I'm not sure I'd be telling her for the right reasons. Afraid that I'd be searching for a reaction, my pathetic heart pumping hope into my bloodstream and turning frigid in my veins when I get nothing in return.

So, it's no surprise that when I'm buzzed through the security gate at Blakely's estate, the ache in my chest is as strong as ever. The pain reverberates like clashing cymbals in an amphitheater, rattling my bones so deep I'm not sure how I'll make it through the night.

I've become a pro at pushing it down. Putting a smile on my face and pretending like Lee hasn't ripped the fabric of my soul apart and shown me all the ways I'm only good enough for second place.

If I'm not good enough for Lee, why would I be good enough for anyone else?

Blakely skips out her front door before I can even turn off my car, my breath whooshing out at the sight of her. A twinge of something *other* than pain slinks into my chest, making my heart skip. It dulls the throbbing, just a bit.

She's so beautiful.

She hops into the passenger seat, energy dancing off her skin.

"Guess what?" she breathes.

"What?" I ask, not able to help the smile the spreads across my face as I take in her flushed cheeks and the sparkle in her amber eyes.

"I snuck out!" she whisper-shouts. "Hurry and leave before Lennox realizes I'm gone."

My brow raises. "Trying to get me in trouble, princess?"

She rolls her eyes. "Whatever. Just go! I don't want him with us tonight."

Her hand reaches over and covers mine on the gearshift, sending tingles racing up my arm.

Nodding, I follow her instruction, leaving her estate and driving to a secluded beach I frequent often at night. There's something about the calm of the sea—staring into an endless ocean as it meets a galaxy of stars that reminds me of how incredibly minuscule we are. How human.

I wonder how it's possible to feel so small while my heartbreak feels so big.

"Are you okay?" Blakely asks as she lays out the blanket I brought, plopping down in the sand.

I turn to her, realizing I've been lost in my thoughts since we arrived, Lee's voice dragging down my memory.

"Sorry, yeah..." Before I can stop it—even though I know it's the *worst* date material to bring up—my mouth vomits out the words. "I got a call before I picked you up and it messed with me a bit." Shaking my head, I lay back on the blanket, rubbing my hands down my face. "Ugh, this is the worst thing to be talking about with you."

A warmth covers the left side of my body as Blakely lays down, curling herself into my frame. My arm wraps around her waist, pulling her in closer until her leg is over my hip and her hand is resting on my chest. She's a perfect fit. Like she was meant to be there all along.

"Tell me," she says. "I want to know you. Even the parts that hurt."

My chest cracks, emotions surging together and mixing

into a volatile cocktail, exploding in my stomach and bursting through my throat, making it tighten and swell.

"It's the girl who always calls you, isn't it?" she whispers.

My chest unravels at her question, the ache coming back full force, my eyes closing at its strength.

I don't want to feel this way anymore.

Nodding, my lips skim the top of Blakely's head, the fruity smell of her shampoo comforting my senses. I take a deep breath, trying to suck in as much of it as possible, hoping it will purge Lee from my system.

"Well..." Her hand rests over my heart, rising and falling with each of my stuttered breaths. "I don't know her, *obviously*. And I don't know what your story is. But if this is hurting..." She taps her fingers against my chest. "I want to be the remedy."

My stomach flips, a tsunami of emotion cascading over my body and capsizing me in their waves. The feeling is so overwhelming, so utterly consuming that I lean down and capture her mouth with mine, desperate to drown in the healing she offers.

As we lay beneath the stars, the ocean lapping at the shore, I let her kiss sweep me away.

And for the second time since being back, I don't think of Lee the rest of the night.

23

BLAKELY

I can tell something is wrong with Jackson from the second I get in the car. His eyes aren't as bright, and even though he gives me that boyish grin, there's something lurking, not letting the happiness reach his eyes. The entire drive, my stomach is tied up in knots, my brain racing with theories on why he's acting so out of sorts. Wondering if it's something I did. Worried that he changed his mind about us and is trying to figure out how to let me down easy.

But once we show up to the beach, there's a shift. He goes from trying to appease me to staring out at the ocean with a tortured look in his eyes.

A look I often find in my own reflection.

And for some reason, that makes my anxiety ease, a need to help him heal taking its place.

I want him to know that I'm here for him, however he wants me to be. That I'm not just some young *princess* brat who has a crush and enjoys his company.

He's been there to catch me every time I've started to fall and I want to be the same for him. *His* anchor.

Jackson surges down to kiss me just as my phone vibrates for the hundredth time, most likely Lennox. I'm tempted to turn it off, but the way Jackson's lips feel against mine—the desperation—is enough for me to ignore it.

I don't want to ruin the moment.

His grip is surprisingly strong, his passion evident in every swipe of his tongue, but still, I can feel the restraint in all of his movements. He's clearly holding back. Going slow, just like I asked.

But my favorite part of Jackson is drawing up his rawness. Shedding his relaxed, charming demeanor until he shows me the man underneath. A shot of adrenaline hits me in the chest, wondering what it would take to make him lose it now.

Then worry creeps in, tightening my stomach. I don't know the first thing about pleasing him. And that's what I want—*all* I want in this moment—is to please him. To take away his worries and his heartache, let him funnel everything he's feeling into me, instead.

Maybe it's inappropriate, our passion spawning from his obvious heartbreak, but if this is what he needs, I want to be the one to give it to him.

I shift into him, pressing my body against his, the blanket scrunching in the sand underneath us. His legs tangle with mine, his knee pressing between my legs, forcing a gasp from my mouth as his thigh slips under my skirt, pushing against my fabric-covered clit.

The need to touch him becomes unbearable, my hand reaching between us to rub against his length. It's thick, and even over his jeans I feel it jerk against my hand, a spike of arousal shooting through me.

A groan rips from his throat and he pushes his thigh harder against my center, his palm coming up to cradle the back of my head. His fingers tangle in the strands of my hair and he tugs, bending me until my back bows, his other hand wrapping around my hip to move me against his leg.

The shift in position is sudden and the firmness of his grasp, the way he's able to mold me so perfectly into exactly what he needs, makes my brain buzz with satisfaction.

A wave of something sharp and hot spirals through me at his control of my body, a ripple of pleasure cascading through every single nerve.

I moan, my eyes rolling back when his fingers tighten in my strands.

"That's right, princess. Get yourself off on my leg."

His words send pinpricks of pleasure skittering along my skin, all of my senses heightened with every pass of my clit on his thigh. Relief flows through me, knowing that he's going to tell me what he wants from me. *He's in control.*

That thought is the last conscious one I have, my mind letting go completely, giving in to the sensations as they blanket every single cell.

His mouth leaves mine, lips trailing down the expanse of my throat, laving kisses along my collarbone as he bends me further backward until the ends of my hair graze the ground.

My hips move under his command, the pressure building until it feels like I'm on the verge of an explosion. I grapple at his chest, finding purchase on the metal chain around his neck, the beads digging into my palm as I hold on, a helpless bystander to his control of my pleasure. Submerged in the solace that's found from the absence of thought.

There is no anxiety.

No panic teasing my insides.

No obsession over what pose I'm in, or what angle may be captured from the cameras. All that matters is the certainty I feel in my bones, knowing Jackson will keep me safe and give me what I need.

"Come for me," he whispers against my skin.

His words sear into my brain and I detonate into a thousand pieces, waves of euphoria crashing through my body. Copper floods my mouth from my teeth biting through the skin of my lip and I swallow the tangy flavor, my core clenching and releasing, desperate to be filled as my body collapses further into Jackson's arms.

His hold is strong and sure and as the pleasure ebbs and flows, I faintly recognize the feel of his hand petting my hair, smoothing over the strands. Closing my eyes, I lean into his touch, a suspended type of bliss skating along my skin.

It could be minutes or it could be hours later when I finally come back to Earth, realizing at some point he shifted us so my head is in his lap. Opening my eyes, I meet his grassy green gaze and my heart jumps, slamming against my chest.

No one has ever looked at me the way he is right now.

Like I'm the only thing he can see.

"That was..." I trail off, a dopey sensation making my brain fuzzy.

He grins, his hand coming up to brush the hair off my forehead. "Beautiful, Blake. That was beautiful."

I smile up at him, a sleepy haze rolling through my limbs, making them heavy. My body relaxes further into him as he smooths his palm over my hair, again and again.

My phone vibrates somewhere in the distance, but I pay it no mind. Instead, I close my eyes and fall asleep in Jackson's arms.

Not a single worry in my head.

24

JACKSON

I hear the engine before I see the car. I don't think anything of it because even though we're on a secluded beach, it's not *technically* private. I assume it's just people driving by, or maybe someone wanting to enjoy the serenity of the ocean, the way I often do.

Still, now that the blood has redistributed to my brain, I realize how stupid it was to get so lost in each other where anyone could have seen.

But I can't say I regret what happened. Being witness to Blakely as she came apart in my arms was by far the most intense sexual experience I've ever had, something I've been reflecting on while she sleeps in my lap—trying to figure out why I react so strongly to everything she does.

Maybe it's because when she looks at me, it feels like I'm the center of her universe. I've had plenty of amazing one-night stands, but there's never been a woman who's given me their complete surrender and seemed so relieved to be free of the burden.

The slam of a car door shakes me out of my reverie and as I watch Lennox stalk over the sandy hill directly toward us, my chest pulls tight, and I'm reminded of exactly who she is and all of the reasons why we aren't supposed to work.

When we're together, it's easy to forget.

Shit.

Glancing down, I rub my fingers across Blakely's cheek. The beats of my heart wax and wane like the moon with the tide and a sadness sweeps through me, not wanting the moment to end. It's been oddly peaceful having her in my lap while the waves of the ocean lap against the shoreline.

Finally brushing the back of my hand against her skin, I lean in close to her ear. "Blake."

She stirs, her lashes fluttering against her cheeks before she blinks slowly, opening her eyes.

"Hi." I smirk, my stomach flipping at her stare. "Lennox is here."

A small grin spreads across her face. "What?" she asks, her voice raspy with sleep.

"Your bodyguard is here," I repeat.

Her eyes widen and she shoots upright, her head whipping around just as he approaches, crossing his arms over his chest and staring down at us.

"Hey, Lennox." She plasters on a beaming smile, stretching her arms above her head.

Lennox's eyes narrow as they dart between us—as he clearly takes in the closeness of our positions. A rock drops in my stomach.

I realize how it must look to others to have a twenty-eight-year-old man sneaking off with a nineteen-year-old girl and not tell anyone where they'll be.

Not that he'd be wrong. She did come on my thigh and fall asleep in my arms, but the accusation in his eyes makes it feel dirty, when it felt anything but. I'm once again reminded of what the rest of the world will think. What her father will think. And while I don't *need* the job with him, he's the key to accomplishing everything I've been working toward for years.

My heart stutters, wondering what I would do if I had to choose between Blakely and my dad's dream.

I'd choose him, of course. I enjoy Blakely, but there's nothing more important to me than fulfilling his dying wish.

Lennox clenches his jaw and jerks his head toward the street. My chest tightens knowing he's about to take her away from me when I wasn't done with the night. Wasn't ready to let her go.

Blakely crosses her arms, stiffening her back. "I'm perfectly fine here, thank you. You can wait until I'm done."

He chuckles and sighs, shaking his head. "Blakely, I'm not fucking around. Get your ass in the car. *Now.*"

A protective spark ignites in my veins with the way he's talking to her. All of the people in her life treat her like an inconvenience they have to manage, rather than an employee on her payroll.

"No." She crosses her arms.

"Do you think this is a game?" he spits. "You think you

can just run off and not tell anyone? That there won't be a cavalry coming after you?"

She scoffs. "It was just *one* night, Lennox."

"One night where *anything* could have happened. I had to track your phone to even find you, Blakely."

"I should have known." She rolls her eyes.

He runs a hand through his hair. "Do you realize I had to call your father? That he went absolutely fucking mental thinking a fan got a little too crazy? Or that someone took you to get to him?"

His gaze narrows as he turns to me. "And you. I understand you aren't from this world, so you don't know any better, and I'll let that slide. I'll even forget to mention to her father, my boss—and yours—that you were the one gallivanting around on a deserted beach in the middle of the night."

My throat tightens.

"God," Blakely interrupts. "I'm sorry, okay? I just wanted to know what it would feel like to be normal, to not have someone watching over my *every. Single. Move.*"

Lennox glares. "That's great, Blakely. I don't really care. The fact is you're *not* normal. You never have been, and you never will be. And when you do stupid shit like this it makes *me* look like I'm bad at my job, and that is unacceptable to me. So grab your shit and let's go."

She sighs, running a hand through her hair, the air tightening with tension as she looks back at me.

My heart falters and I want more than anything to tell her to stay. To tell Lennox to fuck off, that he can wait until we're done. But I don't, because he's right. She's *not* like anybody else, and I *don't* know what this world is like.

Gritting my teeth and blowing out a breath, my hand

runs along my necklace. “It’s fine, princess. Just promise you’ll let me make tonight up to you.”

She gives me a small grin, leaning in to kiss my cheek. “Nothing to make up for, Jackson. I’ll see you tomorrow,” she whispers.

My heart skips at her touch, but as I watch them walk away, a foreboding feeling floods through me like a storm surge, leaving me to wade in rising waters, hoping I can learn how to breathe without air.

25

BLAKELY

The last time I was in trouble, I was ten and my nanny caught me eating brown sugar straight from the bag.

I've always been a rule follower.

The idea of someone being upset with me makes my insides clench up so tight I forget how to breathe. It's why I'm so damn good at subtle selling, because I've been fine-tuned for years to recognize what other people want and have mastered the art of becoming what they need.

But right now, I feel like a kid who got their hand caught in the cookie jar.

Sitting in Lennox's car, the silence presses down on my shoulders and dread crawls in the pit of my stomach.

"You know..." I start, desperate to lighten the mood. "If I would have known pissing you off was the way to get you to talk, I would have started doing it years ago."

He grunts, but stays quiet, his knuckles tightening around the steering wheel.

Well, it was worth a shot.

Huffing, I sit back, trying to meld into the leather seats, hoping they'll keep me safe from his wrath. Glancing around, I realize for the first time that he drove his personal car, and I rack my brain, trying to remember a time before now where I've ever been inside of it.

It's nice. Old, but pristine. It reminds me a lot of Jackson's, and that makes my heart skip as my eyes flicker to Lennox and I try to see other similarities I may have missed.

"This is a nice car." I try again.

Still nothing.

Fine, then.

I stop trying to get him to open up, but the anxiety of having him unhappy with me takes over every thought, and my inability to fix it eats away at my chest. And then I remember what else he said.

Your father went mental.

Funny how it takes my disappearance for my father to remember I was there. The bitterness rolls through my gut, shocking me with its intensity.

My father's not a bad man. He's just busy and broken, and when you're one of those things, you often bury yourself in the other to try and numb the pain.

I would know.

A second still is a second wasted.

My stomach growls, reminding me that even though Jackson brought food for us, we never got around to eating.

Which, if I'm honest, is a relief. My gut was in knots wondering what would be buried in the wicker, whether or not I'd have to come home and adjust with exercise or take the time to explain why I couldn't eat what he was offering. But I know that if I don't eat soon, the urge to binge will be that much harder to control.

We drive through the security gates of my house, and when Lennox pulls into the garage, I notice my dad's Porsche is here. Which means he's home.

A rare occurrence.

Lennox follows my line of vision to where it's stuck on the fire engine red sports car and he sighs. "I'm sure he's here to talk to you." He runs a hand through his dark hair before placing it back on the steering wheel. "Just... don't be stupid again, okay? Don't be so damn reckless. If you want some privacy, let me know. I don't want to treat you like a kid, but you've gotta just work with me here, Blakely."

Regret for causing him problems settles in my throat until I have to swallow around the lump. My eyes drop to my lap and I squeeze my fingers tight, focusing on the bite of my nails digging into my skin.

"I'm sorry, I won't do it again," I whisper.

I realize in the grand scheme of things what I did was stupid. But there's this *thing* growing inside of me that's wild and untamed. Something I've never felt before, and the more I try to tamp it down and stunt its growth, the faster it spreads, making me sabotage things—upsetting the system that *I* helped put in place.

It's making me realize that maybe all of the things I've been working toward aren't the things that will make me happy. That will make me whole. How could they be when I'm so willing to give them up for a single moment in Jackson's presence?

And if it makes my dad come home, well...

As I get out of the car and watch Lennox disappear around the side of the house, I tell myself that I won't be so childish again.

Stepping inside, my stomach tenses and flips with nerves, unsure of what type of conversation I should expect to have with my father. I haven't seen him since he stopped by Donahue Motors last week, and I doubt he's stepped foot in this house until tonight. Or if he has, I haven't seen him.

Walking to the kitchen, I make a snack, my eyes darting around the room and into the hallway with every addition to my plate, my ears straining to hear footsteps.

There's nothing but silence.

Sitting down at the table, I spread peanut butter on a rice cake, taking small bites, trying to prolong the moment, hoping my dad will come to find me. That he *is* actually here for me, and it isn't just a coincidence that the first night he's home in forever is the night I left without a security detail.

But thirty minutes later and there's still not a sound.

I head back to my room, taking the long way, stopping in front of the double oak doors that lead to his home office. Disappointment drops like a lead weight in my chest as I hear his muffled voice and smell the faint scent of cigars. I knock anyway, the metal door handle cold against my palm as I crack it open and peek inside.

He's standing behind his desk, a snuffed-out cigar in the ashtray to his right, tumbler of whiskey to his left, his suit jacket off and shirt slightly rumpled as he stares down at a pile of papers. "Stan, that's fine, but I won't have them producing shit when we're sinking thirty million into it."

His eyes glance up at me and widen. He puts a hand to

his chest, blowing out a breath and shaking his head. Like he's relieved to see me home in one piece.

"I'm sorry," I mouth as I slouch against the doorframe. Hope swells inside of me that he'll hang up the phone to talk. His eyes soften and he holds up a finger, gesturing to the couch on the far wall, like he expects me to wait. Reality crashes back in, reminding me that I always come second to his career.

Smiling softly, I shake my head no and give a half-hearted wave as I head to my room.

I don't want to be his afterthought.

Slipping out of my clothes and into my silk robe, I head straight to my en suite so I can start my nighttime routine. *Mozart's Moonlight Sonata—Third Movement* plays softly through the speakers on the wall, the way it does every night.

Three pumps of cleanser on the center of my Clarisonic, thirty seconds for each side. Then I drop my robe and step on the scale, closing my eyes and slowly counting to twenty-five. Preparing myself.

Like I always do.

Because even though I was successful in my attempt at being sporadic, even though I didn't have a panic attack from stepping outside of my comfort zone—it's the end of the night, and I'm still alone.

And it's the routines that keep me sane.

26

JACKSON

An entire lineup of cars were dropped off early this morning for a new production centered around street racing, which means I've been buried under metal bodies, turning them into stunning beauties.

This is it.

An entire movie showcasing my work. It's what I've been waiting for, and it's why I agreed to take this position in the first place.

Unfortunately, the new workload means I've been heading into Donahue Motors before Blakely shows and not coming up for air until after she's gone. Between that and her busy schedule, we haven't had time to steal a glance, let alone talk.

The first two nights after our date, I tried to call her. I figured if we couldn't hang out, we could at least have a few minutes on the phone, but I'm learning quickly when Blakely says every second of her life is scheduled, she isn't exaggerating.

So, we've been relegated to texts, but even those are few and far between.

I've been telling myself it's a good thing to have some space. At the beach, I was swept away so quickly, the experience between us so intense, I forgot we were supposed to be taking things slow—the way she wants to, and the way I know we should.

Ever since I've given in, there's a desperation clawing its way through my insides, trying to make its way to her, not liking the restraints now that it's had a taste of freedom. But there's nothing I can do to change things, so instead of sitting at home and pining over yet another woman who's out of reach, I've been going to the beach every night and reflecting. Trying to work on myself so I can get back to who I'm supposed to be.

The son my mom deserves.

The man Blakely needs.

Somewhere along the way, I've lost it. Can barely remember what it's like to crack a joke or to truly enjoy everything life has to offer—things that used to be my defining characteristics.

Instead, I've let myself wallow in this pit of misery and loneliness, running away from Sugarlake and trying to figure out why no one wants me, not realizing that I've forgotten how to want myself.

This isn't the first time I've been lost.

After my father's death, there was this well of hopelessness that opened up in the center of my chest, allowing me to sink into its darkness without knowing its depth. By the time I realized how far I had fallen, it was too late, my feet slipping off the grimy walls of grief whenever I'd try to climb my way out.

But my mom needed me to be the man of the house, to be her pillar of support when she couldn't stand on her own, and people treat you different when you don't paste on a smile. So, I hid behind a mask of charm, not wanting anyone to see the monster of despair grabbing my ankles and pinning me down, threatening to eat me alive any time I tried to leap away.

And that's how I've always been known. Jackson Rhoades. The easygoing charmer. No one ever cared to look a little deeper, happy to accept me at face value. And I liked that they didn't try.

I've worked hard at building ladders to climb out of that hole, and I *never* want to be back there again—buried so deep it takes years to see the light. So, I need to figure my shit out before the whispers of sadness grow limbs and wrap around me, dragging me back down.

Starting with the fact that I have feelings for two women at once. Like my heart grew in Blakely's presence, allowing her to sneak in and fill up all the cracks. Now that she's there, everything I feel for Lee is dulled. A ghost haunting the corridors of my memories, hovering between this life and the next.

I still feel her though, like raised flesh on old wounds. Scars don't disappear just because the cuts begin to heal.

The past few nights, I've gone back to the beach, sat in the same spot, and expected memories of Lee to take every thought. *My sweetheart.* I've been surprised to find it's Blakely that floods through my mind instead.

I wonder if she's doing okay. Worry about whether she has someone real with her, or if she's surrounded by the ones who keep her strapped down with "flaws" and "episodes", because they know people who don't believe in themselves are easier to control.

Then I think of how different our lives really are, but how I understand, *so well,* the need to show someone a different face than the one your soul wears.

I think of how it feels to be the person who draws out her candor, who she lets in to wade through her darkness.

A heavy feeling swims in my gut—a shark circling its prey—waiting for realization to hit.

And then it does.

I don't want Lee.

Because even when I've loved her, have pined for her, it's never felt like this.

This soul deep connection, pure in its honesty and raw in its need.

Shocking how quickly it formed. Or maybe it was there all along and my acceptance is what makes it flare so bright. All I know is suddenly it's taking over every waking moment and diving into my dreams, until all I can see, think, taste, touch, *feel* is the need to be with Blakely.

But even with all of these emotions that rage inside of me and spark off my skin, it doesn't take away the pain of my best friend, the one I've loved for years, treating me like a second choice.

The pain morphs at that realization, going from a longing agony to a stabbing ache, my eyes clearing of the fog.

All the things I've been finding in Lee, are things that

fall short of what I deserve. But I didn't know there was more to want.

Blakely, she looks at me like I'm the center of her everything. She listens like I'm the most important person in her world. She trusts like she can see into my soul.

So, no. I don't *want* Lee. Because the way I feel for Blakely? It's pounding through my bloodstream and shocking every cell, showing me all the ways life could be if I experienced it with her.

FOOTSTEPS CLACK along the concrete floors of the garage, making me look up from where I'm sketching out the design for the 1967 Shelby GT500.

James Donahue strolls between the lifts, glancing at the shells to what will become his biggest production of the year. My heart rams against my chest, stomach tensing into knots, hoping he's here for business. Afraid that he can see inside my brain and pull out all the ways I've been daydreaming of doing filthy things to his daughter.

He stops next to my desk, peering over my shoulder, the smell of cigars and wealth wafting through the air and mixing with the silence, making my gut churn.

"Hmm." His hand comes down on my shoulder, patting once before he backs away, leaning against the body of the Cadillac El Dorado. I bite my tongue to keep from asking him to move to a different spot.

"I see the new cars came in." He glances around.

Tossing my pencil down, I turn to face him. "Yep. Can't wait to get started." Excitement spins in the center of my chest like a pinwheel. "This is why I took this gig."

His lips twitch. "Well that makes two of us. The reason I sought you out was for *this* production."

"Oh, really?"

He nods. "There's been a thousand different movies about fast cars and their beauty. I want this one to be different. Your work, Jax... it's special."

Pride fills me up like a balloon and my head tilts as I listen to him get lost in his vision. It's the most he's ever said in my presence, his passion bleeding through every word he speaks. Passion I didn't realize he had until this moment. His excitement is palpable and it soars across the room and implants into my brain, the image so clear it's like I thought of it myself.

The more he talks, the more I see why he's the biggest mogul on the scene.

There are just some things you can tell a person was destined to become. And James Donahue was meant to be the King of Hollywood. The man hiding in the castle and pulling all the strings.

"When does production start?" I ask.

"Five months. Which means I need the cars in three."

I nod slowly, anticipation for the finished product thrumming through my veins. "No problem."

"That's what I like to hear." A genuine smile graces his face, crinkling his cheeks and sparking through his eyes, and I'm taken aback by how strongly it reminds me of Blakely.

The way you don't even realize what you've been shown is a mask until they decide to take it off.

"The other reason I'm here is to alleviate some concerns you may have," he continues.

Confusion draws my brows down. "Concerns?"

"I saw the picture of you and my daughter."

My blood turns to ice, heart slamming against my ribs. "Sir, I—"

He waves his hand. "No, no, none of that. I know how this world works, Jax. Media loves to spin a story even where there isn't one to tell. They don't know I asked you to keep an eye on her." His voice sharpens. "And they definitely don't realize that as my employee, you wouldn't even *think* of taking advantage of the situation."

My gut churns, sensing the warning in the spaces between his words. "Ri—" I clear my throat. "Right. Exactly."

He lifts his chin. "Right." A tense second passes where I hold his gaze, not wanting to break the stare, afraid it will showcase my transgressions.

I *am* taking advantage of the situation, but not in all the ways I *want* to. Guilt sticks to my insides, making bile tease the back of my throat.

"She ran away the other night," he says suddenly, his shoulders deflating.

"Hmm?" I lift my brow, trying to paint a look of surprise on my face. My hand reaches up to grab my necklace, running my fingers along the chain.

How ridiculous that a night on her own is considered "running away."

"Well, she disappeared without her security." He sighs, leaning further into the car's frame. "I don't—it's not like her. She's never been a child I've had to worry about, and now..." He shakes his head.

"With all due respect, sir, she's not exactly a *child* anymore, is she?"

His eyes jump back to mine. "That's exactly what she is, Jax. She's a nineteen-year-old girl who doesn't know what's good for her. If she did, she wouldn't have run off with no protection. Wouldn't be making *stupid* decisions that affect everyone around her. She wouldn't be gallivanting to clubs and showing off her body like a piece of property up for lease."

I cringe. The need to defend her—to remind him that it's *her* body and she can do whatever she wants with it, that she's so much more than he's giving her credit for—rises inside of me, my teeth cutting through the flesh on my cheek.

We both hear the gasp before we see her.

Mr. Donahue turns on his heel, his spine stiffening. My gaze finds Blakely, standing just to the inside of the glass door, her eyes welling with tears and her hand over her chest.

My body burns with the need to go to her. To protect her from the bitter words I know are slicing through her and remind her that opinions don't define who she is.

"Honey, I—" he starts.

"No, it's fine," she interrupts. "Karen told me you were here and I wanted to come say hi." She sucks a ragged breath in through her teeth. "I shouldn't have... I just wanted to know if you'd want me to rearrange my schedule and be home for dinner." Shaking her head, she drops her hands, fists clenching at her sides.

One. Two. Three.

Shit.

She turns on her heel and practically sprints through the door and I wait to see if he's going to follow. To explain that his words were from his worry, not from a place of hate. As an outsider, it's easy to see the difference.

He watches the space where she was for a moment before turning back to me. "As I was saying, she's a *child* in all the ways that count. So, please continue what it is I've been having you do, and just… keep an eye on her."

My heart leaps to my throat, torn between telling him I can't and wanting to race after Blakely and give her someone to fall into.

I don't do either.

I simply nod, a sick feeling plunging through my stomach and clinging to my bones.

27

BLAKELY

"Blake."

Jackson's voice rings out, echoing off the metal stalls in the restroom and I shrink back, my knees practically to my chin as I push further against the tile wall. My trembling fingers press against my mouth, the flesh indenting against my teeth from the pressure. My breathing is sharp. Stuttered, making it almost impossible to stay quiet through the tears.

But I try because I don't want him to see me like this. Don't want it to be yet another time he has to pick me up from where I'm breaking into pieces on the floor.

It was a fruitless mission to seek out my dad, and I knew

it from the moment Karen told me he was here. But there was a part of me that jumped at the chance anyway, wanting to see if things had shifted. If maybe him thinking I was gone would make him cherish the moments with me here.

But those are just visions of a lonely girl who wants her reality to change because she's been shown there's something more.

"Blake."

Jackson's voice is closer now, his shadow swallowing up the flittering light through the bottom of the stall door. A clunking sound rings out, the frame shaking slightly, and even though I can't see to the other side, I just *know* his forehead is resting against the metal.

"Blake," he whispers. "Let me in."

My mouth pinches harder, salty tears dripping between my knuckles as I keep back the noise.

Leasing her body like it's property.

Is that really what he thinks of me?

Is that what *everyone* thinks of me?

The thought spears my chest and my vision blurs.

One. Two. Three.

My fingers tighten around my mouth, the urge to drop my hands and clench them overwhelming, but I stop myself, afraid my hurt will bleed out with the sobs if I don't hold them in.

Jackson sighs and his shadow morphs, his legs coming into view as he slips to a sitting position on the other side of the door.

He doesn't speak for long moments, my breathing comes rapidly and the tension in my chest is a physical ache, like a rubber band about to snap.

His hand appears under the stall.

My gaze zones in to where his palm is resting on the subway tile, the pressure easing now that I have something to focus on. My chest jumps with jerky inhales as my eyes trace the veins on his forearms, pausing at the hairband that's always wrapped around his wrist, an odd sense of jealousy dripping through me when I wonder what it would be like to be a staple in Jackson's life.

Slowly, I move my hand, placing it in his, my manicured nails sliding against his thick, calloused fingers.

He twines them together, and a warmth sweeps through me, brushing under my skin.

I'm sure we look ridiculous. Two people sitting on a dirty bathroom floor, holding hands under a stall. But I don't care. I allow myself to sink into this moment and accept the comfort he provides.

Blowing out a shaky breath, I wipe the lingering tears from where they're dripping off my lashes and smack my head against the tile wall, enjoying the bite of pain that clears the fog from my mind.

I close my eyes.

One. Two. Three. Deep breath in.

It takes twenty-two minutes until I'm okay to move. To *function*.

One thousand three hundred and twenty seconds.

I know because I've counted every single one.

Our hands are still connected, energy sizzling as it dances off our palms, the heat melding our fingers together. A chill rushes up my arm as I break away, my body begging to slip back into his hold. I resist the urge.

This part I'm familiar with.

I know how to pick myself up and slap my frazzled edges back together with tape. It's a shoddy job—my flaws bursting at the seams with the slightest jolt—but it's one that lets me hide the pain in the deepest chambers of my heart, where only I can see the hurt.

Unlatching the stall lock and swinging open the door, I meet Jackson's glassy gaze, waiting for embarrassment to slam into me.

How can he not see how *weak* I am?

But it doesn't come. Instead, a different type of pressure bears down on my chest, spreading to my stomach and flowing through my limbs, filling me with gratitude. For the first time in my life, I feel like someone is at my back.

He sees me even when I don't want to see myself.

Smiling, he reaches out and brushes his hand down my hair, but he doesn't say a word. Doesn't bring up my dad, or how absolutely pathetic I looked begging for his time.

We head back to the reception area, my eyes scanning the halls, hoping I don't run into anyone, not ready to face them until I've built my shield back to full strength.

"If you're looking for a dinner date, I've heard I'm pretty good company," Jackson says, smirking as I walk around and plop into the office chair.

I giggle, his attempt at lightening the mood dulling the throb in my chest, just a little. But then my heart pinches when I realize I have to turn him down.

"I really don't have time, I just..." I trail off, chewing on my lip.

"You just..." He peers down at me, standing so close I can feel the warmth coming off his body. My eyes are level with his groin and heat spikes through me at our position.

"It's stupid." I fidget in my seat, trying to get rid of the sudden throb between my legs.

Jackson leans in closer and my mouth goes dry as his fingers tip up my chin. "*Nothing* you do is stupid, Blake."

My heart slams against my ribs at the absolute certainty

in his words. He's so sure in what he says that I have no choice but to believe him. Because I know Jackson wouldn't lie.

"Have dinner with me," he whispers.

His hand is still on my chin, his eyes peering so deep I swear they touch my soul.

Nodding, my fingers wrap around his wrist. "Okay."

"WE ONLY HAVE a couple hours before my glam team shows up, so I hope you've planned something quick and easy," I tell Jackson as I let him in through my front door.

He smiles and kisses my cheek, the stubble on his jaw tickling my skin. My stomach flips.

Walking into the foyer, he glances around then heads straight to the kitchen, like he's been here for years. Like he's walked these halls a thousand times.

I've lived here my whole life and sometimes *still* have issues getting to where I need to be.

But that's just Jackson. Comfortable in any element. He doesn't have to command the room, because it's intrinsic, the air molding to fit him so perfectly. He owns the space just by existing within it.

"I don't have anything planned, princess. You invited me, remember?" He smirks, leaning against the gray marble island.

My brow raises. "False. You invited yourself."

His grin widens and he sits down on a stool, his chain rustling under his shirt. My stomach clenches, remembering what it felt like to have the metal threaded between my fingers while I came apart in his arms.

My mouth waters and I swallow the saliva, jerking into

action when I realize I'm staring like an idiot, wasting valuable time. I have two hours at best before I'm whisked away, back into my responsibilities.

Usually I'd be in the gym, getting an early evening workout in to cushion unforeseen things—food or drink that I can't avoid. But the urge to spend time with Jackson is stronger than the threat of empty calories, even as the panic wraps around my chest and squeezes, reminding me how easy it can steal my breath.

I'll just exercise when I get back home.

Sleep is overrated anyway. And I'm desperate for some time between Jackson and me where both of us aren't falling apart at the seams.

Part of me wonders if he's attracted to the mess—a scrambled puzzle for him to piece together, then walk away from once I'm whole. But I don't want to think on that either, so I shove it to the back of my mind, determined to enjoy the time together. I've never had a *boyfriend*.

My heart stalls as I think the word, my eyes widening as I stare at him across the kitchen. He's watching me with a sparkle in his mossy gaze, his eyes inquisitive.

"You're far too pretty to look so sad," he says, cocking his head to the side.

"What are we doing?" I rush out.

The easy smile drops from his face and he jumps from the stool and strides toward me. I back up, realizing that he's not slowing down as he comes closer. My stomach flips and my hands grow clammy, my back bumping into the wall.

He presses against me, his hips pinning mine in place. "What do you *want* to be doing?"

I suck in a gasp, butterflies racing from my stomach to my throat, anticipation and arousal surging through my insides. My teeth sink into my lower lip, gnawing away at the flesh.

His fingers grip my chin, his thumb tugging until my mouth parts.

"You'll make yourself bleed," he rumbles.

"Maybe I like the pain," I whisper back.

His eyes flare and my womb clenches even as embarrassment tries to slither its way around me, heating my cheeks. *Maybe I like the pain?* I don't know why I said that, even if I know it's true.

The sting helps me focus, allowing me to feel control even when things slip from my grasp. At least the discomfort is something I'm choosing.

He leans in closer, resting his forehead against mine, his hand cupping the back of my neck until our mouths are centimeters apart. His breath is sweet and I suck it in, wanting him to breathe new life into my bones. Bathe me in his comfort and leave me with his peace, so even after he's gone, I feel him inside me.

"Careful, princess. That almost sounds like an invitation."

The scratch in his voice sends a thrill racing through me, and not for the first time, I wonder what it would be like to give myself to him.

I wouldn't *lease* my body to Jackson. I'd let him own it.

"Maybe it is," I breathe into his lips.

His grip around my neck tightens, his head dipping down to brush his lips against mine. It's soft and teasing, his mouth moving back and forth, creating a friction with every pass that makes my body buzz. Anticipation of what he's going to do next makes every nerve electrified, waiting to explode at his command.

I blow out a shaky breath, closing my eyes and enjoying how small I feel in his big hands.

"Let's eat," he whispers against my lips. He steps back, his hands that were just on my body now adjusting the front of his jeans, and a shot of arousal pools in my belly as I watch him.

"What's on the menu? We could do something easy, like pizza?" he asks.

His question douses me in icy water, the thought of pizza churning my stomach.

Shaking my head, I walk across the kitchen until I'm in front of the white corded phone that's attached to the wall. It's archaic, but my father refuses to change, saying it reminds him of the "good ol' days."

"No, let me call in Eric."

"Who's Eric?" Jackson walks behind me, his arms wrapping around my waist, and his words rumbling into the skin of my neck. Goose bumps spread down my spine as I press into him.

"He's our chef."

"You have a *chef*?"

"Of course we do." My forehead scrunches, wondering why he seems so surprised.

"And you're just gonna have him show up here, even though it's seven at night?"

"Uhh... yeah." I shrug. "It's his job, Jackson."

"What if he's with his family?"

My brows draw together. "Him and his wife both live on the property, it's not a big deal."

He chuckles. "Damn, sometimes I forget how different our worlds are."

Defensiveness swirls inside of me and I twist in his arms to face him. "What's that supposed to mean?"

"You have chefs that live *on your property* and come whenever you call. Bodyguards that find us no matter where we go. It's a different world is all."

Sadness clenches my heart. *Is he judging me?*

"And?" I snap. "It's not my fault this is what I was born into. Hardly fair for you to hold it against me." I push out of his hold.

He shakes his head, gripping me tighter, pulling me back against his chest.

"No." His voice is firm. "I didn't mean it was *bad.* Just different. I've spent the past decade working so I could support my mom and help pay the bills. I learned to cook just so we could taste something other than ramen noodles and rice."

My heart sinks. I can't relate to his experience at all and it makes a sour taste hit the back of my throat.

I've never even thought about things like that.

"But when we're together," he continues. "I get so lost in all the ways it feels like you were made for me, and I forget how different our lives have been." He turns my face back toward him, his hand gripping my jaw tight. "Our circumstances don't define us."

My heart flies, slamming against my ribs.

Leaning down, he presses a kiss against my lips. "I look forward to hearing about your past, Blake. Now, make your phone call so we can eat."

He retreats, walking back toward the island, like he didn't just upend my world with a few words.

My eyes trail after him, wondering what it is that makes him so damn different from the rest.

28

JACKSON

"What was it like growing up here?" My voice echoes off the high ceilings in the dining room, bouncing around the ten empty chairs at the table.

Blakely shrugs, her fingers toying with the edge of the bloodred placemat. "Like anywhere else, I guess."

I snort and she looks up, her eyes sparking. "What?"

"*Like anywhere else?*" I mock, a teasing grin on my face. "That's a good answer for the cameras."

Her cheeks bloom pink and I lean in, resting my elbows on the table. "Now give me the real one."

Slowly, the mask drops, a dark melancholy filling up her eyes. Her entire body slouches, like she's finally giving herself permission to show the weight of perfection that rests on her shoulders.

She swallows. "Lonely."

I'm not surprised at her answer. My gut sours as I try to imagine a childhood through her eyes. With butlers and nannies and no parents in sight. With bodyguards, and the bitter truth of why they're needed.

My mom and I may not have had much, but we always had each other, and I'm thankful as hell to know that's what really counts.

"And what's it like now?" I ask.

She glances up at me. "*Right* now?"

I nod. "Right now."

Her eyes drill through mine, making my stomach flip and my chest fill with... *something.*

"Like you're the only person who's ever given a damn."

She always does this—makes me feel like I'm the most important person in her world. My heart stammers, wanting to jump over the table and hold her under my palms, show her all the ways I care. Words don't seem like they'd be enough.

Before I can say anything else, we're interrupted by Eric, the *chef*, rolling a cart into the room and placing two plates in front of us.

My nose flares at the scent, mouth watering as I take in the panko-crusted baked salmon, a creamy sauce drizzling off the asparagus that sits to the side.

"Damn, Eric. This looks and smells incredible. You free to come cook for me too?" I joke.

He smiles and tips his head, his gray hair flopping on his forehead, but he doesn't answer, just quietly leaves the room.

"Does he not speak?" I ask Blakely.

She giggles, picking up her fork and twirling it. "You may not realize this about yourself, Jackson, but you have a tendency to make people shy."

Grinning, amusement sneaks through me. "Oh yeah? Do I make *you* shy, princess?"

She grins, her eyes dropping back to her plate, bouncing from one item to the next. "Sometimes."

I follow her gaze, noticing how different our meals are.

Did he prepare hers differently?

My brows draw in as I take a closer look. Her portions are definitely smaller, which isn't a big deal considering she's half my size. But her salmon looks plain—no panko crusting, and her asparagus is dry.

I'm about to ask her why she isn't eating the same thing, but before I even open my mouth, there's a visible shift. I can see it in the way her body tightens, a hazy sheen slipping over her amber gaze. And I can sense it, a tense vibration that thins the air, making everything feel on edge. She drops her fists into her lap and I lean back, sneaking a glance under the table, a lead weight dropping in my gut when I do.

She's clenching and unclenching.

One. Two. Three.

My stomach somersaults while my brain races through every second we've had, wondering how many other signs I've missed. Wondering how in the hell I didn't realize, until this moment, that food was one of her triggers.

"I'll just... one sec." She holds up a finger, a pained smile on her face as she jumps from her chair and races out of the room.

She must not go far because even though she's speaking in a hushed tone, I hear her muffled voice filtering through the hall. "Eric, I just want to double-check, you cooked mine without butter or oil, right?"

"Yes, of course, Miss Donahue. I steamed it just the way you like."

"Okay." She pauses. "Okay... I'm just making sure, because I had this thought that maybe you cooked ours together, and I *can't* have any butter or oil."

There's a lingering moment of silence.

"And the asparagus?"

"Same way, miss."

"You're sure?"

"Absolutely sure."

My heart falters as I listen to her beg for reassurance over something as simple as oil.

She walks back in, her posture relaxed, as if the confirmation was all she needed to calm down.

"Everything okay?" I ask.

She slides back into her chair and angles her head, beaming those bright teeth straight at me. "Everything is perfect."

I hum and nod, stuffing a piece of salmon into my mouth. But I watch her closely throughout the rest of the meal. I'm sure my staring is making her uncomfortable, I can see it in the stiffness of her shoulders and the way her eyes dart to every object in the room, but I can't stop, my concern and my questions muddling together until a strain grows behind my eyes.

But she eats all the time. She doesn't seem too thin.

"What?" She sighs, her fork clattering as it drops to the plate.

I lean back in my chair, relief trickling through me that she asked. That she gave me a reason to press her for answers. "What was that?"

"What was what?"

I gesture toward the hallway, raising my brow.

"Oh, I was just double-checking that my food didn't have any of the *extra* stuff." Her nose scrunches.

"Extra stuff?" I cock my head.

"Yeah... you know, all the stuff that's on yours. I don't eat that."

"Like... ever?"

She shakes her head, sipping from her water.

"So, you can't eat salmon and asparagus?"

"You see my plate, it has the same thing as you, doesn't it?" she says sharply.

I lean back in my chair, my solar plexus burning from her tone. I don't want to upset her, and this is clearly a sensitive subject, but this feels too important to let her brush it under the rug. "It was just a question, princess, you don't have to send me to the gallows."

Her lips twitch. "The gallows?"

"Yeah. You know... execution by hanging, for questioning you about your life."

"I don't mind if you ask about my life."

"You sure about that?" My brows rise.

"I just—I eat clean, okay? I exercise. I keep in good shape because my job demands it, and also because it's important to me. I don't like to put things in my body that aren't good for me."

"And what I'm eating isn't good?"

"No, I—Ugh!" She stops mid-sentence, her hands ripping at the roots of her hair. "This is why I don't like eating around people, because nobody understands. You don't know what it's like. You don't *get it*, and that's okay. But don't fucking push me, Jackson, okay? Just be happy with the results like everyone else."

Shock spins through me at her tone and my chest grows heavy. Has nobody ever shown her it isn't her physical appearance that makes her beautiful?

She's so much more than what they see.

Her cheeks are splotchy and her eyes run wild, making me worried that if I continue to press her, she'll spiral.

But I won't stop watching.

I won't stop looking, even when she tries to hide her truths behind her lies.

29

BLAKELY

The rest of dinner is stilted and awkward. Jackson watches my every bite while I try to ignore the way my insides itch at his perusal. It's an odd feeling, wanting to spend all of my time with someone who both comforts and exposes me at the same time.

He strips me bare in a way I've never experienced, leaving me shivering and vulnerable. Standing without a shield, thousands of arrows waiting to fly through the air and pierce my skin.

I expect him to leave after dinner, but he doesn't. He stays, watching as my glam team arrives and transforms me into the picture-perfect image that people pay to see.

And when Sierra pulls me aside—heaping on the praise for getting Jackson to tag along—I meet his eyes across the room and nausea rolls through my gut.

I don't want to use him the way she expects.

The way we had planned.

I want to keep him for myself.

Which is one of the many reasons I'm incredibly nervous to bring him further into my life. Not because he doesn't belong, but because I'm afraid he'll belong too well.

My dad may think I'm naïve—that I need protecting—but I know how this world works. It's impossible to live and breathe it your entire life and stay blind to the duplicity that pulses through its core.

I know once people get a taste of Jackson's charm and his picture-perfect face, they'll crawl hand over foot to be the one who corrupts it. And while I don't think Jackson is easy prey, I'm not sure there's anyone who can outlast the temptation of Hollywood once they set their sights on you.

But I don't want him on my father's bad side, or to think it's because I don't want to spend time with him, so even though there's a foreboding chill that snakes its way around my spine, I don't put up a fight.

"Okay, B, you know the drill," Sierra says, glancing up from her phone as she slides into the back of the Maybach.

Clearing my throat and nodding, I turn toward Jackson. "You'll be okay while I work? Kayla will be here, so you'll have someone to talk to." I cringe as I say it, remembering the jealousy that rained down through my chest last time I watched them together.

Jackson winks, his pinky finger stretching out to run along the length of my thigh, electricity dancing off my skin at his touch. Butterflies erupt in my stomach, my heart shifting into overdrive. It's going to drive me crazy having him close enough to feel but too off-limits to touch.

My gaze darts to Sierra and Lennox, making sure neither of them see.

But I should know better.

My eyes clash with Lennox's and my stomach flips, surging into my throat. His judgment soars across the confined space and scrapes against my skin, waking up the anxiety that lies beneath the surface.

Unease billows in the center of my chest.

He won't say anything.

The real worry is Sierra. I swing my gaze to hers, my heart jolting against my ribs. But she's not paying attention, her head buried so deep in her phone she's in another universe.

I blow out a deep breath of relief, the knot in my solar plexus untangling, and as it does I realize maybe that's why I latched on to Sierra so quickly and allowed her to become the center of my life.

Because she doesn't look close.

She doesn't push.

With Sierra, what you see is what you get, and that's how she views the world.

She doesn't skin me until I bleed, digging up buried secrets like lost treasure. Instead, she adds sparkle and shine as camouflage, keeping the other facets hidden.

Jackson is the first one to come along and search for every angle.

THE NEXT FEW weeks pass before I can blink, Jackson and I falling seamlessly into a new routine.

Time with him moves differently. Faster. And although he's slotting into place, like he was always meant to be here, it leaves less time for other things. Things I *can't* just stop. Like working. Or exercise.

My regime is now relegated to late nights and early mornings, sleep being pushed down the rung until it's rare to get more than one or two hours. I'm used to surviving the deprivation, but I can feel my body starting to crumble, my mind desperate for some rest.

The only time I escape the exhaustion is when I'm with Jackson, each moment rife with a heady connection. It strums through the air and vibrates every single part of me, weaving into my heart and making warmth flare between my legs.

There's just one problem. He won't *touch* me.

At least not the way I want. There's been a few heated moments, and I've memorized the outline of his lips, but there's something holding him back from taking it any further and my need is so thick I can taste it on my tongue.

As I lay in bed, trying—and failing—to fall asleep, I think back to that night on the beach, when he took control and I shattered in his arms.

My nipples pebble beneath the silk of my camisole at the memory, the matching pajama shorts bunching between my legs as my hand drifts down, slipping beneath the glossy fabric and tracing over my clit.

I close my eyes, trying to emulate the feel of Jackson's touch. Trying to imagine it's his fingers ghosting along my center, slowly edging me closer—winding me tighter—until I explode all over his hand.

A shot of desire burns through me, a moan ripping from my throat as my fingers press firmly against my swelling nerves, my shorts growing damp and sticking to the inside of my thighs.

My teeth sink into my lower lip, breaking through the skin. The bite of pain is enough to catapult me over the edge, my body bursting until I see stars, my ears ringing from the force of my orgasm.

Breathing heavily as I come back down, my slippery fingers rest against my pulsing skin as disappointment replaces the temporary blast of pleasure.

Ever since that night, I've laid in bed, trying to recreate the sensations, but nothing has worked.

I'm desperate to feel that way again. For the chains of anxiety to break away as I fall apart in Jackson's arms.

Is that how it always feels with another person?

Curiosity nags at my brain and I know I won't be able to sleep until I find out. So even though it's three a.m., I jump out of bed and grab my laptop, adrenaline rushing through me as I toss it on the comforter and pull up Google.

Floating feeling during orgasm.

The second I type it in embarrassment splatters across my insides, dripping down and pooling in my gut. I throw my head in my hands and groan.

What the hell am I even doing?

But even as I think it, my eyes are scanning articles, my mouse scrolling down the page in a frenzy.

Suddenly, everything stops.

My mouse hovers over a single word, a tugging sensation urging me to click.

So, I do.

30

JACKSON

I'm in deep.

And honestly, it's scaring the shit out of me. I came here to get away from love, and now here I am putting my fractured heart on a silver platter, practically asking for someone to complete the break.

But I can't help it. The things Blakely draws up—the way she makes me feel—it's a maelstrom in the center of my chest, upheaving everything I thought I knew about how someone could make you feel.

It hasn't been easy. Every single second in her presence is a euphoric kind of torment. Being with her is a balm to my wounds. To my loneliness. To the depression that likes to creep up and choke the life out of me at a moment's notice.

But being with her has also been torture. Having to stem the raw *need* that lights up my body like an electrical storm, wanting to touch every inch of her skin. Worship every part of her soul.

I want to consume her. Wrap her in my arms and show her all the ways I can take care of every need. The ways I could bring her to the brink of pleasure and prolong it. The ways I could lose myself inside of her and never come up for air.

She asked to go slow, and so I've been restraining my desires—biting my tongue against the urge to part her thighs and lap up her innocence, drown in the satisfaction of knowing I'm the only man to explore her untouched flesh. And I've also been holding back for myself, worried that once I give in fully, my feelings will explode into complete chaos, blinding me to the reason I'm really here.

To fulfill my dad's dream.

But at the end of the day, I'm still a man. One who's used to using sex as a way to deal with my demons. The ones I don't ever speak of or let anyone know exist. And while the temptation to pick up a random woman is gone, my body still craves the connection, only now the craving is stronger because my curiosity makes me wonder if it will feel different.

I've never had sex with feelings before.

Blakely caught me off guard, spinning me on my axis and making the light hit a different way.

That thought is being pile-driven into my brain right now, as I watch her film content for her platforms.

Blakely's prancing around her pool deck, the tiniest white bikini caressing her skin, being pathetically held together by string that's as small as floss. Her hair is slicked back with product, her skin sprayed with moisture to cast a dewy glow, and my eyes can't stop drinking her in.

My cock is hard as hell in my jeans, but I let it pulse and throb—let myself live in the torment of wanting her and the discipline of holding myself back.

We haven't talked much about her career, beyond her need to look "perfect," and me going with her to paid gigs.

But right now, I'm in awe of her.

She floats effortlessly from one area to the next, intuitively knowing what to do before they tell her, and her aura shines so bright it's impossible to look away. She's a master of attention, a light switch that she flips, her persona beaming strong while she's in front of the camera.

But it's when she's working behind the scenes that she shines the brightest.

In the past few weeks, I've seen a side to her that I never knew existed. At first, before I really knew her, I assumed she was lazy. Spoiled. A rich brat who lived off her last name and her daddy's fortune. And then, once I became part of her world, I thought she allowed everyone else to control her life. A pretty, perfect, useless puppet, dangling until the masters moved her the way they wanted. And while I still see that manipulation, I also see her leadership.

The way she commands a room full of people, demanding their attention while she negotiates terms of a contract. The way her team and all the industry people I've seen come and go watch and listen to everything she says, no questions asked. The way she never loses her temper, how she treats everyone in her world with respect. As an equal.

It makes me wonder if her father just doesn't realize

how much she reflects him in everything she does, or if it's something he's refusing to see.

But he's another thing we don't talk about.

I'll admit, I didn't know anything about it either. I only know social media from an everyday person's perspective, and hardly that if I'm honest. Sugarlake is a bubble, none of my friends subscribe to the social media platforms. Not since everything imploded on Lee and Chase the night of her mom's death, all from a Facebook post.

That was a wake-up call. Personal business never stays personal once you put it on the web. And in Sugarlake, there's no need to be online when you'll hear the gossip from Susan at the church, or Martha at the store.

Suddenly the French doors leading to the pool deck swing open, Sierra bursting through, her mouth pinched and her gaze zoned in on Blakely, a rolled-up magazine in her hand.

Her eyes move up and down Blakely's body critically as she moves toward her, and for some reason, a protective fire starts to burn inside my chest.

Blakely's smile dims as Sierra walks closer, her arm reaching out to pass off the rolled-up tabloid.

Unease circles my gut.

I see the moment the energy shifts, Blakely's shoulders stiffening, her eyes turning down while she stares at whatever is on the cover.

Her hand covers her stomach, then drops to her side, fingers curling into a tight fist.

Without a second thought, I'm up and moving, sensing she needs me without her so much as looking in my direction. I hear Sierra's voice screeching, but I'm focused on Blakely and don't pay attention to her words.

Once I reach them, I snatch the magazine out of Blakely's hand. Her head snaps to me, amber eyes wide.

There's a photo of her on the cover walking into Donahue Motors, a close-up shot where they've zoomed in and circled her stomach.

Is Blakely Donahue pregnant?

I can't stop the chuckle that bubbles out of my throat, the laughter loud as it jumps through the air, clashing with the silence that surrounds me.

"What's so funny?" Sierra snarks.

I look toward Blakely, my heart stalling when I see her fists clenching in threes, and her face a mask of stone.

Sighing, I run my hand over my hair. "Because it's ridiculous." My eyes lock on Blakely. "You're really upset about this?"

Blakely bites her bottom lip, her eyes bouncing from one inanimate object to the next.

"Seriously, Blake. It's insane," I continue.

"Is it? Even gossip has the ghost of truth," Sierra interjects. She backs up a pace, cataloging Blakely with her gaze. "When's the last time you took your measurements?"

Blakely's shoulders stiffen. "I measure every night, Sierra."

"And?"

She pauses. "They caught me in an off moment. They've never been at Dad's company before, so I was unprepared is all. I'm clearly slouching in the picture."

Sierra's hand waves in Blakely's direction. "You do look a little… *puffy*, though."

My head snaps to Sierra so fast my neck twinges, disgust coloring my insides and marring my features. "*What?*"

She shrugs. "I'm just saying. Probably just water weight. Whatever the case, we need to do damage control. There's good ways to keep your name in the headlines, and then there's bad ways, and a nineteen-year-old girl knocked up by a mechanic…" She side-eyes me. "Is not a *good* way."

Blakely curls in on herself, and irritation burns in my gut as I watch the strong woman I've been inspired by disappearing. My jaw tightens as I try to keep my temper in check.

"The headline doesn't even mention me," I say through gritted teeth.

"They didn't have to," Sierra snaps. Her gaze jumps back to Blakely. "I'm gonna go talk to the photographer, make sure we're getting the right angles. We can nip this in the bud, but we'll need to make sure there's *no* room for debate the next few months."

Blakely nods, a flash of pain bolting across her eyes as she watches Sierra walk away.

I walk closer, reaching to cup her face. "Blake, don't listen to that bullshit."

Her arm comes up, batting my hand away as she backs up, sucking in a gasp. "What are you doing? Don't *touch* me while they're here."

My heart falters, twisting until it stings.

Blakely's gaze darts behind me, no doubt searching to make sure no one saw my mistake.

My jaw clenches. "I just want to make sure you're okay."

She clears her throat, tossing her hair behind her shoulders and straightening her spine. "I'm fine, Jackson." She smiles. "Honestly, this is *normal.* And she's not wrong. I've been spending so much time with you lately that I've let other things go. It's my own fault."

Her words have jagged edges and they prick at my skin.

I open my mouth to respond, but she walks away before

I can, joining Sierra and the photographer on the other side of the pool as they lean over his computer.

I'm left with a bitter taste in my mouth and a sour feeling in my gut. If I don't give myself some space, I'll say something I regret.

So, I leave.

And as I drive away, I wonder if she even noticed I was gone.

31

BLAKELY

I watch him as he walks away, my heart throbbing like a pulled muscle, straining to chase after him. But I don't, because now more than ever I want to keep him far away from the shadows of celebrity.

A whisper of a thought trickles down my spine, wondering why I'm so focused on attaining something that I'd do anything to save someone else from.

But that revelation is something I don't have time for, so I push it down. Bury it underneath the goals I've had for years and move along like it was never there to begin with.

I make it through the rest of the afternoon, filming video content for the new platform, and enough branded shoots for the next two weeks. But my heart isn't in it. It's stuck to the tiled pavers where I smacked Jackson's hand and walked away.

My stomach clenches at the memory.

He'll understand. Even as I think it, images of him ruminating over why he was wasting his time on me sends anxiety drizzling through my insides, my brain a muddled mess of "what-if" scenarios.

It makes me jittery and that combined with the pregnancy rumor has me aching for solitude. For a treadmill, or a set of weights. *Something* that will let the heavy twinge of angst seep from my pores and purge from my system until I can't feel the weight bearing down.

My lungs squeeze tighter with every minute and there's tiny cuts in my palms from where I've been relentlessly clenching my fists, but I survive the next few hours until finally, everyone leaves.

I don't waste a single second, flying up the stairs and grabbing my workout gear, desperation acting like sails to my ship, steering me toward salvation. Glancing quickly at my phone, I ignore the way my heart pinches at the blank screen.

No new messages.

Three hours and a shower later, I expect to feel refreshed, but instead I feel the same. I can't remember a time when working out didn't alleviate the bruising grip on my insides, and the fact that it's still there causes panic to spread through my chest.

My eyes bounce from my reflection in the mirror to the pink measuring tape I grabbed off the bathroom shelf.

Over and over again I look, my fingers tightening around the edge of the counter until they ache.

Pregnant. They think I'm fucking pregnant.

Logically, I know they're grasping at straws. Spinning lies into a web of drama, anchoring it on the edges of small truths to make it believable. It's the entire reason Sierra wanted Jax around in the first place. Not *too* close, but close enough to garner interest. I guess she didn't expect it to spiral out of our control—have them run a story we weren't expecting. Worse, one we didn't help craft.

I should be used to it by now. This isn't the first or the last time that my name will be caught up in "bad" publicity. I learned quickly to put up a shield—to not even glance at comments in articles.

I've told myself it doesn't matter what they say. After all, they'll never be as good as I am at tearing me down.

But the truth is their hate hurts. Like a thousand needles slowly bloodletting my body, draining my life source and replacing it with their toxic words.

Sometimes, I think it slices deeper when a stranger throws the barbs.

And when you have a vulnerability, even something rooted in falsity hits the mark. It dives deep and suctions to your insecurities, dragging them to the surface until they're all you can see.

You have been looking a little puffy lately.

The fist that's been clamping my chest grips tighter and I spiral down until I can't see the truth from the lie. The logic from the crippling self-doubt.

Bile teases the back of my throat, nausea churning in my gut as my fingers wrap around the measuring tape, the cloth biting into my fingers as I squeeze it tight.

Panic fills my lungs until I'm gasping for air, the thought of seeing numbers I don't like making me wish I could crawl inside myself and wither away until I'm nothing.

Pathetic.

Suddenly, even though I've just finished an extensive three-hour workout, the need to burn more fat gushes through my veins. My entire body collapses in on itself with the urge to atone for my mistakes. To work harder so I can prove to everyone that they're wrong.

So they never see anything other than what I want them to again.

Stupid, Blakely.

I must be a masochist because there's no other logical explanation for why I grab my phone from the counter and search my name. I know it's a stupid mistake, but like everything else in my life, once I start the spiral, there's no coming back.

Clicking on the first headline I see, I scroll straight to the comments, a burning anticipation swelling in my middle.

Always knew she was a slut.

That bitch ain't pregnant. She's just F-A-T.

Photoshop does her ALL the favors.

Faintly, I hear a muffled voice from somewhere in the house, but I'm too lost in the depth of my self-loathing for it to register.

"Blake?"

F-A-T.

My phone clatters to the heated marble floor and I sink down beside it, the measuring tape still wrapped around my hand. My brain slams against the edges of my memory, trying to remember every single calorie that's passed my lips. Every hour of cardio and weights that I've endured, trying to figure out where I started letting things slip.

There must be something I forgot to write down, something that isn't marked in my daily intake list. Something that would cause me to look so... *puffy*.

My eyes lock on to the glass door of the shower.

"Blake?"

I hear the voice again, but my gaze is stuck, picking out every single imperfection through the distorted reflection.

"Blakely, I..." The voice trails off, footsteps barreling toward me until suddenly, a spicy scent rushes through my nostrils, making my head snap to the side.

Jackson.

My chest compresses until an explosion of grief swells through my throat, stinging my eyelids and burning a path down my face.

"Oh, baby, what's wrong?" His big palms cradle my jaw and I sink into his embrace, my hands clawing at his shirt, suddenly desperate for his comfort.

Like now that he's here, I can finally let go.

My stomach clenches tight as he drags me into his lap, my head resting on his chest while his arms wrap around me. My body trembles with the sobs that wrack through me, staining his white shirt.

His hold is a vice grip around my waist, plastering me to him as he rocks us back and forth.

And that's where we stay. For minutes.

For hours.

My limbs grow lighter and eventually the tears turn to sniffles and then to an occasional hiccup of breath—the last sign that my body isn't under my control.

The purge of emotion is what I needed, the claw that's been cutting into my lungs finally relieving its grasp. The panic has disappeared in the calm of Jackson's arms, but there's still an echo of sadness that reverberates off my insides.

Jackson's hand brushes down my hair. "Is this about the headline?"

My fingers tangle in the chain around his neck as he cradles me and I start to shake my head, but stop before I do. Saying no is a lie. And I don't want to lie to him. "I just... I work *so* hard and it's never enough, you know?"

He hums, the vibration of his voice like a blanket coasting across my skin.

I look at him, craning my neck to swipe a kiss across his jaw, gratitude filling me from the inside out. "Thank you. I don't know why you're back, but... *thank you.*"

He stays silent, the soothing touch of his hand in my hair urging me to curl deeper into his embrace.

"Come on," he whispers, dragging my body up with him to a standing position.

Twisting our fingers together, he leads us into my bedroom. I follow, my eyes stuck on where our palms connect, my heart accelerating in my chest.

He walks us over to my silver floor-length mirror, pulling me until I'm standing in front of him, his hands resting on the curve of my waist.

I cringe as I stare at my reflection, my stomach twisting at how ridiculous I look, dressed in my pink silk camisole and shorts, bloodshot and swollen eyes, my hair tangled from my earlier panic.

My gaze shoots to Jackson's and my heart skips. The difference in our facial expressions is extreme. I'm disgusted and he's drinking me in like I'm water in the middle of a desert.

Tension mixes into the air.

"What are you doing?" My voice cuts through the quiet, sending a tremor down my spine.

His eyes stay locked on mine, his mouth dipping down to the shell of my ear. "Do you know what I love about you?"

I suck in a breath. "I don't—"

"No?" he interrupts. "Let me show you."

His hands drift up my sides, goose bumps leaving a trail behind them. His palm reaches my face and he cups my jaw.

"I love your mouth." His thumb brushes over my lips, his touch lingering until I'm sure he can feel the heat of my skin blooming underneath his fingers. "Every time you speak, the world quiets so I can listen."

My stomach tightens.

His hand moves down, tracing along my neck, his touch branding me with every pass.

Emotion swells in my chest and I squeeze my eyes closed. His hand wraps lightly around my throat and my gaze springs open, a flare of desire curling through my insides at the dominance in his position.

"I love your eyes," he continues. "The way they show me all your truths. No one has ever consumed me with a single look, but you..." He blows out a breath. "You fucking *wreck* me."

I swallow and his grip tightens, making heat pulse between my legs.

What is happening?

His hand slides slowly from my throat, tracing along the edges of my collarbone. My core contracts.

He continues his trek down my arms until his fingers reach mine, twining them together and wrapping them around the front of my waist.

"I love your hands. The way they fit so goddamn perfectly in mine." His fingers weave back and forth between mine, tingles racing up my arms.

My knees grow weak from his perusal and I press

further into him until the back of my head rests against his chest.

He brings up my right hand and I watch our reflection, drunk off the sight of him as he kisses the inside of my wrist, his breath hot against my skin.

My heart pounds against my ribs, anticipation careening off my insides as his palms leave mine, gliding back up until they reach my shoulders.

He squeezes slightly, sending shockwaves of pleasure rolling through me. "I love your shoulders. The way they hold the world, but don't buckle from the weight."

I scoff, my vision blurring. "All I do is buckle."

His head shakes. "Falling down doesn't mean you break, Blake."

My throat swells at his words, tears escaping the corner of my eyes.

"Your strength is when you rise back up," he continues.

Jackson's fingers play along the spaghetti straps of my camisole. My nipples pebble underneath the fabric, heat spiking through my middle and pooling deep in my core. It's surprising how fast it hits considering the seriousness of the moment, but there's a power in his touch that makes me feel more desired—more beautiful—than I ever have in my life.

It's heady.

Alluring.

And I find myself wanting to bathe in the temporary confidence he's dripping onto my skin.

His hand ghosts down until it rests on my chest, the edges of his fingertips teasing the neckline of my top. My stomach tenses, my heart pounding under his palm.

His lips ghost along my ear, his free hand gripping my hip and pulling me tighter against him.

"I love your heart," he whispers. "I would spend the rest of my life *worshiping* at your feet, so long as I got to experience every beat."

My body coils tighter and I wait with bated breath to see what he'll say next. How he'll take the years of bloody wounds and replace them with his words, one scar at a time.

His eyes meet mine.

My breath whooshes out of me, my heart surging into my throat at the intensity that's swirling in his gaze.

His hand presses harder against my chest. "Your worth has nothing to do with how you look, Blake. It has to do with who you are. *That's* what makes you beautiful."

Tears drip off my chin and suddenly, the words of strangers don't seem to matter as much. Maybe they will again tomorrow, when the high of Jackson's touch has slipped off my skin.

But right now, the only thing that matters is this.

Right here, with him.

A single word tumbles through my brain, pushing its way into the middle of my chest and slipping into the fissures of my heart.

Love.

32

JACKSON

I hadn't planned on coming back. Talked myself out of it a thousand times, listed off all the reasons why it was a bad idea. But I couldn't get the vision of her crumbling out of my head. Of watching her try like hell to hold it together while nobody else gave a damn.

And once it was there, I knew the only way to find some peace was to make sure things were right between us. So that I can be the person in her corner, propping her up and giving support, even when she swears she doesn't need it.

Still, I waited until my feelings settled into something that was less hurt and more understanding. Besides, I wanted to give everyone else time to leave. We need to be alone for the things I want to talk about.

I pride myself on being able to read people easily, but Blakely has me second-guessing everything I thought I knew. She's a master of deception, having fine-tuned her persona, threading it so tightly with who she really is that it's almost indistinguishable.

Almost.

I know it's unhealthy to be happy with the fact I'm the only one she shows her realness to. But it's there, warming my insides whether I want it or not. I *like* being the one she runs to. I *like* being the one who loosens her stitching and lets the mask fall away.

But the problem is that the longer she wears the cloak, the more it sinks into her skin. Mixes with who she is and darkens her soul until she believes her own lies. Until she believes *theirs.*

My heart feels heavy thinking of all the effort she puts into appeasing the masses. Of obtaining this ridiculous standard of beauty—of life—all so other people will envy something that doesn't exist.

And maybe that's why, when I find her sobbing on the marble bathroom floor, there's an overwhelming need raging through me to show her all the ways she's truly beautiful.

The ways that can't be shown with numbers, or products, or edited pictures.

My hands glide down her body, pointing out all the ways her soul shines through her skin, and as I do, the air charges with an electric hum, weaving its way between us, injecting the moment with a thick tension.

I feel her body relax more with every pass of my palm, and when I pause on her stomach, she twists in my arms, her eyes clashing with mine. There are a few moments of silence, her amber gaze sparkling with a watery sheen as she looks at me in a way no one else ever has.

My heart beats with fervor, ramming into my chest.

Her arms slide along my shoulders until her fingers tangle in the hair on the nape of my neck. My hands tighten around her waist, waiting for her to make the next move. It *has* to be her.

She rises on her tiptoes, pulling me in, her lips grazing against mine.

"Kiss me," she breathes.

Our mouths collide in an explosion of heat. Groaning, I sink in deeper, my tongue tangling with hers, my fingers gripping her tight and dragging her into me.

My cock hardens when she presses her hips into mine, moaning as she grinds herself against my length.

Months of pent-up tension collects at the base of my spine, begging for release. My intention wasn't for this to happen, but I can't help how my body responds when I touch her.

I thrust against her and she gasps, allowing me to dive in deeper until I can't tell where she ends and I begin. I've never been a big kisser, but the intimacy of our lips melding together has desire twisting my insides and wringing them tight. Her mouth is the sweetest ambrosia coating my tongue.

Goddamn, she tastes delicious.

A groan rips from my throat when she palms my cock through my jeans, making it jerk against her, desperate for more friction.

"Blake," I rasp, forcing myself to break away from her lips. "Wait, we should—"

She shakes her head, her fingers tightening around me.

My eyes flutter from the sensation of having her grip me, even through my clothes, and precum bubbles at the tip, wetting the fabric of my boxers.

I've never gone this long without sex, and while I don't miss the random hookups, my body misses the feel of someone else against it.

"I don't want to wait, Jackson. *Please.*" She surges back up and meets my mouth.

My hands tighten, bunching up the silk fabric at her waist. "You wanted to take things slow," I force out.

"We have been. If we go any slower, I'll die," she responds, her hand rubbing up and down the length of me. "I want *you*."

I walk us backward, her lips never leaving mine, until my knees hit the edge of her bed. I fall to the mattress, her pussy bumping against my hips, making blood rush to my groin, my cock pulsing against my zipper.

"I saw this thing online." Her cheeks heat when she says it, and then she sits on top of me, her chest heaving, lips puffy and red. "When I'm with you I get this… fuzzy feeling."

"Fuzzy?"

"Yeah." Her hips move back and forth over my growing erection, grinding slowly. I imagine her clit swelling with every pass over my dick and my eyes roll from the image.

"It said it's something called subspace."

I freeze. *What?*

"I don't want you to be like… a dom or anything. But I think—" She bites her lip. "When I'm with you like this—when you take control. I like it. It relaxes my brain."

My hands trail along her arms, fingers slipping under the straps of her tank top until they fall, her dusty pink nipples pebbling when her breasts hit the cool air.

My mouth waters, stomach flipping at the view, and I trace along her skin until I'm cupping them in my palms.

Her hand reaches between us, the buckle of my belt clanking as she clumsily undoes it. She raises her hips off me and I move to grab them, a protest on the tip of my tongue, but the words die when her chest dangles in my face. I lean up, sucking a nipple into my mouth and I groan, my dick jumping at her taste on my tongue.

She jerks, her hands stopping their task and grabbing my head to press me further into her. My hands fumble as I rip my jeans down my thighs and kick them onto the ground.

My palms wrap around her waist and I sit up to get closer, my tongue still twirling around her breast, my teeth biting down lightly. She moans, her back arching, the chocolate strands of her hair tickling my hand.

Her hips continue working against me and heat coils low in my gut as I thrust between her silk-covered pussy lips. My mouth breaks away from her hardened nipples so I can tear my shirt off, desperate to feel her skin on mine.

The pressure that's winding through my body tightens like a screw and my abs contort, desperate to sink deep inside her and feel her come apart around me.

But a bit of sense sneaks through when I notice her face is drawn tight, eyes squeezed shut—like she's concentrating.

Even in this moment, she's focused on the control.

She wants me to take it.

Leaning forward, I connect our lips. My hand tightens around her waist, the other cupping the back of her neck, and I flip us, her body bouncing on the mattress.

I hover above her, my eyes drinking her in from our new position, soaking up every inch of her body. The longer I look, the more she fidgets, until her arms move to wrap around her stomach. She turns her head, pink creeping along her cheeks.

Sliding my hands down her body until my fingers entwine with hers, I raise her arms above her head. "Don't hide yourself from me. Let me see you."

Shifting our position, I place both of her palms together, wrapping my fingers tightly around her wrists, gliding my free hand down until it rests at the base of her throat. "Do you trust me?"

"Yes," she whispers.

Her chest brushes against me with every exhale. My dog tags dangle on top of her and I watch her face closely as I thrust my hips against her center.

Her eyes roll, teeth sinking into her lower lip, and I swear to God, in this moment, she's the most erotic thing I've ever seen.

I kiss my way down her body, touching every spot I showed her in the mirror, then doubling back and covering anywhere I may have missed.

Easing my grip on her wrists, I take the shirt bunched around her hips and move it down her thighs until she's left in nothing but her small, pink shorts.

I graze my lips along the hem and then move lower, my heart beating in time to the throbbing of my cock, mouth salivating at the anticipation of having her explode on my tongue.

My thumb presses against her through her shorts, my balls tightening when I feel how damp the silk is.

Fuck.

I lean in, sucking the fabric into my mouth.

She jerks.

My eyes glance up at her, my thumb replacing my

mouth and circling over her clit, her legs trembling around me. "Has anyone ever kissed you here?"

She shakes her head. "No."

Lust floods my system. There's something so primal about the possessiveness that overtakes me, knowing I'm the only man to have the pleasure of being with her like this. Of touching her. Tasting her. *Fucking* her.

My fingers wrap around her shorts and tug, pulling them down her thighs, following their path with my mouth, until I've covered the length of her legs with my lips.

She rises on her elbows, staring down at me with wide eyes and a flushed face.

My palm glides up her thigh, over her stomach until I reach her chest, pushing her back to a lying position. Her legs drop open and my cock stiffens more at the view. I press my hips into the mattress to try and relieve the ache.

Her pussy is perfection, glistening with the arousal *I* caused, I lean in, blowing slightly just to see her reaction.

She gasps and my stomach clenches at how responsive she is.

I bury my face between her thighs, my tongue lapping at her juices and sucking her clit into my mouth.

Goddamn.

The second her taste hits me, I'm lost. Drowning in every whimper, every tense of her muscles, the way she tugs on my hair while she gasps out my name.

I tease her entrance with my fingers, spreading her wetness around and feeling her pussy spasm, her legs pressing in around my head.

"Oh my *god*, Jackson, I think I might..." She trails off, throwing her arm over her face.

My eyes stay locked on her through it all, needing to see

the moment she comes apart under someone else's touch. Under *my* touch. Her tits rise and fall with her heavy breaths and her legs tighten and shake, until suddenly, the world stills.

Her thighs clamp tight around my head and her fingers rip at my hair, making my dick jerk so hard I'm afraid I'll come. A breathy moan spills from her perfect *fucking* lips and her back arches off the bed.

Her body shivers as she comes down and I kiss and suck all the way through it, not stopping until she pushes me away.

"Jackson, *stop*, it's so sensitive." She laughs.

I grin, crawling up her body, warmth billowing through my insides and blanketing every part of me.

It's never felt like this.

Her smile softens as I stare, her hand cupping my jaw. "What are you doing?"

"Memorizing this moment."

She swallows, her throat bobbing with the motion. "Oh."

Her fingers wrap around my necklace, dragging my face down to hers, moaning into my mouth as she tastes herself.

My body drops down, my cock pulsing. I press into her, my eyes rolling as her hips push against me, and as much as I want to strip off my boxers and sink deep inside of her—claim her for myself—I don't.

That's not what this is about, and I don't want her to look back on her first time and have it tainted by the day. By the ridiculous headlines, or how I found her crying on the floor.

I pull back, slowing down our kiss until I can move away.

"I'll be right back," I whisper.

She protests, but I just smile and stand, walking to her bathroom so I can grab a towel to clean her up.

I'm about to head back out when something catches my eye. It's a clipboard, hanging above a scale. I didn't notice it earlier because I was so focused on Blakely sprawled across the floor, but now curiosity pushes my legs forward until I'm scanning all the pages.

And when I do, my chest splits open, heart filling with lead and sinking into my stomach.

There are *extensive* notes.

Daily caloric intake. Daily caloric burn. Measurements. Morning, afternoon, and nighttime weigh-ins.

Suddenly, the conversation from earlier flows through my mind, and the aftermath I walked in on clicks into place.

All the times she's been *obsessively* watching her food.

The three-hour workouts I've witnessed.

This is so much more than a simple overreaction, or a panic attack from a headline she didn't like.

Why has no one confronted her about this?

Walking back out of the room a heaviness weighs down my shoulders and I rack my brain trying to think of the best way to address the situation.

I can't, in good conscience, just ignore what I've seen.

But all my thoughts pause when I make it to the bed, gazing down at a sleeping Blakely. My heart stalls.

I lay the towel down on the nearest chair, sinking into the bed behind her and pulling her into my chest, ignoring the sadness that's swirling in my gut and reaching up to squeeze my lungs.

I'm not sure what it is that she's going through, but I vow to myself that she won't have to go through it alone.

Not anymore.

33

BLAKELY

When I wake up in the morning, he's gone.

I panic for a few seconds, thinking it was either a dream or that he decided I wasn't worth it, until I roll to my side and see a note left on my nightstand. Smiling to myself, I reach out and pick it up, a giddiness dancing through me.

The paper crinkles in my hand as I roll onto my back and read it.

Princess,

Left early so no one would see and didn't want to wake you. Can I see you tonight?

-Jax

My arms and legs smack against the bed as I squeal, happier than I can remember being in a long time.

But the happiness never lasts.

Slowly, the reality of my situation knits its way through the joy, reminding me of all the ways my world is twisted upside down.

Ugh.

Glancing at the clock, I spring from the bed, irritation pricking under my skin from oversleeping. I rush through my morning routine, cursing myself because I know that this is going to throw off my entire day. But there are some things I just can't skip over, and as my eyes bounce from the scale to the measuring tape that's still laying haphazardly on the floor dread stomps my chest like a stampede, the comments from the day before clouding my mind.

It's fine. I just need to work harder.

My insecurities dangle from the gaping hole in my stomach, but I grip the measuring tape in my hand and take a deep breath, preparing myself to get through it.

I already know the numbers have fluctuated.

Of course they have, you idiot.

Sierra's words ring through my head, and even though she said them in passing, they stick to my bones and curdle my insides.

Puffy.

I don't think I've ever hated a word so much.

Rushing through the measurements and trying not to compare them to the other numbers on my wall, I slip into my workout gear and head downstairs to grab a water bottle and get in some fasted cardio.

The smell of fresh-brewed coffee makes me stop short.

Who the hell would be here, drinking coffee?

My stomach tightens and I cautiously place one foot in front of the other until I'm standing in the entryway to our gourmet kitchen.

The breath is sucker punched from my lungs as I take in the sight of my father sitting in the breakfast nook, a cup of coffee on the table and a newspaper covering his face.

I clear my throat, my heart stuttering as I make my way further into the room. Heading to the fridge to grab my water, my eyes trail back to him every few seconds.

The noise must catch his attention because the top right corner of the paper flops down, his dark chocolate eyes gazing at me from across the island.

"Hey, honey."

I swallow, his voice sucking me into my memories. To a time when hearing him speak in the mornings was commonplace—something that happened every week. Then every weekend. Until eventually it whittled down to nothing, and that became our new normal.

Seeing him here now is jarring.

My head cocks as I take him in, wondering what the cause of his sudden appearance is. I already know it isn't me.

It's never me.

"Hi," I murmur, opening up the fridge so I don't have to meet his eyes. "What are you doing here?"

"I live here." His tone is light. Teasing. But try as I might, I can't find it in me to match his amusement.

"You sure about that?" I huff under my breath.

"What was that?" he asks.

I spin from the fridge, gripping the water bottle tight in my hand. "Nothing." I shake my head, forcing a smile on my face. "It's just nice to see you is all."

His eyes light up with his grin and my chest pulls tight. It's so rare to see it, I had almost forgotten it existed.

He places the newspaper down, picking up his mug and sipping. "I thought we could spend the day together."

His request pierces through my skin, squeezing my heart until it's numb to the bruising.

My teeth sink into my lower lip and gnaw, my mind like a seesaw as I weigh the pros and cons, resisting the urge to cancel everything that's on my schedule just to appease him. But then I remember that he's never done the same for me and resentment billows inside of me, wondering why, in a world where money is limitless and everyone knows my name, I can't make my father love me enough to put me first.

My jaw tics and I straighten. "Oh, sorry. I can't today."

His smile drops, a melancholy shadow swirling through the chocolate of his eyes. A sting finds its way to the center of my chest, but I bat it away, letting his voice from the other day play through my head, reminding me of all the ways he thinks I'm up for *lease*.

He frowns. "Can't rearrange your schedule, just this once?"

My brows shoot to my hairline. The irony in his question is rich and it tastes a lot like hypocrisy. How many times have I asked him to rearrange his work schedule for me, and how many times has he actually *done* it?

"Sorry, nope. I know you don't consider what I do work, but it is, and I can't just cancel things. Especially since I'm spending most of my time at Donahue Motors, working for *you*."

He sighs, pinching the bridge of his nose. "That's for your own good."

I cross my arms. "And suddenly you're an expert on what's good for me?"

Hurt flashes across his face and it makes my stomach tighten. I squeeze the water bottle in my hand to keep from apologizing.

"First of all, cut the attitude." His eyes narrow and anger spikes through my stomach. "Secondly, I just don't want to see all of your wasted potential thrown away. You need direction, and I can give you that."

I need a father.

It's on the tip of my tongue, but instead of letting it out, I gulp around the words, my eyes watering from the sting as they drop back down and settle in my chest.

"Look, Dad." I sigh. "The only wasted potential here is our relationship." I glance away as I say it, not wanting to see whether my jab will hit its mark, or worse, if he'll seem unfazed.

"That's not fair."

"Isn't it?" I shoot back. A knot of emotion surges through my throat and teases the back of my eyelids. "You know what's not fair? That I'm doing what you ask. I'm *always* doing what you ask. I've given up my own dreams to placate your wish that I sit behind a reception desk and do absolutely nothing. You want to talk about wasted potential? Let's start there."

My chest heaves as I suck in a deep breath, my free hand clenching into a fist at my side.

One. Two. Three.

His forehead creases. "Let's talk about it, then. What's your dream, Blakely?"

His question catches me off guard, my hand reaching up to rub at the sudden ache in my chest. "It's..."

A pit opens in the center of my stomach when the

words don't come. My rehearsed lines, my goals from the past few years, suddenly none of it seems concrete. Not the way it used to be. Now... now I just feel like I'm wading in murky water, trying like hell to find solid ground.

My spine stiffens and I stick out my chin. "If you don't know that by now then I don't know what to tell you."

My heart squeezes tight when his eyes droop.

"Look," I continue. "I told you I'd do it, but I wish you'd realize I don't *have* to. I make my own money." I smack my chest. "I make my own way."

Desperation oozes out with every breath, willing him to notice all the hard work I put in. How much effort it takes for me to be seen.

He shakes his head. "I'm talking about a *sustainable* career path, Blakely. Not a celebrity flash in the pan." His finger jams into his newspaper. "You think they'll care about you in five years? You think they care about you *now*?"

My throat swells. "Yeah, well... at least they remember I exist."

His jaw snaps shut, the muscle working tight as he stares at me.

I turn around quickly, walking away before he can see the heartbreak he causes sliding down my face.

He doesn't deserve my tears.

34

JACKSON

I don't see Blakely the rest of the weekend, even though she's all I can think about. As usual, her schedule's booked—appearances with her friends, nights on the town, and photo shoots making it impossible for us to sneak away.

Normally I'd tag along and fulfill my "babysitting" duties, but it feels wrong to do her father's bidding when I've had her cum on my tongue.

So instead, my weekend is spent resisting the urge to check her social media just so I can see her and trying to convince my mom to come to California for the holidays.

I don't want to go back to Sugarlake.

Not yet.

Although, the thought doesn't sting like it used to. Lately, I've even found myself nostalgic over the memories, missing the small town and everything in it. Longing for my friends, instead of living in solitude, save for a nineteen-year-old who I'm breaking all the rules for.

It's these thoughts that fill me with hope. With the inner knowing that even if I'm not ready yet, that one day soon I will be.

With Blakely at my side.

A lightness sweeps through my body when I wake up on Monday morning and head into Donahue Motors. For the first time in almost a year, I feel like myself again. My smiles are genuine, not used as a cover for the festering hole inside of me.

I'd like to think it's because I'm healing myself, but that's not entirely the truth.

It's because of Blakely.

It's a dangerous game I'm playing and the logical side of me knows I should put a stop to it. I started bonding with her out of a need for distraction, and if I think on the situation for too long a sense of codependency prods at my fractures—the glue holding my pieces together entirely dependent on Blakely making them stick. I wonder if it's the same for her.

But there's no guarantee we even have tomorrow, so I might as well live for today.

I tinker around with my toolbox, my eyes floating toward the glass doors every few seconds, waiting to see her. But she doesn't show up, and I can only procrastinate work for so long, so eventually I give in and start my day, my excitement twisting into an ache with every passing minute.

I'm beneath the hood of a Cobra when I hear the telltale smack of shoes on the concrete floor. My body thrums with anticipation and I know without even looking that it's Blakely. I can feel the shift in the air, the one that's *always* been there between us. The one I mistook for annoyance, when really, it was my soul scratching at my skin, reaching out to try and touch hers.

I haven't felt like this in... ever.

With Lee, there was always a sense of calm. A warm blanket on a chilly night. One that sends comfort cascading over your skin and warms up your insides.

With Blakely, it's a torrential downpour, making me desperate to cling to everything she is, terrified I'll drown in her absence.

And if this type of feeling is possible, if *this* is how Lee feels for Chase, can I really fault her for her choices?

Something untangles from my chest and floats away at the realization.

"There's a package here for a Mister Jackson Rhoades."

My heart skips at Blakely's voice, a smile spreading across my face. I slide out from under the Cobra, my body shifting into high gear when she comes into focus.

My eyes drink in every inch of her.

"And what a pretty package she is." I wiggle my brows.

She giggles and strikes a pose.

I stand up, needing to wash the grease from my arms, but pause when I'm about to pass by her.

"Hi." I smile.

"Hi yourself." She grins back.

The need to reach out and touch her tightens my stomach. "I wanted to—"

"How are you—" We speak at the same time and her cheeks redden as she brushes a strand of hair behind her ear.

Clearing her throat, she tries again. "You should get over here and say hi to me properly."

I hold out my oil-stained hands. "You don't want me touching you right now, princess. *Trust.*"

"Oh." Her eyes scan my arms and then glance behind her, peering into the main building.

And then she's on me.

Her hands grip my neck, her legs wrapping around my waist as she climbs up my body. My arms shoot out to the side, not wanting to get grease stains on her clothes. It doesn't deter her, she grips me like a vise, her mouth peppering kisses all over my face, before locking our lips together like two perfect pieces of a puzzle.

My stomach lights up like rockets, sparks flying through me. Blood rushes to my groin and I bite back a moan. "Wait." I break away. "Someone could see."

She slides down my body, straightening her outfit and glancing behind her again. "You're right. I just missed you is all."

My heart thunks against my chest. "Did you?"

She smiles wide. "Duh. Plus, I never got to say goodbye and it... it felt weird after—you know."

My mouth waters at the memory of her taste. "Do I?" My brow quirks. "You'll have to refresh my memory."

"Jackson, be serious," she admonishes, her lips twitching.

Laughing, I walk over to the sink, scrubbing the oil from my forearms. "So, where's the package?"

"Oh, I set it on the table over there." She points to the rows of inventory sitting on floor-to-ceiling metal shelves. The perfect place to hide in plain view.

I dry off my arms and grab her hand. "You'll have to show me where."

I weave us through the parts until we hit the shadows, gripping her hips, lifting her up and settling her on top of the table. She gasps, her arms wrapping around my neck as I press myself between her legs. My fingers grip her jaw, forcing her eyes to stay on me. To make sure that *she* stays with me.

"Now I can say hi properly." Leaning in, I capture her lips with mine, my body buzzing from the high of having her in my arms. From the rush of knowing that anyone could come in and catch us. The excitement of doing something so risky makes my cock grow until it's aching for release.

One of my hands wraps around the back of her head, my fingers tangling in the strands of her hair as I thrust my hips, sliding my hardness against her.

She leans back, her mouth parted like an invitation. "Oh my god, Jackson."

My palm moves from her jaw and covers her mouth, pressing firmly as her back bows. "Shh. Quiet."

I lean in, trailing kisses along her jaw and down her throat, forcing her further back until she's flat against the table. "Fuck," I rasp against her skin. "You drive me *crazy*."

My abs tense when her hands graze my stomach, her hips rotating against me. Her palm presses against my erection, stroking me from root to tip through the fabric. My balls tighten and I bite the inside of my cheek to keep from groaning.

"Does that feel okay?" she whispers.

Her question grips onto the little bit of logic I have left and draws it to the surface. Every single cell in my body begs for me to ignore it, but instead, I reluctantly pull away.

My hand releases her hair and reaches down, wrapping around her wrist, stopping her movements.

It's so easy to forget her age. Her inexperience.

"Was I doing something wrong?" she asks, her eyes glancing down to where she's gripping me.

It takes literally *all* of my willpower not to thrust into her palm.

I lean my forehead against hers. "No, baby, I just need a minute, or I'll fuck you on this table."

She smirks. "And?"

My thumb traces down her cheek. "And you deserve more than that."

She sighs. "I can decide what I deserve, Jackson."

"I want to take my time with you." I press my lips to hers and she pushes into me, her tongue licking along the seam of my mouth.

My heart revs and I sink back into her, my grip on her wrist growing lax.

A door slams in the distance and I jump back, my stomach shooting to my throat. Running my hand over my head, my heart rams against my ribs, praying like hell it isn't her dad.

Blakely smiles and winks, righting her shirt and running her thumb along her bottom lip. She slides off the table, and at first glance, it looks like she doesn't have a care in the world. But look a little closer and it's easy to see the tensing of her shoulders and the stiffening of her jaw. The way her hands curl into fists at her sides.

She saunters away and I'm lost, staring after her, adjusting my hard-on and willing it away. My throat is parched, already dehydrated from the loss of her around me.

I start to follow but pause when I hear her voice cut through the air.

"Hey, Karen," she chirps.

My heart stops, Karen watching us the other week flashing through my mind and nausea creeps through my gut, wondering if she's suspicious.

"Miss Donahue, the phone was ringing off the hook and I was getting worried when you didn't come back quickly."

I watch from the shadows as Karen's eyes scan the garage, pressing myself further into the shelving to hide from her view.

"Karen, how many times do I have to tell you to call me Blakely?"

"As long as it takes for you to realize you're wasting your breath," she snaps back.

My stomach sours at Karen's tone.

Has she always been so cold toward Blakely?

I rack my brain, trying to remember other times I've seen them interact, but come up short. In fact, I don't know that I've seen *anyone* in the building give Blakely so much as a smile. My chest twists, regret slicing through me at all the times I was a dick to her, when what she really needed was a friend.

"I'm dropping off the package for Jackson, just like you asked me to, Karen. What's it *look* like I'm doing?" Blakely's voice is sugary sweet, her head tilting with her question.

And that's my cue.

Walking out into the open, I paste a grin on my face. Karen's always been a sucker for the smile. "Hey Kare-bear."

Blakely and Karen both turn toward me.

I force myself to keep my gaze on Karen and lean

against my toolbox. "How come you've been sending someone else to drop off my packages?" I pout.

Karen's cheeks heat, the way they always do when I turn on the charm. My shoulders relax, anxiety loosening its hold around my stomach.

"There's not enough hours in the day, I'm afraid." She smiles but her eyes cut to Blakely. "I can't be the one doing everything around here."

I press a hand to my chest. "I thought *I* was your favorite part of the day."

Karen huffs out a laugh and wags her finger. "Oh, no Jax. *You*, I need to handle in small doses."

I heave a sigh. "Well... I won't lie and say I'm not wounded."

Blakely rolls her eyes.

Karen's smile grows. "This is exactly why. You're incorrigible."

"I think you mean lovable." I wink.

"Well... that too." She grins and turns toward Blakely. "Come on, Miss Donahue, let's allow Jax to get back to work."

Blakely straightens her spine and nods, moving to follow Karen into the main building.

My legs jerk, urging me to go after her, but I force myself to stay in place as I watch her walk away. But then she pauses, her hand wrapped around the edge of the door, and she turns back to me, mouthing, "Tonight?"

I grin, blowing out a breath of relief and jerking my head in a short nod.

Tonight.

35

BLAKELY

Monday is my new favorite day.

After going this weekend without seeing Jax, I'm vibrating with excitement to get to Donahue Motors, just to be around him. Plus, Mondays are *mine.* The one night I've negotiated with Sierra into having all to myself. No putting on a show. No doing or being anything. Just me, my sweats, and a movie, staying as far away from social media as possible.

Because in reality, I don't really enjoy it.

I've never told a soul that, and I don't think I ever will. Even thinking it feels like I'm spitting in the face of the very platforms that have made my career. Social media is the reason why I've been able to avoid being known as just another socialite, with a fat bank and a strong last name.

But Mondays are for me.

And now they're for me and Jackson.

Originally, I was planning on having him over to my place. It's easier that way, no one is ever around, and I don't have to involve Lennox in my secrets. But my father has suddenly decided to be a homebody, and while I'm sure it won't last, I don't want to take the risk of him seeing Jackson. So that leaves me with two choices.

One: I can sneak out again.

Two: I can go to Lennox and plead for his silence. For his loyalty.

Both options make queasiness churn in my gut.

The nausea strengthens when I knock on Lennox's cottage at the back of our estate, my fingernails tearing into the palm of my hand.

The door swings open. "What?" he snaps.

I step back, shocked at his clipped tone. *What the hell?*

His eyes focus in on me and his face smooths, a blank mask dropping over the rage that was just pouring from his eyes.

"Hi." I smile.

He scans the area behind me before jerking his head, opening the door wider for me to walk inside.

I look around, noting the minimalism of everything, wondering why in the eight years that he's been with me, I've never seen his place. Never taken the time to get to know him beyond what he can do for me.

My eyes snag on brown shelves, housing what must be hundreds of books. My legs carry me over before I can think twice, my fingers ghosting across the titles.

I can't even remember the last time I *read* a book.

"Don't touch those." His voice is sharp.

My heart stutters as I spin around, raising my hands in the air. "Sorry, I was just curious is all."

His jaw tics while he stares me down, like he knows I'm not here to get to know him, but because I want something from him.

And as I stare back at him, a knot lodging itself in my throat, I realize maybe he's looking at me that way because he doesn't know to expect anything else.

Have I always been so blind to other people?

"What do you need?" he asks.

I swallow, suddenly feeling guilty over why I'm here—what I'm about to ask him. But seeing Jackson overwhelms my need to suddenly have a conscience about my shortcomings, so I breathe in deep and shoot my shot.

"I need a favor."

His brow lifts.

My stomach tightens, nerves skittering along my spine. "I have somewhere to be tonight, and I just... I'm trying to respect you and *not* sneak away again, but in order to do that, I need to know I'll have your discretion."

His arms cross over his chest, his eyes never moving from mine.

It's unnerving, the way he stands so still.

"No," he finally says.

My heart sinks. "No to the discretion? Or..."

"No to you going at all."

I scoff. "I wasn't asking your permission *to go*. I'm leaving with or without you."

His eyes flare.

It's an empty threat. I doubt I'd be able to escape from Lennox if I tried, but the way he's acting like a warden instead of a bodyguard has irritation snapping at my insides, the need to prove I'm independent wrapping around my chest and squeezing.

My life has never felt like a prison before.

Once again, my direction seems muddled, my compass spinning in circles.

Emotion swells behind my eyes, and even though I try to hold it back, a tear slips through the cracks, falling down my face.

Lennox sighs, his hands running over his face. "*Fine.* Just..." He pauses, walking closer until he's towering over me. "Promise me you're being safe."

I cringe, heat flooding my cheeks. "I promise."

He nods. "I'll take you there and wait in the car."

My lips purse. "Can you drop me off and come back when I call?"

His nostrils flare, his judgment searing into me.

Lennox isn't stupid, and it would be an insult to pretend that he is. He knows exactly where I want to go, and exactly who I want to be with. My breath sticks in my throat, hoping that he doesn't put up a fight.

He gives a short nod and relief pours through me, a smile lighting up my face as I throw my arms around him for a hug.

He stiffens, but it only makes me grip him tighter. "Thank you," I whisper.

He clears his throat, awkwardly patting my back, before he grips my shoulders and pushes me away. "Don't make me regret it, Blakely."

"I won't." I beam. "I'll be ready to go in half an hour."

Skipping out of his front door, I head back to my place, texting Jackson to let him know I'll be there soon. And that once I get there, I'm not leaving.

JACKSON MADE DINNER.

Of course he did.

A knot grows in my stomach, wondering why I didn't think of the fact that this is going to be an issue between us.

I push the food around on my plate, taking a bite here and there, my mind in turmoil over how to bring up the fact that if this is going to work with us, he needs to take my lifestyle choices seriously. That means stick to my prepped meals or having me pre-approve whatever he makes.

God, that sounds ridiculous.

He's chewing slowly, an inquisitive look in his eye as he watches me from across the table.

"Not hungry?" He nods toward my plate.

I shrug, nerves prancing around in my gut. "Not really."

Right on cue my stomach growls. Heat rushes into my face and I lower my gaze.

"Mmhm," he hums, wiping his hands and leaning forward. "Talk to me, Blake. What's going on in that head of yours?"

"I just... you should have asked me if I could eat this." I gesture toward the plate, cringing at how the words come out. "You know I'm strict with what I eat, and it's something that's important to me. I can't have *any* of this." My hand waves over the food.

He nods slowly. "Do you want me to make you something else?"

I sigh. "No, I have some snacks in my bag, I'll just go grab something in a bit." I take a big bite out of the avocado just for show. "The avocado is great, though."

His eyes narrow and I fidget under his stare. *Why is he looking at me like that?*

A phone rings from somewhere in the house, the sound jerking me from his gaze. "Do you need to get that?"

He shakes his head, his attention still on me. "It's probably my mom. I'll call her back."

"Oh." I cock my head, realizing he doesn't really talk about her. That in reality, I don't actually know much about him. Here I am thinking I'm in love and I haven't even taken the time to get to know about his life.

I rest my elbows on the table, propping my chin in my hand. "What's she like?"

He smiles. "She's the best. Charismatic. Hard worker. You know… the usual."

"No," I swallow. "I don't." Sadness slinks through my chest.

His eyes grow heavy, his head angling to the side. "I guess that's right. Tell me about your mom."

I shrug. "You know about as much as me."

His brows draw in. "I highly doubt that."

"You've seen the pictures on the wall." I take a bite out of the burger just to do something with my hands—to have something under my control, because my insides suddenly feel like a storm is ripping through it, tearing up everything in its path.

The juicy flavor of the meat hits my tongue and I pause, my eyes closing as I groan at the taste.

Oh my god. So good.

"Jesus, princess. I'm gonna feed you burgers every day if you sound like *that* when you eat them."

My eyes snap open, the burger dropping from my hands, guilt slamming its way through me.

Breathing deeply I count to three.

It was just one bite. No big deal.

"My mom died in childbirth," I say, focusing on the

pain of never knowing her so I don't focus on the grease that's coating my throat.

His lips turn down. He doesn't apologize like most people, but then again, I wouldn't expect him to. Jackson knows what it's like to have fake apologies thrown at you by people who don't know what the word truly means.

"It's fine," I rush out. "It's not like... not like when you lost your dad." I suck in a breath, hoping I didn't cross into unwanted territory.

Jackson just nods.

"I never even knew her," I continue. "You can't miss something you never had." I lift a shoulder, swallowing around the lump in my throat.

"Really?" he chimes in. "Sometimes I think that makes you miss it more."

I stay silent, my fingers pressing into my palms, trying to slam the door on my grief—keep it locked up tight and forgotten in a corner.

"You sure that phone call wasn't your *sweetheart*?" I lash out, desperate to change the subject.

Jackson's face tightens. There are a few seconds of silence where I think he won't respond. Or maybe he'll tell me to get the hell out and not come back.

"Her name's Alina."

I nod, her name spinning like a cyclone. "Oh."

Alina.

The muscle in his jaw tenses. "Or Lee, that's what everyone calls her. She's one of my best friends, so the phone calls won't stop. She'll always be in my life."

Jealousy scorches through me, squeezing my lungs and piercing my heart. Something nasty sits on the tip of my tongue, like asking why he's friends with someone who clearly causes him so much pain. I pull it back, realizing I have no right.

But I *hate* her.

She took a piece of him and is holding it hostage, somewhere I can't reach.

"And you love her," I whisper.

He takes a sip of water and nods. "We talked about this already."

My chest tightens. "Let's talk about it more."

He sighs, tossing his napkin on the table and standing, walking around to kneel at my feet. His hands squeeze my knees, sliding up until they're gripping my thighs. My stomach burns when he gazes into my eyes and everything in me wants to pull out from under his palms. Demand that he *stop* loving her. That he loves me instead.

But I don't. Because out of everyone I've ever known, Jackson's the only one who's given me peace and never asked for something in return. So, I push down the envy and focus on the parts of him I *do* have.

"Listen to me. I thought I was in love with Lee for a long time." He shakes his head. "For years, to be honest. But what I feel for *you*..." He trails off, his Adam's apple bobbing with his swallow.

His words, meant to be a balm to my jealousy, don't do anything to douse the embers. "I get it."

He chuckles. "I doubt that." He pulls me up from my chair, his fingers tangling with mine. "I'll explain it to you though, if you want."

My teeth sink into my lip and I nod, knowing that if I want to love him fully, I have to love every part of him.

So, I let him lead me into the living room and sit me down on the couch, preparing to hear all about his first love and all the ways she hurt him.

36

JACKSON

I made dinner knowing she wouldn't eat it. Which sounds like an asshole thing, but now that I know there's an issue, I need to test her boundaries. See where things are so I can figure out the best way to approach her. My original plan was to push her for answers, but something in my gut held me back, a whisper telling me if I confront her too quickly, she'll take it as an accusation. Lash out instead of listen and build up barriers that I can't break through.

It's the same thing I did as a kid when people tried to ask me about my father.

So, instead of my original plan, I follow her lead,

allowing her to shift the conversation until it lands on *my* issues.

There's nothing I want to talk about less than my past. But I can tell by the look in Blakely's eyes and the bite in her tone that if we don't, it will just be this thing that festers between us, growing until it pushes us so far apart there's no chance of finding our way back.

If opening up and trusting her is what needs to happen, I'll do it.

How can I ask it of her if I don't do it myself?

We sit on the couch, my fingers tracing the outline of hers as I try to figure out where to start. She asked about Lee, but, there's this tugging in the middle of my body, drawing up earlier times, urging me to start at the beginning. To get it all out now, so she has the whole picture. So there's nothing left of mine she needs to discover.

"My dad died when I was sixteen."

Blakely's eyebrows shoot to her hairline, but she stays quiet.

"Here in California, actually. We knew it was coming, we just didn't know *when*."

"He was sick, right?" she asks.

I nod. "Yeah. Had been for a while. Since I was thirteen." I swallow around the emotion lodging in my throat. "Multiple Myeloma—cancer of the blood. I couldn't believe it. Not him. Not *my* dad. He was a damn Marine, was trained in the toughest of conditions. Had fought in wars, you know? I didn't—" My voice breaks. "I didn't understand how someone like him, someone so strong could get so sick."

A small laugh bubbles out of me, remembering how naïve I was back then.

Blakely smiles, her fingers squeezing mine. "You really worshiped him, huh?"

My free hand reaches up, tangling in the chain of my necklace. "Yeah." I nod. "He was my hero."

"I can tell."

"Anyway, he told me he was gonna fight. And he did. He fought like hell... and he won, just like I knew he would. A year later he was in remission. The relief, Blake—" I whoosh out a breath. "I can't even tell you what that felt like."

"I can't imagine," she says.

"But six months before I turned sixteen it came back, and this time it was too fast. Too aggressive."

The base of my throat swells, the pain of remembering what he went through—what we all went through—making my nostrils flare from the burn. "They gave him two options. Go home on hospice and die in peace, or continue to fight and most likely die painfully, bleeding out in a hospital bed."

Blakely sucks in a breath, her hand covering her chest. "Oh my god, Jackson. That's awful."

I nod, running my tongue over my teeth. "I begged him to fight. But I saw the light in him dim with every dialysis treatment, with every time they shoved a chemo pill down his throat and told us none of it was doing a goddamn thing." My jaw clenches. "And he was *tired*. So, at some point, you have to choose—quality of life or quantity?" I swallow. "Besides that, I could see the guilt eating him alive every time a new hospital bill showed up in our mailbox."

"You didn't have insurance?"

"We did. But the VA is a wreck and cancer is expensive."

She sucks on her lip, her brows drawing in. I don't

expect her to understand struggles for money when money is all she's ever known, but I'm thankful for her listening either way.

"So, he came home?"

I bob my head. "He came home. At that point, he was too weak to work in the garage with me, but he'd come out there, just... sitting in the sun and listening to me work." I envision him on our cracked driveway, his eyes closed and his face smooth, finding peace in his choices. Accepting that he was about to leave us forever. "I was *so* mad at him. I avoided being home, because I couldn't stand the sight of him."

My hand pulls out his dog tags from under his shirt, my palm pressing into the metal. "And then on my sixteenth birthday, while I was at the skate park with my friends, I got a phone call from my mom. He had died." I purse my lips, choking back the sting of tears. "I wasn't there of course." Regret ebbs and flows like a wave inside of me and I shake my head. "Three months later, my mom packed us up and moved us to Sugarlake, Tennessee."

"And that's where you met Alina?" She hesitates on her name.

"Yep." I sigh, a small smile crawling on my face. "She pranced on my porch and shoved her mama's banana bread into my hands. I was a dick to her, because I was just… buried in my grief." I shrug. "But then a few days later, her neighbor Chase came around. And he, well—Chase saved me from myself, I guess." The middle of my chest throbs from old wounds that never healed. "I doubt he knows it though."

"How'd he save you?" Blakely asks.

"By being the asshole that he was." I laugh. "He was so damn broody. He didn't pry, never asked questions. Didn't push me to deal with things I wasn't ready to face. But he showed up in my yard every day and sipped on the beer I convinced Sandra from the corner store to buy us, and just kept me company." I chew on the inside of my cheek. "He gave me friendship when I had nothing and I'll always be grateful to him for that."

As I continue purging my past while Blakely listens, my feelings shift and change, my memory being lent a new perspective.

"So, this guy Chase, he *cheated* on her and now they're back together?" Blakely asks after I finish.

I nod. "Pretty much."

"And he was your best friend."

"Yep." I smack my hands on my legs.

"So, Okay, I'm sorry." Her palm cups her forehead, her eyes squeezing shut. "You're telling me that you were there for this girl for years, held her up through the worst moments of her life. Meanwhile she was keeping major, life changing things from you? And then she picked the guy who not only cheated on her and had it posted all over social media, but broke both of your hearts?"

My chest spasms. "Yeah, pretty much."

"And she just... expected you to be okay with it?" Blakely crosses her arms and huffs, her back smacking against the couch cushions. "No offense, Jackson, but she sounds like a bitch."

I cringe. "No. She's amazing."

Blakely scoffs.

"She is. She's just... not meant for me."

Blakely's teeth bite down on the left corner of her lip and she glances down before peering at me through her lashes. "And you're okay with that?"

"If I wasn't, then I wouldn't be here with you."

I'm not one-hundred-percent honest when I say it. I *am* over my heartbreak. Being with Blakely has opened my eyes to all the ways it's possible to feel for another person, ways that I *never* had with Lee. But it doesn't change the fact that, at least at first, I used Blakely as a distraction to get through the heartache. To bathe in her attention, while I tried to wash away the pain of not being anyone else's choice.

And now…

I forgive Lee. But the thought of Chase is like friction on a rug burn.

It drives me insane knowing that he's slipped effortlessly back into place, like he didn't disappear for the better half of a decade. And maybe, my hurt and anger isn't so much the fact that Lee didn't choose me, as it is that *no one* did. They were both integral to me, but to them, I was just insurance. The spare tire that's kept around, just in case.

And that's one hell of a pill to swallow.

"Are they why you moved to Cali full time?" Blakely's voice pulls me out of my thoughts.

I shrug. "It makes more sense for me to be out here, especially working for your dad. Easier to accomplish everything I came to do." I wink, trying to lighten the mood.

She cocks her head, smiling. "And what is it that you want to accomplish, Jackson Rhoades?"

"Right now?" I lean in, ghosting a kiss across her lips. "I can think of plenty of things."

She giggles and it lights up my insides.

Slapping my chest, she pecks my mouth, her hand reaching up and scratching at the stubble on my jaw. "I'm serious."

I shrug. "I just want my cars in the movies. That's what my dad always dreamed of. What we always talked about."

The corner of her eyes crinkle. "Well, you're already doing that."

"This is true." My palm slides up her thigh, pushing her back until she's flat against the couch, my body leaning over hers, my nose skimming along the expanse of her neck. Arousal jolts through me.

"Are we done talking now?" I whisper, my breath causing goose bumps to sprout along her skin.

She tilts her head to the side, my cock hardening as I drop my hips between her legs.

"Yeah," she gasps. "We're done talking."

"Thank *God*." Our lips fuse together, my heart cracking open, happiness filling every cell.

I told her everything. And she's still here.

She's still choosing me.

37

BLAKELY

I *love him.*

Those are the only thoughts flowing through my brain as his tongue swirls around mine. That I love him, and it's the realest thing I've ever felt. That in a world of superficial, he's my authenticity.

The feeling wraps around me like a cocoon and I burrow myself inside of his embrace, hoping he never lets me go. Hoping that maybe, if I stay here long enough, he'll transform me into something beautiful.

His arms tighten around my waist, and even through the fabric of our clothes the way his erection presses against my core has tingles lancing through my body.

I've never had anyone who made me feel so drunk on lust. Maybe that's why I've held on to my virginity for as long as I have—because there's never been someone around who's made me want to give it up. There's been guys before, I'm not completely innocent, but I learned young that the majority of people are only in my life for what they can get, and my purity was something I could hold on to, make sure it was one thing they couldn't have.

I can't think of anyone else I'd rather give it to than Jackson.

Lifting up my leg, I throw it over his waist, grinding my pelvis into him. He groans, his hips speeding up as they roll against mine.

A rush of power shoots through my body. It's *me* making him this way. *I'm* the one taking up his heart, body, and soul in this moment. But I have no clue what the hell I'm doing. Insecurity spills into my excitement as I think back to all of the times I used to thrive by pushing his buttons, watching him war with himself as I made dirty comments and flirtatious advances. Like everything else in my life, it was just for show. I never would have expected it to turn into this, and I hope he's not disappointed.

Sucking his bottom lip into my mouth, my hand travels down his stomach until I reach the thick outline of him through his jeans.

"I want to taste you," I moan.

His fingers flex against my waist. "*Jesus*, Blake."

Surging forward, I push until he's lying flat on the couch while I hover over his body. I lave kisses along his neck, my hands skimming the hem of his shirt. His chest rises and falls against my breasts, his palms tracing the length of my spine.

Slowly, I lift his shirt until it's off, throwing it to the side.

The silver metal of his necklace glints as it jostles against his chest and I lean in, noticing for the first time that they're dog tags. My heart squeezes, realizing they're his father's.

A rush of warmth expands in my chest when I think about how open he was. How much trust he put in me—in us—when he cut himself open and showed me his past.

My lips dive back in, working their way down his chest. His abs contort when my mouth brushes over them and my core clenches, satisfaction blasting its way through me at how his body responds to my touch.

It's a heady feeling, having the person who is your pillar of strength be at your mercy.

I go to work on his belt, the metal buckle cold against my fingers.

"Blake, you don't have to—"

Smirking, I glance up at him. His eyes are fierce, a dark haze swirling through the kaleidoscope of greens, lust pouring from his gaze.

"Of course, I don't *have* to. I want to, Jackson." His hips lift so I can slide his jeans down his thighs.

His erection tents his boxers and my stomach buzzes with nerves, suddenly worried I won't be good enough to please him.

Swallowing around the insecurity, my fingers wrap around the base of him, using the fabric of his boxers to create friction against his skin. His cock jerks in my hand, making a wave of desire roll through me.

His head falls back against the couch. "*Fuck*."

There's a wet spot forming on his boxers and I lean in, pressing my lips to the cloth, a hint of his taste teasing my mouth. My fingers slip into the waistband, pulling them down, his dick bobbing straight into the air. My heart jumps into my throat before dropping back down, settling into a faster rhythm.

I've always been fascinated by the male anatomy, and although I don't have much experience with men, the few I've seen don't even come close to comparing to Jackson's. My stomach tightens as I take him in.

I've never felt so *wanton* before. Never thought the dirty fantasies that play through my mind alone at night would bleed over into real life, but as I sit and stare at Jackson's rigid cock, my clit swells and desire stirs low in my gut.

There's a thick vein running along the underside of his shaft. I close my eyes, imagining the way it will pulse with his cum. Maybe in my mouth. Maybe inside me. My pussy throbs at the vision, my stomach flipping.

My hand reaches out, gripping him firmly at the base and he sucks in a breath. I glide my palm from root to tip, watching as precum oozes from the head. Leaning in, my tongue slips out and sweeps over the liquid, hunger sparking in my stomach as I taste him for the first time.

Jackson groans.

My body buzzes and my hand repeats the motion, trying to squeeze out another drop. It works, and this time when I lean in to taste him my mouth closes around his tip, sucking.

He moans again, his hands flying down to grip the back of my head.

I glance up at him from under my lashes, suddenly nervous that I won't be good enough. My chest tightens when I think about all the other women who I'm sure have been in my position, my brain starting to spiral, but I pull myself back from the brink. I don't want to overthink this. I just want to be what he needs. "Tell me what to do, Jackson."

His eyes flare, his hips rising slightly, the head of his dick brushing against my lips. "Put your mouth on it." His voice is low. Deep.

My thighs press together to try and ease the ache throbbing between them.

I follow my instincts, pressing a kiss to the tip of his cock, before swirling my tongue around him, lowering my head as my mouth slides down his length inch by inch.

His hands gather my hair into a ponytail, tugging slightly, sending a shiver down my spine.

Squeezing my eyes shut, I marvel at what it feels like to have him between my lips. At the way his salty essence lingers on my taste buds, and how with every pass of my tongue his cock grows harder.

I continue working my way down slowly until the head of him meets resistance, my gut cramping at the thought that I can't take him all the way in.

His finger traces along my jaw. "Breathe through your nose, princess."

Relief from his instruction untangles the nerves, total and complete trust taking its place. My eyes water when his dick pushes into the back of my throat.

"Yeah, *fuck*. Like that," he rasps. "Relax your tongue."

I do.

His hips start to thrust in small movements and even though the physical act is uncomfortable—my jaw aching from being stretched, and my breath stuttered from his girth—the rush it shoots through me is so erotic that arousal drips into my panties, my womb spasming.

I've never been this turned on.

Saliva dribbles from the corners of my mouth, glossing down his cock every time he retreats. His free hand reaches out, grabbing mine and wrapping it around the base of him, the drool making my hand slick as his length pumps through it.

"You take over now." He tugs on my hair. "Like this." Urging me back down, his palm stays on top of mine as he shows me how to twist and stroke in tandem with the bobbing of my head, creating a rhythm. After a few minutes, I grow comfortable—more confident—and his hand falls away, his grip growing lax from where it holds my hair back.

I can feel the moment he gets close, his cock growing in my mouth, his legs starting to tremble around my sides. Suddenly, he tugs sharply on my strands, the sting making me gasp, allowing him to slip free from my mouth.

"Is this... was it not okay?" I ask, my stomach tensing.

He cups my jaw and leans in, breathing his words against my lips. "Perfect. You're absolutely perfect. But you're about to make me come, and I'm not done with you yet. Let's move to the bedroom."

My stomach flips, excitement darting around the deepest chambers of my heart. But as he leads me down the hall and into his room, the self-doubt creeps back in, souring the moment.

Will I be what he's expecting?

What if I'm not any good?

What if he doesn't like what he sees?

It's the last thought that gives me pause, my feet faltering as we hit his bed.

He turns, completely at ease with his naked body, and a pang of envy prickles against my skin from his confidence. His brows draw in as he watches me and his hands come up, pushing my hair behind my ears and framing my face. This is his move, I've realized. He likes to touch me—likes to grab my face and force my eyes to stay on his.

"Are you still with me?" he asks.

Nodding, my teeth gnaw on my lip. "Yeah, I just…" I sigh. "I'm a little nervous."

He nods. "We don't have to do anything you're not ready for."

"No, I'm definitely ready."

"Are you sure?" He tilts his head, his arms wrapping around my waist.

A bit of bravado pushes its way forward, his reassurances calming the panic that's wanting to take root inside of me.

I know if I act like I'm unsure, he'll stop, and I don't *want* him to stop. I want to know what it feels like when he lets go completely. Want him to lose himself inside me and never find his way out.

Rising up on my toes, my lips skim his ear. "Jackson, if you don't, I'll go find someone who will."

His hands tighten around my waist, his grip bruising. He bends, his lips skating along the rim of my ear and sending frissons of excitement tingling down my back.

"The only man that will touch *anything* on you, is me, princess."

38

JACKSON

A foreign feeling whips through my insides at Blakely's threat, and even though I know it's an empty one, the images it produces still drive me half insane.

And that's how I know this is different from anything I've ever felt. Because even when I've been broken over Lee—of her not wanting me—I've never been driven to the brink of absolute insanity at the mere thought of her with someone else.

With six little words, my world is turned on its axis.

I'll go find somebody who will.

Over my dead body.

I'm all she needs.

Suddenly, I'm ravenous, passion and need exploding through my veins and burning away my plans for slow and sweet. I know that I should be taking my time with her. Be romantic and show her all the ways I want to love her right.

But I feel feral. Possessive. This is what she's been pushing me for, what she *always* pushes for—this side of me that stays locked away behind a cool, calm exterior.

My hands grip her waist tight and push her back on the bed. I tower over her as my eyes trail the length of her body. "Strip for me, princess. Let me see you."

Her eyes widen, hesitation swamping the air between us. I could do it for her, could easily reach out and peel off every layer, not stopping until she's stripped completely bare, body and soul. But I need her to be the one to take this step. Need to make sure that she's really as ready as she says she is.

That she trusts me.

She already has so many people taking from every aspect of her life, I refuse to be someone else who does.

She glances around, her arms coming across the front of her stomach and she swallows. "Can we turn off the lights?"

My heart sinks. It's so obvious now, in this moment, that her insecurities go far deeper than just reactionary breakdowns from other people's opinions.

Walking to the edge of the bed, I crawl over her body, leaning down to press my lips against hers. I make love to her mouth nice and slow. Long, tender strokes of my tongue against hers until her body relaxes and becomes supple underneath me.

Good. I don't want her tense for this. It's going to be painful enough without her on edge. This should be all about enjoyment.

Pulling my mouth back, I rub my nose against hers, her breath mingling with mine.

"There is *nothing* you could show me that I wouldn't want to see. I want to be with you because I love what's in here—" I press my hand against her chest. "Not because of what's out here." I run my other hand down her side. "Although, that's beautiful too."

She presses her body further into my hands. "Okay."

"Do you believe me?" I ask.

She nods, her eyelashes fluttering.

"Good." I press another kiss to her mouth, before trailing my lips across her jaw and down her neck, my half-hard cock growing thick from her taste on my tongue.

"So, strip for me, princess."

I move until my back is against the headboard, giving her room and once again, leaving the decision up to her. She has to show me that she wants this. That she's ready.

She surprises me, standing up until she's at the end of the bed. Her fingers grip the bottom of her shirt and drag it slowly up her torso, her skin coming into my view inch by inch, my heart palpitating from the torture of the tease, waiting to be revealed.

My eyes drink her in, greedily gulping the view, and with every moment that passes her body relaxes, her movements becoming graceful. More confident.

I wish I could have her dive inside of my brain so she could see herself the way I do.

My fingers dig into the comforter, grappling with the blanket to keep myself from reaching out and pulling her to me, my cock bobbing in the air as I shuffle on the bed.

Her jeans slide off her legs and then it's just her, encased in black lace—a present just waiting for me to tear into its wrapping.

She's so goddamn sexy.

It's nothing I haven't seen before, the bikini she was wearing for the photo shoot on her pool deck covered less, but the intimacy of the moment has my balls tightening with anticipation.

Her eyes meet mine, the air charging with tension as she reaches behind her back.

Heat collects at the base of my spine and I grip the comforter tighter.

She unclasps her bra and the material slides down, the straps falling off her shoulders. She holds the cups of lace in place, keeping herself hidden from my view. My eyes follow the way her cleavage rises and falls with her heavy breaths. My cock throbs and I reach down, my hand wrapping around it and stroking.

My hand glides up and down, imagining it's her tight pussy creating the heat and not my palm.

A beautiful shade of pink blooms on her cheeks, but she doesn't drop her gaze from where I'm touching myself. Her arm drops, letting the fabric slide the rest of the way off.

Her nipples pebble against the air, and even though I've seen them before— tasted them before—it feels like the first time, blood rushing to my groin as I stroke faster.

"Touch them for me," I rasp.

Her eyes shoot up to my face, teeth sinking into her bottom lip. But she does as I say, her hands slowly rising to her chest as she cups her breasts, rolling those perfect nipples between her thumb and finger.

My insides coil tighter, my heart slamming against my ribs.

"Do you have any idea how *sexy* you look right now?" I groan, my hips thrusting into my closed fist.

My words seem to spark her passion, and she lets out a

moan, one of her hands leaving her breast and gliding down her stomach. My hand tingles with jealousy, wanting to feel her skin underneath my fingertips.

She slips beneath the waistband of her underwear, the outline of her knuckles highlighted by the way she moves them back and forth, touching herself.

"*Fuck*, Blake, does it feel good to touch yourself for me?"

She moans again, her breath stuttering while she nods.

My gaze is locked on the motion of her hand underneath the fabric. Her eyes flutter closed as she moves lower, and my body coils tighter.

"That's right, baby, soak your fingers and then come give me a taste."

The image of Blakely finger-fucking herself in nothing but her thong makes me pull my cock harder, tendrils of pleasure winding through my body. My balls draw up and I relax my grip, trying to stem the urge to shoot all over my hand before I've even touched her.

"Come here," I say.

Blakely's eyes pop open and she slides her fingers from her panties, sauntering over to me, an air of confidence surrounding her—something she didn't have when we first came to the room.

Her middle finger is glistening with wetness and my mouth waters, my stomach squeezing with the need to suck it into my mouth and clean it of her juices.

She stops when she's right in front of me, her body pressing against mine, and without coaxing, she raises up her hand and slides her finger along the seam of my mouth.

My gut flares, precum steadily oozing out of my cock as it throbs between us.

I slip out my tongue to lick her flavor from my lips and

she takes advantage, her finger slipping inside of my mouth.

My hand shoots out, grabbing the lace of her underwear in my palm and pulling harshly, making it stretch against her skin until it rips. She jumps, squeaking in surprise, but the action is drowned out by the animalistic lust that's flooding through my veins.

Gripping her hips tight, I drag her on top of me, her legs coming down on either side of my body, the heat from between her thighs settling in my lap. My eyes roll when I feel her bare against me, her arousal so thick it drips down the length of my dick.

Her arms wrap around my neck, forehead resting on mine as she jerks her hips forward then slowly moves them back. Our mouths skim as she rocks, an electric sensation scorching through me as my shaft glides between the lips of her pussy, my cock pressing against her swollen clit with every forward motion.

It's the most delicious type of torture and I swear to God I have never been more turned on in my entire life. "Goddamn, Blake, I need to feel you."

"So feel me." She pushes down harder, my tip slipping to her entrance and prodding against the hole.

I bite my cheek so hard I taste blood, my nails digging into her sides as I flip us around on the bed.

My hand brushes down her body until I find her clit. She sucks in a breath, her legs falling open as I circle my thumb on her swollen nub, feeling it pulse underneath my touch.

She's close.

Good.

My finger teases her opening, collecting her wetness and using it as lubricant to easily slip inside of her.

She moans, her back arching. Her pussy is tight as hell and my cock twitches as I imagine what it will feel like to have her wrapping around me like a vise.

Her legs start to tremble, a gush of liquid seeping out of her and coating my hand as I add another finger, her walls fluttering around them.

She covers her mouth with her hand and I grab her wrist, pushing it above her head and tangling our fingers. "Don't. Let me hear you."

She nods, her clit swelling underneath my fingertips.

"Give it to me, baby," I breathe.

And that's all it takes.

I watch, enraptured by her beauty as she explodes, detonating around my hand. Her body shakes, her pussy clenching and releasing around my fingers, clit pulsing in time to the spasms under the pad of my thumb.

Any remaining blood rushes to my groin as I watch her come undone and I lift my hips off the bed, worried the friction will make me come.

She slowly relaxes, her breasts rising and falling as she tries to catch her breath.

I take my fingers out of her, bringing them to my lips and sucking them into my mouth, licking every drop of her cum from my hand. "Delicious."

She giggles, the back of her hands brushing against her cheeks. "I'd never imagined you being such a dirty talker."

My brow quirks. "I'm full of surprises," I say as I climb up her body.

My cock is leaking steadily, throbbing from the torture of being teased for the past hour and finding no release.

I grip myself in my hand, rubbing the head of my dick along her slit. She jumps, gasping, her pussy still fluttering against me from aftershocks of her orgasm.

"Are you sure about this?" I ask again.

She wraps her arms around me, pressing her lips to mine. "I've never been more sure of anything in my life."

"Do I need a condom?"

She shakes her head. "No. I want to feel you."

Pressing a kiss to her lips, I press into her slowly, stretching her inch by inch.

Immediately her body tightens and I pause, my arms resting on either side of her head.

"Are you okay?"

She nods, her eyes closing.

My hand brushes across her lids. "No, baby, keep your eyes on me. I need to see you. Need to make sure you're here with me."

She snaps them open, a thousand emotions swirling out of her gaze, matching the intensity of how I feel inside.

And suddenly, I know what this is.

This is love.

39

BLAKELY

The sting is *real*, and as he pushes in further, it feels more like he's splitting me in half rather than making love.

But I breathe deep, allowing the pain to keep me grounded.

My arms slip down from around his neck, my nails digging deep into the muscles of his shoulder as he continues to press in.

He pauses again, allowing me to adjust.

"Just do it," I force out, my hands trying to drag him into me.

His muscles tense under my hands and he surges

forward, blinding pain racing through my core and up my middle as his hips rest flush against mine.

"*Goddamn,* you're tight," he moans, looking down at me. "Are you still with me?"

I open my mouth to speak, but words don't come out because the truth is, this fucking *hurts*, so I settle for a nod.

My legs wrap around his hips, holding him close, worried he'll second-guess what we're doing. That he'll stop because it's clear I'm in pain.

After a few minutes, the agony eases into a tolerable throb. He must sense the shift in my body because he slowly starts to move, dragging his hips back, his cock rubbing against my walls as he thrusts in a slow and steady rhythm.

There's a slight sting that remains, but I can tell that he's holding himself back.

I don't want him to.

Lifting my head, my lips ghost across his neck. "Jackson… *fuck* me."

"I don't want to hurt you, baby," he grits out.

"You won't." My hand reaches between us, my fingers brushing against his balls. "I want to feel you come."

His entire body jerks and he plunges in deep, making me lose my breath. Pleasure curls around the edge of the discomfort, and I give into the sensation, losing myself in the moment, my chest swelling with emotion as I give myself to the first person who's ever seen me for *me.*

Heat simmers low in my abdomen. My hand moves down to rub my still-sensitive clit, my fingers skimming the sides of his dick as it moves inside of me.

I want to know what it feels like to orgasm around his cock. I wonder if it's even *possible* through the ache of being stretched until it burns.

His eyes lock on to where I'm touching myself and he

rears back, gripping under my calves and sliding down to my ankles, raising my legs until they're spread wide in the air.

I whimper, the new position making him hit impossibly deeper.

"Where do you want my cum, princess? *Fuck*, you feel good." His words come out sharp, in time with his thrusts, and his dirty mouth is gasoline to the fire that's growing inside of me.

I increase the pressure of my fingers. "Don't stop talking," I breathe.

His chest glistens from the sheen of sweat that coats his body, his abs tensing with every slap of our groins. My body jostles on the bed, my fingers rubbing furiously back and forth.

"Are you gonna make that pussy milk it out of me, Blake? Do you think you can?"

His words are a challenge and I take it to heart, pressing my hand down hard and rubbing in sharp circles, the bundle of nerves swelling with tension from every pass of my fingers.

He drops my legs, his body coming down on top of mine until his slick chest rubs against my nipples, his necklace cold against the flush of my body.

My arm is mashed between us and his body weight lends an increased pressure that has my insides coiling so tight my legs shake.

"Do you want to feel me come inside you?" he whispers against my ear.

Goose bumps sprout along my overheated skin.

"Want me to shoot so deep, you can never get me out?"

My stomach tenses. "*God*, yes. Put your cum in me," I plead.

Jackson's hips falter as he buries himself to the hilt inside of me. I can feel his cock pushing against my walls rhythmically as he comes, and the feeling catapults me off the cliff of ecstasy.

My body seizes, thousands of stars dotting my vision as I explode around him, the pain of tender skin giving way to an electric pleasure that sparks off my skin like lightning, crashing through the air around me.

My breaths come in pants, my forehead slick with sweat as I slowly float back to earth. Jackson is pressing soft kisses all over my neck, his body trembling as he lays against me.

And I feel... relaxed.

Happy.

Whole.

An hour later we're still lounging in bed, only having left when Jackson grabbed a towel to clean me up and then forced me to use the restroom, saying if I don't pee after sex I'll get an infection.

But now, we're back under his sheets, our naked bodies lazily strewn against each other, his fingers tracing along my spine, holding me like I'm the only thing that matters in his world.

Right now, it feels like I am.

I've never been so comfortable around another person, *especially* not naked, but after so many times of him finding beauty in all my pieces, I think I'm starting to believe him. And he made me feel so... *sexy.* When I stripped down as he stroked himself and watched, I felt empowered.

I felt *seen*.

As we lie in his bed, relaxed and satiated, I think about our earlier conversation. The ache between my thighs doesn't come close to the ache that split my heart as I listened to his memories. The agony bled out in his words as he talked of his friends who never cared to put him first. Of his father and all the ways he loved him.

"Sometimes I'm happy my mom died before I could know her," I blurt out.

Jackson's head turns toward mine, his eyebrows raising in question.

I huff out a laugh, covering my face. "I know, that sounds terrible. It's just, I was thinking about what you told me earlier, about your dad, and... I can't imagine having to go through what you did. Knowing what it's like to have him and then to lose him, I—" My voice catches, emotion blocking the airways in my throat.

He lets out a heavy breath, pressing his lips to the top of my head. "Don't compare our grief, baby. You don't have to know something to mourn its absence."

I chew on my lip, sadness knitting together like a blanket in my chest. "Do you think that's why my dad works so much?"

"Because he lost her?"

Swallowing over the lump, I nod against his side.

He shrugs. "Only he knows why he does the things he does. But I know this, and I'm not sure you want to hear it."

My stomach sinks. "What is it?"

"He loves you."

I huff out a laugh.

"You can scoff at it all you want, Blake, but if he didn't love you, he wouldn't force his employee to tag along wherever you go, just to make sure you're with someone he can trust. He wouldn't assign security with so much tracking that it's impossible to sneak away. He wouldn't look so broken whenever you walk out of the room."

My eyes sting. "He does?"

"He stares after you like he doesn't know how to reach you."

The cracks in my heart split open, bleeding into my stomach, creating a burn so intense I lose my breath.

"He loves you." Jackson's hand tilts my chin up to his face. "How could he not?"

I roll my eyes with a small grin, trying to hide the fact that his words make me feel like I'm breaking. A tear slips out, sliding along my cheek, and Jackson's thumb wipes it away.

"I don't know how anyone could be in your presence and not fall in love with everything that you are."

My heart stalls. "Are you..." I hesitate, my voice wobbly with emotion. "Are you saying *you* love me?"

A slow smile creeps on Jackson's face, so perfect it makes my chest ache.

"Yes, princess." He presses a chaste kiss to my lips. "I love you. I didn't know what love was *until* you."

My heart soars, flying so fast it makes me dizzy.

He loves me.

Suddenly, a giggle bubbles up my throat and I let it out, delirious from the gamut of emotions I've felt in the past few hours. "I love you too, you know."

He smirks. "Oh, I know."

Scoffing, I lift up on my shoulder, peering down at him. "You are so cocky."

He laughs, dragging me down until I'm laying half across his chest. "But you *love* me."

I grin. "I can't help it. Turns out, you're extremely lovable."

He hums, the vibration from his chest skittering across my skin. "You think so?"

There's a serious tone to his voice that wasn't there a

moment ago, and I realize we've run over a pothole in an otherwise smooth road. A vulnerability you don't even realize exists until you're falling into it.

It makes my stomach sour, pissed the hell off that anyone has ever made him think he wasn't worth it.

I crane my neck to meet his eyes. "I know so."

"Does this mean you're mine?" he asks.

My hand reaches up, scratching at his stubble. "Only if you're mine, too."

His face warms and he dips down, pressing our lips together, showing me all the ways he loves me.

40

BLAKELY

"So, are you prego?" Kayla asks, sipping from her orange juice.

My mouth waters at the sugary drink, and like usual, jealousy sears my insides.

Must be nice.

"Are you seriously asking me that?" I level her with a glare, leaning back against the metal chair.

We're at brunch. I took the day off from Donahue Motors, specifically for this outing. I miss having girl time with Kayla, and ever since I've taken on this role for my dad, our daytime lunches have become nonexistent. Add to that fact, Sierra has been begging me to get some "Kodak moments" of the new Adidas line. So here we are, acting casual, like we don't see the horde of photographers standing across the street, huddled around the sidewalk, waiting for their moment.

As usual, we're the ones who called them.

Kayla shrugs. "I don't know, you practically disappear from my life overnight and you..." Her eyes trail up and down my body. "You seem different."

My insides smart at her words.

"Well, no. I'm not *pregnant*, for Christ's sake," I snap.

She raises her hands in surrender. "I didn't think so. I mean, I told him... who would you even have been with? That would mean you lost your V-card, and I know for damn sure you wouldn't do that and not tell your best friend."

She eyes me over the rim of her Chanel sunglasses.

I fidget, my fists curling around my thighs, tempering the urge to clench them and count to three on repeat in my head. "That's what you told who?" My head cocks.

"Hmm?" she asks.

"You said 'that's what I told him.' Who is *him*?" My chest pulls tight. Is she gossiping about me in her free time? Does everyone talk about me behind my back, even the people who I'm close with?

No.

"Oh." She laughs. "Uh, Jake. It popped up on TMZ and he asked if it was true."

I'm about to ask when I get to meet him when she takes a piece of bread from where it's steaming in the middle of the table and plops it on her plate.

My stomach curdles as she smothers it in butter, popping a gigantic piece in her mouth. "Mmmm," she moans. "The bread here is the best, dude. Are you gonna have any?"

A hole burns through my chest at her question, and I can practically taste the way the butter would melt on my tongue, but I know there isn't enough room left in my daily intake to squeeze in any extra carbs. And even if there was, the thought of not knowing how they make their butter—what exactly is in it and how much—makes anxiety prick against my lungs.

Shaking my head, I make a show of taking a big bite of my Kale salad.

Kayla glances at the half-eaten bread in her hand and drops it to her plate, her nose crinkling in obvious disgust. "Ugh, I would kill to have your dedication."

I don't respond, not sure how to since she always says the same thing, and I never know what to tell her other than "so *have* it."

"What are you getting into tonight?" she asks.

I shrug. "It's Monday."

"And?" Kayla's eyes widen.

"Mondays are my days to do nothing." I try to bite back the smile when the thought of Jackson pops in my mind, but I can tell from the way Kayla's eyes spark that I'm not successful.

"*Nothing* sure looks like it's gonna be fun." Kayla wags her eyebrows.

Should I tell her?

It would be nice to get it off my chest. The secret of Jackson and me is heavy, every day spent with him like a new brick being laid on our foundation, the urge to share my happiness with someone making me burst at the seams.

"I'm seeing someone," I blurt.

Kayla's eyes widen.

"No one can know," I rush out.

"Okay." Kayla nods. "Who is it?"

I cover my face with my hands. "I can't tell you."

"Um... excuse me, bitch? I think the fuck not. That's the equivalent of saying guess what and then never mind. You better tell me."

I chew on my lip, debating whether or not I can trust her. If I can't tell my secrets to my best friend, who *can* I tell them to?

"Jackson Rhoades."

She stares at me blankly. "I'm sorry, who?"

Rolling my eyes, I lean forward. "Jackson. Blond, hair in a bun. Insultingly good-looking. Tags along to the clubs."

Her eyes flare as she sighs, pushing her sunglasses on top of her shiny brown hair. "That's who I thought you meant." Her forehead creases. "Isn't he kind of old?"

I shrug, disappointment trickling through my veins. "Twenty-eight. But Kayla, he's... *everything*."

"Does Sierra know?"

My stomach jolts at her question, surprise flickering through me that her first reaction is to ask if my manager knows. I'm not sure how things like this usually work, but in my head, I imagined telling her and us gushing together, my excitement bleeding into hers until she demanded every detail, her joy solely because someone is making me happy.

But maybe that's not how girlfriends work in real life.

The pinched look on her face brings me back to reality quick and I shake my head. "No, Kayla. I told you, you can't tell anyone. I don't want the public to butt their way into our relationship." I chew on my bottom lip. "Besides, he works for my dad. I don't want to get him fired."

She chokes on her orange juice, smacking her chest. "I forgot about that. Jeez, really slummin' it this time around, huh?" She smiles as she says it, but annoyance stomps its way through me, slamming against the walls of my heart.

"I don't care about his money," I say, my gaze narrowing.

Kayla raises her hands in surrender.

Sighing, I close my eyes, feeling the panic start to unearth itself from where its buried, stretching its claws toward my chest.

One. Two. Three.

I open my eyes. "Kayla, promise me you won't say anything. I told you because I wanted someone to confide in. I don't want this getting out, okay? It's important. *He's* important."

She mimes zipping her lips closed and throwing away the key. "My lips are sealed, babe."

But even with her reassurance, anxiety dances along my spine, humming with a warning.

A few hours later, it's still there, tension having weaved its way into every breath, my brain on high alert and my body on edge.

Lennox drops me off at Jackson's house with a pinched look and a sigh. "I'm guessing I won't be hearing from you until the morning?"

I smile sheepishly, heat flooding my cheeks. "That would be a safe bet."

He runs his hand over his buzzed head, his fingers coming down on the steering wheel and tightening. "You're really putting me in an awkward position, Blakely. I hope you know that."

Pressure weighs down my chest. "I do," I whisper.

"Do you?" he asks. "I work for your father, not for you. And it worries me you're spending your small amount of free time with this guy who is *way* too old for you, and most likely looking for a way to latch on to your success."

Annoyance makes my back stiffen. This is only the second conversation I've had with someone about Jackson, and already I'm exhausted from defending him. "He's not like that."

Lennox's jaw clenches. "If you say so."

The rubber band holding me together snaps. "Listen, I appreciate the concern, but honestly, you're right. You *work* for my father, and you're overstepping your boundaries. Caring about my personal life is above your paygrade. Try not to forget that next time," I hiss.

His nostrils flare and he bites the inside of his cheek.

Regret immediately slices through my stomach. "*Shit,* Lennox, I—"

"No." He shakes his head. "You're right. It's not my place."

And with that, he waves me away.

Despite the way my body feels like a live wire, sadness at the fact that no one else seems to approve of Jax and me, I walk up to his house with a skip in my step, excited to be spending time with him again.

Mondays are really the only chance we get to be alone together. It's tiring having to constantly pretend like my soul isn't tearing through my skin to latch on to his.

But if we go public, things would be much, *much* worse. That was made more than obvious to me today. So, I'm going to drag this out as long as possible and hope I can convince him to keep things between the two of us for as long as I can.

I may want to show him to the world, but I don't want the world to steal him away.

41

JACKSON

I've never been in a relationship before.

I'm not sure anyone knows that about me, not even Blakely. It's honestly never something I've cared about until recently. Until Blakely came into my life and took over every waking thought.

And now that I'm in one, I'm not sure what to do. It's not like I can look at normal relationships and draw from their experience or reach out to my friends back home and ask for advice.

All of them are out in the open. They don't need to hide behind metal shelves or beg their bodyguard to sneak them away in the middle of the night.

Maybe I can Google *How to secretly date a socialite*, see what hits I get.

I thought it was exciting at first, sneaking around, but the novelty wears off fast, and ever since I told her I loved her a month ago I've had to keep myself from bringing up the fact that I want to say fuck it and go public.

Because with every day that we don't, it feels more and more like *I'm* the secret. And even if Blakely isn't meaning to, it's hard not to feel like I'm left in the shadows, waiting for a second of her time, while she gives hours to everyone else.

To the millions of people who don't even care to really know her.

It's torture tagging along with her in public and not being able to touch her. To watch my Blakely disappear and the one she gives the world rise to the surface.

In private she's everything I could ever ask for. She showers me with love and light, and just… fills me up with happiness until I'm screaming on the inside, wanting to shout to the world that she's mine. But she's so worried about people catching on, she barely gives me a second glance when we're around others, and while I get why she's doing it, it doesn't make it hurt any less.

But I haven't brought it up, because how can I cause waves when we've just started dipping our toes in the water?

There's nothing I can do except surrender to our feelings, follow my instincts, and pray for the best. Take comfort in the fact that this is temporary and figure out a plan of action, so when we *do* decide to go public, we're prepared for the possible fallout.

Mainly, with her father.

The one who just left the garage, reminding me *once again* that my job with her is to be his eyes and nothing more. He was here to surprise her, to let her know that after considering what she's been telling him, he no longer expects her to work here.

My stomach's been in upheaval ever since, worry battering against my brain as I think about what that means for our time together. Will not being here every day mean she has more free time or less?

How much of it will include me either way?

Tonight will be the fourth Monday since we made things "official" and while being with her is like a drug, the in-between moments are thick in withdrawal.

There's an undercurrent of tension eating away at the space between us, the weight of our secrecy dissolving the air like acid, making it harder each day to breathe. And maybe that's why I haven't brought up my concerns over her eating habits, too afraid to mar the little amount of time we have together with something that I know will put her on the defense.

I've spent the past month watching her. Taking mental notes and paying attention to how often she works out (three times a day), to how regimented her diet is (every single bite).

She's been bringing over packed and prepped meals, "saving me the trouble of having to cook," not realizing how obsessive she is when she eats her food and robotically enters it into her phone.

I see her through the glass windows as she spins in her reception chair. She looks bored out of her mind and happiness lights up my chest as I watch her. But it's quickly replaced by sadness that weighs me back down as I realize this is her last day and she hasn't taken the time to come and tell me.

The thought sends heat flaring in my veins and I drop

the terry cloth towel from my hand as I storm inside, irritation fueling my movements.

Her eyes swing my way, a gigantic smile gracing her face. My heart pinches at the sight.

"Hiya." She waves.

I stop once I'm in front of the desk and take a deep breath, trying to calm the storm that's raging in my stomach.

"Hi," I grit out. "Bored?"

Her grin widens as she spins dramatically in her chair. "What gave it away?"

My lips twitch, wanting to laugh at her antics, but with every second that passes where she doesn't tell me her news, anger brews like a melting pot in the base of my stomach.

"Were you planning to tell me?" I cock my head.

Her smile droops a little. "Tell you *what?*"

My fingers wrap around a brochure that's sitting to my right, just to have something to grip so I can channel my anger there instead of having it bleed out into my words. Because I feel upset. Irrationally so, and I have no idea where it's coming from other than the fact I feel caught off guard by the information her dad told me, and I'm unsure why it didn't come from her—why she didn't immediately come to tell me. Especially when she's supposed to be mine.

"Your dad stopped by today."

She nods, her brows furrowing. I see the moment it hits her, her eyes widening slightly before panic swirls through her gaze. "Jackson, I was going to tell you. I just found out. Probably right before you did."

"I don't like being in the dark about things, Blake."

"I wasn't *trying* to leave you in the dark," she whisper-shouts. "When did you want me to tell you? While Karen was up front with me for the first half of the day, training my replacement? Or maybe while my father was still here, huh?"

I shake my head, but she's on a roll and continues her tirade. "Yeah, that would have been just *perfect.* 'Hey, Dad, don't mind me, I know that I've been trying to get you to see things my way for months, and now that you finally have I should be happy, but... you see... there's this guy, who happens to be your employee who I'm in love with, and the thought of not seeing him every day has my insides splitting in half and leaking out onto the floor.'"

She sucks in a breath, her eyes glistening as her hand comes up to cover her mouth.

My heart falters, my stomach sinking as the weight of her words hit me. My anger dissipates into thin air, my arms straining with the need to take her in my arms and console her. Let her know that it's okay, that once we tell everyone this won't be so hard.

I start to walk around the desk to be next to her, but before I can make a move, Karen walks into the room. My jaw clenches, annoyance lancing through my chest. I *hate* having to stop what I'm doing in order to put on a front for other people.

It feels a hell of a lot like lying.

Blakely glances over at Karen and back to me, apology shining in her eyes.

"Tonight?" I whisper.

She nods.

Turning around and walking back out to the garage, I dream of the day where I can show the world she's mine.

I stay at work late, not wanting to go home and wait like a pathetic lapdog for her to show up. For the first time since coming to California, I long for my friends back home. At first, I was happy for the distance, needing to separate myself from the guy who fucked anything that moved and pined for Lee in silence. Needing to gain some clarity. I have that now, at least where Sugarlake is concerned, but it's replaced with a different type of limbo.

I turn my wrench too hard at the thought, cursing when my hand slips, my knuckles nicking against the metal.

Standing up, I lift my shirt to wipe off the blood.

"Lookin' mighty fine there, Jackson Rhoades."

My heart stalls in my chest as I slowly turn around.

"Holy *shit*."

42

BLAKELY

I called Jackson to let him know I was on my way over, but he didn't pick up. And when I went to his place, there was no one there to answer the door. I know I'm a few hours earlier than usual, but there's been a pit gnawing at the center of my stomach ever since our conversation today, so after my workout, I asked Lennox to drive me.

Glancing at Lennox as he idles in the parking lot of Donahue Motors, I cringe, guilt's sharp edges prodding along my insides. He's basically become my chauffeur, taking me to secret rendezvous spots whenever I snap my fingers.

Jackson's Mustang sits in the parking lot and my heart

jumps, unease trickling through me at the fact that he's still here, which means he's either buried beneath a car or ignoring my phone calls.

Is he really that mad I didn't tell him right away?

Fear that he's going to leave me surges through my chest, thoughts spiraling as I think of having to go back to life before him. Nothing sounds worse than having to learn to live without him, he's quickly twined himself to my soul, stitching us together until I can't tell us apart.

I know he wants to go public.

He hasn't said it, but it's there, lingering in the silence of everything he does. And I *see* him. The reason we're drawn to each other in the first place is our ability to shed the other's exterior, peeling away layers like an onion and finding the raw truth underneath.

I sigh, turning toward Lennox. "Give me a few minutes, I'll come back out and let you know whether I need a ride."

He gives a short nod, pulling out a worn paperback from the center console, ignoring me completely. He's been gifting me the silent treatment ever since our talk three weeks ago, and I've been trying to work my way back in his good graces ever since, but he's a tough nut to crack and there aren't enough hours in the day.

Walking up to the front door, my eyes scan the parking lot, looking to see if anyone else is here, not wanting to explain why I'm back after my sudden last-day departure. But it's deserted, only Jackson's lone Mustang in the lot.

The garage doors are closed and the front door is locked, but I enter the code on the keypad and walk inside, heading straight to where I know he'll be.

And then I stop short, my stomach surging to my throat.

Jackson is leaning against the driver's side door of a

cherry red sports car, a beautiful grin spread across his face as he talks animatedly with a girl.

A very pretty girl. One who I've never seen before. I have no clue why she would be here after hours on a work night with Jackson.

My mind races, the illogical part of my brain jumping to a thousand different conclusions, my lungs squeezing tighter with every breath, and I stumble back a step as my fists clench at my sides.

Deep breath in. One. Two. Three.

It doesn't help, the spiral has already started, sprung from the anxiety that's been growing inside of me for days at the unknown of this situation. My mind races, hoping like hell that whatever is happening is innocent, but not wanting to stick around to find out.

My heart feels like it's being squeezed until the vessels burst as I trip my way to the front of the doors and rush out to Lennox's car. Somehow I make it, my stomach tossing like a ship in a storm and slide into his front seat, my body shaking and my face hot.

"What's wrong?" Lennox is suddenly on high alert, sitting up straight, his arms coming out to touch me but then pulling back.

I can't focus enough to talk, the sharp pain in my chest becoming more acute with every passing second, my eyes watering from the loss of air. Leaning forward, I place my head on my knees, trying to stop the dizziness.

"Blakely, Jesus Christ, do I need to take you to a hospital?"

Lennox's words strike an even stronger chord, one that vibrates down my insides like nails on a chalkboard, and I muster all of my remaining sanity and strength to rasp out, "Just drive."

Deep breath in. One. Two. Three. Deep breath out.

My stomach heaves with every bump in the road, visions of honey-blonde hair and the perfect smile on Jackson's face torturing my thoughts, making them spin webs of situations that, if I were in my right mind, I would know better than to believe.

But I can't focus on any of that.

Right now, all I can focus on is my breathing.

Sweat drips down my forehead as I ramp up the intensity of the treadmill, pushing the incline to seven and letting the lactic acid pour into my muscles. If I focus on the burn, then I won't focus on the last three hours.

How I'm not where I want to be.

How I'm all alone instead of lying in Jackson's arms.

My phone has been ringing off the hook, Jackson's name flowing across the screen every few seconds, and call me petty, call me insecure, but I just can't find it in me to talk to him right now. Not until I get the giant node that's tangled in my chest to release its death grip on my lungs.

Once I can breathe again, then I'll call him back.

I overreacted. I knew it even when I was in the midst of my panic, but there's nothing I can do about it now other than move forward and try to keep a level head. Make sure I'm in the calmest state possible to talk to him.

And I'm not there yet.

As the miles tick up on the treadmill and the burn of muscles mutates into fatigue, the knot loosens, disappointment settling heavy in its place. He's never given me a reason not to trust him, and at the first sign of something not going my way, I lose it.

Pathetic, Blakely.

My insides cramp. I never realized that loving someone meant giving up such a huge amount of control. And where Jackson is usually the balm to my wounds, has been the anchor keeping me grounded, tonight he was the catalyst to my destruction. The tornado I let ravage through my system and rip up everything in its path.

It caught me so off guard, there was no time to find shelter.

My legs are numb and lethargy trips them up, so I reluctantly turn off the treadmill, guzzling water before walking back up the stairs, my legs like jelly as I hold on to the wooden railing.

Once I'm back in my bedroom, I strip out of my clothes, preparing to go into my en suite to start my nightly routine.

The one that I don't feel the need to have whenever I stay at Jackson's.

Anxiety punches my gut as I step into the shower.

And as water beats down on my back, hiding the tears that stream down my face, I realize that for the first time since he came into my life, once again, I feel alone.

43

JACKSON

My heart has stalled and then kickstarted its way back into beating.

Alina May Carson stands at the entry between the garage and the main building.

"Sweetheart, what the hell are you doing here?" I ask, shock coloring my words and flowing through my veins.

Part of me is happy to see her, it's impossible not to be, especially when I was just thinking of all the ways I longed for my friends back home. But the bigger part is irritated. Upset that she *never* listens when I tell her that I need space. That she's here for some reason, when she should be back at home in Sugarlake.

She walks further into the room, her eyes scanning the rows of cars and the shelves of inventory, eyes glinting as she comes to stand in front of me.

"What, you think you can ignore my calls for months and I wouldn't get on an airplane for the first time in my life *just* to make sure you're still alive?" She grins.

I sigh, running my hand through my hair. "Sweetheart, this is..."

Her smile droops and a pang of guilt worms its way through my annoyance.

"Are you not happy to see me, Teeth?"

The nickname makes my annoyance wane, missing the way she always jokes about my smile. Blowing out a breath and placing my hands on my hips, I level her with my stare. "I am. I'm *always* happy to see you, it's just... I told you I needed space for a reason, and yet here you are. *Still* not listening to me."

"Hmm..." she hums, nodding her head. "I'll get my ears checked once I get back home."

Huffing out a laugh, I roll my eyes.

"But in the meantime," she continues. "I figured you could show me around, let me see how things are goin' out here on the West Coast."

She walks around me and peers into the Cobra, whistling as she takes it in. "This car gonna be in the movies?"

Pride flares in my chest as I nod, turning to watch as she peruses the body, taking in my hard work.

"You know it," I say.

"Well, dang, Teeth..." She pauses, chewing on her lip. "It seems as though all your dreams are comin' true. But I think you've forgotten about us little guys back in

Tennessee." She crosses her arms over her chest. "You care to explain yourself?"

A pang hits my heart. "I already have. I didn't forget about you, sweetheart, I just needed some space."

Her face grows serious, eyes dropping to the ground as she toes the concrete with her shoe. "Because you *wanted* to forget?"

I sigh, exasperated with this conversation already, but coming to terms with the fact that she's here, whether I want her to be or not, and I know she won't leave until she gets what she came for.

"Because I wanted to move on from you."

My words rush out, lingering in the air. She sinks her teeth into her bottom lip, biting hard, and the gesture sends a knife through my gut, realizing it's the same nervous habit that Blakely has.

Shit. How the hell am I going to explain this to Blakely?

"And how's that goin'"? She cocks her head.

Blowing out a breath, I walk over to my workbench, pulling out a stool to sit down. Blakely flashes through my mind again—to be honest, she never leaves—and a prickling sensation works its way through my insides, my soul tapping its impatient fingers, wanting to be next to her.

"Surprisingly well, actually." I smile at Lee, her blue eyes sparking.

"That's good to hear 'cause I don't know how much longer I can wait to have my best friend back."

"You never lost me." I shrug. "Not really, you just... you're not good at realizing how you affect people sometimes, sweetheart. How your *actions* affect people."

She scoffs. "You sound like Eli."

I smirk, curiosity at how her relationship with her

brother has changed since he moved back to town right when I was leaving.

"Well, Eli has a point."

"Yeah, so I've been realizin'," she mutters.

My brows draw in, wondering what she means, but not wanting to get into a drawn-out conversation right now. My eyes flick to the clock on the wall and back down, my chest squeezing when I realize it's a little past seven and I'm still here instead of heading home to wait for Blakely.

Standing up, I walk over to the Cobra, leaning on the driver's side door. "How'd you even know where to find me?"

"I'm nothin' if not resourceful." She nods. "Honestly, I went by your place first, but no one was there, and then we looked up Donahue Motors and came here. There was a nice lady leavin' when I got here and she let me right in... told me where I could find you."

My heart stutters, my stomach kissing my chest before sinking back down. "*We?*"

She sucks her lip into her mouth again, gnawing on the flesh, her fingers brushing her long hair behind her ears. "Yeah, uhh, Chase came with me."

My nostrils flare, the resentment rising through me like a flash flood. "And where is he?" I glance around like he's waiting, lurking in the shadows, ready to pop up at any moment.

"He ain't here." She lifts a shoulder. "But you know how he gets, he wouldn't let me come alone, and I had already bought the ticket. It's been almost three months since we talked, Teeth, I needed to make sure you were okay."

"A trip to my mom's house would have been a lot less expensive," I snap, suddenly over this conversation.

She brought Chase. As soon as she forgave him, she just expected the world to agree. But I don't forgive him. Not for what he did to her, and not for what he did to me.

"Your mama never tells me anything you don't want her to, and you know it." She grins. "Listen, don't be mad, okay? I wanted to surprise you, thought it would be fun to see where your new life is. And Chase, he... well, you know how he is. But he knows you won't wanna see him. He's just here for me."

I snort. "Better late than never, I guess."

Her eyes narrow. "My problems with Chase are my own. I'm here for *you*."

Old resentment billows and unfurls like smoke, tarring up my lungs and making me choke. "And I didn't *ask* for you to be."

Her eyes grow glassy, and like muscle memory my heart pangs, wanting to wipe away her tears. Only now, the feeling she inspires in me isn't the love I thought it once was. It just feels like friendship.

Once again, my stomach clenches thinking about how Blakely and I left things. About how I snapped and let my emotions get the best of me. Let my insecurity over no one knowing about us bleed into my reaction to something that, in the grand scheme of things, isn't even a big deal.

I need to talk to her.

Snapping the hairband on my wrist, I walk toward my toolbox. "This is just..." I sigh. "I wish you would have let me know first."

"Oh, because if I had called, you would have answered?" she retorts, following behind me. "Teeth, you're not even answerin' Becca's phone calls."

I shrug my shoulders. "That's because she's annoying."

A giggle bursts out of Lee's mouth and it makes a smile jump onto my face.

"Look, sweetheart, I'm happy to see you, I really am. But I can't do anything tonight, I have plans." I hesitate, wondering if I should tell her about Blakely. Now that she's here, desperation tugs at my insides, wanting to tell her. Wanting her to know so that I can gain some outside perspective. So that she knows that I finally get it. I *know* what the 'can't eat, can't breathe, can't sleep' kind of love feels like, because I found it in this amazing woman.

Still, something holds me back from speaking up. "How long are you here for?"

"Just through tomorrow." She grins. "I know it's not good timin' with it bein' Monday and all, but we need to be home on the weekend for our meetin's."

My eyebrows draw in. "Meetings?"

She nods. "Yeah, every Sunday, Chase runs a group for families of addiction. I've been goin'." She beams and a warm content feeling swims through my veins.

She's really working on herself, and even if Chase is part of the reason, I can't be mad at that.

All I ever wanted was for Lee to be happy.

I wipe my hands on a terry cloth towel and grab my keys off the shelf, turning to look at her. "I'm assuming you need a ride back to wherever you're staying?"

She smiles a big, toothy grin. "Honestly, I miss that car more than you. It's the real reason I'm even here."

A loud laugh bursts from my throat and I shake my head. Walking toward the garage door to set the alarms for the night I throw my arm over her shoulder. "Come on, sweetheart. Let's get you back."

An hour later, I'm sitting in my living room, going over everything that's happened in the past few hours.

My phone is resting on my thigh, faceup, in case I get a text or a call from Blakely, and a pressure weighs down on my chest with every minute that the screen stays dark.

Earlier tonight, I missed her calls. And her texts.

And now it's radio silence.

Where is she?

It isn't like her to ignore my calls. Even when she's in the midst of her busy schedule, she always responds. Lets me know that she's still there. That she's thinking of me.

Lennox gave me his number for emergencies a while back, before we even got together, and I'd be lying if I said this was the first time I thought about using it to get him to let me in the house.

He's the reason I was able to get to her after the day on her pool deck, when I found her almost catatonic on her bathroom floor. But these days her dad spends more time at home, and the last thing I want is to run into him before he knows about us. And that leaves me completely helpless. A ball of anxiety churning in my gut as I wait for some type of recognition.

Something that lets me know she's okay.

But all I get is silence.

44

JACKSON

The next morning, I wake up before my alarm, my sleep being plagued by nightmares of Blakely needing me and being all alone. Unease circles in my stomach, the need to talk to her overriding every other thought in my brain.

I reach to the side table, grabbing my phone before my eyes are fully open, wanting to see if I missed a response from Blakely.

Nothing yet.

Calling into work, I tell the temp at the front desk that I won't be in today, my stomach souring at the reminder that Blakely no longer works there.

Brushing the thought aside, I pick up the phone and send her a good morning text before dialing the number I've been avoiding for months, figuring that if Alina is here, I might as well take the time to be with her. She's never traveled outside of Tennessee. Never been on a plane. Her coming here at all is a big step for her.

I just hope Chase stays away.

My jaw clenches at the thought of him. At the sheer *audacity* of him tagging along. But I won't lie and say that part of me doesn't want him to force his way into the time, make amends for all the ways he let me, and our friendship, down.

But I know better than to hope. If he wanted to, he would. And so far, he hasn't.

"Good mornin', Teeth!" Lee's chipper, her voice like sunshine peeking through blinds, and a smirk creeps on my face before I can stop myself. It's good to hear her talk, and it's even better not feeling old wounds bleed whenever she does.

I think my heart is mended. Now it's another girl who's responsible for the beats.

"Hey, sweetheart. Ready to get some Jax lovin' in today?" I joke, falling easily into the banter that flows so effortlessly between us.

"Yes!" she squeals. Energy rushes my body, suddenly excited to show someone from back home my neck of the woods. My mom won't come to Cali, the memories too rough for her to relive, and it's been lonely out here, not being able to share my present with anyone from my past.

"Okay." I smile. "I'll be there in an hour to pick you up."

"I'll be wearin' bells and whistles."

I open my mouth, ready to tell her not to let *him* tag

along, but I hold back, deciding to let things play out, see if the jealousy will show the way it used to when we were kids.

But to my surprise, he stays in the hotel.

Lee hops into the passenger seat of my car, grinning from ear to ear, a short jean skirt and a Dixie Chicks tee on her small frame, her honey hair pulled up in a giant bun.

I bounce my hand on top of it and she bats me away, scowling. "Quit that."

"Cute." I smirk.

She kicks off her flip-flops, throwing her feet up on the dash without a care in the world. And once again, my mind is brought back to the time when Blakely did the same thing, worried that I would be upset. Apologizing for the simple act of being comfortable in a car.

My chest pulls tight, realizing that it's nine a.m. and I still haven't gotten a text back. I soothe my worries by telling myself it's her first day of not having to be at Donahue Motors, and maybe she's sleeping in, catching up on time for herself after a lifetime of living for other people.

"What just happened?" Lee asks.

I side-eye her as I pull onto the street, heading back to my house. "What do you mean?"

"Your face got all wonky."

I bite the inside of my lip. "Wonky?"

"Yeah, you know... droopy in the corners, like you just thought of somethin' sad." The air grows thick the longer I stay silent. "*Are* you sad, Jax?"

My grip tightens on the steering wheel. "I'm actually really happy, sweetheart. I uh... I met someone."

She squeals, the sound so harsh in the quiet of the car

that my hand jerks on the wheel, making us swerve over the dotted white line.

"I knew it! Tell me *everything.*"

My chest warms. "Let's get back to my place first."

Lee nods, leaning back in her seat, a goofy smile on her face and her shoulders slightly less tense than when she first got in the car. It's nice seeing her this way. Reminiscent of her youth, before her mom died and Chase disappeared. Before her dad became a raging alcoholic and she had to carry the weight of his secrets on her back.

It makes me miss home, a twinge of envy for everyone who's gotten to see her rebloom.

My phone vibrates in my pocket and at the next red light I pull it out, relief swarming every part of me when I see Blakely's name is on the screen.

I text her back quickly, not wanting to miss my opportunity, and the tension loosens from my shoulders as we pull into my driveway and head inside.

I give Lee a brief tour, but my place is small and bare, never really having taken the time to turn this house into a home.

"So," she says, chomping on the Doritos she grabbed from my pantry. "Tell me all about her. What's her name?"

Sighing, I rest against the kitchen counter, snapping a hairband against my wrist, trying to figure out where the hell to start.

"You remember me telling you about Blakely?"

Her forehead scrunches. "That bratty girl you always droned on about?" Realization lights up her eyes. "You're tellin' me *she's* the girl you're with?"

I nod.

"Ain't she nineteen?"

Sucking air in through my teeth, I nod again.

"Oh." She pauses, licking her orange fingers clean before diving in to grab another chip.

My entire face screws up. "*Lee,* that's disgusting."

Her brows furrow. "What is?"

I gesture to the bag. "You just licked your fingers and now you're double-dipping."

She laughs, shrugging her shoulders. "And you're deflectin'." She points at me. "Tell me, Mr. King of one-night stands, how did the girl you used to hate come to be your *lovahhh.*" She draws out the word, wiggling her eyebrows.

I chuckle, my fingers playing with the chain of my necklace. "I don't know. It just kind of... happened. Her dad asked me to watch out for her, and when I did, I realized that she was so much more than I thought."

"Weren't you already babysittin'? You used to call it that all the time." She narrows her eyes at me. "Back when we used to talk every week."

I cringe, remembering all the times I complained about Blakely. Back then, she was just some young girl who got under my skin and pushed all my buttons. But that was before my irritation for who she pretends to be transformed into passion for who she is.

"Maybe I spoke it into existence." I grin, moving around and reaching in the bag to grab a chip. "You once told me I'd find the everything kind of love... that it would knock me on my ass. Do you remember that?"

Her eyes gloss over as she nods, her hand coming up to rest on her heart. "Jax, are you tellin' me you're in love with this girl?"

Something warm and tender fills up my chest. "Yeah, sweetheart. She's my everything."

45

BLAKELY

I wake up later than normal on Tuesday morning, and while I feel more rested than I have in years, my brain automatically goes into flight or fight mode, racing around the room like I have somewhere to be.

Every still second is a second wasted.

It isn't until I'm halfway through my fasted cardio that I remember I *don't* actually have somewhere to be. But instead of freedom, I feel the sting of sadness wrapping itself around me. The only reprieve I get is knowing that because I haven't told Sierra of my freed-up schedule, I have the day to just… *be.*

I don't know the last time I've ever spent a morning

doing absolutely nothing. The thought shoots an uncomfortable tingle down my spine, but I ignore it. My stomach tightens around nothing, the emptiness of fasted cardio always bringing me a sense of accomplishment, and I grasp onto the fiery burn, hoping it will propel me through the rest of my day.

Or at least until the next workout.

I jump off the spin bike the second I hit one thousand calories and rush my way back up to my room where I left my phone, unable to stem the urge that's pushing at my back, telling me to man up and just *read Jackson's messages.*

Unlocking my screen, my breaths still coming in sharp gusts from exercise, I open up the string of texts.

Jackson: Sorry I missed your call. You still heading over?

Jackson: Hello?

Jackson: Blake, are you okay? I'm starting to get worried.

Jackson: Good morning. Please call me.

Nothing after that.

My chest sparks with regret, shame flaring because I couldn't keep it together when I saw him with that girl. That instead of handling it like an adult, I spiraled into the mess that I try so hard to hide from the world.

The part that I hate about myself the most.

At the first sign of something not going my way, I fall apart at the seams. I don't *want* to be this way. I'm sick of feeling like a malfunction. A broken doll that's patched together to try and fool the world.

Blowing out a deep breath, I text back.

Me: Hi. I'm sorry. I was a mess last night and I should have responded sooner. Can we talk today?

I don't expect an immediate response, but before I can

even set my phone down, three bubbles pop up on the screen. My heart jumps.

Jackson: A friend from back home showed up in town so I'm taking today off to spend some time. Do you want to meet her?

The first thing I feel is relief. Every crazy scenario that looped through my brain all night disappears like they never even existed, because he didn't hide her from me. He's being honest and open. But then, as the words sink into my brain, my insides tighten like a drawstring, wrangling like a noose around my throat.

A friend from back home.

Chewing my bottom lip, my fingers tremble as I type a reply.

Me: Who is it?

The three bubbles pop up and then stop over and over, and each time they do, my stomach screws tighter until it feels like it might crack from the pressure.

Jackson: Lee.

Jackson: I really want you to meet her.

I lay down my phone, my chest lighting up so quickly my face turns hot, my heart hurling itself against my rib cage.

Deep breath. One. Two. Three.

Me: Does she know about us?

Jackson: No, but I'd like her to.

My mind races, wanting to meet this girl, but not sure I'll be able to control myself. I want to slap her for hurting him. I want to throttle her for showing up and taking away the small amount of time that we get.

But leaving them alone together while I sit and wonder where they are and what they're doing feels like the worst type of purgatory.

So, it really comes down to picking which version of hell I want to sink into.

Me: I'd like to meet her. Can we do it somewhere private? Why don't you two come here?

Jackson: Is your dad going to be there?

Me: No, he left town this morning.

Jackson: We'll be there.

Jackson: I love you.

Anxiety twirls like a ballerina in the center of my stomach as I write him back.

I love him too. I just hope he doesn't remember how much he loves *her*.

JACKSON TEXTED around two that they were on their way, and my insides have been raging in protest ever since. I thought about calling Kayla just to have someone to vent to, but she hasn't been anywhere near supportive of Jackson and my relationship and I cower at the idea, not wanting to deal with having to defend him *again.*

Besides, telling her about Jackson and Alina feels like a breach of his trust.

The intercom buzzes in the kitchen and I spring up from my spot where I've been staring into the security cameras, waiting impatiently for them to arrive.

My stomach squeezes as I open the gate and let them in.

One. Two. Three.

I prepared some snacks, things that I know will fit into my daily count, and food that will hopefully keep Alina from judging me too harshly. I'm already on edge from meeting her in the first place, and new people *always* have something to say about the way I eat.

Walking to the front door, I swing it open just as they land on the top step, Jackson's car parked in the circle drive behind them.

I paste on a big smile, the one I use for the cameras, and Jackson walks up and grabs me around the waist, pressing a tender kiss on my lips. A little bit of tension seeps out when he does.

He pulls back, his eyes looking so deep in mine I feel like they're trying to draw out my soul. "Hi, princess."

"Hi yourself." I smile. My heart swells at his attention, but my nerves are stinging me with every motion, reminding me there's a lot to feel nervous about.

He steps back, running his hand down my arm until our fingers tangle together, turning so that he's standing next to me and facing his friend.

My gaze follows his and I hold my breath as I take her in. She's *gorgeous* and when she smiles my chest tightens with envy.

Her baby blues land on me, a shade of curiosity crossing her features, her head tilting the slightest amount. It would be unnoticeable to the average person, but I've been trained since birth to learn how to read people, to know what they're thinking before they've even finished the thought, and I can tell she's sizing me up. Making sure I meet her standards. That I'm worthy enough for a man like Jackson.

Spoiler alert: I'm not.

Slowly, a smile spreads across her face. "You look familiar," she says.

My stomach cramps.

"Do I?" Keeping my smile in place causes so much

strain it pulls the muscles in my cheeks.

"Yeah, I don't know... somethin' about you." She glances behind me, her eyes widening as she takes in the expansive foyer and the ornate chandelier hanging above our heads. "Dang, this place is massive. You ever get lost when you're tryin' to get around?"

Her thick accent paired with her unfiltered words catch me off guard, not used to people who aren't polished and proper, especially during introductions, and whether I like it or not, a tiny sliver in the center of my chest warms.

The corners of my lips twitch. "Not since I was a kid. Come in, please."

I move to the side, tugging Jackson's hand to make more room, and Alina walks in, whistling as she peers down the hallways.

She spins back around, her hands in her back pockets as she glares at Jackson. "Teeth, I think you and introductions are a lost cause. You're terrible at 'em."

He chuckles, squeezing my fingers and gesturing toward her. "Blakely, this is my best friend, Alina, but you can call her Lee. Lee, this is Blakely."

"I've heard a lot about you." It's the nicest thing I can muster, my insides split down the middle, raging between wanting to be mean because she broke Jackson's heart, and wanting to be nice because she clearly means a lot to him.

And I'm instantly jealous of the way they are with each other.

There's an obvious comfort to them. One that only exists when you've known each other for years, and a niggle of doubt worms its way into my brain, wondering if there was more to the story of them than Jackson wanted me to believe.

Her smile widens, her golden hair shining underneath

the lights. "I'll be honest, I can't say the same, but I'm just dyin' to get to know you."

Surprise pushes into my stomach, stealing my breath away.

She wants to get to know me?

Is this some kind of trick?

Keeping the grin in place, my free hand clenches at my side, confusion spinning my brain in circles, trying to figure out if she's being genuine or if she's putting on a show. I'm not used to dealing with someone outside of Hollywood, and years of learning to think the worst of people have whittled my ability to trust a stranger down until it's barely a nub.

Jackson clears his throat when I don't respond right away, pulling me into him and kissing the side of my head. Satisfaction buzzes through me at the fact that he's not afraid to touch me in front of her.

I watch Alina close, looking for a sign—something that shows me she's bothered by his affection. But her eyes soften as they take us in, a peaceful look covering her face, and if I didn't know any better I could swear she was close to tears.

"Let's go sit down somewhere," Jackson says.

"Yeah, I set out some food if you guys are hungry." I move forward, walking briskly into the kitchen, my mind jumbled and my heart palpitating. I've only known her for two minutes, but she's already so different from the image I had in my head.

As we reach the kitchen, I take a deep breath, telling myself that I'm going to be mature about this.

I'm going to give her a chance.

Because I love Jackson, and Jackson loves her.

And I'll just have to find some way to be okay with that.

46

JACKSON

I see the tension leaving Blakely's shoulders with every minute she spends in Lee's presence, and as it does the rope that's been knotting around my stomach eases. I won't lie and say that it didn't make me nervous to bring her here, especially since things have felt so off between Blakely and me.

But Lee has a way about her, she forces her way into your life and makes herself at home. So if there's anyone who can walk into a mansion with someone I'm dating in secret, acting like it's just another day, Lee's the girl.

I sit back and watch as they interact, Lee shoving food

in her mouth and asking a million questions about Blakely's career, fascinated by the fact she's a social media influencer.

"So, you get paid to post photos or what?"

Blakely shrugs. "Yeah, it's a bit more involved than that, but basically, people pay me to promote their brand or be seen in their clothes. Things like that."

"How many followers do you have?"

Blakely shrugs again. "A lot."

Lee scoffs. "Girl, come on now, don't be shy. I don't even *have* social media. I gotta get my jollies somehow, you know?"

Blakely's nose scrunches. "You don't?" She turns to look at me. "What *is* it with you people in that town not having any contact with the outside world?"

I smirk. "Sugarlake is a unique place, princess. The kids all use it, but for us, there isn't really anything you can post that the town doesn't already know." I glance over to Lee. "Unless you work *really* hard at keeping it quiet."

Blakely's head cocks. "Wow. I honestly cannot imagine life like that. It sounds..."

"Borin'?" Lee pipes in.

"Peaceful." Blakely sighs.

My heart spasms in my chest, surprise flowing through me. This is the first time I've heard Blakely insinuate that she doesn't enjoy what she does, and it gives me hope that she'll be more receptive when I bring up how I think it's her environment exacerbating her issues. The ones that manifest in front of my eyes and become worse whenever she's surrounded by people who constantly tell her how they'll improve her looks "post production."

Lee laughs, covering her stomach with her hands. "I'm so sorry, y'all I—" She wipes under her eyes, taking deep breaths. "The thought of Sugarlake bein' peaceful is..." Her giggles continue to trickle out of her. "Well, it's just a little funny, is all. But yeah... if you're used to the whole world bein' in your business, I'd guess that small-town drama wouldn't come close to comparin'."

Blakely's lips turn up, her face warm and open. "You're so different than I thought you'd be."

Lee's head cocks. "I don't know if that's a good thing or a bad thing."

"Definitely a good thing." Blakely reaches over and squeezes my thigh. "Can I be honest?"

"I hope you're never anything else," Lee responds.

"I thought you'd be a bitch."

Lee's eyes widen and she leans in close. "Who says I ain't?"

They both burst out in giggles and I bite back my smirk, a warm, gooey sensation filling up the center of my chest and spreading until my entire body is consumed by the feeling. I've never seen Blakely look so calm. So carefree. So... *happy*. And the way her and Lee have hit it off, despite the way I bled my heart out into her palms—it makes me feel more confident than ever in our future.

"What are you doin' tonight, Miss Celebrity?" Lee asks. "We should all go out to dinner." She glances at me from her peripheral and my insides clench tight because I know where this is headed.

"*All* of us?" I narrow my eyes.

She sighs. "Look, Teeth, I know you don't wanna see him, but I was hopin' y'all could sit down while he's here, and you know, work things out."

I purse my lips.

Blakely's eyes bounce between us, her brows drawing in.

My palm covers her hand that's still on my thigh, suddenly wanting her support while Lee brings up someone

I'd rather have left out of the conversation. "Can we not talk about this right now?" I grit out. "We've been having a good day and you're ruining it."

Lee jolts back, raising her hands in surrender. "Ugh, fine, Jax. Have it your way."

Blakely fidgets, clearing her throat. "Probably best I don't come along with whatever you guys have planned tonight anyway. I have a meeting at the house with Sierra, and besides..." She glances toward me. "It wouldn't be smart to be seen somewhere that we can be photographed."

My stomach flips and drops to the floor. I had *almost* been able to forget while we were here.

It felt so nice. So *normal* to be with her like this, not having to worry if I was looking at her for too long or touching her too much.

Lee's eyes lock onto mine. "Y'all aren't plannin' on goin' public?"

I try to speak around the sudden lump growing in the center of my throat. "We're just being careful."

"For a couple reasons," Blakely chimes in. "One is because things get crazy when you're in the limelight and I don't want Jackson to have to deal with it." She looks toward me again. "Literally hundreds of cameras in your face at every turn, and gossip rags digging into your past, using it to sell a story. Which they *will* do."

She says it like I haven't already thought of that. Like I haven't gone over every single scenario in my head a thousand times and decided that as long as I get to be with her none of it matters.

"Besides, my father would lose his mind, and I would never forgive myself if Jackson lost his job, his chance at making all his dreams come true, because of me."

I give a soft smile through the throbbing ache in my

chest, reminding myself that everything she's doing is out of concern for *me*.

But it doesn't help to blot the sting of truth in her words.

"Yeah, so, speaking of…" I angle my head and look at Lee. "Don't tell anyone back home."

"Who would I tell?" She chomps on a cracker.

"Becca. Eli..." I take in a breath. "Chase."

She sighs, putting her food down on her plate. "Jax, I don't know if I can keep this from Chase. He's gonna ask what we did today, and we're always one-hundred-percent honest with each other. It's the only way to keep communication open and trust in place. But I promise I won't breathe a word of it to anyone else."

Grinding my teeth, I give a short nod back.

My stomach tenses as we leave, happy that I got to see Blakely, but still feeling like something is shifted slightly out of place.

Lee gives Blakely a giant hug on her way out, telling her to not be a stranger.

I stay behind, pushing Blakely up against the wall beside the open door.

"What are you doing?" she breathes.

"Kissing you." I dive into her lips, moaning as her taste touches my tongue, my body pressing her against the wall. Her arms come up around my neck, squeezing me tight, and I groan, getting lost in everything she is.

Finally, I break away, my forehead resting against hers. "Goddamn, princess, you make it hard to leave."

She giggles, her finger coming up to trace the edges of my mouth. "Are we okay?"

My heart squeezes. "Yeah, baby, we're okay."

I wrap my hands tighter around her waist. "Lee leaves

tomorrow, and I *really* want some time alone with you. Do you think we can figure something out before next week?"

She nods. "We'll figure something out."

Pecking her lips one more time, I force myself away from her and walk out the door.

47

BLAKELY

Alina—*Lee*—was different than I expected, and as they leave out of my front door, I feel a sense of peace that I haven't had since hearing her name. They love each other, that much is clear, but Jackson doesn't look at her the way he looks at me.

And I find comfort in that.

She's genuine in a way that I only learned people could be when Jackson came into my life, and it makes me curious to know if everyone in their small town is just as nice, or if it's something unique to the two of them, and maybe that's what drew them together in the first place.

For the rest of the afternoon, I bask in the relaxation

that comes along with being able to hide away from the world, no one knowing where I am or what I'm doing. I try to sit down and watch something, but the only thing on is reality TV and it makes my stomach turn as their drama plays out on the screen.

None of its real.

I'm just as guilty, making people long for a make-believe world.

A few months ago, I never would have thought twice about it. I guess that's the funny thing about life. It just takes a moment for your world to flip upside down. A shift in altitude that changes your view. Gives you a new perspective.

Sierra sits across from me on the couch, racks of clothing being brought in for me to choose from for the next two weeks. This is a routine thing. It takes hours, and usually I enjoy it. But now, just like with everything else that comes along with my job, I can't seem to find the enthusiasm. Because really, who fucking *cares* whether I pick the crotchet crop top or the bright pink jumpsuit. The finished product everyone sees will be different than what it actually looks like anyway. A false perception, molded to trick the public, just like every other second of my life.

"So." Sierra tucks her legs underneath her on the couch. "Let's talk publicity."

"Okay." I nod, sipping from my water bottle.

"DJ Andelo's team has been reaching out *incessantly*, wanting to hook something up between the two of you."

I scrunch my nose, the memory of the handsy DJ from a few months back making me cringe. "What do you mean, 'hook something up'?"

"I mean they want to put you two together out and

about in public. Get people talking... asking questions." She pauses. "I think it's a good idea."

My stomach constricts. "Like fake dating?"

Sierra clicks her tongue. "You two are both in the clubbing scene, and it would be great promo for both your careers. I wanted to run it by you first, but I'm about to call them back and say we're on board."

"No," I snap. My voice comes out quick and sharp.

Her eyes narrow. "What do you mean, *no*?"

I shrug. "I mean *no*, Sierra. It's pretty simple. I don't want to. DJ Andelo was hella gropey the one time I shared a stage with him. I'm not comfortable doing anything that involves spending one-on-one time."

She rolls her eyes. "Guys grope, B. That's what they do. Especially when you wear your cute little outfits and prance around on stage with your tits and ass in their face."

My chest burns. "Excuse me? Are you saying it's *my* fault he got handsy?"

"I'm saying you should know by now what to expect with who you are and the reputation you put out to the public." She brushes a strand of hair from her forehead.

"You're the one that picks my damn outfits, Sierra!" I shriek, pointing to the racks of clothes. "You think I want to be seen in this shit? I don't care about any of it. *Any* of it."

Sierra's eyes widen and she sits back against the couch cushions, blowing out a slow breath. "Well…" she speaks slowly. "That's something you should have realized before you chose this career, Blakely. And correct me if I'm wrong, but a few months ago you had *zero* problems with any of this, and now all of a sudden you don't care?"

My fists curl in my lap, wondering how we got so off track. My original plan was to dive headfirst back into the game. Make up for the lost time that was spent wasting away at my dad's shop. But, being back doesn't feel as gratifying as I thought it would.

"No," I sigh. "I *do* care, I just… don't you think it's all a little meaningless?"

"It's that mechanic," she spits the word.

My heart stutters, my eyes shooting to her face. "W-what?"

"Blakely." Her gaze narrows. "Don't play stupid with me, okay? Cut the shit and keep it real. I *know*. You really thought it was something you could keep from me?"

"No, but—" I shake my head back and forth, confusion tumbling through me.

How could she possibly know when we've been so careful?

I can only come up with one possible conclusion. Someone told her.

All the air is sucked out of my lungs. "How do you know?"

"That's not important." She waves her hand.

My fist slams down on my knee, my jaw squeezing so tight it feels like it's bruising. "*How* do you know, Sierra?"

With every second that goes by, the balloon of tension grows, waiting for her to say the words—a prick to ignite the explosion.

She sighs. "Kayla called and told me."

Boom.

My ears ring from the fury that erupts in my veins, something dark and thick oozing from every orifice.

"She was worried about you." Sierra moves in closer, placing her hand on my leg. "Both of us are."

I snap, my hand reaching out and tossing Sierra's away roughly, my body shaking from how hard I'm tensing my muscles to try and maintain control. I want to race across the city, hunt down that backstabbing bitch and throttle her.

How could she?

My mind spins like a merry-go-round, lost in my madness, and I know that if I don't get it together, I'll crumble where I sit.

And I don't want to crumble right now. I want to find Kayla and demand to know why.

I stand up so fast my head spins, my fists tightening against my sides.

One. Two. Three.

"What are you doing?" Sierra asks, her voice rising in pitch.

"Leaving."

"You *can't* leave, Blakely, we have tons to do tonight."

"I don't care, Sierra. You're spending your time trying to set me up on a date with a sexual harasser and telling me not to be with the man I love, and for *what*? Because he doesn't fit some bullshit standard?"

"That's exactly why!" she screeches. "He doesn't fit the standard, Blakely. *Your* standard. He's too old, and too middle-income. It doesn't look good. It *won't* look good. When you started your career you had two choices. Do you remember? You either become someone they can relate to, or someone they wish they could be. And you chose the latter, so guess what, you can't have everything you want. Because dating some nobody who is almost a decade older than you? That's not something most people wish for."

My hands reach up and tug on my strands. "This is *so* stupid."

She shrugs. "It is what it is."

Huffing out a laugh, I try to ignore the Mack truck

that's barreling through my insides going a hundred miles an hour. "Yeah, Sierra. It is what it is. I'm leaving."

I walk away without a second glance.

The urge to head straight to the gym is strong, but the need to hunt down Kayla is stronger. So, even though I told Lennox he could have the evening off, I stomp back to his cottage, the quickness of my blood pumping through my veins making my face hot with anger.

I can't believe she told Sierra.

Maybe later, when my mind clears of its red haze, I'll be able to look back on my friendship with Kayla and find where we veered off course so badly—when she became someone I couldn't confide in and turned into this person who would go behind my back and ruin the only good thing I have in my life.

Or maybe she was always playing a role for me, the same way I play a role for the masses.

My fist pounds against the front door to Lennox's cottage, waiting for what feels like hours until I hear shuffling and muffled voices.

Shit. Does he have company?

Sucking my bottom lip into my mouth, I wait, guilt pressing down on my chest for being so selfish. For running back here when it's clear he's taking advantage of the night off I gave him.

I turn around to leave just as his front door swings open.

He's shirtless, his tattooed abs and corded muscles on full display. But that's not what shocks me into stunned silence, my chest tightening and my spine tingling with suspicion. It's his look of surprise that morphs into guilt as he stares at me.

He jerks his head in a nod. "Are you okay?"

"Hey." I cringe. "I'm so sorry to bother you." I gesture

toward the door. "I just... I was hoping you weren't busy and could give me a ride to find Kayla. I umm..." I pause, wringing my fingers together. "Never mind. I can wait until tomorrow." Casting him a sheepish glance, I turn to leave.

I was *so* close to never knowing. But then I hear a different voice and I spin around, my heartbeat surging to my throat.

"Is that—"

He stiffens, his eyes closing.

Shock forces me back a step. "Is that Kayla? Is she *here?*"

The thought of her with Lennox reignites the fire in my veins and I shove by him, pushing the door open. He doesn't put up a fight.

Kayla stands in the middle of his living room, naked, save for a white bedsheet around her body, her wide eyes staring at me across the space.

My mouth opens and closes a few times as my eyes bounce back and forth between them.

In any other situation, I probably wouldn't have cared. But after tonight, all I can see is betrayal as it flows from her and soars across the room, wrapping itself around Lennox and binding them together. Emotion clogs my throat and stings the back of my eyes, my knuckles white from how tightly my fists are pressing against my sides.

One. Two. Three.

"Why, Kayla?" I force out.

She cocks her head, her lips turning down. "You know I've always liked him, Blakely."

I cut my hand through the air. "Not that. Not Lennox. I don't give a *fuck* about him. Why would you tell Sierra about us?"

Her eyes light up with recognition, and if I fool myself I

can almost imagine the regret that flashes behind her eyes. But it's gone in a millisecond, replaced by a smirk.

"Why not?" She shrugs.

"I'm sorry," Lennox cuts in. "You did what?"

I spin and face him. "Oh, she didn't share that during pillow talk? I confided in her about Jackson, and she ran and told Sierra out of *concern* for me."

Lennox's brows furrow, his head turning sharply toward her. "What? Why would you do that, Kayla? That's not your place."

"Because she's going to ruin *everything*." She glares at me. "You don't appreciate how things are handed to you on a silver platter, when the rest of us are out here working our *asses* off trying to make it half as big as you."

I nod slowly as I take in what she says, flashbacks of our friendship playing on a loop in my mind, showing me all the ways she's been bitter over who I am.

"I'm looking out for you, Blakely. That man will ruin you. You can't just go around secretly dating anybody you want and think everything will be okay."

"Wow." I laugh. "You're saying this to me while wrapped in my bodyguard's bedsheet. '*Jake*' I presume. Pot meet kettle."

She breaks eye contact. "That's different."

"Oh?" My eyebrows shoot to my hairline.

"I love him," she states, her shoulders lifting.

I grin, my face tilting toward the ceiling, the trembling inside of my body vibrating through my bones, making me feel unsteady. It's a miracle I'm still holding it together when everything around me feels like it's starting to collapse.

The curtain has been pulled, showing me that I've been living happily in my bubble for who knows how long, letting these people dictate my entire life when really, they've all been doing whatever the hell they want anyway.

I close my eyes.

"Blakely." Lennox's voice is a deep rasp.

I lift my hand, stopping him from speaking as I work on slowing down my heart rate, trying to regulate my breathing.

One. Two. Three.

Opening my eyes, I walk over to Kayla, my hand coming up and whipping across her face, the sharp sting of my palm satisfying every single cell in my body. Her head rolls to the side, a surprised gasp leaving her lips.

"What the *fuck?*" she squeals, her hand covering her cheek.

I point at her. "That's for making me think you were someone I could trust."

I turn around, shouldering past Lennox, and slam the door behind me.

48

JACKSON

I'm dropping Lee off when my phone rings. Blakely's name flashes across the screen and a spike of concern shoots through me. It's odd for her to call when she's supposed to be working the rest of the night. My car is idling on the curb in front of the hotel, and I hold up a finger to Lee so I can answer.

"Hey, princess." It's silent on the line and I pull the phone away from my ear, checking to make sure it's connected. "Hello?"

"Jackson." Her voice is strained—a pained whimper that has me sitting up straighter in my seat.

Lee looks over, lips turning down when she sees my shift in position.

"What's wrong?" I ask.

"I just—I need..."

She pants into the line, and my heart surges at her shortness of breath.

She hasn't had a panic attack in over a month. At least, not any that I've seen, and the sound of it happening when I'm so far away is a sledgehammer to my insides, making me feel as though, once again, I'm not with the people I love when they need me the most.

"What do you need, baby? Are you okay?"

"I ne-need you to come get me." She hesitates. "Please."

"On my way. I'll be there in about twenty minutes. Do you need to stay on the phone with me?"

"No, I just... I can't be here anymore." Her voice breaks and my heart cracks along with it, wishing I could fly there instead of having to depend on four tires and a road.

"Okay. Deep breaths, yeah?"

She breathes deeply in and out on the other end of the line. I hang up, suddenly desperate to say my goodbyes to Lee and make my way to where Blakely is. To take her back to my house and hold her in my arms until she works her way through her panic.

"Is everything alright?" Lee asks.

Shaking my head, I snap my hairband off my wrist, using it to throw up my hair. "No. Blakely needs me. She..." I trail off, not wanting to spill all her issues into the open. Even though it's Lee, and I know secrets are safe with her, it still feels wrong.

It's Blakely's story to tell, when and if she chooses to tell it.

"Say no more." Lee smiles, her eyes shimmering. "She's amazin', you know? Young." She laughs. "But amazin'. You did good, Teeth."

My chest inflates with happiness. Lee always told me when I fell in love she'd be front row, cheering me on the hardest.

"Leave it to you to fall for a girl who lives her life in the spotlight. If you ain't careful, Hollywood's gonna try and snatch that pretty smile right off your face." Lee grins, reaching out and pinching my cheek.

I bat her hand away, laughing, my eyes glancing to the dashboard clock, anxious to say goodbye and head to where I'm needed.

"Yeah, yeah," Lee says. "I see you starin' at the clock. I'll leave. But you gotta answer my phone when I call, okay? And call Becca too, she misses you."

I nod.

"Promise me, Jax." She sticks out her pinky finger.

I loop mine with it and swallow. "I promise."

Opening the door and stepping onto the sidewalk, she looks back, smirking. "Here's to goodbyes, so we appreciate the hellos."

"You're never gonna let me forget I said that are you?" I chuckle.

She shrugs. "It's a good line."

"Be safe, sweetheart."

She smiles and when she closes the door and walks away, it feels like we also closed a chapter. Moved into a new space where I don't long for her the way I once did—where we can love and support each other the way we were always meant to.

I wait until she's inside the building before I leave,

shifting onto the road and hoping Blakely will be okay until I get to her.

When I pull up to her estate, I see a hunched form curled against the outside of the gates and realize it's her.

My stomach somersaults, wondering what the hell could have happened from the time I was here until now. It's only been a few hours. I move to put the car in park and grab her, but her tear-stained face looks right at me and she hops up, running to my car. Black smudges contrast against the pale skin of her face. She throws herself across the center console, wrapping her upper body around me.

"Princess, what happened?"

She sniffles, her body trembling in my arms. Cradling her to my chest tighter, my hand brushes down the back of her head.

"Kayla told Sierra about us," she whispers. "It was bad."

My stomach jumps at her words, but hope swells inside of me. I didn't even realize Kayla knew, so the fact she did tells me that maybe Blakely is more open to going public than I originally thought.

And if Sierra knows... then the only person left to tackle is her father.

But now isn't the time to focus on that, so I push it to the back of my mind and hold her tight. She falls apart in my arms, like she was waiting for me to show up so she could, and I catch all of her pieces, waiting until she gets through the worst of it to drive home and help put her back together.

When the worst of it has subsided, she moves back into her own seat. I keep her hand locked with mine while I shift gears, letting the nighttime air flow in from the windows, hoping the wind will help calm her thoughts.

Her body still trembles as we walk to my front door and concern snakes up my spine. I grab her before we move inside, drawing her into my chest and bringing my lips to hers for a chaste kiss. She grabs my shirt and wrenches me closer, her tongue diving into my mouth.

I give in, my hands reaching around her and gripping tight, showing her that she can use me for whatever she needs.

"Thank you," she whispers against me.

Leaning back, I kiss the tip of her nose. "Nothing to thank me for, princess."

We go inside and I draw a bath in the clawfoot tub, wanting to give her some way to try and relax—quiet her mind.

She slips out of her clothes and submerges her body under the bubbly water as I light the candles I keep on the shelves just for her.

"This is always so nice," she croons. "Why don't I ever take baths at home?"

"Never too late to start." I move to sit next to her, dipping my hand in the water and swirling my fingers around.

"Are you gonna get in with me?" Her eyebrow quirks.

I smile. "I thought you'd never ask."

Pulling off my clothes, I sink in behind her, the heat of the water causing goose bumps to sprout along my exposed skin. My legs settle around her body, her ass nestling against my groin. The intimacy of the moment isn't lost on me *or* my cock, and despite wanting this to solely be about comfort, I start to harden against her.

Her head leans against my chest as I wrap my arms around her waist, kissing the side of her head. "What happened, princess?"

She sighs. "Sierra found out about us and she's... *not* happy."

Of course she isn't. "No offense, but I could give a fuck about what Sierra thinks."

She chews on her bottom lip, sinking farther into me. "Yeah, I guess you're right."

I tangle our fingers and bring them out of the water, staring down at how perfectly they fit together.

How can someone who feels so perfect for me have so many people against us?

"Blake... I want to talk to your dad."

Her upper body twists toward me. "What for?"

My chest pulls tight. "What do you mean what for? So we can be together. *Really* be together." I pause, my stomach turning with nerves as I think about how to say what I need. "I love you. But I don't know how much longer I can keep doing this in secret."

Her eyes water.

"It's *killing* me, Blake."

She sucks her bottom lip into her mouth, her eyes staring into mine, softening the longer they stay locked on my gaze. "Okay."

My heart skips. "Yeah?"

She smiles, leaning in to kiss me. "Yeah. Fuck them."

Her hand slips under the water, reaching between us to palm my growing erection. The water sloshes as she strokes me, her fingers slipping up and down my length, coaxing me to grow until I'm throbbing in her hand.

"Baby," I groan. "As good as that feels, are you sure you don't want to talk first?"

"Mmm," she hums, her hair rubbing against my collarbone as she leans against me. "I just want to feel you." Her free hand grabs mine and moves it down her body until I'm cupping her pussy. "Touch me, Jackson."

I listen, the air charging with a thick tension as my fingers slip between her folds, caressing her clit in small circles.

She sucks in a breath, her hips pushing against my hand, starting a slow grind. On every backward motion, her ass grazes against me, making me jerk, desperate to fuck her until she can't speak from the pleasure.

My free hand cradles her jaw, head dipping down so I can mold my mouth to hers. She grips me tighter, her hand massaging me until suddenly her touch disappears. She moves forward, standing in the tub and then getting out, her naked body glistening under the lights of the room.

"You coming?" She looks back at me.

After the past couple days of us feeling off, and then everything that happened with her tonight, I just want to take care of her. Show her that I'm what she needs.

I jump out of the tub and follow her into the bedroom, water dripping off our skin. Catching her around the waist I throw her on the bed, crawling on top of her and then diving down to sweep my tongue up her neck.

She moans, her legs wrapping around my waist, my dick twitching against her as she rubs her pussy along the length of my shaft.

Our tongues weave together, a type of carnal passion infusing itself into the moment, overwhelming me with the lust that's burning through my insides.

I kiss her deeper, hoping that she'll taste it on my tongue and swallow it down to feel it in her soul.

My cock leaks, precum creating a sticky mess between us as she continues to work herself against me, and my gut coils tight.

I need to be inside her.

My hand wraps around my dick and I stroke it once before angling the head to rub against her clit, tingles spreading up my length.

"Goddamn, princess. Do you want me inside you?" I run my nose along the side of her neck.

"Jackson," she mewls.

Positioning myself at her entrance, I plunge to the hilt, my body tensing from the pleasure of being surrounded by her heat.

Fuck. She feels so incredible like this.

I work up a steady motion, thrusting in and out, long, deep strokes that send shivers racing up my spine.

Her hands push against my chest, moving me back on the bed where she can climb on top. My abs tense as she hovers over me. Inch by inch, she drops down until I'm fully inside of her. My cock throbs, pushing against the walls of her pussy, aching to paint her insides with my cum.

My hands grip the cheeks of her ass, squeezing hard as she moves back and forth, her clit rubbing against my pubic bone with every pass of her hips.

She's close. I can feel it in the way her walls clench and release, fluttering around my dick, her wetness gushing out until it soaks my skin. Heat collects at the base of my spine, my balls drawing up so tight they hurt.

Cum rises through my shaft and pumps out of the tip in rhythmic pulses, my cock flexing inside of her. My head hits the pillow, vision going black from the pleasure that's cascading through my body in waves.

She moans and throws her head back, her pussy squeezing out every drop as she explodes, shattering around me.

Incredible.

Pulling her to me, I try to catch my breath.

And as we both come back down to earth, my body buzzes, happy as hell this is the last night we'll have to hide.

She's choosing me.

49

BLAKELY

Jackson always makes me feel better, but there's still this ball of anxiety that's pulsing in the center of my stomach, making me agonize over our earlier conversation.

Go public.

Yeah, but why not? Everyone's trying to make decisions based on what *they* think is best for me, and I'm no longer interested in the things they have to say. If others insist on lighting my world on fire, I might as well enjoy the burn.

After we finished making love, I fell asleep, exhaustion wringing my bones. But now it's almost midnight and I'm wide awake, stomach growling from emptiness, my body feening for a workout. I left in such a rush—was in such a state of panic—that I didn't bring anything with me.

Getting out of bed as quietly as possible to not wake up Jackson, I head to the bathroom, staring at myself in the mirror. I cringe at what I see, shame clinging to my insides. Black mascara tracks down my face, my foundation streaked, showcasing the path of my tears.

I look around, trying to find something to clean my face, my muscles tightening until they push uncomfortably against my skin, my body ticking as I try to shake off the feeling.

This is the first time I've been at Jackson's house and felt the urge for my routine.

But there's nothing I can do about it, so I close my eyes and count until the need simmers to something manageable.

It's fine. Everything will be fine.

I settle for a water wash, taking a hand towel to help scrub the grime off my face. When I'm done I lay the towel down, my face raw from where I scrubbed too harshly, and I stare at myself in the mirror. My finger traces my reflection, an odd sensation filling my gut.

I don't like the way it feels so I snatch my hand back and leave the room, heading to the kitchen to find something I can eat.

I'm squatting down, searching the bottom of the pantry, my stomach winding tighter with each second as I search for something edible. The last thing I need is something to screw me up tighter and make me snap.

Where is all his food?

"Looking for something to eat, princess?"

My heart jumps into my throat at his voice and I spin around from my crouched position. "Yeah, I didn't bring anything with me, but your food choices are literally nonexistent. What have you been eating when I'm not here?"

He purses his lips. "You're staring at a full pantry."

I force a laugh, the ball of energy spinning faster in my gut. "This hardly counts as food." I wave my hand toward the shelves. "I need something I can eat, Jackson."

He sighs, running a hand through his tousled locks as he walks closer, leaning his back against the kitchen island. "Don't you get exhausted from all of this, Blake?"

My chest squeezes. "Exhausted from all of what, exactly?" I stand up and cross my arms, my defenses quivering from overuse.

He points to the pantry. "All of this. The never being able to eat anything other than what you've prepared. The constant fear of anything—*anything*—other than one-hundred-percent clean food entering your body. It's no way to live, princess."

My face grows hot, the earlier tension reigniting in my veins. "Are we really doing this right now? You *know* what my career demands. How important being healthy is to me." I spread my arms to the sides. "This is how I live."

His eyes turn down and he shakes his head. "Baby, this isn't living."

My heart stutters, disbelief dousing my insides. *Is he really fighting with me on this?* I clench my teeth, fury trickling slowly into my veins like the drip from an IV. "You've been with me for months, Jackson, and you haven't said a word. And you choose *now* to do this?"

"You're right." He nods. "I should have said something the second I realized."

"Realized *what?*" My voice rises.

He exhales, reaching his arms out for me, but my ire is stronger than my need for him in this moment—earlier betrayals making me see things through a fogged-up window, distorting the words before they hit my ears until I only hear accusations.

I step away, my back pressing against the cabinets on the wall. "Don't touch me right now. Just tell me. You realized *what*, exactly?"

His Adam's apple bobs, his hands paused midair. Slowly, he drops them to his sides. "Realized that you have an issue, Blake. That you need help."

Tears sting the back of my eyes, disgust at what he's saying rising through me like rapids, choking the breath from my lungs until I'm spinning from the lack of air. "I'm *fine*."

"You're not." His voice is firm, his eyes glassy. "How many times do you work out a day?"

"I—"

"When was the last time you just ate for pleasure, or hell, not even for pleasure, when was the last time you didn't track every single thing that went into your mouth?"

Anger smolders inside my chest as he attacks, the smoke swelling my throat. My insides pull and release, the ball of nerves in my gut churning so fast it sends sparks to singe my edges.

I can't deal with this right now. "I don't want to talk about this anymore."

He groans, his hands running over his face. "You *never* want to talk about it."

"Because there's nothing to talk about!" I yell. "I'm done with this conversation. I'm leaving."

"You're—wait, you're what?"

"*Leaving*, Jackson. I've had a shitty day and I come here just to be attacked by you? I—"

A sharp pain radiates through my chest, the sting so sudden I hunch forward, my arm grasping the countertop.

One. Two. Three.

Closing my eyes, I focus on my breath, knowing I'm on the edge of collapsing. Of spiraling so fast I won't make my way back out.

I need to leave. Go home to my gym and have my routine.

Normally, Jackson is enough to ease the storm raging inside, but for the second time in just as many nights he's furthering the spiral.

"Blake, please..." He touches my back, his hand smoothing up and down my spine, and I don't have the energy to push him off me. Opening my eyes, I fumble to the living room where I left my phone and do the first thing I can think of to get out of here.

I call a cab.

Grabbing my purse and wiping the few tears that have escaped with the back of my hand, I push past him, twisting once I hit the front door.

My eyes are lasers, hoping I can slice him through the middle from my hurt. "*Don't* follow me, Jackson. I mean it."

He's standing behind me, arms outstretched, his jaw clenched. But he breathes in deep and nods.

I storm outside, a cataclysmic boom of thunder reverberating in the air, echoing the way I feel inside—like everything is imploding.

The dark skies open and sheets of rain fall, sharp against my skin.

Fitting.

My stomach heaves as I stand in the downpour, praying the water will wash away everything that happened today.

That I can go back to before all of this, before *any* of this, and just be Blakely.

The girl with no mother, and a father who still made it home for dinners.

My nose burns, raindrops and tears marring my face.

"What are you doing?" Jackson sounds panicked as he rushes from his front door, his voice strained and desperate.

"I already told you," I force out through my inhales. "I'm leaving."

"Come on, Blakely. Let me drive you."

I spin, rainwater dripping off my lashes and into my eyes. "*No*. I need you to give me space, okay?" My voice chokes on a sob, my hands coming down to cover my stomach.

This whole time—*this whole time* Jackson has been judging me.

I thought he loved me. Thought he accepted me for who I was, but he doesn't. He's just like everyone else, not accepting my choices and thinking he knows best.

Bile hits the back of my throat.

Headlights appear around a corner and my heart leaps, my stomach clenching and releasing along with my fists as I make my way toward the cab.

I feel the heat of Jackson at my back, can practically taste his need to grab me tight and not let me go. But I ignore it, throwing open the back door and jumping inside. Fumbling through my words, I spout off my address, watching as Jackson grows smaller in the back window—his wet hair sticking to his face, shirt soaked to the bone, and his hand covering his heart.

Maybe tomorrow I'll regret my rash decision, but right now all I can focus on is holding it together while everything around me crumbles to dust.

By the time I get home, the panic has crawled through my chest and wrapped around my lungs, clicking into place like a chain with padlocks. Jackson's words have been on repeat, my brain latching onto them, stirring the melting pot of rage that's brewing in my gut.

I feel *sick.*

"*When was the last time you ate something without counting every calorie?*"

Fire licks up my spine, my breaths so stuttered it hurts to inhale. My head is spinning so fast I'm worried I may pass out, and like a helpless bystander, I'm relegated to a dark corner as panic overtakes my body.

He thinks I don't eat anything? Well fuck him.

I made the cabbie stop at the corner store and I filled up an entire cart with whatever my hands could grab. I slam the food down on the counter and rummage through the bags, my hands shaking as I tear through the plastic to prove a point.

I don't need help.

Tears blur my vision as I grab the first thing on the counter, not even registering what it is, my fingernails ripping into the cellophane and tossing the wrapper to the side as I shovel it into my face.

The sweetness explodes on my tongue, but I don't enjoy it like I should. Instead, nausea turns my stomach, my inner voice screaming at me to stop, but my brain already lost to the first bite of sugar I've had in years.

I don't even know what it is I'm inhaling. But it doesn't matter.

Everything fogs over, and on autopilot I continue to eat, Jackson's accusations and the internet's cutting words ringing through my ears and fueling my need, every memory another bite that slides down my throat.

She's pregnant.

Photoshop does everything for this girl.

You have been looking a little... puffy.

You need help.

I let out a scream, my hands slamming down on the marble, smashing the food underneath my fingertips, my chest stretching so thin it feels like it will shatter into a thousand pieces.

"Blakely, are you...What the *hell?* Are you okay?" My father's voice cuts through the air and everything in me freezes. He's not supposed to be here. He's supposed to be out of town.

Turning around, my breath lodged in my throat, I lock on to his shocked face, his eyes wide as they scan the demolished packaged items and the ripped-up plastic strewn all over the kitchen.

"Blakely."

His eyes lock onto mine, and for some reason, his gaze starts to calm the inferno and I slowly come back to myself. But as I do, reality hits. I turn and look at what I've done. My eyes scan over the destruction. "Oh my god," I breathe.

The second I speak, my stomach churns, my hands coming up to cover my mouth.

"Blakely," he repeats. "What is this?"

"I think I... I'm going to be..."

My heart slams against my chest so hard it cracks with each beat. I push past him, rushing up the stairs, flying past the pictures of my mother and straight-lining to my bathroom.

I barely have time to get my fingers down my throat before everything surges up, my body rejecting the food on its own. And with every heave of my stomach, control creeps back into my grasp, my fingers tightening around its reins.

When it's over—the acidic remnants of bile burning my esophagus—a sense of peace cascades down my body.

Because at least now, in this moment, I don't feel like I'm breaking.

50

BLAKELY

Waking up the next morning, my body feels empty, drained of every single molecule, leaving behind a hollow shell. But as I head down to the gym for my fasted cardio, the numb gives way to a thick, dark substance that weighs me down until my legs feel sluggish, and it feels a lot like shame.

I threw up last night. I *made* myself puke. Lost control, ate thousands of calories, and then purged. Like a...

Shaking my head, I don't even finish the thought.

You need help.

The morning sun shines light on things that were shrouded in shadows the night before. Jackson was only trying to tell me what, deep down, I already know about myself.

I have issues with food. And with exercise.

With control.

Anything that isn't under my thumb at all times, if I'm honest.

It's been there for as long as I can remember, but as I've become more popular in the spotlight, it's gotten worse. Other people's judgments and opinions are so far out of my reach, that I grasp onto the things I can—dependent on the feeling of perfection.

I shouldn't be surprised. Repressions often grow wild when they're unchecked in the dark. But I never thought I'd get to the point I did last night. And I won't ever let myself get there again. I don't think I need outside help, not convinced it's as serious as Jackson believes, but I'm anxious to see him. To tell him that I get what he was saying, and I'm sorry for my overreaction.

Since I've been ignoring Sierra's calls all morning, still too pissed off and emotionally drained to even think of dealing with her, my plan is to shower and then head to Donahue Motors so I can see Jackson and apologize. I don't want him to go through the entire day with thoughts of last night running through his head.

Hopping off the treadmill, I make my way to the kitchen, unease swimming through me at the thought of eating.

I'm not sure what I expected to walk into. Maybe for the evidence of my late-night binge to be strewn across the counters, making me atone for my mistakes in real time. But everything has vanished. Disappeared like it was never there in the first place. A pang hits the center of my chest, wishing I could erase my memories just as easily.

What I *don't* expect is my father, sitting at the kitchen island, his laptop open in front of him, his jaw tense and his brows furrowed.

I had forgotten he was here.

Nerves jumble in my stomach.

"Good morning." I peer at him from my peripheral. My heart spasms when his eyes meet mine, a darkness swirling in them that I haven't seen in years.

It makes me feel like I'm about to get in trouble, which is absurd because I don't know what I've done, other than eat ten-thousand calories and rush out of the room without answering his questions.

My stomach curdles at the thought. *Stupid, Blakely.*

"Feeling better this morning?" His chin raises.

I force a timid smile. "Much, thank you. I'm sorry, I just... I had a rough day."

"Hmm." He nods, his fingers rubbing the stubble on his jaw.

My stomach sinks.

Something's off.

But if he isn't going to come out and say whatever's bothering him, I'm not going to pry it out, so I move further into the kitchen, opening the fridge and grabbing a fresh water. I glance around for Eric, wanting him to make me an egg-white omelet.

"Where's Eric?"

Dad sips from a coffee cup, before gingerly placing it down on the counter. "I gave him the morning off."

I wait for him to elaborate, but he doesn't, he just sits there, staring.

"Okay." I spin back around to grab the eggs and spinach, a tense energy crackling through the silence.

"What did you do last night?"

My hand freezes on the fridge handle, my heart stalling in my chest. Clearing my throat, I turn toward him. "What do you mean?"

"I mean before you came home and..." He gestures to the counter. "Did you do anything fun?"

"I uh..." My heartbeat slams against my ribs, a bite of foreboding snapping at my stomach. "The usual, I guess." I shrug. "Why do you ask?"

He graces me with a closed-mouth grin, beckoning me over to his side of the counter, turning his laptop.

"You know, I had the most interesting conversation with Karen the other day. She was convinced that you and Jackson Rhoades were *friendlier* than what she felt was appropriate."

My breath catches and as I walk toward him my steps are slow, wary of his eerie calmness, not sure what to expect when I reach his side. But out of all the scenarios that raced through my mind, this wasn't one of them. My stomach plummets, my hands dropping the bag of spinach to the floor as I see what's on the screen.

Pictures. *Lots* of pictures, all of Jackson and me.

Embracing in his car. Holding hands. Kissing on his front porch.

"Oh my god," I breathe.

"There's an article, too, if you're curious. An anonymous source and a taxi driver, both *eager* to part with your secrets for what I'm sure was a hefty check."

His voice is cutting and I feel every slice as he knifes lacerations into my chest.

"Dad, I—"

"How long, Blakely?"

"Look, it's not—"

"I asked *how long*?" His hand smacks the counter.

Swallowing thickly, my fists curl into themselves, my eyes glancing down. "Not that long," I murmur.

"Before or after I asked him to watch out for you?"

My heart clenches. "After."

His eyes flare. "Did he force you?"

"What?" I gasp. "No, Dad, it isn't like that. I love him."

He laughs, running a hand through his dark locks. "You love him. Of course you do. Well, I hope you can love him from afar because after I'm through with him, he'll never step foot in California again."

My breath stutters, his words reaching in and clamping down on my soul, a different type of panic rising up inside of me. *No.*

"Dad, no. This has nothing to do with you."

"It has *everything* to do with me," he snaps. "I'm your father. I trusted him, and he disrespected me by going behind my back and taking advantage of a child."

Scoffing, resentment billows in my gut. "Oh, please," I bite out. "I'm not a child anymore. But you're gone so often, I'm not surprised that you haven't noticed."

He stiffens. "That's not fair."

"That your favorite phrase?" My eyebrow rises. "You're unbelievable, you know? You jet around to your fancy business meetings and stay gone for *weeks* at a time doing God knows what, avoiding this house and everything in it. Including *me.* And now, suddenly I'm a child? Suddenly, I need protecting?"

He opens his mouth, but I slash my hand through the air, continuing. "I am so *sick* of everyone thinking they get to determine the outcome of my life. None of you have spent a single second trying to understand what it's like to live in my shoes."

"Blakely."

"Did you know that I have panic attacks?"

His mouth parts, shock flickering through his eyes. "What?"

I bite my lip, my nostrils flaring. Maybe I shouldn't have blurted it out that way, shouldn't use my troubles as a weapon to prove a point. But if my father has the audacity to walk in here and act like he has any right to judge Jackson and my relationship, then he can sit and listen to everything else he hasn't taken the time to see over the years.

"Yeah." I lift a shoulder. "Terrible ones actually. So debilitating that I struggle to do anything that's not scheduled in advance. So intense when they hit that sometimes they make me feel like I'm physically going to die."

Tears spring to my eyes and I swallow, ignoring the painful squeezing of my lungs. "And everyone around me watches it happen, calling it "an episode" and brushing it to the side. Calling me melodramatic. A perfectionist. Do you *know* what that's like? To have your mind collapse in front of everyone and have them ignore the fall?"

"Blakely, honey, I didn't know. We can—"

"Jackson," I interrupt again. "Is the only person who has ever given a damn. He's the *only* one who saw through the bullshit." I pull at my designer workout clothes. "He saw the real me. The one I forgot existed. He held me when I was drowning, *every time*, and he loved me through every fall." My voice catches, regret for how things went last night swarming like a thousand bees, the sting radiating through my body.

Something flashes in my dad's eyes, and for just a moment, I think what I've said has gotten through. But then he stands and closes his laptop. "That doesn't change the fact that he's twenty-eight. And my employee. I can't just give him a pass."

Fear clamps down on my shoulders, its icy fingers trailing along my neck. "Are you saying you're going to fire him?"

"I'm saying he's never going to set foot on a Hollywood set again, Blakely. And neither will his cars. He's lucky that's all I'm going to do." His phone rings, buzzing across the counter, and I watch in frozen disbelief as he picks it up and answers.

"Tom, just a moment." He presses a button and looks toward me. "Stick around for a bit, okay? I want to talk more about what you just told me. About the… attacks. But I'm not going to change my mind on Jax. And you need to stay away from him."

"If I do, will you keep him on?" The words rush out before I've even registered that I've said them, but I don't take them back. I can't. I refuse to be the reason that Jackson loses out on his dream. On his father's dream. It's the only thing that's ever mattered to him.

Resolution flows through me, filling me with a melancholy confidence, and my spine straightens as I stare my father down. "Dad, if I stay away from him. If I make it clear that we'll never speak again, will you keep him?"

He sighs, his lips pursing as he looks at me for long, strained moments. And then he nods.

Relief pours through me, mixing with the heavy acknowledgment that what I have to do will shatter me entirely. But I've lived years of my life alone, and I'd rather live a hundred more than be the reason why Jackson's dreams don't come true.

"Okay." Blowing out a breath, I shake my head through the ache that's piercing through my chest. "Okay."

And just like that, I've lost my father's attention. He's already gone back to his full-time life, leaving me alone and forgotten in the dust.

There's a weight pressing down on my chest as I come to terms with what I've just done. What I've agreed to. The realization that in order to give Jax his dream I have to break both our hearts, reaching up and clawing at my throat, strangling me in its choke hold.

Closing my eyes, I breathe.

One. Two. Three.

And then I call Sierra and tell her to contact DJ Andelo.

51

JACKSON

My phone is hidden inside at the reception desk. I didn't want to put it away, but I *had* to, to stop myself from obsessively checking if there was anything from Blakely.

I don't know how to feel after last night.

When I woke up, it was to a pit festering in the middle of my stomach, worried that I ruined everything by being a complete dumbass. Only finding the courage to confront her issues on the same night she's had her life blow up in her face. It was bad timing, but I don't regret the things I said.

Still, there's a lot I don't know, and the more I think on

what happened, the more I realize there's no way *to* help her. Not until she wants to help herself. And where does that leave us? Because as long as I stick around, pretending that everything's okay, walking on eggshells to keep from sending her into a spiral, I'll be enabling.

And that in itself is detrimental to her well-being.

But the thought of not being with her—of not seeing her—is a hundred serrated knives drawing their jagged blades through my chest. If something happens, and I'm not there when she needs me, I'll regret it for the rest of my life.

Flashbacks of my father's death and me not being by his side roll through my head, and I drop the wrench from my hand, struggling to breathe through the sudden pain.

I can't leave her.

We'll go public and then I'll do whatever it takes to keep opening her up to the idea of help. We'll do it together, as a unit. The way we're meant to be.

I work for another hour before giving in to the incessant prodding of my mind, needing to check and see if there's anything from her. I walk inside and grab my phone from the corner, smiling at the young temp who replaced Blakely.

My chest squeezes when I unlock my phone and see there's still nothing.

Turning to head back to the garage, I pause when I hear Blakely's name on the TV as it drones quietly in the corner.

My heart stutters in my chest. I turn around, gazing up at the screen.

And there she is.

Beautiful as ever, prim and proper, not a hair out of place. Looking absolutely perfect, the way everyone expects her to. There's a smile spread wide across her face, sunglasses covering her eyes, and she looks... like she's perfectly fine.

My chest squeezes, knowing that I'm wearing our fight on my skin and she's somehow been able to hide it beneath the surface.

She's so good at acting that I *almost* believe she isn't affected at all. That it didn't even happen.

And then, blood freezes in my veins, my stomach pinching so tight that acid rises up my throat, because walking out of the restaurant next to her is that douchebag DJ. The one I almost throttled when he played grab-ass on stage. I didn't even realize they talked.

What the fuck is she doing with him?

An ache spreads through my ribs, my heart pummeling against the walls of my chest. Everything in me is screaming to turn away, but I ignore it, enraptured by the sight of her.

"Wow, I didn't know they were dating," the receptionist says.

I glance at her, my hand reaching up to tangle in my necklace. "What makes you think they are?"

She nods toward the TV. "Says it right there."

My eyes fly back to the screen, scanning the words on the bottom that, until now, I paid no attention to.

Blakely Donahue and DJ Andelo an item? CONFIRMED.

Like a hammer to my gut, my breath whooshes out of me, my mind trying to catch up to what my heart already knows, trying to make sense out of something that just makes *no fucking sense.*

She wouldn't...

Like a train veering off track, I continue to watch, the vision of them together striking against my heart.

"Blakely! Blakely! Do you have anything to say about you and DJ Andelo?"

She smiles, her hand looping through his arm, leaning in close like she's meant to be there. Like it's *him* that she fits perfectly with, when I know that it's really me.

"Just that we're happy, and finally ready to go public. Tell the world." She gazes up at him, a beaming grin on her lying face.

Douchebag smirks down at her, and I want to reach through the screen and cut off his oxygen until I feel the life leave his pathetic body. My heart thrashes under my skin, disbelief pouring through me.

Something's not right.

"What do you have to say about the recent pictures of you and Jackson Rhoades?"

My heart stalls like a stuck clutch, my breath sticking in my throat as I wait to see what she says. *They know who I am. They have pictures.*

I look closely, searching for a sign, some signal that she's struggling. That it's a performance. That she'll call me later with an explanation. I'm desperate to see *something* that explains why she's choosing someone else over me on national television.

But there's nothing. Not a single flinch or counted breath.

"Jackson Rhoades is a family friend," she says.

I scoff, nausea curdling in my stomach.

"Someone doing my father a favor while he was too busy to watch out for me himself. While I enjoyed his company, there's nothing else to tell." She shrugs.

"What about the pictures?" another reporter yells out.

I hear a gasp to the side of me, the receptionist staring at me with wide eyes. "Isn't *your* name Jackson Rhoades?"

My jaw clenches, but I ignore her and keep my eyes locked on the screen, a hole burning through my stomach like battery acid.

Blakely giggles and my chest pulls tight. "This is embarrassing, but it's just a case of a few too many drinks and bad decisions. A mistake on both our parts, and one that I've already apologized for to the people who matter." She caresses DJ Andelo's arm, and he grabs her hand, bringing it up to kiss.

Rage shoots through me like an arrow, ripping open my chest and flaying my skin.

"The truth is," she continues. "He's twenty-eight and a glorified mechanic. There's nothing there that interests me. And now that my father's back, you won't be seeing any more of Jackson Rhoades." Her eyes find the camera, staring through the lens and setting my soul on fire, disintegrating it to ash. "*That* I can promise you."

The reporters seem to be satisfied, moving on to ask other questions, like what she just said didn't shift the earth under my feet.

"Are you okay?" The receptionist's hand grazes my elbow.

Her touch shocks me back to life and I clear my throat, pasting on a smirk. "I'm great. Hey, I'm leaving for the day, okay? Let Karen know."

She gives a thumbs up, her eyes wary, and I race out of the front door, my heart racing faster than my feet can carry me, determined to find her and figure out what the hell is going on.

It's been three hours of me calling and Blakely hasn't answered a single time.

I try again, my head falling into my hands, this time an operator coming on the line and telling me that her line has been disconnected.

"Fuck!" Throwing my phone on the coffee table, I stand up, pacing. Frustration reaches up and clobbers my chest with its fists.

How could she do this?

I grab my keys from the counter, deciding to drive to her house and refuse to leave until she lets me in. Maybe that means I'm unhinged, but since my world has imploded anyway, what's the worst that can happen?

Buzzing the intercom once I'm at the gate, anxiety lines the base of my stomach like fire ants, the sting shooting from my gut to my throat.

My fingers press the button again and again, but nobody answers, and I slam my fists against my steering wheel, defeat clawing through my chest and pulling my muscles tight.

How am I supposed to figure out what the hell is going on if I can't *get* to her?

My phone rings and I jump to answer, an unknown number flashing on the screen.

"Hello?"

"Mr. Rhoades, this is Blakely Donahue's manager, Sierra."

My teeth grit. "Sierra, is Blakely with you?"

She sighs. "That's none of your concern, I'm afraid. But she did ask me to make this courtesy call to let you know that your presence is no longer necessary."

Her words go off like a gunshot, blasting holes through my middle, blood seeping out onto the floor. "Bullshit. This is *bullshit*, Sierra." My palm smacks the steering wheel. "Let me talk to Blakely."

"I'm afraid that's just not possible. And if you don't stop *harassing* her, I'll contact the police and put a restraining order in place. I'd hate to have that tarnish your stellar reputation. Have a good day, Jackson."

Click.

My breaths are deep as I stare at my phone, my brain zooming through every encounter I've ever had with Blakely, wondering what I missed, or where the fuck things went so wrong.

Why is she doing this?

I can only come up with one possible conclusion.

She's a coward, and if I ever needed to know whether she would choose me or her career if it came down to it—now that answer is crystal clear.

I'm second choice. *Again.*

I thought I knew heartbreak when I left Sugarlake, but that was just a graze—a scrape—compared to the severed limb of Blakely giving up on us. Of the realization that maybe I never meant much to her at all.

That maybe, I was always just a safe place for her to land.

A visceral pain shoots through the width of my chest, my heart squeezing until it bursts, the glued-together pieces ripping apart until my love is no longer recognizable.

Now, it's just shredded paper.

"Jax."

My head snaps up. I'm not sure how long I've been idling outside of her estate, but clearly, it's been long enough for someone to notice I was here.

I come face-to-face with my boss, Mr. Donahue. He looks disappointed, his eyes narrowed and his lips turned down. I'm not surprised. If our pictures are all over the internet, then I'm sure he knows the truth.

Or at least some twisted version of it.

He sighs, jerking his head toward the house. "Come in, let's have a chat."

I drive my car through the gates, parking in the circle driveway, hoping this goes quick so I can lick my wounds in peace. I thought things were finally slotting into place, when really, they were dangling on the edge of a cliff, waiting to tumble and smash on the concrete.

Being here hurts. Everything from the gold-framed pictures on the walls, to the expensive chandelier hanging from the ceiling reminds me that Blakely's no longer mine.

I'm not sure if she ever was.

Mr. Donahue gestures for me to follow him inside and we walk down the hallway to his office in the back.

Everything is a dark cherry, bookcases lining the walls from floor to ceiling, and on the back wall, a gigantic glass case filled to the brim with awards.

It's a fitting office for a king.

He sits in his chair, lighting up a cigar and watching me through the smoke. I stand straighter, refusing to cower under his gaze.

"You fucked my daughter." His words are crass and they make my muscles tense.

I shake my head. "No, sir."

"No?" His brows lift.

Snapping the hairband on my wrist, I walk forward, sitting down in one of the wingback chairs. "Well, yes, *technically.*"

His jaw tenses but he stays quiet, rolling the stogie between his lips.

"I fell in love with your daughter. And I'm sorry I did it

behind your back. Believe me, I tried like hell to stop it, but there was nothing I could do. She's... everything."

Was.

My stomach churns, emotion swelling in the center of my chest. I push it down. I'll have time to break later, when I'm alone.

He grunts. "My plan was to fire you. Kick your ass out of my shop and make sure your name never made it onto any credit. The bigger part of me *still* wants to."

Biting the inside of my cheek, I nod. I've been prepared for this moment. Countless hours have been spent weighing the pros and cons, figuring out what I'd do if I ended up blacklisted from Hollywood, unable to see my dad's dream come to fruition. Sure, there've been some of my cars in movies. But none of that took the spotlight. Not like the upcoming feature film showcasing dozens of beauties, all handcrafted by me.

For Blakely, I would have given it all up. Gone back to flipping my own cars and finding peace in the fact that my dad would want me to be happy more than he'd want me to be alone and miserable creating fake shells for prop cars.

And as much as I love my father, I can't keep living for a ghost.

"But," Mr. Donahue continues. "You're the best. And if you promise to stay away from my daughter, then I'll let you stay on." He smiles, like he's giving me a gift.

Irritation at the audacity of everyone in Hollywood—everyone in this vapid, senseless town, drizzles through me, igniting the rage that's been percolating underneath the remnants of my heart, waiting for its chance.

I shake my head. "Thank you, sir, but I think I'm good."

His smile drops and he leans forward in his chair. "Excuse me?"

"I said, I think I'm good."

He laughs, placing his cigar in the crystal ashtray to his right. "Son, I don't know if you understand what it is you're doing, but you're ruining the chance of a lifetime."

I shrug.

"This is all for some girl?" His fingers push against his head. "Think about this, kid."

Some girl.

Giving him a thin grin, I stand up, brushing the wrinkles out of my clothes. "With all due respect, Mr. Donahue, your daughter is far from *some girl.* Maybe you should realize that before it's too late."

My heart pumps cyanide, poisoning my bloodstream. "And just for the record, I would have given up *everything* for her."

His face screws up.

"Thank you, truly, for the opportunity. But I quit."

He's silent, a mask of discontent across his face. Shaking my head, I turn to go. It's not until my hand touches the doorknob that he speaks.

"Wait." His voice is strained.

I pause.

"Tell me..." He swallows. "Tell me what to do to help her. I want—" He closes his eyes. "I don't know what to do."

Emotion clogs my throat, but I bite it down, realizing that after this moment, Blakely Donahue is no longer my problem.

"She needs help. Help that neither of us can give her."

"Jax, *please,* give me more than that. I just… she won't talk to me, she'll never let me in."

The venom of heartbreak in my veins wars with the love that still flows freely. I blow out a breath. "She has panic attacks. Bad ones. And she struggles with food."

He closes his eyes, a look of defeat dragging down his face. "Thank you," he whispers.

Choking back the tears, my tongue runs over my teeth as I nod.

And then I'm out the door, and I know exactly where I'm headed.

Home.

52

BLAKELY

I've always thought of myself as weak. A pathetic shell of a person who breaks apart and shatters at the first sign of distress. My emotions are wild, frequently revolting against the box I keep them in, leaping out like a caged tiger, its razor teeth snapping as it shreds everything in its path.

Standing next to DJ Andelo and looking into the camera, hoping Jackson was watching while I spewed the biggest lies I'll ever tell...

That was the strongest I've ever had to be. The biggest test of my control.

But where there's a play of strength, there's the comedown after the show.

And when I go home and find the rest of the leftover junk food stacked neatly in the cabinet, my inner demons jump in glee, breaking free of their shackles until I've consumed every last bite. Thousands of calories in under twenty minutes. And even though I promised myself it wouldn't happen again, I race up the stairs and force it all back up, the sharp edges of control slotting back into place with every single heave.

Just like the time before.

So, no. I'm not strong.

I'm still just a fraud.

I lay on the floor next to the toilet, allowing the heated marble to warm my chilled skin, hoping that maybe the warmth will shock some feeling back into my body—make me able to experience something other than this bone-deep ache.

Forcing Jackson out of my life was the right choice. But I didn't expect it to hurt this bad. Like there's this giant, rotting wound in the middle of my body, sucking up everything in sight until nothing is left.

Maybe if I lay here long enough, it will suck me up too and I'll cease to exist.

Eventually, I pull myself up from the ground and head downstairs to grab some water, my mind on autopilot. There's a type of numbness that comes with the acceptance that this is my lot in life. This is my reality.

Muffled noise comes from the family room and light from the TV flickers into the darkened hallway.

Curiosity pushes me forward until I'm standing behind the oversized couch, staring at my father as he watches home videos on the TV.

My cracked and bleeding heart splinters more as I watch my mother walk and talk right in front of my face.

"James, stop." She laughs, pushing the camera and smiling.

My stomach clenches tight, my breath sucking in on a gasp. I didn't even know we *had* home videos. I would have watched them every day.

My father's head snaps around, his eyes dark as he looks at me. I'm not sure if he wants me to leave and honestly, maybe I should, but my feet are stuck to the floor like glue, desperate to stay right here. Maybe if I close my eyes, I can pretend she's standing next to me, brushing back my hair and telling me things I've always imagined a mother would.

After a few moments, he smiles softly and gestures me over. A thread loosens in my chest and I trudge to the couch and sit down, my eyes flickering back and forth between him and the screen.

He's wearing plaid pajamas, a glass of water in his hand, and I rack my brain trying to remember the last time I've ever seen him look so relaxed.

The only one that comes to mind is when I was six years old and I came down on Christmas morning expecting to see my nanny, but found him instead.

The screen flickers, drawing my attention back, and the footage goes grainy before popping a new image on the screen. My mother sits in a rocking chair, rubbing her swollen belly and singing a lullaby. Tears spring to my eyes, my battered heart seizing in my chest.

I swallow, not able to tear my gaze away for a second. Her face looks up to the camera, beaming. "James, she's kicking like crazy! I think she likes this song."

Closing her eyes, she hums, putting her hand out in the space between them. "Come here, feel her move."

The camera jostles as it's set down, angled toward my mother, and suddenly, my father walks into the frame. A younger version, without the graying at his temples and the frown lines, but still, the same. He kneels in front of her, both of his hands coming up to wrap around her belly—around *me*—his eyes shimmering, his mouth parting on a gasp.

"It never gets old, does it?" my mother says, her fingers running through his hair.

He leans in, kissing her stomach before resting his cheek against it and smiling. "Hello Blakely Alexandra. We can't wait to meet you."

My stomach flips and tightens, my throat burning.

"She was so excited to have you," my father says from beside me, his voice low and deep. "We both were."

My teeth chomp down on my lip so hard it breaks through the skin, the tang of blood trickling into my mouth.

"Your mom was an actress," he continues. "Did I ever tell you that?"

The tears I've been trying to hold back overflow like a broken dam, my vision blurring. "No," I whisper. "You never talk about her."

"You never ask."

I'm quiet, my legs coming up to curl into my chest, my arms wrapping around them. "I'm asking now."

He smiles. "She was an actress, that's how we met. A terrible one." He chuckles. "But that's what I loved about her. She was..."

"Beautiful," I cut in, watching her twirl effortlessly around as she dances on the screen.

He audibly swallows. "She was definitely that. But she was *genuine*. And in my world, that was something rare. Almost unheard of."

My gut cinches like a corset, pushing the breath from my lungs. "Yeah, tell me about it," I mumble.

"She wanted nothing to do with me." I glance over at him and see his eyes shining, fat drops of emotion lining his lower lids. "But I was persistent and had a ring on her finger in less than six months."

My chest compresses. "I wish I could have known her."

His hand reaches over, patting the top of mine, and my eyes drop to the motion, trying to remember the last time I felt his touch.

"So do I, honey." He hesitates. "I'm sorry I've never let you."

My fists clench against the couch cushions. "It's okay."

He shakes his head. "It isn't."

Something loosens in my chest, dropping down into my stomach and disintegrating. "You're right, it isn't."

"Anyway, your mother's bad acting was my favorite feature on her. She wasn't able to hide a thing from me, you know?" His eyes glance at me from his peripheral. "Not like some people, who can hide the world behind a smile."

"But it also meant that when she'd fall down, people would see. And your mother… she fell down a lot."

My heart skips. "What do you mean?"

"She had depression. *Severe* depression that would hit out of nowhere and take her down for months. She'd go from this smiling, happy person, to a shell who couldn't even get out of bed. I watched everyone in her life brush it off and tell her to get her act together. To just *decide* to be happy."

The hole in the middle of my stomach widens, sadness coating its edges.

"But I saw her." He wipes a tear from his chin. "More than anyone else, I saw her. And I was there every day, helping her shower and holding her when she cried." His voice breaks as he turns to me. "I think the biggest regret of my life will be not doing the same for you."

My mouth parts, shock freezing everything in my body, unable to process his words. Not sure if I should even believe them.

"She would be ashamed of what I've become. Of how I've let others raise you. How I left you alone with your demons instead of helping you learn to navigate their shadows."

Tears steadily roll down my face, my nose burning and chest throbbing from his words.

"You've always been so damn self-sufficient, and I... I have no clue how to do life without her." He nods his head toward the screen. "Almost twenty years and I still wake up with a hole where my heart should be." He inhales deep. "I let work take over my life because the alternative is admitting to myself that she's gone, and because of that, I've failed at taking care of the greatest gift she ever gave me."

I suck in a stuttered breath, my face screwing up as the tears stream from my eyes, dripping over my lips and dissolving on my tongue.

He turns toward me fully and takes both of my hands in his. "I know it doesn't make up for it, but I am *so* sorry, Blakely."

The little girl inside of me bursts with joy, but the woman spawned from his abandonment pushes back. "What if it's too late?" I choke out. "What if you waited too long and now I don't need you?"

He bobs his head. "Everybody needs somebody, Blakely. I'm begging you to let that person be me. At least until we can get you help."

My spine stiffens.

I try to pull my hands back, but he tightens his grip. "Your mother had the same reaction, a straight back and a defiant look on her face before I even finished getting out the words."

I scoff. "But I'm *fine.*"

He shakes his head. "There's no shame in getting help, Blakely. Sometimes, you have to put yourself first, admit that you need someone to help you steer through the choppy waters."

My chest caves in at his words.

"Your mom went to therapy, four times a week at first. She went on anti-depressants and she had to work *every day* at digging herself out of the hole she fell into. It didn't make her less of a person. It didn't make her less worthy. It just made her human."

His words filter through my cracks and I stare at the TV, watching her love my father. Watching her love *me.*

His hand squeezes mine. "It's okay to be human, Blakely. Let me help you. *Please.*"

Raising my chin, I swallow back the sob. Closing my eyes, more tears squeeze from the corners and stream down my face. Thoughts of Jackson filter through my head, of him begging me to get help—for me to just open my eyes and see.

"This isn't living, baby."

I gulp in air, the slight aftertaste of vomit—despite brushing my teeth—still lingering, the shame resting heavy on my tongue.

I close my eyes.

One. Two. Three.

And then I nod.

53

JACKSON

It took me two days to drive back home from California, only stopping for sleep and gas, desperate to be as far away from there as possible. There were paparazzi lined up outside of my house, and they watched, their cameras flashing like strobe lights as I packed up my essentials and tried not to run them over as I left.

I pray they don't follow me back home.

As the miles tick up on the speedometer, the memory of Blakely haunts my thoughts, reminding me of all the ways I had her, and how easily she tossed me to the side. She caved and let others dictate her life.

I don't buy for one second that she's really with that

prick DJ. And the more I think about it, the more I realize that Blakely just couldn't find it in her to stand up for us when it counted. After all the ways I stood for her, holding her up, she let me fall at the first sign of trouble.

Her letting me go was a blessing. But that doesn't make the sharp ache in my chest dull.

Pulling into my mom's driveway, I'm hit with nostalgia, remembering all the times I worked on this very car over on the shady patch of grass off the gravel drive. I was determined to make this beauty purr, finish the job that my father and I started—before he got too sick to turn a wrench.

I didn't tell my mom I was coming home. I didn't tell anybody. Didn't want to have to explain things before I had a chance to let them settle within myself.

Sucking down a deep breath and forcing the sadness down, I leave my car, spinning as I hear the screen door creak open.

My mom's hands are over her heart, her wavy blonde hair blowing in the breeze, a beaming smile on her beautiful face.

"Jackson!" she yells, racing off the front porch and hurtling herself in my arms. I wrap my hands around her, breathing in her scent. She smells like *home* and I sink into her embrace, suddenly feeling like a little kid lost in his grief, desperate to have her take away the pain.

She leans back in my arms, her hands coming up to rest on both sides of my face, gazing into my eyes.

My chest throbs, a lead weight heavy in the bottom of my gut.

"What did I do to deserve this?" She smiles, her eyes crinkling in the corners.

I force a grin. "*Surprise.* I'm home."

Her brows furrow. "What do you mean you're '*home?*'"

"I mean, I'm home." I shrug.

She backs away and I reach into the back seat, grabbing my duffel bag and following her in the house. I throw it next to the coat rack, following her into the kitchen.

She grabs two mugs from the counter and starts the kettle before spinning to face me. "For good?" Her brow quirks.

"Yep." I snap the hairband on my wrist, pulling out a chair to sit at the round kitchen table.

She sighs, her gaze looking right through my tough exterior. "What the hell for?"

I bark out a laugh, not surprised at all by her line of questioning. My mom's never been one to mince words, especially when she's trying to drag out information. The carpool moms loved to gossip whenever we moved to a new state, calling her crass, but she paid them no mind. Growing up with a military man as a husband forces a thick skin. So does fighting cancer.

Sighing, I run my hand through my hair. "California wasn't everything I dreamed of, I guess."

"But what about *your* dream, baby?"

The teakettle whistles, and she pours us both a cup, walking over and placing one in front of me before she takes a seat at the table.

"Dreams change." My stomach churns.

She hums. "Don't give me that nonsense. You've been working toward this your whole life. Back when you were sixteen and *begging* me to let you get your hands dirty at the shop."

I roll my eyes. "Mom, I got that job because we *needed* it. You were working yourself half to death, and I wanted to help. Not because it was my dream."

Her forehead scrunches as she leans back in her chair. "Baby, I wasn't working myself to death because of money. I was doing it so I didn't have to face the truth of being alone. If I worked, I could pretend he was still coming back home."

My jaw clenches, fingers tightening around my mug of tea, allowing the burn from my fingertips to distract me from the throbbing in my soul. "Well, so was I."

She blows on her tea, nodding. "That's fair."

We sit in silence for the next few minutes, sipping on chamomile and enjoying the quiet. Or maybe we're both reflecting on the ways we've handled life ever since Dad's death. Going over all the things we did right, and all the ways we could have done things differently.

Then, even though I try to fight it, my mind wanders to Blakely. And despite the betrayal that swirls in my gut—the hurt that clamps around my lungs with every breath—I wonder how she's doing. If she's maybe, possibly, missing me as much as I somehow still miss her.

Sighing, I force the thought away, mad at myself for not being able to push her to the side as easily as she did me.

My mom's hand reaches across the table and covers mine. "What's wrong, Jackson?"

I smirk. "Who says something's wrong?"

The left side of her mouth lifts. "A mom always knows."

I've always kept my problems close to the chest, not wanting to dump my issues on her when it was clear the load she carried was close to making her knees buckle from the weight. With Dad gone, it was my job to be the man of the house. And the man never crumbles beneath the pressure, he's there to hold everyone else up.

But as she looks at me with questions in her eyes, my heart yearns for understanding, so I blow out a breath and give in, desperate to have someone in my corner who I *know* will choose me. Someone who loves me without conditions.

"How did you survive after losing him?" I ask.

At first, I don't think she'll answer, that she'll change the subject like she usually does.

Her mouth parts, her eyes growing glassy. "A minute at a time. And when that didn't work—a second."

My fingers tangle in the chain around my neck, telling myself that if my mom can get through Dad's death and somehow make it to the other side, I can get through losing Blakely. At least I know she's still out there, living. My chest squeezes, hoping her father shows up for her. That the look I saw in his eyes wasn't a trick of the lighting—that he heard me when I told him she needed help.

I can't bear the thought of her being all alone when she's in need.

"I'm sorry I wasn't there," I blurt out.

My mother's brows draw in. "What on Earth are you talking about?"

"With Dad." I swallow, the lump in my stomach surging through my chest and into my throat. "I should have been there. Should have—" My voice cracks and I shake my head. "I missed his last moments."

"Oh." Her chin wobbles as she sucks in her lower lip. "Honey, he never blamed you for that. Neither of us did."

A tear slips out of the corner of my eye, my hand reaching up to brush it away.

"Your dad... he was *so* proud of you, but it was because of who you were, not because of what you did." She takes a slow sip of tea. "And you did more than your fair share. More than you ever should have had to."

"No, Mom, I—"

"No." She shakes her head. "We all have our burdens to

bear, and letting you be the one to shoulder him when he couldn't stand is one of mine. But if you've been holding on to this... skewed version of yourself, out of some type of guilt over not wanting to see him in his final moments, I'm here to tell you that, baby, you've *got* to let that go."

My throat feels raw as I swallow. "I don't know if I can," I whisper.

She sighs. "You've always been a nurturer. Ever since you were a little boy. I used to take you with me to the hospital and show you the nursery. Do you remember that?"

I shake my head. "No, I don't think so."

"Oh, well that's a shame. You *loved* it." She laughs. "Always wanted to go in and hold them. Asking the nurses if you could help."

I smile, trying to force the memory, but coming up blank.

"You have a heart that gives until it bleeds, Jackson, and that's a quality to be proud of. But it's not your job to pick up everyone else's pieces." She blinks, her eyes watery. "And if I've let you live your life thinking you somehow let us down by not doing enough, by not being there..." She goes quiet, glancing down at the table. "Well... I guess we both have some self-reflection we need to do, huh."

I don't respond and she doesn't say anything else. We simply sit and drink tea in silence, her hand grasping mine, and me doing what she says we should.

Reflecting.

And the longer I do, the more I think that maybe behind the heartbreak, behind the hurt of everything that's happened in my life, there's a single catalyst.

Me, trying to atone for my past mistakes.

Filling the hole left by my father with this urge to be

what everyone needs, heartbreak suctioning to my bones and leaching all the marrow, desperate to cling to *something* that feels real.

So, while losing Blakely guts me, the thought of ever loving someone else like a carotid artery that's been splinched, I know that placing all the blame on her isn't entirely fair. And it isn't going to help.

I'll live through the break and somehow I'll learn to move on.

54

JACKSON

I spent the rest of the day testing out the waters, slowly immersing myself into the public around town, worried there would be people hounding me for information, desperate to know if Blakely Donahue was the reason I came back.

But then I realized, this is *Sugarlake.* A town filled with primarily older generations who could care less about celebrity gossip. There's no need when there's enough drama going around our small city streets to light up the whole town.

As I walk through the grocery store, perusing the

shelves, my shoulders relax because nobody questions a thing.

"Be still my beatin' heart."

My stomach jumps at the voice and I spin around, a smile growing on my face. "Rebecca Jean, how did I know you'd be the first person I'd see?"

She smirks, her bright red curls swishing as she shakes her head. "You're an asshole."

I raise a brow, pointing at myself. "Me?"

"You ignored my calls, *dick*, and then you come back here and don't even tell us? Honestly, the nerve."

Laughing, I drag her into my arms. "I'm sorry, Becs. I have a lot to make up for."

She hugs me back, speaking into my shirt. "Yeah, you bet your ass you do. Does Lee know?"

Guilt weaves its way through the cracks as I think about how Lee doesn't know. But with her knowledge comes questions, and I'm just not ready to answer them yet. "No, I just got in. Thought I'd surprise you guys."

"Baby girl, I—" A tall man with honey-blond hair walks around the corner and my eyes widen slightly as they take him in.

Elliot Carson. Lee's brother. I had forgotten him and Becca hooked up.

Eli's voice trails off as he sees me, his eyes taking in my arms as they wrap around Becca's waist.

His lips turn down and he slowly walks toward us. "Jax?"

Becca steps away and he pulls her into his side. His posture screams possession and I smirk, amusement spinning through my chest that he thinks I'm a threat. *Good.*

I'm not, of course. Becca's one of the only girls around here that I haven't been with, but Eli abandoned Lee when she needed him the most, and I still haven't forgiven him for that.

"What is this?" I point between them. "You two a couple now?"

Becca blushes and nods in response to my question and jealousy sears my insides as I watch her gaze up at him with love, him tipping up her chin and pressing a kiss to her lips like they're the only two people in the room.

I *dreamed* of having that with Blakely. Of being able to touch her and kiss her in public. How fucking pathetic.

"Well, we're having family dinner over at Chase and Lee's tonight and you're comin'."

I'm ripped from my thoughts with Becca's statement, dread pooling low in my gut. I run my hand through my hair. "I don't know, Becca. I'm tired. I was planning on spending tonight with my mom."

She narrows her eyes. "You're comin', Jax. You're part of this family, and now that you're back, I won't let you sneak off and hide."

I huff. "I'm not hiding."

"No?" Her hands go to her hips.

"Rebecca, leave him alone," Eli chides.

She quirks a brow at him. "When have you *ever* known me to do that?" Her eyes come back to mine. "Is this about Chase?"

My chest pinches and I shrug, suddenly remembering why I avoided her calls. She's so damn pushy and she sees *everything*.

She sighs, her finger twirling in the strands of her hair. "Yeah, I figured as much. Listen, I'm no fan of the man either, but he's... he's different now."

"Good for him."

"He *is*, Jax." She pauses. "Come to dinner. Lee will keel

over and die from happiness. She's been missin' you somethin' fierce."

"She just saw me." I cross my arms.

Becca's brows draw down. "For like, a day. That ain't the same thing and you know it."

Sighing, I nod, knowing that once Becca puts her mind to something there's no getting out of it.

A few hours later, I'm bouncing on the balls of my feet, nerves tangling together in my stomach as I stand at the front door of Chase's place. It's ridiculous that even though I spent the best years of my life with this group of people, I feel as though I'm a stranger walking in, hoping they'll accept me.

The door swings open and I come face-to-face with my ex-best friend. The one who left town and didn't bother to mend our fences when he came back. His hazel eyes spark when they see me and he runs a hand through his jet-black hair, tousling the strands. He tips his chin. "Hey, man. Welcome."

Resentment churns through my insides, my teeth grinding as I force a small smile.

He stands there for a few seconds, his eyes watching me, waiting for a reaction. But I won't give him one.

Sighing, he moves to the side. "The girls are in the kitchen."

I shoulder past him, animosity radiating off my body like lightning rods, and head to find Lee and Becca, hoping that being around them will allow me to relax. I paste a smile on my face, doing my best to hide my heartbreak behind the charm as I walk into the kitchen. "Ladies, have no fear, the *sexy* one is here."

Lee turns around and squeals, running over and grabbing me into a hug.

Becca stands at the counter with a knife in her hand, smirking. "Good Lord, I did *not* miss your lines, Jackson Rhoades."

I wink at her as Lee pulls out of my arms and smacks me in the chest. "How could you not tell me you were comin' back?"

Because I didn't plan on having my heart ripped from my chest.

Shrugging, I swallow, biting down the pain. "Surprise."

Her eyes catalog my reaction, growing dark as she takes me in. Her lips pinch but she doesn't say anything, choosing to walk back to the cutting board instead.

"So," she starts again. "How long are you in town for?"

Sitting down at the set table, I sigh, rubbing the back of my neck. "For good."

Becca spins back around and Lee stops mid-chop. "I'm sorry, what?" she asks, her voice rising.

My eyes meet hers, begging her to not push—trying to show her without words that I'll tell her later, when we can talk alone.

"Things just weren't working out in California anymore." Nausea rolls through my gut as a sharp bite of pain drops through my middle.

Lee's eyes darken, her shoulders slumping, and I can see in her gaze that she understands what I'm saying. She presses her lips together and clears her throat, resuming her cutting on the board. "That's a real shame, Teeth. But we're glad to have you home."

Home.

Eli shows up not long after and then dinner's ready, everyone sitting down and digging in. But my appetite is gone, lost somewhere between realizing that Blakely felt more like home than Sugarlake ever did, and having to douse the irritation that cuts across my skin whenever I see Chase's face.

Of course, nobody else recognizes the tension that stretches the air thin across the table. Or maybe they do, and they're choosing to ignore it. Focus on the fact that I'm here, instead of admitting that none of them have *ever* recognized that Chase didn't only leave Lee.

He left me too.

"So, tell us about California," Becca says.

Lee's eyes meet mine across the table as she shovels a bite of mashed potato into her mouth.

My gut churns, wanting nothing less than to talk about what I've left behind. "Nothing to tell."

Becca's nose scrunches. "Okay, weirdo. Keep your secrets."

Eli clears his throat, standing up. "We're stopping by Dad's after this, Lee, do you want us to take him some of this food?"

Lee smiles and nods, jumping up. "Yeah, lemme put some in a container for y'all to take. Remind him I'll be there tomorrow mornin' to pick him up for his AA meetin' over in Sweetwater, okay?"

I sit back, happy to have the attention off of me, but a sadness pressing down on my chest seeing that while I was so focused on needing space their lives continued without me.

As everyone starts to move around, Chase sits at the head of the table watching me, not saying a word. Suddenly, he stands up and walks to the fridge, grabbing two beers and sitting down in the seat next to me.

Silently, he slides one over.

My jaw tics, but I lean back in my chair and take small sips, the fizz burning as it slides down my throat. And for the first time since I stepped into the house, the knot in my stomach unravels the tiniest bit, because I know that out of everyone here, Chase won't push me for answers. He won't make me talk when there's nothing I'd be able to say.

Just like when we were kids, he sits there in silence.

Keeping me company.

And whether I want to or not, I feel a little less alone.

Time continues to pass and eventually I fall back into a routine.

But the days are long with nothing on my agenda, and while my mom's company is nice, after so many days in a row she's driving me absolutely *insane.*

"Why don't you take over the rent at my place?" Becca says, after I bitch to her and Lee while we meet for Saturday brunch.

It's an old tradition, one that we used to do religiously every Saturday for years. Back then it was a way to keep Lee from sinking too deep in her depression. Now, it would seem, the two of them think I need the same type of help.

I still haven't been able to bring myself to tell Becca about Blakely. Some wounds are just too painful and I'd rather forget altogether. Allow myself the space to move on without her constantly being brought into conversation.

My mouth screws up. "And live with you? *Pass.*"

"No, dumbass." She rolls her eyes. "Eli's been beggin' me to move in with him for the past month anyway. Ever since he decided to claim me for himself." She grins like the cat that got the cream. "I've been holdin' off because Doc says it's important to go slow, but... to hell with it, ya know?"

"Dang, Becca," Lee groans. "Can you *please* quit talkin' about my brother and your extracurricular activities? It makes me gag."

Becca sips from her mimosa. "We're all adults here, Lee. You don't hear me complainin' when you drone on about Chase fuckin' you six ways from Sunday."

Lee's nose scrunches. "It's still gross."

"Can we stay on track here?" I cut in. "You're just what… planning to ignore your therapist's advice so I can have a place to live?"

"I'm nothin' if not a giver." She puts a hand over her heart.

I chew on the inside of my cheek, contemplating her words. It would be nice to have a place of my own while I figure out what it is that I want to do.

"What are you plannin' to do about work? You gonna flip cars again?" Lee asks.

My heart twists. The thought of working on cars makes my stomach roll. While I love what I do, the entire reason I worked so hard to get into the industry—to make a name for myself—was to see Dad's dream come to fruition. And I guess, technically, I've accomplished that. I may not ever see them featured the way I'd like, but they're there in the background, and that will have to be good enough.

But the passion that once flowed through my veins and seeped from my pores is missing, replaced with a fear that everything from the carburetor to the engine will remind me of Blakely.

And I'm doing all that I can to forget.

I shrug. "I don't know. I'll just take it easy for a while. Relax."

Becca sighs. "Must be nice to be so loaded you ain't got to work."

She's not wrong. Despite what Blakely and everyone around her seems to think, being the best at flipping cars is an extremely lucrative career. One car can bring in upwards of six-hundred thousand dollars. In fact, I took a pay cut to work for her father. But I've had several years to amass millions and have invested wisely, my portfolio manager calling me once a month to keep me up to date.

Lee scoffs. "Like you're one to talk, Miss Thang. Eli has more money than God. You'd just have to snap your fingers and he'd make sure you never worked another day in your life."

I chuckle, shaking my head. "It's so weird that you two are together."

Becca balls up a napkin, throwing it at me. "Get over it. He makes me happy. Not all of us are meant for the bachelor life like you."

I smirk, but her words strike a chord—sharp and out of tune, it reverberates inside of me, scraping under my skin, reminding me of how close I came to not having to settle for a life alone.

It's been almost a month and still, my broken heart beats for her.

55

BLAKELY

Turning Pointe is an exclusive, resort-type rehabilitation center, hidden away in the hills of California, specifically centered around celebrities who need privacy while they heal.

My dad, of course, "had connections" and was able to get me in for a thirty-day treatment.

I agreed without a fight. I'm so tired of being tired. Exhausted from pretending like I'm okay when it's clear that I'm just a bunch of shattered pieces held together with warped tape.

Sierra, however, is not on board, scoffing at the notion of me disappearing for an entire month.

"Do you know what that will do to your career?" she snaps over the phone.

I sigh. "Sierra, I don't *care*. I need to take care of *me*."

"I never would have leaked to the press if I would have known the result was you having some come-to Jesus moment."

My heart stalls in my chest. "What did you just say?"

She breathes harshly over the line and my stomach drops to the floor. I had assumed the anonymous source was Kayla. Through everything that's happened over the past few days, I've never *once* questioned Sierra's loyalty. Always been under the assumption that she had my best interests at heart, she just didn't know the best way to approach them.

Clearly, I've been a blind idiot.

"You're fired."

"What?" she gasps.

"You heard me. This..." I rest my forehead on the counter, letting the cool marble chill my overheated skin. "I'm done letting you make choices for me. Poisoning my mind to think I need to be something other than what I am."

"You *pay* me to do that."

"No, Sierra. I pay you to manage my schedule. To keep things organized. To be my right-hand woman. *Not* to make me feel like nothing is ever good enough. Like my flaws are worth ignoring, like it's worth sacrificing fucking *everything* to make it to the top." Fury burns through me, my words sharp as I hiss them down the line.

"That used to be *your* dream, too."

"Yeah, well… dreams change."

"So that's it? You're just done with me?"

"That's it." I smile as I breathe out the words. "I'm just done."

I hang up the phone, twisting to face my father as he leans against the wall, spinning car keys around his finger. "You ready, honey?"

Sucking in a deep breath, I nod, fear chomping down on my insides at the unknown. "Yeah, I'll meet you out there, I just... I have something I need to do real quick."

He nods, walking away, and I turn, staring down at my phone like it's about to reach out and strangle me to death.

Who knows, maybe it will.

I place the phone in its stand and press record, my chest whirling with anxiety.

For the first few seconds, I'm silent, staring at my unfiltered, makeup-free face, wondering what the hell I'm doing. Bile surges into my esophagus and I close my eyes.

One. Two. Three.

"Hi, everyone." I smile into the camera, even as dread snakes down my spine and wraps around my hips. "You're not used to seeing me like this." I gesture to my face. "Honestly, *I'm* not used to seeing me like this." I glance down at my fists clenched in my lap, and back up to the screen, my heartbeat pounding in my ears. "I've been lying to you. You see, I've spent *years* showing you all my perfects. Not letting you see what happens behind the screen. And you deserve better than that." A tear drips down my cheek. "*I* deserve better than that."

Blowing out a shaky breath, I continue. "So, I guess this is my apology. I'm sorry for making you think I'm something I'm not. Spoiler alert: the internet isn't reality. What you *see* any of us do is edited. Set up. It's *bullshit.*"

My fingernails cut into my palms, my head growing dizzy.

"The truth is, I'm a wreck. And maybe someday soon, I'll find the courage to share more of that with you. But first, I need to take care of me." My voice cracks. "Thank you from the bottom of my heart for all of your support, I truly cherish every single second I've spent getting to know you, and I'm sorry that I let the genuine beauty of people connecting over the internet turn into something so... processed and fake." I lift my eyes to the ceiling. "So, for now, this is goodbye. Hopefully, when you see me again, I'll be a better version of myself."

With shaky hands, I snatch up my phone, uploading the video before I lose the nerve. Before I break from the thought of people peering inside and not liking what they see.

COGNITIVE-BEHAVIORAL THERAPY.

I've been at Turning Pointe for twenty days, and my life now revolves around psychotherapy. My psychiatrist, Dr. Janice Dean, sits me down every day and we work through the behaviors, thoughts, and feelings that accompany my urges. My issues with food and exercise. My panic. My need for control.

When I first arrived, I was poked and prodded, tested for thyroid issues—which apparently can create similar symptoms to panic attacks—and asked to fill out a questionnaire. A very *invasive* questionnaire that made me feel like ants were digging holes under my skin and crawling around through my veins.

Turns out, I have OCD. *Who knew?* Obsessive, irrational thoughts that spiral into compulsive behavior. In my case, excessive exercise and extreme control over the routines in my life, which lends itself to Orthorexia. A type of eating disorder that I didn't even know existed.

But tackling my disorders are the least of the hard work.

It's the recreation of my panic attacks that make me feel like curling up in a ball and begging for death. But still, I show up every day, and we work through it.

A safe space where we purposely recreate my triggers, causing panic to happen in a repetitive manner so Dr. Dean can walk me through the symptoms. Force me to face the root of the cause. And every day we take away more of the fear, so I can learn how to cope when they hit.

It's intense. Grueling. Masochistic. And it involves a level of self-reflection that I spent years trying to avoid.

But I'm here. And I'm doing the work.

I *want* to be better.

When I'm not in therapy, I'm meeting with a dietician. One who works with me on building a healthy relationship with food, so I stop associating my happiness to what goes into my body. I keep a daily affirmation journal too, and that combined with the behavioral therapy to retrain how I think of myself is… a lot.

Every morning, I take an anti-depressant. It's not a miracle cure, but it helps curb the darkness that threatens to swallow me whole.

Evenings are filled with group sessions, all of us in treatment coming together to share our experiences. It's easy to see the ones who are desperate for help, and the ones who can't admit they have a problem. And as I take them in, guilt slugs me in the chest, because I know that's how I was with Jackson.

I've burned a lot of bridges.

Kept up ones that veered me in the wrong directions.

By the time my thirty days are up and I walk out of the

front doors, I'm ready to grab the bricks and lay a new foundation, one by one.

I'm not out of the woods, I'm not even sure there is such a thing. If there is, then I have a long way to go, and will most likely be in therapy for the rest of my life. But I find peace in that.

For the first time, I don't feel the need to be *seen.*

Because I see myself.

I expect my father to be waiting outside to pick me up, but he isn't there. In his place is Lennox.

My stomach jumps, my breath sucking in through my parted mouth.

Time to start rebuilding bridges.

56

BLAKELY

It's silent on the car ride home, Lennox glancing at me every few minutes and then staring back at the road.

My hands are clammy and I rub them on my pant leg, wanting to break the tension but not knowing where to start.

As far as people who have wronged me, Lennox was unfairly placed in that category. It's easy to see now, after some separation, that he's been one of the most loyal people to have ever existed in my life.

"Do you love her?" I blurt out.

His jaw tenses as he looks at me, his knuckles tightening on the steering wheel. He blows out a breath and nods.

I bite on my lip, processing that information. "That's good," I finally say.

"It is?" His voice is surprised.

I nod. "Yeah. Makes it easier to forgive you."

He huffs. "You have nothing to forgive me *for*, Blakely. I'm not required to tell you about my personal life."

I press against the back of my seat. "I guess that's true."

He hums, rolling down his window, the breeze whipping gently across my face. "But I am sorry for keeping it from you. The way everything went down was..." He cringes. "Not ideal."

Laughter bubbles out of me and I snort, leaning my head against the headrest. "You can say that again." Our talk dies down and a sadness fills my chest, wondering if I'll ever be able to forgive Kayla for the things she's done. I like to believe that at one time she *was* actually my friend. Maybe she still is, and she was just misguided in her actions. Or maybe she's lost in the clutches of fame, losing the girl she once was in the process. If that's the case, I hope she finds her way out. I know all too well what that feels like.

I've been staring at my reflection for days, thanking God that the girl inside of *me* didn't disappear for good.

She's still there. Battered and bruised and rising from the darkness. *Stronger.*

"Do you think she regrets it?" I ask.

He blows out a breath. "You'll have to ask her that."

My stomach churns at the thought. "I'm not ready to talk to Kayla. I don't know if I ever will be, she's... a painful part of my past, and honestly, I'm worried that if I spend time with her now I'll get sucked into bad habits. Negative thinking." I tap my head. "I've been working really hard to change that around." Just the thought of seeing her again causes emotions to whirl around inside of me. "Yeah." I shake my head. "Definitely not ready to see her."

"Neither am I." Sadness tinges his voice.

I think he's saying he doesn't see her anymore, even though he loves her. Empathy sneaks from my chest and pours into my heart, knowing all too well what that feels like.

Turning onto a back road, I take notice of where we are and sit up straighter. I thought we were heading home, but this is on the other side of town, headed toward...

"Where are we going?"

"To meet your dad. He's at Donahue Motors, so that's where I've been instructed to drop you off."

My heart flips, stomach sinking at the thought of running into Jackson. I had come to terms with never seeing his face again, learning to live just like my dad does —with a hole where my heart should be.

The thought alone sends a spike of panic through my chest. I recognize it immediately, but instead of trying to push away the feeling, I grasp onto it, closing my eyes and breathing deep. I tense up every single part of my body, stiff as a board and then slowly relax, focusing intensely on the relief of each muscle as the tension melts away.

There have been numerous types of relaxation techniques I've tried since being at Turning Pointe, but my favorite, the one that works the best, is progressive muscle relaxation—or PMR.

"Are you okay?" Lennox's voice rises in alarm.

I don't answer until I've finished the routine, feeling the stabbing panic fall away, control rising in its place. "Yeah, I'm okay. Just keeping the panic at bay," I reassure him.

Lennox glances at me. "He's not there."

My chest pinches. "Who?"

"Jax. He left town right after you humiliated him on live television."

My insides cramp. "I did *not* humiliate him."

Lennox pulls into the parking lot of Donahue Motors, driving to the entrance and pulling to a stop, the car idling. He twists his body toward me. "Blakely, be real. Any man would be humiliated by what you did."

My defenses start to rise. He doesn't understand why I did what I did, no one does, and that's fine. I can live with that because I still don't have to live with the guilt of knowing that I was the reason Jackson didn't get the one thing he's always wanted. "I did it to save his dream, Lennox."

He clicks his tongue. "I don't think he'd see it that way."

My heart stalls as his earlier words filter through my brain. "Wait, did you say he left town? As in he no longer works here?"

"I did. It was all over the internet, I'm sure you can look it up if you want to see."

Nausea rolls through me in tumultuous waves. "Paparazzi?"

Lennox nods.

"*Damnit.*" Frustration billows inside of me. "So everything I did was for nothing? He just left town anyway and threw away his dream?"

Lennox tilts his head, a sad smile creeping along his face. "Maybe his dream didn't seem as sweet without someone there to share it with."

Sadness and guilt mix together, forming a lethal cocktail, and I gulp it down like water, allowing the burn to flow through my insides and poison my blood.

It's what I deserve, after all.

Forcing a smile, I lean across the center console, giving

Lennox a hug. He stiffens but doesn't push me away, and in Lennox's world, it's as good as if he squeezed me tight.

"Thank you," I say. "For being you. You're one of the most important people in my life. One of the only ones I can trust."

His nostrils flare, the right corner of his mouth twitching as he nods.

"Are you waiting out here for me?"

He shakes his head. "Your dad said to drop you off."

"Okay, well... see ya later. Thanks for the pep talk."

He laughs, waving me off, and I get out of the car and make my way inside, searching for my dad.

I find him in the garage.

As I walk through the glass doors, memories spin like a record. Every corner of this place reeks of Jackson and I have to bite back the tears, an intense longing exploding inside of me—the whip of regret striking new lacerations against my heart with every step.

My dad is standing next to a man who's loading the cars on a truck. My eyes scan the area, taking in the scene. "Hey. What's going on?"

He spins, his smile blinding as he beams from across the room. "Hi, honey." Walking over, he pulls me into his arms. It's a new thing of his—hugging. He visited me every week at Turning Pointe, and each time he'd grip on so tight I worried he might leave bruises.

I sink into his embrace, allowing his warmth to wrap around me like a blanket.

Pulling back, his hands on my shoulders, he sighs. "Let me look at you."

I roll my eyes, but my chest warms from his attention. "I was only gone for thirty days, Dad. And you saw me last week. I'm hardly different."

He lifts up my arm, his finger poking my sides. "Hmm... I don't know, you seem different to me."

Giggling, I wrench out of his grasp. "Stop it. What's all this?" I wave to Jackson's work as it's loaded onto the truck, worry tearing through my insides, hoping that he isn't taking them somewhere to be hidden away, covered in dust, never to be seen again.

I'll never forgive myself for ruining things when it didn't make a damn difference in the end.

My dad's face grows serious, and he leans against the red toolbox Jackson apparently left behind. "This is me, taking the last of Jax's cars and putting them on set."

My breath stutters, hope sticking to my insides like cling wrap. "You're using them?"

He nods. "I'm using them. And I'll be paying him for it, too." His jaw clenches. "I never should have used his career as an ultimatum. I just... well—" He lifts a shoulder. "I don't really have an excuse. I was angry. Protective. Not able to see past my ego to recognize that sometimes two people fall in love even when the world tells them they can't."

My heart throbs against my ribs, my abdomen flaring.

"You feeling good?" He lifts a brow. "Strong?"

I straighten my spine, pride filling every pore at all the work I've been putting into myself. "Yeah, Dad. I'm feeling strong."

He nods, sucking on his teeth. "Good. Because I have the jet geared up and ready for you."

Confusion spreads through me. "Uh... for what?"

"To go get him back."

I laugh, nerves lighting up my insides like a Christmas tree. "I'm sorry, to get *what?*"

"You never would have gone through with that ridiculous charade if I hadn't pushed you." He grabs my hands. "Let me help you make it right. You love him?"

Choking back a sob, I nod, my hand coming up to cover my mouth.

"He saw you when everyone else was blind... the way I saw your mother." He shakes his head. "You don't let something like that slip through your fingers."

I sigh. "Dad, there's no chance—"

"You *fight*, Blakely. And only after you've given it your everything, do you admit defeat."

"I don't..."

"Do you want him back?" he asks.

"Well, yes, but—"

"Then take the jet, there will be a car waiting for you when you land. You go to him and you show him that you see him too."

Sucking in a breath, determination attaches to my spine, rooting me in its confidence. In its strength. "Okay."

"And Blakely…" he tips up my chin. "I'm sorry."

My eyes sting with tears, fragments of my heart being sewn back together. "I forgive you." I glance around. "So, guess I'm going to Sugarlake?"

He nods. "Guess you're going to Sugarlake."

57

JACKSON

It's been four weeks of Friday dinners, and they each end the same way. With Chase grabbing two beers and sliding one to me, sitting down, and not speaking a word.

Tonight, I'm outside on the back deck. The sliding door opens behind me and a fresh beer appears. I grab it, watching as Chase rests his forearms on the railing and stares up at the sky.

"Do you ever look at the stars and feel small?" he asks.

My stomach jumps at his voice, surprised that he's finally decided to talk. I lift my head, gazing up at them. "All the time."

"Yeah, me too." He chuckles, sipping from his bottle.

"There's only been a few other times in my life where I've felt that small."

I swallow, unease molding to my cells.

"For instance, when my mom left my sister and me at a gas station and never showed back up? I felt small as fuck then."

My gut sinks. It's no secret that Chase is adopted—that his mom was a junkie who left him and his sister, Lily, when they were young, but I never knew the details. Chase isn't really one to verbalize his issues.

I peer at him from my peripheral, wondering what else I don't know about him, and then I snap out of it, reminding myself that I truly don't give a fuck.

"The second time... was when my best friend dropped me without a second thought, not even waiting to hear my side of the story. Choosing to slide into my place as he tried to fuck my girl."

My entire body freezes, the beer poised at my lips.

"I've been waiting for fucking weeks to see if you'd ever apologize. I thought maybe that you'd extend an olive branch. Thought that if everyone else had taken the time to let me back in, then maybe you would too. But here we are, with *me* being the one who has to do all the talking." He points a finger at me. "You *know* I fucking hate talking."

Disbelief rains down my spine, wrapping around my chest and squeezing. "Are you seriously standing there and trying to say that *I'm* the one who hurt *you?*"

He nods. "That's exactly what I'm fucking saying. You were my best friend, Jax. My *only* friend, and instead of being ride or die, through thick and thin, you jumped ship."

"You treated her like *shit!*" I yell, waving my arm toward inside. "You fucked another girl and posted about it on

Facebook on the same night her mom died, and yet I'm the bad guy?"

He shakes his head. "You have no idea what the fuck you're talking about."

"No?" I raise my brows. "So explain it to me."

He puffs out his chest. "You don't *deserve* an explanation. Eight years ago? Yeah, I would have spilled my bleeding fucking heart out, telling you how my stupid ass fell for some bitch's manipulations because I was fucked up over Lily almost dying in my arms and then running away." He runs a shaky hand through his hair. "Eight years ago, I would have told you how that *same* stupid bitch snuck into my bed when I was asleep and took a few pictures." He pauses, his eyes swirling with hurt. "But today? Today you don't deserve shit."

I swallow, his words shooting through my skin like bullets and burrowing into the holes they carved out.

"I get that I let you down. That you're pissed off at me. That you've held onto a grudge for all the ways I've fucked up. And I'm sorry for that. No one knows more than I do about how I wasn't the man I needed to be back then." He runs his hand through his dark hair. "I've spent years atoning for my mistakes. Growing and learning, and working every *fucking* day to try and be a better man."

He gulps down his beer. "But you were *my* friend first. And I needed you, too."

"I didn't know," I say, my mind whirling.

His jaw tics. "You didn't *want* to know."

My stomach rolls as I think back to eight years ago. To how I became enamored with Lee. How every time I drove her to visit him in college, I fell a little bit more, and let the resentment for Chase grow until it wedged between us.

How I'd see them love each other so hard it hurt to watch, and dream of having her love me the same.

It's possible I let my infatuation with her affect our friendship long before he messed things up himself.

A tsunami hits, clarity washing over me like icy water, my chest pulling tight as I stare at him. "I don't... I don't know what to say."

"Say the truth. That you've blamed me for everything. For eight fucking years, not realizing that *you* were being an asshole."

My brows rise and I stumble back, dropping into the lounge chair behind me, my fingers tangling in my chain. "Well, shit."

Chase's lip twitches.

He rolls his head back, staring at the sky, and I'm stunned into silence. My mind flips around, looping a complete one-eighty, leaving me nauseous from the spin. All of my anger toward him was because he didn't reach out—didn't try to fix something that, turns out, he wasn't solely responsible for breaking.

"Are you still in love with her?" he asks, still gazing at the stars.

My stomach drops to the floor, my mind picturing Blakely. But then I realize he's asking about Lee. *His Goldi.*

"No." I swallow.

"Good." He nods, sucking on his teeth. "Then, we'll be okay."

My brow rises. "Just like that?"

He walks over, sitting down next to me. "Life is too short to hold on to grudges." He sighs. "But you fucking hurt me."

I glance down, watching the condensation drip down the neck of my bottle. "Yeah, well, you hurt me too, man."

"Yeah. I know." He tilts his beer toward me. I hesitate before bringing mine over, clinking it against the glass.

The conversation doesn't take away the years of resentment between us. But it's a start.

My phone rings as I'm leaving my mom's place. It's been nice, having so much time to relax and reconnect with her and everyone else.

I've been roped into every Friday night dinner and Saturday brunch for the past five weeks, and while the comradery of friends helps ease the ache of missing Blakely, it doesn't make it disappear.

But I've realized in her absence that neither of us were in a healthy place for a relationship. I was an enabler, having her use me as therapy, instead of supporting her while she found tangible solutions. And in return, she allowed me to sink into the role of a hero, as if being there whenever she needed would make up for the fact I wasn't there for my dad.

A toxic cycle, where one hand washes the other, but both of us never quite get clean.

I've tried like hell to avoid going online and searching her name, but I'd be lying if I said I hadn't.

Ironically, that's been the only thing that has brought me clarity through the past month. Allowed me to look at our relationship from a different angle and see how, sometimes, no matter how hard you love someone, they just aren't in a place to receive it.

I've watched that video of Blakely, tearfully saying goodbye to her fans, a thousand times, the sewn together pieces of my heart fraying as her beautiful face crumples as she finally shows her truth. Pride fills my chest, followed closely by grief, because I wasn't what she needed to make that final step. Part of me wonders if it was my absence that finally helped her start to heal.

I don't look at the missed call until I get home, my brow furrowing as I realize it was Becca. Odd, since I'm planning to see her in less than an hour for dinner.

Pulling up her name, I press call.

"Hey, what's up, Becs?"

"Jackson Rhoades, you mother*fucker*."

I roll my eyes. "What did I do now?"

"I had the most interestin' conversation ten minutes ago, with the most *interestin'* woman."

My stomach flips, a tingle of warning shooting through my middle. "Oh? And this is my fault... how?"

"Because she was lookin' for *you*."

My muscles freeze, my hand halfway through my hair. "Who?"

"A pretty young thing. Blakely somethin' or other. Showed up at my school in a bright blue sports car, askin' where she could find herself some Jackson."

My heart slams against my ribs, my head growing dizzy from how fast my world spins.

She's here.

I try to swallow around the sudden dryness of my mouth. "What did you tell her?"

"I told her to come to dinner, of course."

My breath sputters. "You *what?*"

"Oh, was I not supposed to do that?"

"Jesus Christ, Becca, you can never just stay out of it."

"Well, maybe if you had *told* me anything about her, I wouldn't have had to resort to such drastic measures! Anyway, she's sittin' pretty right here in her car, waitin' to follow me and Eli on over. I just thought I'd give you a heads-up. Let you get your shit together."

My jaw clenches as I hang up on her, frustration burning a hole through me as I pace back and forth, contemplating not showing up at all.

But I know that won't solve any problems, and despite my brain telling me that nothing she can say will make a difference, there's a rope attached to my soul that's being tugged, the other half still tethered to her.

Besides, if I don't go, I can't demand the answers that I deserve.

So, with a deep breath, I pick up my keys and head to dinner.

Pulling into the driveway, my eyes glance around, my heart in my throat as I check for Eli's Jeep or a bright blue sports car.

Nothing.

I hustle up to the walkway, not bothering to knock as I open the door and walk in. There's this urge to talk to Lee, just to have someone with me who knows her and can give their two cents on the situation.

Rushing around the corner, I run into Chase, my shoulder slamming against his.

"*Fuck*, goddamn, Jax. Where's the fire?" He rubs his shoulder.

My chest heaves, trying to catch my breath. "Where's Lee, Chase? I need to talk to her. It's important."

His brows draw in. "She ran to the store to pick up wine. She should be back soon."

"Shit." I run my hands through my hair, my nerves ricocheting off my insides at the thought of having to face Blakely.

"What's wrong?"

Sighing, I lean back, banging the back of my head against the wall. "Blakely's on her way here."

His brows raise. "Blakely as in, the girl you were fucking around with in California?"

"I wasn't *fucking* around." I glare at him. "But yes."

He smirks. "So, what's the problem?"

My mouth parts. "The problem is she dropped me at the first sign of trouble."

He hums. "Oh, kind of like how you did with me?"

"No, I—" My stomach cramps. "This is an entirely different situation."

"I would hope so. Unless you've been in love with me all this time and just haven't told me." He grins.

"When did you become the smart-ass in this friendship?"

He shrugs. "Probably when you became the broody prick."

Sinking down to the floor, I rest my arms on my knees.

He slides down beside me, his head clunking against the wall. "Love sucks sometimes."

I laugh. "You're telling me."

He shakes his head. "Fucking painful."

The doorbell rings but he doesn't make a move to go answer. "Life is full of regrets, Jax. Don't let this be one of them."

My heart falters. "So, I should what, just forgive her?"

"I didn't say that." He shrugs. "Only you know what you can live with."

"Sage advice," I snark.

He smiles, dimples popping in his cheeks. "I'm a fucking treasure trove of good advice these days. You're welcome."

Smacking my knee before standing up, he walks down the hall.

My mind races, my stomach soaring then diving to the floor. Reaching up to grab my dad's dog tags, I close my eyes and pray for some guidance.

And then, I stand up and walk to the front door.

58

BLAKELY

I've never felt so normal.

Pulling off the highway when I see the sign for Sugarlake, I stop at the first building, which happens to be Sugarlake High.

I'm worried I'll be recognized, and it turns out I'm right, because the first people I see are two girls sitting in the front office when I walk inside.

One looks up, her jaw dropping as she nudges the other with her arm. Sighing, I paste on a smile, walking over to take selfies and chat, before asking them to please not mention to anyone that I'm here.

They swear they won't, but I don't have high hopes.

Glancing around and not seeing anyone else I can ask for help, I head back out to the car, calling my dad on the phone and letting him know I made it safe. Just as I'm hanging up, a woman walks toward me, her hand shielding her eyes.

"Hi. Can I help you with somethin'?" she asks.

I lock my gaze on her, taking in her curly red hair, and slip my phone into my back pocket. "Oh, hi." Nerves buzz around my stomach like bees, my teeth sinking into my lower lip. "I'm not sure."

"You new in town?"

Laughter bursts from my chest, because yeah, technically, she's right. "I guess you could say that. I'm looking for someone, but now that I'm here I'm not quite sure where to look. I just stopped at the first place I saw." I gesture to the school building. Apprehension snakes its way up my middle, gripping my throat. "He doesn't exactly know I'm here."

"Surprise visit?" She smiles, her green eyes sparkling.

I grimace, second-guessing my decision to hop on a plane and fly here on a whim. "Something like that."

"Well, who ya lookin' for? Maybe I can help. Small town and all."

"Jackson Rhoades." I say it fast, his name rolling off my tongue before I lose my nerve entirely.

Her eyes widen. "You're lookin' for *Jax?*"

My chest wrings tight. "I take it you know him?"

She grins. "Even when I wish I didn't." Her eyes scan up and down my body. My head grows dizzy, her perusal making anxiety slam down on my lungs.

I focus on my breath and practice PMR.

One. Two. Three.

I hope she doesn't notice that I've suddenly gone stiff

right in front of her, but I'd rather her think I'm awkward then see me in a full-blown attack.

"How'd you say you know him again?" she questions.

My heart palpitates. Obviously, he's never mentioned me. Not that I can blame him. "He worked for my dad out in California. I just... there are some things I need to tell him."

Recognition hits her eyes. "You're that girl he was always complainin' about," she mutters.

A tendril of amusement works its way through my nerves and a small smile lifts my face. "I was an expert at pushing his buttons."

She throws her head back and laughs, walking right up to me and linking our arms. "Well then, I think we'll get along just fine. Come on, now, we're about to head to meet him for dinner. You can follow us there."

My stomach somersaults. "Really?"

She smirks. "I ain't never told a lie. I'm Becca, by the way. And *that's* Eli." She points to the black Jeep pulling up behind my Maserati.

There's something about her that draws me in and I find myself smiling—trusting her before I even really know her. "I'm Blakely."

Her eyes sparkle. "Nice to meet ya. Now you just hop in that fancy car and follow us, okay? It's a straight shot to the middle of town."

Nodding, I walk around and sink into the driver's seat, my hands brushing against the wheel. It's been a long time since I've had to drive a car, and my gut churns, wishing my dad had picked something less flashy.

Oh well, too late now.

My stomach is tense the entire drive over, lost in my head, running through all the things I want to say. I barely see the scenery as it passes me by. But there's a sense of calm in the air, a peace that doesn't exist in a big city. And I get the feeling that being here for a few days could lift years of tension off my shoulders.

The Jeep parks in a driveway and I pull onto the curb, my hands trembling as I turn off the car and get out, closing the door.

What the hell am I even doing?

My heart pounds against my ribs as I walk over to Becca and Eli and I force a smile on my face, hoping that my nerves aren't showing themselves too strongly.

Eli grins. "Hey there."

I'm so nervous I could puke, so I don't open my mouth, just lift my hand in a wave and walk behind them to the door.

"I called Jax on the way over," Becca says.

"He knows I'm here?" A heaviness presses against my chest.

She nods. "Yep."

The door swings open and my stomach swings with it, flying into my throat. A man with dark hair and a sharp jaw stands in the frame, his eyes glossing over Becca and Eli before landing on me.

"You gonna just stand there all day or you plannin' on lettin' us in?" Becca snarks.

I bite back a giggle, a little bit in awe of her fiery tongue.

The man doesn't speak, just moves to the side and lets them push past, moving back before I can follow.

"Oh, I..." My knees tremble. "I'm here to see Jackson?" My voice rises like a question and I curse myself for sounding so unsure.

Strong, Blakely.

"Chase." Jackson's voice filters from the hallway and my breath sticks to my lungs.

I've been working *really* hard the past month, learning every day to manage my panic, but right now, it's a true testament to how far I've come. Because even though I feel the spiral forming like a funnel cloud, I don't give in. I just close my eyes and count to three. Practice my PMR and ride the wave until it recedes.

"Is she okay?" someone whispers.

I hear shuffling and what sounds like the closing of a door, but I keep my eyes closed until I'm sure I'm in control. And when I finally open them, my gaze clashes with forest green.

"Jackson," I breathe.

His nostrils flare. "Are you alright?"

A small smile creeps on my lips. "Yeah, I'm okay."

He sighs, running a hand through his hair. My stomach winds tight like a screw. *He looks so good.*

"What are you doing here, Blakely?"

"I came to talk to you."

He crosses his arms over his chest. "So talk."

His demeanor is cold. Detached.

My throat is suddenly parched and I swallow, licking my lips. Jackson's eyes drop to where my fists are curling at my sides.

"I'm not going to lose it, if that's what you're worried about."

He shakes his head, his hair grazing his jaw. "That's not what I'm worried about."

"It isn't?"

He groans, rubbing his hands over his face. "Blakely, please. Get to the point."

My chest compresses. "Right, sorry. I uhh..." I scratch

my cheek and then smile at him. "This is harder than I thought."

"Can't be any harder than going on camera and lying to the world."

I flinch, his words like needles that pierce through my skin. "You're right. You didn't deserve that." My throat clogs. "And that's why I'm here, I guess. To explain." I look at him through my lashes. "If you're open to hearing it."

He jerks his head in a sharp nod.

I breathe a sigh of relief. "My dad he—he saw the pictures of us and made me choose."

His forehead creases. "Made you choose *what*?"

The words tumble out of me. "He was going to fire you, and all I could think was that you'd lose *everything* you had worked for. All the years you'd been pouring into your dad's dreams." I snap my fingers. "Gone in a second. Because of me." Regret sloshes inside of me. "So, I made a deal. I'd make sure we never spoke again as long as he kept you on."

Jackson's gaze narrows. "That wasn't your choice to make."

"And I knew you'd say that." I smile, shaking my head. "I knew if I told you, then you would choose me."

He throws his arms to the sides. "So what was the problem, Blake?"

"I didn't want you to *hate* me!" My voice rises. "Five, ten years down the line, you'd resent me for taking away the one thing you had left of him, and I couldn't—" I gasp, emotion climbing up my esophagus and pouring out of my mouth on a sob.

"*Shit.*" Jackson walks closer until he's right in front of me. "Don't cry."

His hands grasp my face, his thumbs wiping my tears, and even though I know it will make things hurt more when he walks away, I sink into his touch, reveling in all the ways he makes me feel.

Sniffling, I nod. "I'm so sorry." I pause, taking in a deep breath. "I made a mistake. A *terrible* mistake, and if I could take it back I would, but I—I know I can't."

He sighs. "It's so easy to forget how young you are."

My breath hiccups. "Do you think you can forgive me?"

He backs up, his fingers scratching the stubble on his chin. "I don't know, Blake. There's... you really hurt me. You gave up on us, and then you shut me out. You didn't *include* me in choices that affected both of us."

I nod, the slices in my heart bleeding with every beat. "I know," I whisper.

"Where's Sierra? She know you're here?" His voice is sharp.

My chest burns with betrayal and I shake my head. "I fired her."

His brows shoot to his hairline. "You did?"

"Yeah, right before I went to rehab."

He rocks back on his heels, his eyes widening. "Rehab, huh?"

"Yep. Turns out, I'm a basket case. Who knew?" I laugh, running a hand through my hair, but it dies down quick when I see he isn't amused.

"Did it help?"

"The rehab?" I smile. "More than I ever thought it could. Therapy is... life changing, to be honest. And so are the anti-depressants. I still have my moments, but what's life without a little struggle?"

He nods, the left side of his mouth rising into a small smile. "Good. That's—I'm really happy you're healing, princess."

The nickname is a sucker punch to my bruised-up

heart. "Look, Jackson… I don't have any fancy words. I'm not good at speaking things and making them sound pretty. I just have my truth. The one you've always seen."

My eyes well with tears, the pressure in my chest feeling like it will burst at any moment. "And I couldn't go on without you knowing that I see you too."

His jaw clenches and I step forward. "I've made mistakes, and I'll probably make a thousand more. But I'll spend every day of my life trying to make it up to you if you'll let me."

His eyes are glassy as he stares.

"Do you think you'll ever be able to give me another chance? To give *us* a chance?" I ask, taking another step forward.

His eyes darken and the air charges with his answer before he even speaks. The hope drains out of my body, dissipating into the air.

My dad said to fight like hell, but sometimes, things are too damaged. Totaled.

Wrecked.

Nodding, my hand comes up to rub my chest. "Right. It was stupid to think you'd—"

"Would you just *stop* making decisions for me before I even have the chance?" he interrupts.

My breath stalls in my lungs.

He moves closer. "You messed me up, okay? I haven't been able to sleep. I haven't been able to eat. My every waking thought is of you. And that infuriates me because I should hate you. I *wanted* to hate you."

My chest caves in, despair stretching its wings, preparing to wrap around me and shroud me in its darkness.

He moves again, his shoes touching mine.

His hand cups my jaw. "But I can't hate you. I love you too damn much."

I gasp, my stomach flipping as his lips come down to meet mine. I don't waste a second, jumping up and wrapping my legs around his waist, my tongue swiping across his lips, desperate to taste him after going so long without.

He groans, his arms wrapping around me.

He breaks away, holding me tight against him. "We're still not okay."

I nod, leaning in to peck his lips.

"I'm serious, Blake. We have to communicate. I need to be able to trust you."

I nod again. Another kiss.

"And I want you to make a video, telling the world that we're together."

My heart soars.

"Well, glad to see I missed the fight and made it back for the party." Lee's voice shocks my system, heat flooding my cheeks as I hide my face in Jackson's shoulder.

I try to slide back down but his arms lock me tighter against him, keeping me in place.

"Hi, Lee," I mumble, peeking at her.

She smirks. "Hiya, Blake. Nice to see you again." She walks right by us and up to the front door. "Dinner will be ready in twenty."

My stomach clenches when she says dinner. Food is still a struggle, and some days are easier than others. But *every* day I try. And that's all anyone can ever really do.

"Is that true?" I ask Jax once she's inside, my hands gripping behind his neck. "Am I sticking around?"

He smiles, finally letting me slip down his body until I'm pressed up against him. His hand glides down my arm and tangles our fingers together.

"That's right, princess. I want you to stick around."

Happiness blooms inside of me, growing like a weed and spreading through every atom.

And as I follow Jackson inside the house, being greeted by hoots and hollers, I've never felt so at home.

EPILOGUE

SIX MONTHS LATER

Jackson

Rolling over in bed, my arm touches silky skin and I groan, pressing myself against Blakely's warmth.

She pushes back immediately, like even in her sleep she aches to be close and I lean in, pressing a kiss to her shoulder.

"Good morning," she breathes.

Trailing my lips up her neck, I nip at her ear. "Good morning, princess."

Her hand reaches behind her, palming my morning wood, bringing it close until it rests between her legs. My abs tense as she slides back until the tip of me spreads apart her lips and sinks inside of her pussy.

I groan, my hips immediately thrusting in and out, tingles of pleasure racing up my spine as I work my cock inside her.

Her hips move in tandem with mine and she lets out a moan, grabbing my hand, our fingers interlocking as she brings it up to cup her breast.

My head stays buried in her neck, enjoying the closeness of our position, loving that I get to wake up like this every morning and go to sleep with her every night.

She never left Sugarlake.

For the first couple of weeks, she stayed at the bed-and-breakfast on the edge of town, until we both admitted it didn't make sense. She was spending all her time with me anyway, so she checked out and moved in with me.

It's crazy.

Moving so fast it makes my head spin.

But tomorrow isn't guaranteed, so you might as well live life with the one you love.

It was that thought that ran through my mind when I pulled her in my arms all those months ago and forgave her mistakes.

Some people think I gave in too easily, but when you go through the grief of death, forgiveness is easier to grasp. And I'd forgive her a thousand times over if it meant I could spend the rest of my days by her side.

She made a video the next day. Her first official post in over a month, telling everyone what happened. The truth this time, and then professing her love for *me*.

Surprisingly, people didn't care that I worked on cars, or that in their minds I wasn't worthy. Mainly, it's been an overwhelming amount of support. And it's because of the positive reaction that she decided to stay an influencer. But even though she's still posting selfies and making videos, it's a different world compared to what she used to do.

Now, instead of photoshopped pictures and staged outings, she posts her realness. Videos of how her therapy is going, and how she deals with side effects of her anti-depressants. How she still struggles daily with her relationship with food and exercise. She takes people on her journey and lets them know they aren't alone. And I think it helps her to know that she isn't either.

She still has panic attacks, and there are times where she breaks down in tears, caving to her obsessive thoughts and wanting to slide back into old habits. But no one is expecting perfection, and instead of hiding it from the world, she shows how it's okay to embrace the things that make you *you*.

I've never been more proud to call her mine.

Her pussy flutters around me, soft moans ringing through the air. Heat races up my spine, my balls tensing as I come deep inside of her, my teeth biting down on her neck, groaning through my release.

Eventually, I roll onto my back and look at her. "Do you want breakfast?"

She smiles. "Yeah, I want pancakes." Standing up, she sways her hips as she walks to the bathroom, my heart swelling as I watch her go.

There's not a day that goes by where I regret taking her back.

My phone rings, bringing me out of my trance, and I pick it up when I see it's Chase. I'm surprised to have him calling so early. After he proposed to Lee two nights ago, I expected them to be MIA, celebrating their engagement.

"Hey, man."

"Hey. I need a favor."

Sitting up in bed, I run my fingers through my hair. "Sure, what's up?"

He sighs. "Do you remember when I told you about that private investigator?"

My brows furrow. "Yeah, Mason or whatever, right? The one you hired to look for Lily?"

"Right. Well, he called me the other day. And Jax, he fucking found her." His voice pinches. "He knows where my sister is."

My breath whooshes out of me. Lily ran away back when we were kids and I had given up hope that she'd ever be found. "Holy fuck, Chase."

"Anyway, he tried to be stingy with info, because he's a giant fucking prick. But eventually, after I promised him I wouldn't do anything rash, I got an address out of him."

"And?"

"And obviously I was lying. I'm on a plane to Arizona in three hours to find her, but Goldi woke up puking her guts out, and I... *fuck.* I need you to come with me."

My stomach tightens. "Today?"

"Yeah, man." His voice breaks. "*Please.*"

Standing up, I head to my dresser. "When do we leave?"

"Is Mason meeting us here?" I ask, looking out over the run-down apartment complex. We're hiding across the street, behind a row of unkempt bushes.

"No. I told you, I promised him I wouldn't come."

I roll my eyes. "But here we are."

Chase glances at me, raising his eyebrows.

It's hot, the sun beating down on my neck, and my stomach is ten seconds away from eating itself out of hunger, but I don't complain. I just sit here with Chase while his eyes bounce back and forth, his foot constantly tapping on the ground.

"Hey, man." I put my hand on his shoulder. "It will be okay. We'll find her."

He nods.

My stomach jumps when something hits my back, and I spin around, a red ball rolling on the ground next to me. I bend over to pick it up.

"Hey, mister! Over here!" My eyes follow the voice until I see a young boy running over in black shorts and a Spider-Man tee. Definitely can't be older than four or five. *What's he doing alone?*

Grinning, I hold up the ball. "This yours, kid?"

He smiles. "Yep. Thanks. Sowwy."

"No worries." I toss him the ball.

"Mommy!" the boy yells, waving his hand at a woman who's racing across the street toward us.

Chase gasps beside me, his hand shooting out and gripping my arm tight.

The woman stops short when she reaches us, her eyes wide as she holds out her hand.

The boy races over, grabbing onto her leg instead. He beams up at her, his chubby cheeks rounding out with his smile.

And it's only then that I take in his features, my heart jerking as it slams haphazardly against my chest.

Jet-black hair. Piercing hazel eyes. A dimple that pops in his cheek.

Just like Chase.

Just like...

"Lily."

THANKS FOR READING!

Enjoy Beneath the Hood? Please consider taking a second to leave a review!

<u>Get First Looks and Exclusive Sneak peeks</u>

Join Emily's Facebook Group: THE MCINCULT

Want text alerts? Text **MCINCULT** to 833- 942- 4409 to stay up to date on new releases!

ALSO BY EMILY MCINTIRE

THE SUGARLAKE SERIES

Beneath the Stars

Beneath the Stands

Beneath the Hood

Beneath the Surface

THE NEVER AFTER SERIES

A Collection of Dark Romances Where the Villain Gets The Girl

Hooked: A Dark Peter Pan Reimagining

Scarred: A Dark Hamlet Reimagining

Wretched: A Dark Wizard of Oz Reimagining

Twisted: A Dark Aladdin Reimagining

Crossed: A Dark Hunchback of Notre-Dame Reimagining

COMPLETE STANDALONES

Be Still My Heart: A Romantic Suspense

ACKNOWLEDGMENTS

Three books in and this never really gets any more real to me.

First, I have to give the biggest acknowledgment to my best friend, Sav R. Miller. Writing is vulnerable. It's hard. Having someone there to pick you up and talk you through the rollercoaster is SO important. For me, that's Sav.

Thank you for reading my words before anyone else and for checking Goodreads when I'm too emotional to look, for telling me that I'm *that* bitch, and to not second guess myself. I love you even though you continue to call me bufflehead.

Can't wait to sip mimosas in the Smokies.

To my PA, Brittni: Thank you for keeping my life in line, I don't know how I survived so long without you.

To my Alpha Readers: Sav R. Miller, Lee Jacquot, and Anne-Lucy Shanley. You've all been with me since the very beginning with Beneath the Stars, and this series wouldn't be what it is without you. Thank you so much for reading while I write. You get the rough, raw version and help me craft a beautiful story, and none of this would be what it is without you.

To my Beta Readers: Kayleigh King, Michelle Chamberland, Ariel Mareroa, AV Asher. Thank you for working on my ridiculous schedule and being such an integral part of my process. I am so grateful for you.

To my ARC Readers: Y'all make me NERVOUS! Thank you so much for wanting to be in my corner, and loving my words enough to want to read them before everyone else. I value your opinion and your time more than you know. My books only do as well as they do because of your support.

To my Street Team: I LOVE YOU GUYS omg. Thank you for being the best hype team in the world. I don't know what I'd do without you.

To my Editor and Proofreader: Ellie and Rosa with My Brother's Editor. For making my words clean and pretty and not getting mad that I overuse commas and misuse apostrophes.

To my cover designer, Clarise with CT Creations: You're brilliant! Thank you for always working with Amazon's ridiculous guidelines and making my visions come to life.

To my husband, Mike: For always knowing what I need before I ask, for bringing me flowers and Sephora gift cards for no reason, for being the best dad to our daughter that anyone could ask for. For your support. I love you the most. Thank you for being my real life book boyfriend.

To my daughter, Melody: Everything I do is for you. Out of all my creations, you will always be the greatest.

And finally, to you, the readers: I am so blown away that you want to read my words. Thank you from the bottom of my heart for your support. I'm so happy I was able to let you escape into my imagination for just a little while, and that you wanted to stay there.

ABOUT EMILY

Emily McIntire is a *USA TODAY* bestselling author known for her Never After series, where she gives our favorite villains their happily ever afters. With books that range from small town to dark romance, she doesn't like to box herself into one type of story, but at the core of all her novels is soul- deep love. When she's not writing, you can find her waiting on her long- lost Hogwarts letter, enjoying her family, or lost between the pages of a good book.

Made in United States
Orlando, FL
18 December 2023

41259847R00253